STEAL ACROSS
THE SKY

TOR BOOKS BY NANCY KRESS

STEAL ACROSS
THE SKY

NANCY KRESS

TOR

A TOM DOHERTY ASSOCIATES BOOK
NEW YORK

This is a work of fiction. All of the characters, organizations, and events portrayed in this novel are either products of the author's imagination or are used fictitiously.

STEAL ACROSS THE SKY

Copyright © 2009 by Nancy Kress

All rights reserved.

A Tor Book
Published by Tom Doherty Associates, LLC
175 Fifth Avenue
New York, NY 10010

www.tor-forge.com

Tor® is a registered trademark of Tom Doherty Associates, LLC.

ISBN 978-0-7653-5956-8

First Edition: February 2009
First Mass Market Edition: February 2010

Printed in the United States of America

0   9   8   7   6   5   4   3   2   1

*For Marty,
King's pawn to King's pawn 4 . . .*

Now the day is over,
Night is drawing nigh;
Shadows of the evening
Steal across the sky.

—SABINE BARING-GOULD

History . . . is indeed little more than
the register of the crimes, follies, and
misfortunes of mankind.

—EDWARD GIBBON

It ain't necessarily so.

—IRA GERSHWIN

PART I

THE CRIME

1: LUCCA

"Well," Cam said, rising on her toes and leaning toward the bridge's main screen, "there they are."

Lucca, despite the tightness in his throat, was startled into laughter. All the hoping to be chosen for this insane mission, all the agonizing over the Atoners' unknown selection criteria, all the complicated family reactions and media furor and governmental observation, all the tension on the voyage out—and then Cam greets the alien star system with the most mundane understatement possible. And this was *Cam,* an American who thrived on flamboyance like vineyards on sun. Although perhaps that was the point. Cam was making an uncharacteristic effort to be careful.

Soledad scowled. Lucca understood: Soledad had to be viewing the Kular System with mixed emotions. She was the alternate Witness, and neither Lucca nor Cam had died on the trip to Kular. Neither had fallen ill, gone insane, changed his or her mind. Cam and Lucca were going down to the twin planets below, and Soledad was not. Nonetheless, Soledad was generous enough to purge the scowl from her face and say, "I wish you both luck." Lucca took her hand and squeezed it.

He didn't touch Cam.

On-screen, Kular A and Kular B sparkled with the magnificence of the remote. The binary planet system rotated around a common center of gravity, 1.4 AU from their G5 star. At some time in the unimaginable past they had formed from the same dust cloud, and their composition and gravity were similar. That much the Atoners had told their human surrogates.

Neither planet had any moons, although each would dominate the other's sky. On Kular A, the pole end of the one giant continent was obscured by a massive dust storm, but the rest shone clear with blue seas and green flora. Clouds drifted over the one inhabited continent on B. Or maybe it wasn't the only inhabited continent any longer. The Atoners had not, they said, visited Kular in five hundred Terran years. They would never visit it again. That's what human Witnesses were for.

"Let's go to the shuttle bay," Cam said. More mundane speech. But she was right; commonplace words were what was needed right now. Procedural speech, unambiguous speech, careful speech that didn't imply grandiose emotions that could only prove embarrassing later. Speech such as, for instance, *I will love you forever.*

"Yes," Lucca said carefully, "let's go to the shuttle bay."

Soledad led the way; she was, as of the moment the two shuttles launched, mission coordinator. Cam followed eagerly, looking beautiful as ever but so different in the rough tunic, leggings, and boots that the Atoners had supplied, her wild black hair loose to her shoulders. He was used to her in inexpensive American clothes, trashy and sexy. But then, he probably looked just as outlandish to her. Only Soledad, her stocky body clothed in jeans and a sweater, looked normal.

Lucca trailed the two young women, glancing back once more at Kular A. In a few more hours he would be down there, a Witness for the Atoners of Neu, a part of the aliens' grand, remorseful, incomprehensible program to repent of long-ago sins against humanity, sins that humans themselves hadn't even known had been committed.

It started to go wrong the minute the shuttle hit the atmosphere. Insertion was supposed to happen with the same minimum disruption to passengers as all the other Atoner craft. Lucca didn't understand Atoner engineering—nobody on Earth understood it—but he'd been assured that the shuttle would go down "smooth as good chocolate." He'd been so startled to hear that phrase from the Atoner in the Dome on the moon—what did the Atoners know about chocolate? They must have learned the words from American television. *Smooth as good chocolate.*

Lucca screamed as he was flung violently against his webbed restraints. The shuttle lurched crazily. On the comm-link Soledad shouted, "Lucca! Lucca!" but he couldn't answer her. Pressure closed his throat, burst capillaries in his eyes, took his ability to speak or move. *I'm going to die—Ave Maria, piena di grazia . . .*

Later, he would not remember that he had prayed.

He wasn't dead, even though the shuttle was now silent as the grave, and as dark. Lucca hung upside down in his webbing. His eyes burned and his left leg ached. But pressure no longer tortured him, and he was able to free his arms.

"Soledad?" he said aloud. No answer; the shuttle comm-link wasn't functioning. *E che cazzo.* He fumbled inside his rough woolen tunic for the portable commlink on his belt. "Soledad?"

Barely any delay; the Atoner ship empty of Atoners orbited only three hundred klicks above the planet. "Lucca! What happened? Are you all right?"

"The shuttle crashed, I think. Or not exactly crashed—" If it had, he'd be dead. "—but came down too hard. Something malfunctioned. Where am I?"

"About a thousand klicks north of where we'd planned. At the southern edge of the dust storm, actually. Are you hurt?"

"No, I . . . yes." Lucca unfastened the last of his webbing and fell to the ceiling of the shuttle, which was now the floor. It took all his effort not to scream again. "I think my leg is broken."

Soledad swore in Spanish. "Shall I come and get you?"

"No!" Abort now? He had been on Kular less than ten minutes! "I'm going to use the med kit to set my leg. Call you when I have anything to report." He thrust the commlink back into his hidden belt, his fingers brushing bare skin. All at once that brought up an image of Cam, naked in his bunk aboard the ship, which in turn brought up an image of Gianna, equally naked.

Not now.

The med kit was stored during flight in a metal cabinet now so twisted and smashed that Lucca couldn't get it open. Several minutes of groping in the dark determined that. All at once panic, the genuine unlovely thing, split his heart down its center seam. He hit the controls for the shuttle door, then pulled and pushed at it, but it wouldn't open. He was trapped, a sardine in an alien can whose workings he did not understand.

Cam carried a laser gun. Lucca could have had one as well, but he'd refused all weaponry even though he was far more proficient with firearms than was Cam. The Atoners had agreed without comment. But the Atoners hadn't imagined him trapped in a prison of their own making.

Or had they? Surely aliens with the technology for star travel must have made that technology trustworthy? If they could adapt ship controls and screens for human use, if they could send those humans light-years away in weeks, then they could . . .

No. This was an accidental malfunction.

He pushed away the paranoia and splinted his broken leg with the arm of his chair, which twisted off more easily than he expected. The Atoner implants in his body released painkillers and, he assumed, healing meds as well. From a cabinet not twisted shut Lucca extracted and ate some protein bars. He checked the commlink, personal shield, and translator, each in its separate tiny pouch on the belt under his tunic. And then, since there was nothing else to do, he waited in the dark.

An hour passed.

Then another.

Or maybe not—it was difficult to judge in total darkness. But he knew the passage of time by the deepening blackness in his soul.

This was his real enemy, and it didn't come from being trapped in an alien machine, on a mission he could never have imagined and had not even remotely expected to be chosen for. The depression was an old and accustomed companion, as well known as the feel of his growling stomach or the taste of his mouth when he awoke each morning. This gray fog, this low-grade fever of the mind, had been with him since childhood, banished only for the three glorious years with Gianna. When that London lorry had rolled off St. Martin's Lane, onto the sidewalk, and over his wife, the blackness had howled through Lucca like a typhoon, and had not abated for an entire year. But that shrieking grief had almost been preferable to the deadened aftermath.

He'd told the Atoners all of that during his recruitment interview, stumbling through the simplest words in an attempt to be honest: "I am a widower. My wife died in an accident three years ago. I become depressed." Did the Atoners even value honesty? No one knew. They/he/she/it, whoever was behind that impenetrable screen, had not commented. *They won't take me,* Lucca had thought, and hadn't known which was greater, his disappointment or his relief.

But they had taken him, and here he was, and not even a trip to the *stars* had banished the soul-blackness. Nor had that stupid affair with Cam, nor would anything ever except the impossible, having Gianna back.

Time dragged on. Eventually, he slept.

He woke to pounding on the hull, to pounding in his head, and to muffled shouts. *Kularians.*

Lucca reached under his tunic and turned on both the translator and the personal shield. He felt hot and feverish—a side effect of the implanted meds?—and the loud hammering of his heart rivaled the banging on the hull. He banged back.

The pounding stopped. After a while it resumed, steady and purposeful. The Kularians were, with excruciating slowness, cutting him out of the shuttle. *Tools able to work metal.* His first observation as a Witness.

A long time later, a meter-square of hull fell inward, clanging on the shuttle floor. Lucca braced for the weapon that would follow, although of course nothing they could have would penetrate his shield. Would it be a spear? A club? An automatic rapid-fire gun? They had had ten thousand years, after all. The Atoners said that neither Kular A nor Kular B gave off electromagnetic signatures of any kind: no radio transmissions, no television, no microwave towers, nothing. Presumably that meant, at most, an early-industrial society. But on Earth, the Gatling gun, capable of getting off two hundred rounds a minute, had been patented in 1862.

A head poked through the opening in the shuttle. Just that—an unprotected head.

The head said something.

Lucca smiled. The translator needed native language, a reasonable amount of language, before it could decipher anything. Lucca pointed at his leg and made a grimace of pain. The head vanished.

A half hour later they had him out. By then his whole body ached, feverish. It was daylight, although with the blowing sand, that could have meant dawn or dusk or anything in between. Grit blew continuously against everything, coating shuttle and clothing and tools with coarse dust. There were eight Kularians, and they worked with a cooperative energy that involved much arm waving, heated discussion, and foot stamping. There didn't seem to be a formal leader. At no time did they show anything that Lucca could interpret as fear. They seemed intensely interested in getting a task done, and not at all hesitant about whether it should in fact be done in the first place.

Once they understood that Lucca's leg was broken, they became more careful in handling him, although never really gentle. Finally, with a good deal more shouting and foot stamping, they loaded him onto a kind of travois, which at first Lucca thought they would pull themselves. But then someone led an animal from around the other side of the shuttle, a slow and seriously ugly beast like a shaggy elephant, ruminatively chewing God knew what. The animal's yoke was tied to the travois, giving Lucca a clear view of its hindquarters. He saw no anus, but the beast smelled terrible. It lumbered forward, led by one Kularian, while four others walked protectively beside Lucca.

Lucca looked up into the face of the Kularian nearest him and smiled. *Thank you.*

The man nodded. A swarthy man with deeply weathered skin, a long black mustache, very dark eyes, and one front tooth painted dull red. The man wore a hat of animal skin with flaps now shoved onto the top of his head, tunic and leggings not unlike Lucca's own although of coarser cloth, and clumsy skin boots. He carried nothing, which was unusual for a man in anything but an advanced culture. More primitive humans away from their homes usually had things that needed carrying: weapons, baskets, stringed instruments. But this was indubitably a human, just as the Atoners had said. A human being whose ancestors had been kidnapped from the plains of Earth and brought here ten thousand years ago, as part of the huge experiment for which the Atoners now dripped with inconsolable remorse.

2: TRANSCRIPT, "WITNESS" INTERVIEW

Property of the United States Air Force

Classification: Secret, Level 8
Recorded: April 18, 2020
Interviewee: Camilla Mary O'Kane, ID # 065-453-8765274
  [personal data and background check attached]
Interviewer: Atoner, identity unknown
Place: Atoner Luna Base
Recorder: Col. John Karl Stoddard, USAF Intelligence
Present: Interviewee, Recorder, Atoner behind usual screen,
  all usual restrictions in place

ATONER: Good day, Ms. O'Kane.

O'KANE: Good day, sir. [NOTE: DESPITE EXHAUSTIVE PREINTERVIEW BRIEFING, INTERVIEWEE IS RESPONDING COUNTER TO SUGGESTION WITH HONORIFIC CHOICE. ATONER GENDERS REMAIN UNKNOWN.]

A: I hope your flight up to Luna was pleasant.

O: Yes. Your shuttle was smooth and fast. I never flew on a plane before.

A: You have been chosen from a large number of applicants for this interview. Why do you wish to become a Witness?

O: So we're going to plunge right in? Okay. I'm going to be honest, sir. I'm twenty-three years old and I've always held pretty crappy jobs. Right now I'm a waitress. I was smart in high school, but afterward I couldn't afford college, and the way things are in the United States right now . . . Do you know what I mean by that?

A: Yes.

O: The way things are, the best I can get are jobs where I can't make any decisions or learn anything important or have an impact on anything. And I live in *Nebraska*. I don't understand why anyone *wouldn't* want to be a Witness! Here I am on the moon, something I never dreamed possible for me. And to go to another planet, see a whole different— Haven't you had applications from all over the world?

A: Yes.

O: And that's only from countries that permit their citizens to apply! I heard that on a podcast. If the repressive countries let their people apply, you'd probably get millions more applications.

A: What do you think are your qualifications to witness for us on another planet?

O: I'm intelligent, strong, and healthy. I'm brave. I don't rattle easily—I really don't. I notice everything. And even though I'm not trained or anything, I want to do this so much that I'll study anything you want, do anything you tell me to.

A: You notice everything?

O: Well, maybe not everything—please don't hold that statement against me!

A: What would you do if we told you to do something you think is morally wrong?

O: [long silence] Then . . . I guess I wouldn't do it. Does that disqualify me?

A: No. You say you are intelligent and strong and able to learn well. Why don't those qualities enable you to create a life better than "crappy"?

O: [long silence] I think—forgive me, sir—that despite what you said before, I think you don't understand the United States right now. The economy sucks. The environment is going down the toilet. Even rich and educated people are

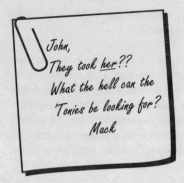

John,
They took _her_??
What the hell can the
Tonies be looking for?
Mack

scrambling to stay all right, and for somebody like me . . . You think intelligence and grit can succeed by themselves, but I'm telling you that's a pretty illusion.

A: Thank you for your interview, Ms. O'Kane.

O: What? You mean that's it? That's all the time I get? [NOTE: INTERVIEWEE IS STRONGLY ACTING CONTRARY TO PREINTERVIEW BRIEFING.]

A: What more would you like?

O: Can *I* ask some questions?

A: [long silence] Yes. [NOTE: THIS SILENCE OF 6.3 SEC-ONDS HAS BEEN NOTED IN NO OTHER INTER-VIEW RECORDED BY USAF INTELLIGENCE OR BY THOSE COUNTRIES PARTICIPATING IN THE ALIEN DATA-SHARING INITIATIVE.]

O: Why do you want to send human Witnesses to those other planets anyway? You're the ones with starships, why not go yourselves?

A: We cannot answer that.

O: You mean—and I say this with all due respect, sir—that you choose to not answer it?

A: Yes.

O: Well, okay. Then . . . you call yourselves "Atoners." What are you atoning *for*? [NOTE: STRONGLY ACTING CONTRARY TO PREINTERVIEW BRIEFING. INTER-VIEWEE WAS SPECIFICALLY AND REPEATEDLY

INSTRUCTED NOT TO ASK THIS, AS A MATTER OF DIPLOMATIC RELATIONS.]

A: Were you told to not ask that question?

O: Well . . . yes.

A: Then why did you ask it, Ms. O'Kane?

O: Because I . . . Oh, fuck, I really blew it, didn't I? You're not going to accept me as a Witness. So I don't have anything to lose, but I still would like to know. Shit, the whole *world* would like to know! What are you atoning for?

A: We choose to not answer that.

O: Okay. Your right. Anyway, thank you for the trip up here. I never thought . . . This is something I'll remember my whole life. And I wish you luck, sir, with your project, whatever it is.

A: Thank you.

DATE: May 16, 2020
INTERVIEW RESULT: Interviewee Accepted

3: AVEO

The soldiers came for him at his son's burial. Aveo saw them on the other side of the pit, which was already half-filled with wrapped bodies. Although a few of the green burial cloths were spider-silk, smooth and glossy, most were only coarse sarel fiber. The corpses of the very poor were barely wrapped at all, merely wound with two token strips of rough cloth around chest and head. Over all the dead, of whatever caste, lay the clumps of lime that partly masked the reek of decay. Ojea had not yet been covered. Aveo's son's strong young body, decently wrapped in green to please the Goddess that Aveo did not believe in, lay on top of several shovelfuls of white lime, a pristine bed.

Ojea had always valued cleanliness.

The soldiers were silhouetted against the moon, rising huge on the horizon. They marched along the edge of the pit, four of them in bronze breastplates and helmets, plus a *cul* with the royal slashes of blue painted on his bare breast. The mourners around Aveo, none of whom had come for Ojea, melted away. Aveo didn't run. It would have been undignified, and useless.

"Aveo ol Imbro." It was not a question. They did not give him his title.

"I am Aveo ol Imbro."

"Come with us."

Aveo did, a little surprised that he was not struck, or tied, or even touched. The four soldiers formed a square around him and marched him toward the city. The wind followed, smelling of death and lime and loss.

Death lay on the hot land as well. Fields that should have been bursting with grain near harvest had already been stripped. Broken stalks poked at the sky. Empty *gleisin* pens, shorn orchards, all gone to feed the army. What would the city eat this winter?

He would not be alive to find out.

At dusk the silent procession entered the West Gate. Beggars and slaves shrank from the soldiers; market women cast down their eyes and made themselves small. To Aveo's surprise, the *cul* didn't lead him toward the prison close against the city wall. Instead the *cul* marched toward the palace, through its gates, and—yes—to the Hall of the Goddess of All Green.

Aveo had been here before, many years ago, when everything had been different. A reception for scholars from the university. Wine, laughter, smiling slaves in white skirts serving delicacies. Uldunu Three had been on the throne then, not his murderous son. Before the assassination, before the war, before the university had been closed and the slaves stripped and branded. Before.

They marched into the Hall. His Most Sacred and Exalted King Uldunu Four sat on the Green Throne. Advisors in their red robes clustered behind him. Aveo recognized Ilni and Omoro, and looked away. *Which of you betrayed the university, betrayed the city, betrayed my son?*

Aveo and the *cul* halted before the throne, sank to their knees, and crossed their arms over their breasts. The soldiers, who were not people but only utensils, remained standing. They had no souls and thus were incapable, like animals or plants, of meaningful homage to the Goddess of All Green and Her son, Uldunu. Aveo gazed at the king's toenails, painted with tiny green swirls and encased in green sandals set with gold.

"Up," Uldunu said.

Aveo rose.

"Raise eyes. You are a traitor, Aveo ol Imbro."

It was not permitted to speak, since Aveo had not been

asked a question. It was permitted, now, to gaze, and he and the king studied each other. Aveo saw a young man fantastically painted, every inch of his bare-chested body in intricate green designs, petals inside petals, sensuous curving vines and lashing textured branches, a strong and brutal body turned into a support for the living world. The king's short skirt was green spider-silk. His eyes were bluer than those of the father he had murdered.

What did Uldunu see? A coarse brown skirt instead of the red Aveo had once worn, no caste paint, a man neither young nor old but infinitely more aged than before grief had broken him.

"You are a traitor," Uldunu repeated. "You advised my father, and your son led a pathetic uprising against me. You deserve to die as he did, and in the same agony. You deserve that your soul, like his, should lie forever fallow, never blooming in Her sight. But the Goddess of All Green has another task for you."

Aveo failed to keep surprise from his face.

"You were a scholar," the king said, his voice full of contempt for such a pursuit. He waved his hand at the advisors behind him. "These men tell me you studied the languages and customs and false gods of those cities that are our enemies. You have lived among them."

They had not been enemies then. Nor had their gods proven any more or less false than the Goddess of All Green. But a man like the king could never understand how Aveo had come to believe that, nor the emptiness that lack of belief left him with now. *Ojea . . .*

"You will use this traitorous knowledge now for the glory of the Goddess. In Memenat a woman has hatched from an egg fallen out of the sky. She cannot be killed by spears or fire, so perhaps she is an evil goddess from an enemy city. But she cannot kill those who attack her, so perhaps she is not a goddess. You will go there and talk to her in your enemy languages and find out why she is here."

Aveo blinked. Accustomed as he was to the stupid and blood-hungry childishness of the king, and to the endless foolish talk about religion and goddesses, this was something new. A woman from an egg, a egg from the sky . . . He had heard no rumors that Uldunu Four was mad.

"You will also discover how we can kill her. If you fail to discover that, you will die a far worse death than your traitor son. Go."

The *cul* pushed Aveo, not hard, and he fell to his knees. The green-and-gold sandals below thick legs moved away. When he had gone, Aveo rose, a little dazed.

Evidently Uldunu Four not only held the power of life and death, he could also change the essential nature of the real. Aveo had been a traitor and a condemned man but no longer a scholar. Now he was still a traitor, no longer a condemned man, and restored to being a scholar. Also, apparently, something else: an emissary to a woman hatched from an egg fallen out of the sky.

Just before the assassination of Uldunu Three, Aveo had composed a treatise on the relationship of reality to kulith, the game played ubiquitously in the city by everyone from advisors to slaves. How much of what we believe, this treatise asked, is shaped by the objects in common use around us? Would we have numbers in tens if we did not have ten fingers and toes? Would we try less hard to outwit each other if we did not play kulith? Would we think slavery so natural if one could not buy and sell some—but not others—of the variously colored stones in a kulith game, which represented men and women? Aveo had stopped short of asking the question really in his mind, which was: Would we even believe in the Goddess of All Green if belief were not shaped by the objects that, even in kulith, must be given to Her in daily tribute?

Despite omitting that final question, with the wealth of examples he had gathered to support it, the treatise was a dangerous one. At the university, old Ubapa had urged

Aveo not to let it be read or copied or archived. It could get him imprisoned. Aveo had not listened, and Ubapa had been right, and here was Aveo walking too fast along a hot and dusty road, emissary to a goddess he did not believe could exist.

They had been on the road four days. The moon, green and blue, now filled the sky. Aveo, not a soldier, was unused to the exertion or the pace. His feet burned in their worn sandals, his muscles ached, his face burned from the sun. Sweat matted his skirt to his bony shanks. He stank.

"With pain comes delusion." That had been Ibrix, writing three centuries ago, and the Sacred Scholar had been right. Sometimes, trudging along on feet that blossomed into fire, his head light, Aveo thought he saw Ojea in the heat shimmers of the road ahead. His son was a child, a man, an infant in the arms of the King's Torturer. Aveo cried out. A soldier reached out to cuff him, stayed his hand, and scowled.

On the fifth day they arrived at Memenat. That city had been captured, sacked, and burned. The bulk of the army had moved on, but two entire detachments of soldiers had remained, encircling the fallen sky egg with a makeshift city of their own. Aveo passed through wooden gates set into high dirt walls. He crossed plank bridges over deep trenches dug by newly enslaved Memenati. This shoddy city of tents and clay was nonetheless rich with plunder, and Aveo noted the jewels and rich robes on the prostitutes, the roasting meats beside the cook tents. His stomach ached with hunger.

Despite the new riches, the shadow city showed surprising order. The prostitutes were confined to one area, the dirt streets were swept, the soldiers on duty stood sober and at attention, their breastplates polished. When Aveo was marched through the staring camp and turned over to its commander, he saw why.

"Rem Aveo ol Imbro," the commander said, and Aveo raised his eyes in astonishment. It was illegal to give him his scholarly title. Was it done from fear? A superstitious soldier might well be unsettled by events here: An egg fell out of the sky, a woman could not be pierced with a spear. Things were not as always supposed, and anything could happen next, the ground itself might well give way as just another illusion. Fear could make such a man overly careful, unwilling to invite divine retaliation in any quarter.

Commander Escio ol Escio was not such a man. He was short but very muscular, his bare chest painted with the blue whorls of his rank. Escio's eyes met Aveo's squarely. Light gray eyes, measuring, neither easily frightened nor easily duped. Aveo said, "Is it permitted to ask questions?"

"Yes. But would you first like to sit and to eat?"

Something broke in Aveo then, from fatigue and hunger and grief, and tears filled his eyes. He turned away. When he had mastered himself, the tent was empty, which almost brought the shameful tears again. When had he last encountered that much kindness?

The commander returned with a steaming plate of meat and stewed fruit. He busied himself while Aveo sat on a three-legged stool and ate it. Then Escio sat opposite him, hands on the knees exposed by his blue skirt. Escio's voice was controlled, quiet. "The egg fell out of the sky eleven days ago. We attacked, but neither spears nor fire so much as blackened it. The next day the woman came out. She has come out every day, usually between noon and dusk. She just stands before her egg. For four days we attacked, and the spears slid off her and fell to the ground. Fire didn't touch her. Then orders came to stop attacking and wait for a scholar from the king."

Aveo risked a question. "Why did you attack her?"

"Those are my orders. Immediately attack all enemies and traitors."

Aveo himself was a traitor. "Has she spoken?"

"No."

"Does she carry a weapon?"

"Not visibly."

"Describe her, please."

"She dresses like a farmer of the north, in leggings and boots and brown cloth tunic. She bears no paint, of any caste. She is about as tall as you, and stands without fear. She looks young. She has dark skin, black hair, dark eyes."

Dark, with boots rather than sandals. Aveo had a sudden hope that she might be from Pular, far to the north. He spoke Pularit.

But what kind of Pulari could fly through the sky in an egg? The Pulari were unsophisticated farmers and trappers, their huts made of mud and their kulith pieces of uncarved stone.

Aveo studied the commander, and took another risk. "You said your orders are to attack all enemies and traitors. Why did you decide the woman must be an enemy?"

Escio said, with the air of a man who knew full well what he was revealing, "I knew that the king would think she must be an enemy."

"And you, Commander—what do you think she is?"

"I think as the king's soldier."

Disappointed, Aveo looked away. When the commander rose, he did, too. Escio said, "I will take you to the inner gate and wait with you until the woman comes out of her egg."

"Thank you."

"Rem Aveo. I play kulith at the sixteenth level. I read your treatise on kulith and reality, about how what we believe is shaped by what is around us. The egg is not an illusion. It is here."

Aveo turned in surprise—such reading and observations from a soldier!—but Escio was already leading the way out of the tent, toward the woman fallen out of the sky.

4: LUCCA

He dreamed, while the alien medical devices did their work inside his body.

Lucca was vaguely aware of the jolting of the travois, vaguely aware of his own methodical mind forming questions: *Does the travois mean they haven't discovered the wheel? How long have these beasts been domesticated?* But in and out of the questions, of the fevered dreams, flitted shadowy forms, illusions. Gianna, alive and well, strolling through the Maduro vineyards and laughing at him over her shoulder. Cam, naked in his bunk aboard the Atoner ship. He tried to tell Cam about his dead wife, but she put out a hand, laughing, to stop him, and the hand grew long and leafy like the Tuscany vines and Lucca cried out and woke himself.

The man with the long mustache leaned over him and spoke, and the implant whispered in his ear, "Are you well, fellow-traveler-on-the-first-road?"

The translator had listened to the Kularians while Lucca slept. Now it whispered into his ear implant as the man spoke, and then it whispered again, giving Lucca the meaningless sounds he parroted aloud. The process was clumsy and slow, despite Lucca's intense practice on Luna and during the voyage out. Finally he managed, "I'm fine," and then, all at once, he *was* fine. The fever vanished like a blown match, and he was enveloped in a sudden glow of neurological well-being. Also the result of the Atoner meds? He hoped not; he wanted to see everything as clearly as possible, free of chemical illusions.

He expected the Kularian to continue the conversation, to ask Lucca's name or where he came from or why he'd been trapped in a silver metal egg in the middle of nowhere. But the man walked away, striding ahead of the rest toward some structures distant on the endless scrub plain.

Lucca could see his breath; the air held the cold tingle of coming snow. Heavy clouds blotted the sky. Had Kular B risen, and had Cam landed on it successfully, or had her shuttle malfunctioned, too?

They neared the settlement and Lucca saw that it consisted of a circle of flimsy animal-skin tents that looked easy to take down and move. As people came curiously toward the travois, he saw they were all men and adolescent boys. *Temporary hunting or trading camp on a steppe-like northern plain in late autumn.* The men all had one red-painted front tooth; the boys did not.

The group all talked at once, waving their arms and stamping their feet, and the translator couldn't keep up. It offered Lucca random phrases: "found in a metal *skrog* (untranslatable)" and "broken leg" and "three *guwats* (untranslatable)" and then, three times in rapid succession, "traveler-on-the-second-road." Lucca detected no hostility or fear toward himself and only minimal curiosity— how was that possible?

Everyone went into the largest tent except for two boys, their mustaches as yet only downy fuzz, who grinned at him, stamped their feet, and blushed.

Dusk was falling, the late and lingering northern twilight of a nineteen-degree axial tilt. It suffused the air, still laden with dust from the passing storm, with a silver-gray glow. Kularians emerged from the large tent, laughing and talking. They walked a short ways out to the plain. The two boys picked up the poles of Lucca's travois and pulled it after them. Everyone, including Lucca, formed a circle, and one man walked into the middle of it.

Lucca raised himself on his elbows where the boys had plopped him flat. A hunting-celebration ritual of some

kind? An initiation, or a religious rite? Or just the equivalent of a university club, with what Cam had called *horseplay,* now that the men were away from their women?
Probably very mild horseplay; Lucca couldn't see these
genial, incurious people engaging in hazing or orgies or
dangerous dares.

The man in the center of the circle sat down. So did
everyone else, except for a big man Lucca had noticed
before. No one spoke. Lucca had the impression that whatever needed to be said had been taken care of in the large
tent. The big man sat next to the man in the center. Everyone smiled and nodded, probably prevented from foot
stamping only because they were all sitting down. As native rituals went, this one wasn't very colorful.

The big man drew a long knife and cut the other man's
throat.

Lucca gasped. His hand groped under his tunic, at his
belt, suddenly frantic to make sure the personal shield was
still activated. Blood spurted from the Kularian's throat
and flew through the air, like projectile vomiting. The victim made horrible gurgling sounds for a few seconds, waving his arms in a grotesque parody of his earlier friendliness.
Then he collapsed and the large man let the body fall to the
ground.

Everyone smiled and one of the teenage boys laughed
happily.

It was darker now. The boys seized the poles of the
travois and pulled it back toward the tents, then inside
the largest, leaving the flap open. There was nothing inside the tent except piles of blankets, some fur and some
woven. One by one the men straggled in, stamping their
feet and chatting easily. Bowls of stew were brought in
from the cook fire outside. The man with the long mustache, who seemed to have assumed charge of Lucca, sat
beside him, and a boy handed each of them a bowl.

Lucca couldn't eat. The smell of the stew, fragrant in
itself, turned his stomach. He reminded himself that he

was safe, that nothing short of nuclear weapons could penetrate his personal shield, that the Atoners wanted him back safely to "witness," that the Atoners knew what they were doing.

But it was an Atoner shuttle that had malfunctioned, breaking his leg and marooning him on this steppe.

The Kularian said, "Fellow-traveler-on-the-first-road, are you warm enough?"

"Yes, I . . . yes. Thank you."

"Eat. Jikelioriatwe makes good stew, and tomorrow we head home."

"Yes . . . What is your name?" Maybe manners required guests to ask first.

"I am Hytrowembireliaz."

Lucca would never remember it. He said, "I am Lucca."

Hytrowembireliaz threw back his head and laughed, a joyous sound untinged with hysteria. He said to the tent at large, "His name is 'Lucca'!" and everyone shouted happily. The translator said helpfully, "His name is cooking ladle."

It was a great joke. Everyone made several jokes about ladles, the contents of ladles, women, and ladling things into other things. The tent grew noisier, smellier, more crowded. Lucca couldn't tell who was talking to whom, including whether they addressed him as he lay on a pile of reeking furs in the corner. His hands shook as he tried to eat a few spoonfuls, and then he was furious at himself for shaking, and then he grew afraid again and that was worse.

Out the open flap of the tent he could see, by starlight, the abandoned corpse. No attempt was made to bury it or guard it from animals.

Eventually the tent quieted, several people left, and the remainder lay down to sleep. Hytrowembireliaz squatted beside Lucca and covered him tenderly, saying, "There—you will be warm enough now." The tent flap was closed. In the darkness, men snored.

He wanted to talk to Cam or Soledad, but he couldn't link with either the ship or Kular B until he was alone. All he could do was lie here and go over and over in his mind the friendly benevolence, the many nods and smiles, the native Good Samaritans taking hours to rescue a stranger. And then the man willingly—even happily—taking his place in the center of the circle so the other could slice open his throat. All the genial joking afterward. Who were these people, and what did the Atoners want Lucca to perceive about them? The man in the center of the circle, the sweet smiles, the knife and the blood . . .

Hytrowembireliaz never had asked Lucca who he was or where he came from.

In the morning Lucca again felt equal to his task. Sleep, plus whatever the Atoners had put into him, fortified him. He was here to witness. Many primitive cultures practiced ritual killing, and sometimes it was an honor to be chosen to die. Or death might have been a punishment that even the victim thought he deserved. Lucca would find out which.

Not even the sight of the corpse shook this resolution. During the night the body had been chewed and mangled by animals. Lucca's gorge rose, but the Kularians barely glanced at the pulpy horror. With cheerful efficiency they took down the tents, loaded them and a huge pile of furs— evidently this *had* been a hunting expedition—onto travois made of the tent poles, and hitched up their reeking, ponderous beasts. The procession moved at about three miles an hour, making conversation easy. The men chattered, sang, waved their arms. Hytrowembireliaz appeared beside Lucca's travois to say, "Do you want some water?"

"Yes, please." Hytrowembireliaz passed him a leather water bag. Communal, but Lucca expected that and tried not to think about all the other mouths that had been on it before his.

"Last night," Lucca began, and waited. The less he said,

the less obvious his ignorance would be, and Hytrowem-bireliaz might spontaneously offer information.

He did; evidently these were not a reticent people. "A good crossing, yes. Chytfouriswelpim is very happy."

"Why?"

Hytrowembireliaz frowned slightly. "What do you try to say?"

Careful. Something here is a given. "Why now?"

Hytrowembireliaz's face cleared. "His wife has gone on the second road. His sons moved to the south, to farm. Chytfouriswelpim wished to set out on his journey."

So it had been a voluntary death. Something hard and angry formed in Lucca's chest. The dead man had been hale and laughing, not sick, not even old. A widower, yes, but widowers adjusted, went on. No one knew that better than he. Even in his blackest moods, Lucca hadn't killed himself. He'd endured, had at least tried to be too strong for that easy escape.

These people were cowards.

And deluded as well. The "second road"—a belief in an afterlife, probably the single largest aberration of the human mind. The Kularians threw life away here, from the illusion of something better later. "Pie in the sky," the Americans said. They were right. Squander this life now, in everything from joylessness to suicide bombing, and collect your rewards in Heaven, in Asgard, in Paradise, in Hades, in the Fields of Yalu. Untold light-years away from Earth, separated from the rest of human culture by ten thousand years, and Kular still came up with the same pathetic illusions.

"Yes," Lucca said, and hoped his forced smile didn't hold too much of either contempt or pity. He was not here to judge. He was here to witness.

One more night of travel, and the land became more irregular, rising to become foothills of a low mountain range. The sky didn't clear and the air grew colder still.

Trees appeared, strange wide plants with many trunks, intertwined branches, and purplish-green leaves falling off even as he watched. Each tree stood separate, no more than three meters high but covering up to a half acre, a miniature forest. Small strange creatures darted in and out.

Finally they reached a village of miniscule stone huts surrounding a much larger stone building, all set beside a clear, swift river flowing down from the mountains. Women, children, and old men rushed out, and there was much foot stamping, arm waving, and laughing. Temporarily forgotten, Lucca climbed carefully off the travois, pleased and astonished to find that he could stand as long as he didn't put too much weight on his splinted leg. Whatever the Atoners had put inside him, it was wonderful.

"Welcome, fellow-traveler-on-the-first-road," a woman said to him. Like the men, she wore pants, boots, and tunic. Her hair, cut very short, curled wildly around her broad face as if electrified. She had one red tooth. Her dark eyes were kind. "Come inside."

He limped after her, Hytrowembireliaz, and three children into one of the stone huts.

"I think I'm a guest for the winter," Lucca told Cam. It was such a relief to finally get away from the amiable Kularians. He sat on the ground beside one of the miniforests, just out of sight of the village. Snow fell, one desultory flake at a time. He'd already reported in to Soledad and uploaded the contents of his translator with whatever it had learned of the Kularian language.

"Well, you're doing better than I am," Cam said. "I still haven't made contact. Unless you count the spear-and-fire attacks, and they've even stopped doing that. I go outside the shuttle every damn day, stand in the middle of this entire army camp they've built around me, and nothing happens. *Nothing.* Christ, why did the Atoners tell us that we can't go to the natives until they approach us first?"

"Why did the Atoners tell us anything they said? Your personal shield works?"

"Like I'm encased in Lucite. The spears just slide off me and I don't feel a thing. Haven't you had a chance to test yours yet?"

She didn't listen. Just to him, or to anyone? For the hundredth time, Lucca wondered why the Atoners had chosen Cam as a Witness, and why he allowed himself to get so irritated by her. Yes, they'd had that brief stupid affair on the ship, but even as he'd entered her beautiful body Lucca had known he wasn't going to love Cam. He wasn't going to love anyone except Gianna, not ever again, and when he'd come inside Cam it had been with a bitter wrenching shudder that was barely pleasure at all.

He said, "No, I haven't had a chance to test my shield. I told you, these are cheerful people, hospitable, not easily agitated. Except when they're cutting each other's throats in assisted suicide, they're *nice*."

"And that's bad?"

"No, of course not." But Lucca knew that all that niceness bothered him. He didn't like it, although he didn't know why.

"Nice and peaceful sounds good to me right now."

He didn't believe her. Cam relished the attacks that could not touch her, relished being the omnipotent and mysterious stranger around which a whole encampment of soldiers had been built. Whereas Lucca was mostly forgotten except when he was in the way of Hytrowembireliaz's busy family, at which point they smiled at him and stamped their feet and forgot him again. He was fed, given warm clothing and a comfortable bed, and asked nothing. It was incredible. He was practically invisible.

"So ask them things," Cam said.

"I do. There is only one answer: 'over the mountains.' The grain for porridge comes from over the mountains, in trade for furs. The family loom comes from over the mountains, in trade for furs. But as far as I can tell, 'over the mountains' functions exactly like here, except for a different climate. The language has no word for 'city' or any form of government, no word for 'king' or 'president' or even 'leader.' How can there be no form at all of any word for someone in charge?"

"Anarchy," Cam said.

"Anarchy is actually a sophisticated form of social organization, Cam. It requires strong cultural ties to reinforce taboos against violence and stealing, and communal institutions to teach those taboos to the young. Here there are no institutions, no schooling in abstract ideas, and, as far as I can figure out, not even a written language. This is the thinnest culture possible on all possible axes. There aren't even any interesting rituals beyond cutting each other's throats when they decide it's time to die!"

Silence on the other side of the commlink. Lucca heard his own tone, lingering in the air like miasma. Finally Cam said, "Well, excuse me for not having a college education. And you're taking all this way too personally, Lucca. I thought anthropologists were supposed to be objective."

It was such a Cam-like remark that Lucca put his head into his hands. He wasn't an anthropologist, having dropped out of graduate work at Oxford when Gianna died, well before he'd finished his degree. And anthropologists weren't "objective," whatever that meant, because they were human and thus inevitably equipped with the lenses of their own culture. And of course he was taking this personally. Lucca had told Cam, had told the Atoners, had told the UN interrogators, that he believed the personal was all one had. Personal vision and personal thoughts, filtered through the lens of one's biology and background, until sickness or old age or a renegade lorry took those things away and the self vanished. Cam never listened.

He said, "I must go. My ass is cold from sitting on the ground."

"Me, too. Not my ass—it's sweltering hot here. I mean

I have to go and stand in front of the shuttle so nothing can happen. Again. If I didn't have Soledad to talk to all the time I'm inside this damn shuttle, I'd go mad. It's weird, you know—two emissaries from the stars, and two planets just ignore us. Who'd have thought?"

Despite himself, Lucca laughed. He closed the comm-link and looked up to find Hytrowembireliaz's middle child, Chewithoztarel, watching him. The little girl, who looked about ten, had not yet had her hair cut short or her front tooth reddened, so perhaps both were puberty rites.

"What are you doing, Lucca?"

She must have crept up on him from around the stand of trees. No—of "tree." He sat beside one of the tangled half-acre stalks and vines that were all one plant. Her dark eyes gazed at him with the first curiosity he'd seen since he landed. What would she report to her parents? That the stranger talked into a tiny box?

Counter an unwelcome question with another question. He said, "What are *you* doing here?"

"Ragjuptrilpent told me you were here."

He didn't know the name; probably one of her little friends. "What else did Ragjuptrilpent say?"

"She said you washed in the shed and pissed in the corner."

Pleasure flooded Lucca. Unable to stand his own stink any longer, he had indeed washed in the lean-to behind the stone hut where the water tubs were kept. As soon as he'd undressed, he'd needed to piss and, shivering with cold in the unheated shed and unwilling to dress again and make the trek to the privy, he'd gone in a corner and covered his urine with dirt. But the shed was closed on all sides, and no little girl with an unpronounceable name had observed him. Furthermore, Kularians never entered other families' huts, which were so tiny they contained room only for piles of sleeping blankets and changes of clothing. Cooking, eating, and socializing all took place in the village lodge, where nearly everyone spent all non-sleeping time. If Lucca had been observed at his hasty and frigid bath, it had not been by the unknown Ragjuptril-pent but by Hytrowembireliaz's middle daughter herself.

So Kularians sometimes lied.

It was the first crack Lucca had found in the surface image of happy, simple natives. So perhaps it wasn't much—it was still something. A culture that developed lying had things it wished to hide. Chewithoztarel had lied, and she had asked a question out of curiosity. Finally, Lucca had an informant.

He scrambled up off the frozen ground and put a hand on the little girl's shoulder. "Will you help me walk back to the hut, little fellow-traveler-on-the-first-road?"

"Yes!"

Maybe he would find out something—anything—worth witnessing, after all.

5: FROM *REWIRED AND HACKED IN,* EDITORIAL COLUMN

Marketing a Thunderbolt

At first, of course, they thought it was a joke, those few Internet roamers who visited the new website. Maybe it came up far down a list at Google or Ask.com, or maybe they just stumbled across it during a session of bored, late-night conspiracy surfing. It was just one of the thousands of bogus sites that sprang up hours—maybe minutes—after NASA released the shattering news that probes had detected an alien spacecraft approaching the moon. Some of Earth's population panicked; some rejoiced; some urged attack; some joked.

So no one believed the website was real. Come on, now—a classified ad for human "Witnesses" to some colossal alien crime? The site didn't even look very inventive: just sixty-seven dry words, unadorned by even basic clip art:

> We are an alien race you may call the Atoners. Ten thousand years ago we wronged humanity profoundly. We cannot undo what has been done, but we wish humanity to understand it. Therefore we request twenty-one volunteers to visit seven planets to witness for us. We will convey each volunteer there and back in complete safety. Volunteers must speak English. Send requests for electronic applications to witness@atoners.com.

But after the aliens made radio contact with SETI and then proceeded to talk freely—if circumspectly—with anyone whose communication equipment could reach the moon, everything changed. The Atoners mentioned the website. Within minutes, it took millions of hits, and everything—panicking, rejoicing, attacking, joking—ramped up exponentially. Suddenly the B movies and the old comic books and the paperbacks with tacky covers were all *real*.

And, in retrospect, the Internet was the perfect way for bona fide aliens to recruit humanity for the stars, for at least five reasons:

1. A website is accessible by anyone with a computer. If you want to reach a whole lot of people simultaneously, 24/7, this is the way to do it. Radio and TV broadcasts must change frequencies across borders, adjust to time differences, pre-empt Monday night football. The Internet is always there, always ready, everywhere at once.

2. A website bypasses the filters of government censorship, spin, posturing, and rhetoric. Instead of being told what aliens said, we can see for ourselves.

3. This website demonstrates formidable technology. It apparently joined the Web without human agency and has resisted all attempts to remove, block, modify, or hack into it—and trust me on this, the best computer minds on Earth have tried. We *know*.

4. A website reaches those people who are most computer-literate—the young—whom the Atoners apparently wanted to reach. Everyone "accepted" so far has been under thirty. Space is usually considered a game for the young, educated, and intelligent. Nothing like knowing your target audience.

5. The website *works*. Millions of "applications" have been filled out and sent.

As the entire planet waits to see who else is accepted—and whether any means really is provided to take them to the moon, let alone to other planets and back—one fact emerges about the Atoners: Madison Avenue could take lessons from them. Their sales approach is logical, attention getting, and effective.

Except, perhaps, for one thing—we still don't have any idea what they're selling.

6: CAM

Cam checked on the shuttle displays to be sure that no soldiers lurked just outside, ready to rush in the second she opened the door. They couldn't hurt her, of course, but they might have done all sorts of damage to the inside of the shuttle. Or maybe not—this was Atoner property, after all. And a rush by some soldiers would at least liven things up. Cam was really sick of twenty-three-hour shifts in a six-foot-diameter round box with nothing to do but talk to Soledad, whom she'd never gotten along with all that well in the first place. Lucca didn't know how lucky he was, broken leg and euthanasia whackos and all.

Who would have guessed witnessing for aliens, on an alien planet, could be so *boring*?

Well, maybe today would be the day. Cam checked her equipment, activated her personal shield, and opened the shuttle door, blinking in the bright hot sunlight. Two men walked toward her from the dirt walls that circled the shuttle a hundred yards away.

Well, this was more like it!

One was a soldier, deeply sunburned like all of them, in short blue skirt, breastplate, and helmet. For an insane moment Cam wondered, not for the first time, what they wore under those skirts. Then she snapped herself into Witness mode, relaxing her body posture to look unthreatening, smiling so hard that her face felt like it might crack, trying to note everything at once.

The soldier had short dark brown hair and, like most of the Kularians she'd seen, light-colored eyes. Muscular arms, swirls of blue paint on forearms and cheeks, the same height as she, neither young nor old. The other wore a longer skirt of coarse brown cloth with very worn sandals. No body paint. He was much older, with straggling untended gray hair and deeply lined face. He stank and he limped. Clearly not another soldier, so what was he? He seemed too poorly dressed to be an official ambassador or a ruler or anything like that.

The translator needed samples of native language, so Cam couldn't respond to whatever he was calling to her. But when the two reached her and stopped, she was startled by the old man's eyes. Deep blue, they were speckled with silver, like muted stars in an evening sky. Cam knew she wasn't particularly sensitive to other people's moods; she'd been told it often enough by friends and family. But *these* eyes—although they watched her with sharp intelligence, they struck her as the bleakest things she had ever seen.

The old man, getting no response, sensibly stopped his torrent of words. He touched his chest and said, "Rem Aveo."

Cam repeated it, touched herself, and said, "Cam O'Kane." How could she keep him talking? Maybe by asking for more words. She reached out to pluck at his tunic and ask for its name; immediately the soldier stepped between them, a wicked dagger in his hand, and scowled. A bodyguard?

"Sorry, I didn't mean to hurt him. Is this your leader? No, of course not. Look, I need you to *talk*."

The old man watched her intently. All at once he began a flow of words. How had he known? It went on for a few minutes while the guard, expressionless, watched. People also watched from the ramparts, a circle of silent and wary eyes. It spooked Cam a little. But then the translator began to whisper fragments into her ear: "Come from . . . sky . . . peace . . . soldier . . . you . . . Are you a soldier come from Pular? *Cooz.*"

"*Cooz,*" Cam said aloud, parroting the translator and assuming the word meant "no."

"From where? . . . Sky . . . where?"

"From the sky, yes," she subvocalized and then repeated the sounds in her implant. "I'm not from here." She watched those navy-blue-and-speckled-silver eyes sharpen even more. Complete incomprehension on the soldier's face, although he didn't look stupid.

Rem Aveo was speaking a language the soldier didn't know.

She let him ask several more questions but didn't answer, letting the translator process vocabulary and grammar. Then Cam pointed to things, encouraging him to name them, to offer her sentences about them. She tried to look as if she understood but simply chose not to say anything herself, but it was clear he wasn't fooled. Finally the soldier spoke sharply. The old man turned to him and spoke, and Cam's implant translated, "She is Pulari. She doesn't speak our language."

The tricky old son of a gun.

But what should she do? She didn't even know if the translator could handle two separate languages; the Atoners hadn't said. Fuck! Why hadn't they prepared her better? Well, she would just have to do the best she could.

She said to Rem Aveo, "I am not Pulari. But you want this soldier to believe I am Pulari."

If he was startled, he didn't show it. "Yes," he said. "It is kulith."

The translator offered her nothing.

He said quietly, "You don't know kulith."

No, but the soldier did. He had the look of a man who finally recognized one word in a sea of incomprehensibility. Aveo said more words, many more, and the translator finally offered, "Strategy. Life or death strategy."

"Whose death?" Cam said.

"Mine," Aveo said. He looked at her with those sad, shrewd eyes, and all at once Cam realized he was younger than she'd first thought. The sadness and boniness and gray hair had misled her. But there was strength in his gaze, his stance, his natural authority. Middle-aged maybe, but no more.

She said, "If I am not Pulari, you will die?"

"It is not that simple."

She smiled. "It never is," she said, all at once feeling wise and powerful. This poor man. Why not play along, until she had the situation better figured out? She had to pretend to be from somewhere; pretending to be Pulari could save a life. And if the translator could handle both languages, then maybe the ones not speaking "Pulari" would talk more freely in front of her, and who knew what she might learn that way?

"Pulari," she said to the soldier, and pointed to her own chest. Then, in English, "Hello."

Cam walked through a wooden gate and out of the shuttle enclosure. The pale-eyed soldier must be more than just a bodyguard, might even be some sort of commander; he said something and more soldiers fell in behind them in perfect rows, perfectly quiet. As they moved through neat, cleanly raked dirt streets between straight rows of tents, the silence began to unnerve her. She glimpsed non-military people, men and women and even a few children, but none of them made any noise, either. All were bare chested, even the women. Most wore skirts of various colors and lengths, but some were completely naked. Nobody looked happy. Because of her?

Then a child threw a rock.

Cam just happened to look up as the small brown arm let fly. The boy—or maybe it was a girl, she couldn't tell—perched on top of an earthen wall. The throw was awkward, without force, and the stone landed several feet in front of Cam, plopping into the dust. It was no bigger than a pebble.

Immediately a soldier leaped onto the wall, grabbed

the child by the neck, and thrust his short sword into the little belly.

The child screamed, a high inhuman shriek like an animal caught in a trap. The soldier tossed the body, gushing blood as soon as the sword was withdrawn, from the wall. The child continued to scream, but the woman who darted from behind a wagon to snatch him to her made no noise. To Cam, staring in horror, that was the most terrible part: The mother didn't dare yell or wail or cry. She huddled over her child in complete silence, both of them covered with blood, until through the inadequate shield of her arms Cam saw the little body stop twitching and the solitary scream stopped.

Cam trembled. She tried to stop the movement in her legs and arms but she couldn't, she just couldn't, it went on and on. Then Rem Aveo's arm came around her shoulders, she was clamped to his side, and his hand gripped her wrist and held it steady.

Everyone watched her.

Rem Aveo spoke and the translator said in her ear, "Do not fall over."

"I'm okay," she gasped. After a moment she pulled away from him. Her trembling stopped. The procession moved forward, through the dusty streets, and she, Rem Aveo, and the commander entered a large tent, where the trembling began again.

Cam swore. She hated herself for this, it was stupid, she was supposed to be an impartial Witness no matter what happened, it was what she'd been sent here for . . . that child, no more than a toddler, really, spitted like a chicken and that poor mother too afraid to even cry out . . .

Cam was sitting on a stool, holding a metal goblet. Rem Aveo had one, too—yes, that was right, the soldier had poured them both from a leather bag. Rem Aveo drank his.

The commander stared at her frankly, speculation in his pale eyes.

Rem Aveo said quietly in Pularit, "You come from a place where such killing does not happen."

"Yes," Cam choked out, even as part of her mind thought, *No*. Such killing happened all the time on Earth, she read about it in the flimsies, saw it on the newscasts. Soldiers casually murdered children all the time in Africa, in Asia, in South America. But not in Nebraska, not on Cam's small-town street, not in her sight.

"Where," Rem Aveo said skeptically, "can such a place be, if people live there?" And she stared at him over the rim of her goblet, not knowing how to answer. Wondering for the first time if she really could do this, or if the Atoners had not made a terrible mistake in choosing her, so shaken by a single death, to witness whatever incomprehensible thing it was that they needed to know.

7: AVEO

"What is she?" Cul Escio said in a low voice to Aveo.

Aveo said, "I don't know." It was the truth, although he saw that Escio didn't believe him. Also that Escio didn't not believe him. But the man was a soldier, a commander; he liked certainty. A scholar's ambiguity was distasteful to him. And yet—Escio had read Aveo's treatise on reality and kulith.

"Tell me, *rem,* what you think she is."

The two men stood at the doorway of Escio's tent. The woman from the sky sat on a stool, holding a goblet of wine. The tent darkened with the sky, but no slave came to light the lamps. The camp lay as if deserted, deathly silent.

Aveo said carefully, "She speaks Pularit and says she is Pulari."

"So you have said." Again, belief and disbelief mingled. "The Pulari play kulith. They do not have such sky eggs. And the Pulari can be killed. She must be a Pulari goddess."

"It is possible. I will need to talk to her further."

"Do so. Did you see that, *rem*?"

Aveo had been watching Escio, not the woman. "See what?"

"She reached inside her tunic for a moment, drank some wine, then reached inside again. What could that mean?"

"I don't know." He should stop saying that; Uldunu Four was not keeping him alive in order to profess ignorance. "Perhaps it is a Pulari drinking ritual."

"You don't know. Yet you lived among the Pulari."

Aveo stared levelly at the commander. "But not with one like this. Let me talk to her alone, please."

Escio left. Aveo brazenly took the only other stool in the tent, the commander's own, and pulled it close to "Cam." What a name—it sounded like an animal, or a vegetable. The names of people began and ended with open sounds. Even Pulari people.

Surprise was a time-honored kulith attack. "Ostiu Cam, a moment ago you reached into your tunic before and after drinking your wine. Why?"

She looked startled. This one could hide nothing. She was not a goddess, nor an emissary, nor a soldier, nor a scholar. All those were devious.

She said, after a long hesitation, "I have weapons."

"Of course. You touched your knife. Why?"

"Not a knife." And then, in steady decision, "Spears slide off me, fire can't burn me. The soldiers told you that, right? I am protected by . . . by invisible armor. Touch me. Go ahead—touch me."

She held out her hand and Aveo slid a bony finger along the back of it. Slickness like the finest metal, but also a very faint tingling. He lifted her hand and studied his finger against it in the fading light. A small gap between their two skins. He touched her lips, too dazed for propriety: the same slickness and tingling. Aveo fought for calm.

"I see. You . . . dismantled the invisible armor to drink. Nothing can get through this armor. But when a hard thing is struck very hard, as you were by spears, it staggers and falls. You did not."

"No."

"The armor roots you somehow to the ground. And the fire? Smoke cannot get through, either? How do you receive air for breath?"

But he had asked too much. He felt her withdraw from him, protecting the rest of her secrets, perhaps regretting that she had said so much. Aveo chose another kulith strategy: the presentation of vulnerability to lure an opponent closer. "Ostiu Cam, your presence is puzzling to us all. We have never seen anything like your egg, or you. The king himself, Uldunu Four, sent me here to see you and tell him what you are. I have said to Cul Escio that you are Pulari, not only for my own sake but because that is something he can understand. I cannot understand what you are or what I must do without your help. I will do whatever you say. Do you understand me?"

She smiled radiantly and Aveo saw that she believed every word. Her dark eyes sparkled, her well-fed body leaned toward him. An innocent, such as Aveo had not seen in a very long time, not in what the world had become. Innocent, and a little stupid.

She said, "I come from much farther away than Pular, Aveo. From a place you have never heard of, where we have things you haven't yet invented, like the invisible armor. I'm here as an observer only, to see everything I can and then tell my own people about it. That's all. We're curious, like scholars are curious. I know you can understand that."

It was impossible not to believe her. And yet—was she so stupid that she didn't know how she sounded? *Here to see everything and then tell my people about it . . . like scholars.* But invading armies, too, needed to know as much as possible about their potential conquests, and they sent spies to discover this. An army of soldiers who could not be speared or burned or knocked over . . . Uldunu Four's reign would fall. But how much else with it?

Aveo could be the means for all his people to be slaughtered.

She might be an innocent, but who might be using her without her knowledge?

His head swam. Just as she said, "It's so dark," a slave entered the tent and lit the lamps. In their glow the slave, a naked girl barely budded, looked terrified. She knelt, trembling, before Aveo and crossed her arms across her thin chest. "*Rem,* the *cul* sent me . . . to wait on you and the goddess. . . . The *cul* will sleep . . . I don't know where, not here, he . . ." Terror brought her near tears.

Aveo said in his own language, "Make two beds on either side of the tent, and bring food from the cook tent."

"Yes. . . ." She was gone, skittering through the tent flap so quickly she barely moved it, although even so Aveo saw the guards that Escio had set outside.

Her fear had, perversely, emboldened Aveo. He said, "*Ostiu,* you must continue to pretend to be Pulari. A trader from Pular, I think, here to offer commerce in invisible armor. That way you will not seem so threatening."

"Good idea. If I'm going to sell armor to your king, he'll want to see me, right?"

"Yes." With Aveo as translator, and thank his own forethought that she must have a translator. He could not imagine what her unbridled tongue could say to the king.

"That girl—she's a slave?"

"Yes."

"Where I come from, there isn't any slavery anymore. It's wrong."

Stupefied, Aveo stared at her—at the clear dark eyes, the invincible body—and decided he would not ask who, without slaves, did the menial labor in her country. There were more subtle ways to learn her. And learn her he must, because if there was truly a nation of Cams somewhere on the other side of the world, then changes were coming such as Aveo had never dreamed. Nor anyone else.

The slave returned with two plates of food. Hastily the girl made up two beds. Cam reached inside her tunic and kept one hand there as she reached for the plate Aveo had already picked up. Gently she took it from his hand and began, one-handed, to eat.

So three more things learned: She was not completely trusting after all. She could be poisoned. She didn't have the sense to cloak her suspicion in deception.

They ate in silence, and afterward Cam removed her hand from her tunic. The slave had once more fled. Aveo guessed that Escio used her at night; he had the fastidious look of a man who traveled with his own bedslave rather than use the much-soiled camp prostitutes. The lamps glowed softly on the walls of the *cul*'s tent.

"I want to be taken to the king tomorrow," Cam said, "but first I have more questions. That is, if you don't mind."

"In time," Aveo said, and she frowned. But he was firm. Rising from the stool, he pulled between them the tent's one low table, with its beautiful inlaid box, and opened the box. "First, Ostiu Cam, there is something you must do. If you are to be someone who has lived with the Pulari, and if you are to see the king, you must be able to present yourself properly. This is completely essential. You must—"

"What are you doing, Aveo? What are all those little bits of wood and stone?"

"Game pieces. I am going to teach you to play kulith."

8: DATA ANALYSIS

Property of U.S. Government

(page 1 of 16)

Witness	Hans Kramer	Camilla Mary O'Kane	Jeanne D'Arles	John Elijah Jones	Amira Gupta	Lucca Giancarlo Maduro
Age	29	23	29	27	28	27
Sex	M	F	F	M	F	M
Nationality	German	American	French	British	Indian	Italian/British (dual citizen)
Residence	Bonn, Germany	Jay, Nebraska, U.S.	Lyons, France	London, U.K.	Mumbai, India	Cortona, Italy
Religion	None	Methodist	Catholic	Jewish	Hindu	None
Education (U.S. equiv.)	B.S.	High school	High school	M.A., Ph.D. candidate	Ph.D., Yale	Graduate work (Oxford)
Occupation	Chemist	Waitress	Factory worker (cheese)	Student	Asst. professor, U. of Mumbai	Family firms (multiple)
Military service	Yes	No	No	No	No	No

Criminal background	None	Shoplifting, plus juvenile, sealed	Grand larceny	None	None	None
Psychiatric hospitalization	None	None	None	2 months, depression	5 days, anxiety disorder	None
Marital status	Married	Single	Divorced	Single	Single	Widowed
Family	Child, parents, 3 siblings	Parents, 1 sibling	Parents, 3 siblings	Parent, no siblings	Parents, 6 siblings	Parent, 2 siblings
Politics	Christian Dem. Union	Unregistered	French Socialist Party	Labour	Bahujan Samaj	Greens
IQ	145	105	Unknown	Unknown	Unknown (estimated high)	Unknown
Languages (besides English)	German, French	none	French	Some Hebrew	6 Indian dialects	Italian, French, some Russian
Date applied	April 10	April 9	April 13	April 10	April 11	April 21
Date accepted	May 12	May 16	May 12	May 11	May 15	May 16

Summary

Analysis program #1. Identified Patterns: NONE
Analysis program #2. Identified Patterns: NONE
Analysis program #3. Identified Patterns: NONE
Analysis program #4. Identified Patterns: NONE

9: LUCCA

He dreamed, yet again, of Gianna. She walked across the Kularian steppe, walked right through one of the complicated and multi-rooted trees, and came to him, naked. Her smooth flesh gleamed insubstantially, but her eyes were her own, alive and sparkling, as she said, "I'm still with you, Lucca, even if I am dead. I—"

"Lucca! Lucca!"

He woke to Chewithoztarel crouching over his pile of blankets. Only by her voice was he sure it was her; the tiny hut was so dark that he couldn't see even the outline of her small form. Hytrowembireliaz snored loudly, in counterpoint to his wife's softer wheezing. Somewhere in the close, smelly dark, the other two girls also slept.

"You screamed," Chewithoztarel said, from somewhere between fear and concern. "What's wrong?"

"Nothing's wrong," Lucca said. It came out as a gasp. "Go back to sleep."

"People don't scream when nothing's wrong," the child said logically. She didn't move. Lucca had wished for curiosity among the Kularians, for a deeper connection to them, and now here it was and all he wanted was for her to go away. *Gianna, walking toward him . . .*

Chewithoztarel said, "Are you sick?"

"No." *. . . naked and insubstantial, walking through trees and . . .*

"Are you going to start out on the second road?"

"No! Go to bed!" *. . . naked and she said, "I'm still*

with you, Lucca, even if I am dead" . . . lies. All lies, delusions to comfort the desperate and the gullible. She wasn't with him, would never be with him again, and he hated the dreams that offered lies instead of truth. There was no comfort in lies, and it was cruelty for his mind to cloak the lies in Gianna's vanished love.

Chewithoztarel crept away. He heard her settle back into her own pile of rugs, and he smelled the fresh reek in the air as the blankets were disturbed. He would have liked to go outside, but that would surely wake everyone, and it was bitter cold out, and if the sky was overcast he wouldn't be able to see anything in the vast, unlit dark. So he stared sightlessly at the ceiling and tried to hang on until morning.

"I don't know if I can stand the whole winter here," he said to Soledad on the commlink. It was the first time Lucca had made this admission to her, and maybe to himself. He hated saying it.

"If you're absolutely strained to the limit, I'll come get you," Soledad said. "But I think you can make it to the end."

"What end?" Lucca retorted. He and Cam were supposed to stay on their respective planets until they had "witnessed something that needs witnessing," probably the vaguest instructions in all human history. On Kular A there was nothing to witness, nothing to report except endless fishing and hunting and dancing and winter sleeping so prolonged it was nearly hibernation. With his leg healing but not yet whole, sleeping was the only one of these activities that Lucca could take part in. But sleep brought the cruel, lying delusion that Gianna lived.

"Whatever end arrives," Soledad said. "Are you sure you can talk this often? Where are you?"

"I'm nowhere, Soledad." He sat on a blanket in the middle of empty space, white on the ground under a white cloudy sky, out of sight of the village and in sight of absolutely nothing else. Chewithoztarel had a way of sneaking up on him, but not here.

"Aren't the Kulari suspicious that you go off three or four times a day to talk to me? What do they think you're leaving the village for?"

"I don't know. They're never suspicious, never curious."

"You know, I would change places with you in a minute."

"I know you would, Soledad." He was conscious of overusing her name, of making it an anchor in the blank frustration of his days. She *was* his anchor. He didn't want to commlink Cam, off having dramatic adventures on Kular B, and Soledad didn't tell him much about Cam. She had tact, Soledad. Why hadn't he slept with her instead of Cam, so typically brash and American, on the voyage out?

Because Cam looked a little like Gianna, even though no two women could have been more different, and Lucca had clutched at her like a drowning man. *Stupido.*

Soledad listened carefully to the translator uploads he sent as often as possible; she knew everything that happened—or, rather, didn't happen, in this static environment—on Kular. She said, "I really do think you can manage this, Lucca. You're stronger than you think."

"Thank you. I better get back now. My ass is freezing."

She laughed and clicked off. Bored—she must be so bored up there in orbit. But, of course, so was he down here. Hytrowembireliaz had said that spring would bring a trading trip over the mountains and, Lucca fervently hoped, a more complex and interesting society to "witness." But Soledad had given him his coordinates on the planet; his shuttle had crashed pretty far north. Spring was a long time away.

Limping, leaning on his crude wooden crutch, he made it back to the village. Everyone was in the community lodge, where they spent most of the day. Shivering, Lucca crawled into his bed pile in Hytrowembireliaz's hut, willing to trade lunch for privacy. But he wasn't alone long.

Chewithoztarel bounced into the hut, bringing with her snow and cold. She sat at the bottom of Lucca's bed pile and leaned toward him, grinning. One of her front teeth had fallen out this morning, and her gap-toothed smile might have looked cute to anyone who liked children more than Lucca did. Or who wasn't so frustrated.

"I saw you!" the little girl said gleefully. "I saw you coming back from way over the hill! And Ragjuptrilpent saw you, too!"

Not Ragjuptrilpent again. Of all the parallel customs that could have evolved in Kularian childhood, why was the winner "imaginary friends"? But . . . what matter if Chewithoztarel had seen Lucca return from the plain? No one else would ever question him about it and she wouldn't follow him, or if she did, he could just send her back. Kularian children were obedient to adults. Lucca's private and sanity-saving contacts with Soledad could go on, privately.

Chewithoztarel said, "What is a 'soledad'?"

Sleep-talking. An easy explanation. In some unremembered dream he had called out Soledad's name, and Chewithoztarel had overheard. The child denied this, looking a little frightened at Lucca's savage expression, and he forced himself to smile. "I said 'Soledad' when I was asleep, didn't I?"

"No. You said it outside. Ragjuptrilpent heard you. She told me."

Lucca willed patience. "All right, she heard me. What else did she hear?"

"Just funny noises. Not real words. But you said 'soledad' many times and she remembered. What is a—"

"It is nothing," Lucca said, and turned away. He didn't like her listening to his sleep-talk. So often his dreams were of Gianna, who did not belong on Kular A, who no longer belonged anywhere in the universe.

Chewithoztarel said, "*Nothing* is nothing," disgust and bafflement in her child's voice.

The next time he went out on the plain, he called Soledad *amica,* which he had never done before. If Soledad was startled by this, she didn't say so. Maybe she thought he was cracking up. Lucca said the word carefully and slowly, ten separate times. He had decided on it as he trudged out of sight of the village, and he had never called Gianna that. Or anyone else. It was a stupid and unnecessary experiment, but then, what else did he have to do with his brain?

When he returned, he found Chewithoztarel in the community lodge. She had just come in from building snow spikes, or whatever they were supposed to be, outside with her friends, and her little face was flushed rosy. Lucca sat down next to her.

"Did you have fun outside?"

"Yes! Did you see our *seclis*?"

The translator didn't recognize the word, but Lucca nodded. "Yes. Very nice. Did Ragjuptrilpent help you build it?"

Her dark eyes widened. "No! She was with you!"

"Of course. With me."

"She likes you," Chewithoztarel said with her gap-toothed grin. Her mother called to her and the little girl jumped up, but Lucca put a hand on her arm. He kept the personal shield turned off all the time now; these people were not dangerous.

"Chewithoztarel, did Ragjuptrilpent hear me say 'Soledad' again?"

"I don't know. I have to go now, Lucca, Mama wants me."

He released her arm and she bounced off. But then she threw over her shoulder, "Oh, she just told me. You didn't say 'soledad.' You said 'amica.' Bye!"

She ran to her mother, and he sat there, shattered and, all at once, unexpectedly afraid.

Telepathy. It was the only thing his dazed mind could come up with. This must be what the Atoners had sent him here to witness. Had it evolved everywhere on the planet, or just here? Had it evolved at all? It must have, and he could see certain evolutionary advantages . . . better coordination of hunting parties and . . . and . . .

His thoughts shimmered like heat waves in the vineyards of home. He couldn't seem to fasten onto any one idea, couldn't seem to follow it logically through— Could these people read his mind? Was that why they were so reticent with each other: privacy taboos to compensate for no mental privacy?

No, there was still Chewithoztarel. If she could read his mind, she would have seen the image of Soledad and not had to ask what a "soledad" was. So she hadn't seen into his mind. Perhaps the telepathy was language dependent, which would explain why all she had was a word, no images . . . or did she— What if the ability only came with puberty? Or maybe disappeared with puberty? Or if . . .

He couldn't think. This was too large, too all-encompassing. It smothered his thinking, like snow smothering grass on the steppes. He needed to tell Soledad, tell Cam— Did the telepathy exist on Kular B, too? He needed to—

He needed to think. And he couldn't seem to.

Nor could he get away to commlink anyone. It had begun to snow in earnest, thick white sheets that made even the closest huts invisible out the lodge window. Lucca would get hopelessly lost if he tried to go out on the plain. And if he went to Hytrowembireliaz's hut, that monster child would surely follow. He would have to wait to spill this amazing news.

The dancing and foot stomping had resumed. Lucca sat in his corner, leaning on his wooden staff, watching the dancers. The women leaped as exuberantly as the men, their short hair crackling around their faces, their red teeth flashing. What did they know, what could they do, that he could not—and what did it have to do with the Atoners' self-alleged crimes?

10: CAM

It made no sense. Aveo wanted to *walk* to the capital.

They lay on their beds in Escio's tent, Aveo still asleep, in the very early morning. The naked little slave girl had crept in with water practically the second that Cam sat up and stretched on her pallet. The girl must have been lurking outside, which made Cam uncomfortable. Had she been there all night? The tent was warm enough, but most likely outside had turned cold, with no blankets and no clothes.

"Hello," Cam had said, but of course it was in Pularit and the girl didn't understand. She put down the two heavy pails of water, one by Cam's pallet and one beside Aveo's, and scurried away before Cam could rise.

Was Cam supposed to bathe in front of Aveo? Not going to happen. But she did turn off her shield to wash her face, neck, and hands, by which time the girl was back with two bowls. This time Cam caught her by the arm and held her fast.

"Cam," she said, pointing to herself and smiling like an idiot. "You?"

The girl trembled. Up close, she looked even younger, maybe no more than twelve or thirteen. Cam caught the pungent odor of semen.

Son of a bitch. Escio? Most likely. Every terrible story she'd ever heard of slave owners' abusing their "property" raced into her mind, followed by a hatred so bilious she could taste it on her tongue.

Aveo awoke. "Let her go, Ostiu Cam. She's frightened of you."

"It's not me she should be frightened of! That bastard raped her!"

Aveo looked puzzled, and Cam realized that they'd hardly given the translator any vocabulary for either "raped" or "bastard." Or maybe Aveo just looked like that because he was part of the same rotten society that sold children into sexual slavery.

All at once she flashed on a sudden image of *herself and Lucca naked in his bunk aboard the Atoner ship and her saying, "You're too innocent, Lucca." Because despite his having been married, his sexual repertoire seemed a lot more limited than hers. But Lucca had laughed and said, "I'm innocent? Oh,* cara, *you have no idea how much you don't know about the world outside Nebraska."*

Aveo said, "Let her go, please."

"Not until I at least get a name for her! She's not an object!"

Aveo said something to the girl, who replied shakily. Aveo said in Pularit, "Her name is Obu."

"And tell me how to say thank you in her tongue."

"Dzazni."

"Dzazni, Obu," Cam said, and released her. Obu looked as if she'd been slapped. She ran out of the tent.

Aveo said, "We could debate slavery, Ostiu Cam, all morning, but it would be better if you ate your breakfast. We have a long walk ahead of us."

"Walk?" she said blankly.

"To the capital. Did we not agree last night that you wish to go there, that Cul Escio conceives it as his duty to take you, and that I am to translate?"

"But not walk! We can go in my ship, of course."

"Ah, you call it a 'ship,' not an 'egg,' " Aveo said.

That was what the translator had decided to call it. For a brief moment Cam felt adrift; she didn't understand the sounds she mouthed, and it was really the Atoners, through their translator, that were in control here. Then the unpleasant sensation passed. She possessed the translator, and the shuttle, and her personal shield, and no one on Kular could force her to do or go or be anything she didn't choose.

Aveo, looking patient, said, "The 'ship' would, I think, frighten the king."

"Frighten him? Why?"

Aveo said, "He does not possess such a miracle himself."

Of course not. Cam had the impression that Aveo was saying much more than his actual words. She had that impression a lot, and she didn't like it because it made her feel stupid. He was a difficult old man.

Aveo struggled to pull himself off the pallet. Cam saw the flailing movements of his thin body and pushed away pity. This was not some pathetic old geezer in a nursing home. Aveo was smart, wily, and patient. She had learned that much last night, as he taught her to play kulith.

He said, "We cannot go in your ship. It's impossible."

"Why?"

"Many reasons." He reached for his bowl eagerly, like a man who hadn't eaten well in a long time. "First, Cul Escio will not travel without a heavily armed guard; we are at war. Second, I doubt he would set foot in your ship because he could not control what might happen there. Third, if that egg from the sky landed in the capital, King Uldunu Four would immediately conclude that you are very dangerous and should be killed."

"He can't kill me."

"He can kill me."

It was said calmly, without drama, but Cam felt a shiver along her neck. Somehow she had become responsible for Aveo, and maybe for Obu as well. Nothing she had planned on. She said grudgingly, "How long a walk is it?"

If he felt triumphant, it didn't show. "Five days."

"Then there must be a lot of open country around the capital."

"Yes. Ravaged, but open."

"Then you and I will go in my ship to within one day's walk of the city and wait for Escio and his troops to join us there."

He stopped eating, a piece of some breadlike thing suspended in his hand halfway to his mouth, and stared at her. "You . . . and I?"

"Yes. That way you'll be safe and we'll get there faster. You can't tell me that you can keep up with those soldiers, Aveo. You look like someone who just got out of the hospital."

"The . . ."

"Like someone who's been sick a long time."

He didn't answer. Into the pause Cam said, "And Obu. She comes with us, too."

He ate the last of his bread, after sopping up the last of the juices in his bowl. "Ostiu Cam, you have missed the point of kulith last night."

"*Kulith*? What does that have to do with anything?"

"It has everything to do with everything. I thought you understood. You played fairly well, for a beginner, so—"

"I played chess in high school."

"—so I thought you understood. You cannot rush too fast at the opposing army, or you will lose."

"Oh, rats, Aveo, that's just a game."

They stared at each other in mutual incomprehension. Then Cam got another idea. "Obu—does she belong to Escio personally? Or to the army?"

"I don't see the relevance of this."

"Just tell me! Who does she belong to?"

"To Escio, I imagine."

"Then I can buy her from him, right?"

"*Buy* her?"

"Yes! I can make him an offer." She had trade goods on the ship, valuable things that Atoners had supplied. Her mind became fired with the idea; she could set at least one slave free. Maybe even more.

Aveo said quietly, "If you even make such an insulting

offer, he would be within his rights to try to kill you. Or me."

"Why?"

But all he said was, "We must play much more kulith, *ostiu.*"

"Oh, fuck kulith! He—"

Escio entered. Aveo looked at her pleadingly, and Cam shut up. Obu could be discussed later, as long as Cam kept the girl with her in the meantime, so Escio couldn't rape her again.

The two men spoke. Cam stayed quiet, letting the translator gather vocabulary and grammar for this second language. But something was wrong. Escio's hand rested on the hilt of his knife, and although his back was to her, she saw the tension in the hard muscles of his bare back. Aveo, facing her, also tensed his thin body, but his face all at once sagged and his eyes turned bleak. Without moving his head, he slid those hopeless, silver-flecked blue eyes sideways to Cam's face, and no effort was needed to cross two cultures, ten millennia, or hundreds of light-years to read Aveo's meaning: "Good-bye." Escio's hand tightened on his dagger, even as he talked on.

With one swift motion and no forethought whatsoever, Cam reached into her tunic, switched off her shield, pulled out her laser gun, and fired. Escio's knife had just cleared its sheath. Flesh sizzled, smelling of burnt meat, and the *cul* fell. The hole in the back of his head was so small that it wasn't even visible through his hair.

Aveo looked at her from uncomprehending eyes.

No no no no she hadn't . . .

But she had. And now she must keep going. Swiftly she reactivated the shield, grabbed Aveo's arm, and pulled him toward the tent flap. In his ear she said softly, "Keep walking. Don't say or show anything."

Outside the tent Obu waited. Cam grabbed her, too, and dragged her along. The child opened her mouth to scream, but Aveo said something sharply to her and she scurried into file behind him. "Let her go," he said quietly to Cam, "and she'll follow."

It seemed endless miles, endless hours to the ship. But no one stopped them, no one questioned the orders that Aveo snapped at the gate guards. Halfway across the enclosure, shouts arose behind them. "Run!" Cam said, and sprinted forward, dragging the old man. She got them inside as the first spears were thrown, flung herself in after them, and closed the shuttle door.

She had killed a man. She, Cam O'Kane, who swerved her car to avoid snakes on summer roads. She had killed a soldier of the king and now she stood in an inhuman ship, staring at two humans with whom she had absolutely nothing in common, wondering what the fuck she was supposed to do next.

11: AVEO

If ever Aveo would have thought that this woman was a goddess, it would have been at this moment. Standing beside her in an impregnable silver egg, having watched her kill Cul Escio without any weapon actually touching him, seeing the strange and frightening objects around her— even to him they were frightening, and the slave girl had been terrified into numb rigidity—he knew that Ostiu Cam was not of this world.

But not a goddess, either. No. A goddess would not look so distraught, so scattered. Even the Goddess of All Green, said those who followed her, killed with the impartial necessity of frost on the fields, meat for the table. But Cam, despite the hard and clear simplicity that was her usual manner, had been badly upset by killing the *cul*. This was a human woman, not some supernatural figure. Aveo knew so beyond doubt, and in knowing felt a sharp stab of something between disappointment and relief.

There might be worlds beyond this one, but they held no goddesses to conduct one to the beloved dead. *Ojea* . . .

"Just . . . just sit down," Cam said, her voice quavering.

At the sound of her voice, Obu screamed, began to wail, and tore at her hair.

"What . . . Aveo, tell her to stop!"

"She won't, *ostiu*. She is mourning her dead."

"What dead? Do you mean *Escio*? He raped her!"

"I doubt she sees it that way. In kulith—"

"Oh, damn kulith! Just shut her up!"

Definitely not a goddess.

Aveo grasped Obu's arm and spoke to her in a low voice, the only words that would quiet her: Cul Escio lives with the Goddess of All Green, he feasts in her Hall of Warriors, Obu will one day see him again, and if she did not stop wailing right now then he, Rem Aveo, an important scholar, would intercede with the Goddess so that Obu would never be allowed into the Hall during all eternity. Instead, she would be doomed to perpetual slavery digging the Goddess's coldest fields, where nothing grew but frozen and withered roots. Fortunately, Cam was not listening.

Cam talked to a section of the wall, which answered. That was frightening enough, although it was possible a person was concealed behind the wall. But Aveo also realized something else. Always before, Cam's speech had been hesitant, with a small pause after every few words. Now it gushed forth in an uninterrupted torrent. Why?

"Soledad, I killed him. And I— don't— I'm in the shuttle and . . . What? No! Don't you understand, I—" The sounds made no sense to Aveo, and neither did the answering sounds from the wall. But slowly the *ostiu* calmed. Obu, too, now sat quietly on the floor, head between her bent knees, terrified into submission. Aveo, listening hard, caught a few repeated sounds: "Lucca" and "Kular" and "witness." None had meaning.

Finally Cam said "okay"—another meaningless sound— and turned away from the wall. Her gaze fell on Obu. "What did you do to her?"

"Nothing. She is mourning."

Cam grimaced. "Well, that's the worst thing about slavery, isn't it? It brainwashes . . . deludes . . . the slaves into buying into the system . . . into agreeing with the . . . the word for . . . Never mind."

Aveo had to not mind. Nothing she said had been rational. Keeping a tight grasp on his own rationality, he said, "What shall we do now, Ostiu Cam?"

"We still have to get to your king. And now we're going to have to fly."

"Fly?" That word had been all too clear. Still, Aveo's mind rejected it. Fall from the sky, maybe, things could fall from a great height. But fly . . . only birds flew. Then Cam spoke another word to the wall and it lit up with an army.

Despite himself, Aveo gasped. Uldunu Four's soldiers, attacking the egg . . . no, not irrational sorcery but only some kind of window, showing the outside. Spears and fire besieged the egg, and the terrified faces of brave men loomed close.

"Bye-bye, tin warriors," Cam said. Aveo felt the floor lift beneath him. The soldiers outside fled, then grew smaller. Obu crumpled into a faint. Ground flowed beneath them like water. They were flying.

Aveo, for the first time in many years, had to consciously resist crossing his arms over his breast in the sign of submission to the Goddess.

"Here's my plan," Cam said, "unless you have a better idea. We land the ship just outside the city and walk in, since you think the ship will scare the king so much. Then we—"

"No," Aveo said. The ground still rushed away beneath them so dizzyingly that he had to look away from the window-that-was-not-a-window. He must hold steady; she clearly needed him. Or somebody. She was like an unbroken animal that ran blindly around a room, knocking over furniture and slamming into walls.

"No?"

"No. If you leave the . . . the ship outside the city, Uldunu Four will know of it before we reach him and be just as frightened. Spies are everywhere. Also, a thing reported at a distance can be misrepresented, but a thing seen close to the capital and by men he trusts cannot. Thus, you may as well land it on the roof of the palace and invite him to enter it, as you have me and Obu."

Cam glanced at Obu, curled into a corner and refusing to uncurl, and sighed.

"Also," Aveo said, "if I walk with you, I will be dead within two minutes of leaving the ship. I am a traitor, and I do not have your invisible armor."

"You're a traitor? Really? What did you do?"

Not a woman: a child. Did she really think he could, or would, answer that? Apparently she had learned nothing playing kulith. What kind of place did she come from, that such stupidity was not already dead? Instead of answering her, he said, "Ostiu Cam, what is a 'lucca'?"

"Lucca— Oh, you overheard me on the— No word for it. Okay. Lucca is the name of my friend."

"And 'kular'?"

"That's what we call your world."

Again, nonsense. The world was the world. "And 'witness'?"

She frowned. "That means 'to see something and report on it.'"

"You are a spy."

"No. Yes. I mean, a spy is looking for information to help win a war, right? I'm just here to see something else, and to report on it to . . . to some other people."

"Report to what people?" Aveo asked.

"I've never actually seen them."

"Report on what?"

"I don't know."

"You are here to 'witness' something you cannot identify to people you've never seen?"

Cam ran both hands over her face, pulling the skin into a grotesque stretch and then releasing it. "It sounds weird, I know. But we were told we would know it when we saw it. Although so far that hasn't happened."

"And you believed these people that you will 'know it when you see it'?"

"Yes. The ship is theirs, not ours. So they— Look, Aveo, this doesn't matter now. We need to decide what we're doing. Look, there's the city."

It was true. Aveo saw the city wall, the West Gate, the palace towers rise over the horizon like a real ship nearing land. In so short a time! Again that swooping vertigo, that sense of unreality, took him, and again he fought it off.

She said, "So you think Soledad should land the shuttle on top of the palace? Is it that big building there? I see a flat section of roof."

"Yes. Are you . . . aren't you steering the egg?"

"No. Soledad is. My other friend." Then more strange sounds to the wall, answering sounds, and Aveo watched in fear and awe as the egg slowed over the palace and lowered itself gently to the rooftop.

"Come here, please, Aveo, I want to try something," Cam said. "Really, stand as close to me as you can."

Every impulse in Aveo resisted. But he stood and she moved next to him, reaching inside her tunic. Then she moved even closer. As tall as he was, she bulked larger, and she smelled of clean hair and female skin. To his horror, Aveo felt his old member, long unused, stir even as he pulled back from her foreignness, and was ashamed of doing so. He was—had been—a scholar. The strange should intrigue him, not repel him.

For the second time Cam reached inside her tunic, and Aveo felt a faint tingling along the side of his body beside hers. He drew back sharply.

"No, don't do that. I'm trying to see if the shield—the invisible armor—can cover us both. It covers my gun"—a meaningless sound—"but I don't know how much area it will— Fuck it, why didn't the Atoners give me more information?"

More meaningless gabble, but he was slightly shocked

to hear the crudest of all words for copulation come from her mouth.

"Okay, I'm going to shove you against that cabinet handle— Do you feel that?"

She pushed his chest against a piece of metal protruding from the wall. Aveo gasped, "No!" She shoved harder, and still he felt nothing except a fear he could not shake, like a low fever. Again and again she experimented with various parts of his body, pushing and pulling at him like laundry in a boiling pot.

"Okay, now we know. You can be inside the shield but only if you stand behind me and really, really close. Otherwise, the force field . . . the mechanism . . . *it* just snaps you out. Can you do that, Aveo?"

"I can. I will not."

"You *will not*? What are you, crazy? Otherwise soldiers are going to run you through like butter! Look!"

She waved at the wall window. Warriors poured onto the roof from below, a full battle group without the discipline of Escio's men but far more heavily armed.

"I am a scholar of the Hall of Scholars," Aveo said. "I will not go before Uldunu Four like a child clinging to its mother's skirt."

"Would you rather be dead? I need you to translate because *you* spoke only Pularit to me. And you owe me, Aveo. I already saved your life once!"

"And took Cul Escio's."

"Saving *you*! God, you people! Now you come with me or I'll just . . . take you out to the countryside someplace safe, dump you, and start all over learning whatever the fuck language it is that your king speaks!"

He could imagine that: Cam, alone in the court of Uldunu Four, unable to speak the language, ignorant of even the most basic protocol, insulting the king from the first move on the kulith board. Aveo himself wandering the countryside, hungry and very soon dead. But what matter? All life was ephemeral, all death eternal, and saving one man did not atone for the killing of another because atonement itself was irrelevant. In the vast reaches of time, nothing really mattered any more than moves in yesterday's kulith.

But it mattered to him. Even though whatever scholarly knowledge he gained from this bizarre adventure would die with him, anyway.

He said quietly to Cam, "I will come."

"Good! Now hang on tight. I'm going to open— Wait, what about Obu? She'll have to stay here. There's no way safe for her— Wait, in that supply cabinet."

Obu wouldn't go. The moment Cam touched her she came to life, shrieking and flailing. Finally Cam jammed Obu inside the metal chest and slammed it shut. The girl continued to scream. Cam looked near tears.

"It's for her own good! Tell her!"

Wheezing with exertion, Aveo said, "She is too terrified for any words to reach her."

"Fuck it! Let's go!"

She opened the egg's door. Soldiers, thick as vermin, first fell back and then surged forward, hurling spears and rushing in with daggers. Aveo clung close to the woman from the sky. Amid raining weaponry and soldiers' shouts, he waddled to a stairwell in the city where he had been a scholar and a traitor and an emissary and was now a translator for a girl who did not know what she was looking for, in a place she could not even begin to understand.

She had called him crazy. Aveo thought Uldunu Four to be crazy. But no one—no one—could be crazier than this woman, unless it might be those masters she claimed to have never seen but who had sent her here on this craziest of all journeys.

They reached the stairwell and began to descend.

12: PRESS CONFERENCE

June 4, 2020

PRESS SECRETARY MATTHEW STEYART: Ladies and Gentlemen, the President. [sounds of shuffling as reporters rise]

PRESIDENT: Thank you. I'd like to make a brief statement, and then I'll take your questions. If there's one value that has shaped our country, it's freedom. For nearly 250 years we have guaranteed our citizens unprecedented freedom of thought, of religion, of privacy, of movement, of actions within the law. These freedoms have yielded for the American people unparalleled social richness, unparalleled peace within our borders, and unparalleled contacts with other nations. During the last three years, my administration has made every effort to protect and defend these individual freedoms. For this reason, I firmly believe that allowing United States citizens to *choose* to accompany the Atoners to the moon, and beyond, is their right and our legacy. We must wish the twenty-one "Witnesses," both those who are our fellow countrymen and those from other nations, Godspeed. And we must hope that the knowledge they bring back from their journeys will enrich us all. Okay . . . Sandy?

SANFORD GARDNER, CNN: Ma'am, how would you answer those critics who say that you are risking having these so-called "Witnesses" converted to some strange philosophy or hostile military intention and so returning to the United States as brainwashed or otherwise altered spies?

PRESIDENT: You mean they might want to ask intrusive questions of the White House? [laughter] Seriously, as I just said, the United States does not limit the thoughts of its citizens. We of course limit actions, for the good of us all. But those Americans who have volunteered to travel with the Atoners are as free as the rest of us to be exposed to, consider, and adopt any thought they choose. If, however, they return and perform actions that in any way endanger this country, of course that will be appropriately addressed at the appropriate time. But the Atoners have approached us in peace, as friends, and as friends we accept their overtures, which, I'd like to remind you, are part of the most stupendous event to affect mankind in centuries. *Centuries.*

[MANY VOICES]: Ma'am! Ma'am! Madam President!

PRESIDENT: Yes, Kyle?

KYLE YOUMANS, NBC NEWS: You've been praised and condemned both for mobilizing the National Guard the moment that the anti-Atoner riots began in four separate American cities. Sixteen people are dead as a result of either those riots or subsequent Guard actions. Do you now consider that mobilization premature or in any other way a mistake?

PRESIDENT: I do not. Most of us are not going to the stars, at least not just yet. We barely have a human presence on the moon, even with Selene City and China's Village of Heaven and the commercial base of Farrington Tours. Most of humanity lives *here,* on Earth, and here where we live, order and law must be preserved. Jenna?

JENNA JOHNSON, FOX NEWS: Madam President, your handling of the entire Atoner crisis has resulted in low— lower—approval ratings for your administration and for you personally. Do you think this reflects an understanding on the part of the American people that their leader has sold out to aliens?

PRESIDENT: I do not. Chris?

CHRIS DEFAZIO, *THE NEW YORK TIMES:* What sort of knowledge do you expect that the Witnesses will bring back to us?

PRESIDENT: How can we know yet? Let me tell you a story. In the nineteenth century, Queen Victoria summoned the scientist Michael Faraday to Buckingham Palace. Mr. Faraday had just formulated important laws related to electricity, and the queen was curious. She watched his various demonstrations and listened to his explanations and finally asked, "But Mr. Faraday, what use is this 'electricity'?" Do you know what Faraday answered his monarch? He said, "Ma'am, what use is a baby?"

We don't know what knowledge will come to us from beyond the stars. But like a baby, it should be nourished and watched as it grows and develops.

CHRIS DEFAZIO: Follow-up question, please! Ma'am . . . If you weren't the president of the United States, were young enough, and had a chance to become a Witness for the Atoners and visit another planet—Would you have gone?

PRESIDENT: [long pause] In a heartbeat.

13: LUCCA

It snowed heavily for three days and three nights. Village and steppes piled with white. The Kularians, laughing, dug paths and tunnels from huts to community lodge to storehouse to privies. The winter didn't seem to change their mood at all; they were no more affected by cold and monotony and boredom than were rabbits or badgers on Earth.

Nor was Lucca any longer bored. He set about cautiously, trying to arouse no suspicion, to investigate Kularian telepathy. From the day he'd landed, twenty-eight days ago, the natives had assumed that he was just like them. Lucca didn't want to disturb this notion. He wasn't sure what they would do if they discovered he was not telepathic.

How did it work for them?

He feigned sleep until long after Hytrowembireliaz and his family had left for the lodge and another day of communal cooking, dancing, gossiping. Then he sat up and concentrated on an image that Chewithoztarel could never have seen: the rich Tuscany vineyards of Vino Maduro in Cortona, where Lucca had grown up. In loving detail he pictured the vines heavy with purple Sangiovese grapes, the pale fields dreaming in the sun, the tall, thin cypresses spiking the blue sky. He went back to the sights and sounds and even the smells of childhood, before Oxford and London and Gianna. As he concentrated on the images, he thought over and over the Italian word *vigna*. After at least fifteen minutes of this, he fought his way through the snow to the community lodge.

It was more subdued than usual. No one was dancing, and the adults sat in small groups, talking quietly. Those children not outside played a betting game with stones or wove ribbons on their small handheld looms, a current fad. Chewithoztarel, however, sat alone in a corner, staring at her fingers, uncharacteristically silent.

"Chewithoztarel?" Lucca said, sitting beside her on the usual pile of smelly rugs. "Are you ill?"

"No."

"Is something wrong?"

"No."

"You look sad."

"I am."

He waited. Often, saying nothing prompted people to talk—although not usually Kularians. Was this sadness somehow connected to his images of gorgeous scenery the little girl would never see? That seemed a pretty sophisticated concept for Chewithoztarel, but Lucca didn't know for sure. He didn't know anything for sure anymore. His heart thumped and he had to make himself breathe normally.

Chewithoztarel, maddening as always, said nothing.

Lucca thought hard about the *vigna*. Maybe one had to be physically closer to a receiving telepath in order to get through . . . but then how had Chewithoztarel "heard" what he'd been saying to Soledad far out on the plain?

Chewithoztarel said nothing, staring down at her own fingers.

Hytrowembireliaz approached, crouched beside his daughter, and said sharply, "Small heart, stop this."

Lucca blinked. It was the first time he'd ever heard anyone in the village speak harshly to a child, or in fact to anyone. Hytrowembireliaz looked at Lucca. "I apologize for my child. She is young, and they were good fellow-travelers-on-the-first-road."

"Friends, yes," Lucca managed. Who were good friends? Someone must have died. As Hytrowembireliaz moved

away, Lucca surreptitiously counted the villagers. All
adults were present. How many children were out in the
snow? He had to know. Laboriously he arose and walked
outside.

It took him a while to count the kids because they were
playing some game that involved hiding in a sprawling
acre-wide tree, behind huts, and in snow holes, but eventually they tired of this and trooped inside to eat. All the
children were accounted for. And when Lucca went back
inside, Chewithoztarel had joined a group of girls gig-
gling in one corner. Clearly there were no vineyards in her
exasperating mind.

He sat beside Blanbilitwan, the child's mother, who
smiled at him with the same impartial, low-key good humor she offered everyone else. Her red front tooth was
slightly chipped, yellowed enamel showing through. Tentatively Lucca said, "Chewithoztarel will miss her fellow-
traveler-on-the-first-road."

Blanbilitwan's smile didn't waver. "Yes. But she will
learn."

Learn what? Before he could think of what to say next,
Blanbilitwan added, "I remember when my sister started
down the third road. I cried, too. So silly! But it was past
time. If Ragjuptrilpent hadn't been so young herself, she
would not have stayed here so long."

Ragjuptrilpent. Chewithoztarel's imaginary friend: a
real girl who had died. Yes, it did make sense for a child
to pretend her friend was still alive. But—

Ragjuptrilpent told me you were here.

She said you washed in the shed and pissed in the corner.

*I saw you coming back from way over the hill! And
Ragjuptrilpent saw you, too!*

Cold slid along Lucca's spine. He said to Blanbilitwan,
"When . . . when did Ragjuptrilpent start on . . . on the
second road?"

She wrinkled her forehead. "I must think . . . yes, in
Trem. You had not yet come to us."

"Trem" meant nothing to the translator. "How many days ago?"

"Oh, many. At least five tens. She was always late, that girl." Someone called to Blanbilitwan and she moved away.

Before he arrived here. Ragjuptrilpent had died, and then . . . what? Hung around as a ghost, lingering on "the second road," to spy on Lucca and giggle with Chewithoztarel over Lucca's activities? Ridiculous. Lucca didn't believe in ghosts. There was another explanation for all this, and he would have to find it. This was, must be, what the Atoners had sent him here to witness. There was an explanation.

He made his way to the door, smiling at everyone he passed, and went back out into the cold. In Hytrowembireliaz's hut, he crawled under blankets, his own plus a few of other people, and commlinked Soledad. To hell with discretion and tact and not contaminating the two-planet double-blind experiment. He had to know if Cam was encountering anything like this, and what she and Soledad made of it. Anything to help make sense of the unthinkable. Anything at all, from anyone, anywhere.

14: CAM

If the bastards would only stop rushing at her!

Cam took another step down the palace stairwell. In ten minutes, she had advanced six steps down the straight staircase squeezed into a passage so narrow that only one person could descend at a time. Or two, if the second was Aveo, clinging to her back like a humiliated monkey. For each step, she had to wait until no soldiers were trying to stab or spear or punch either of them, so that she could press the manual override on her shield control, which briefly stopped whatever forces rooted the shield to the ground. If she didn't stop the rooting, she couldn't move forward; if she did, the fucking soldiers might push her down the stairs and Aveo might come loose from the protection of the shield.

But it was the shouting that was the worst, constant hoarse war cries like this was Little Big Horn or something. "Shut up!" she screamed in English, which only added to the clamor. She could feel Aveo tremble on her back, but he said nothing. Brave old man! She'd be damned if she'd let him make her look bad.

They came at Cam in a steady stream from both above and below, until finally she couldn't stand it anymore and shoved at the one standing in front of her, who was trying futilely to slice open her belly with a knife the length of his forearm. He staggered and tumbled backward, knocking over the man behind him, and on down the rest of the stairwell they fell like a line of dominos. Cam laughed out loud, from nerves and relief and fear, and was appalled when the laugh became a sob.

Aveo breathed in her ear, "Turn left at the bottom of the stairs, through the curtain."

She did, and what had been a rough stone passage abruptly became a wide gallery open on her left to a garden lush with alien flowers. And they *were* alien, the first truly alien thing she'd seen on Kular. Not that she could spare attention to examine them closely! But she was aware of the plants' weird shapes, pungent scents, and above all that some of them emitted a constant rumbling, very low and somehow unsettling— *Were* they plants? Animals of some type? Dangerous?

"Straight ahead," Aveo said, as more soldiers rushed them and Cam was forced to stand still, rooted. The wall to her right was set with thousands of tiny colored stones, but the patterns looked odd to her, somehow *off,* like that modern art she'd never liked at home. Home . . .

Not now.

"Last door on the right," Aveo said, and all at once that sounded to her so much like directions to a bathroom that she laughed again, not a sob this time, and felt her confidence return. She could do this. She was doing this. Only . . .

I don't want to have to kill anyone else.

"That may happen, *ostiu,*" Aveo said dryly, and Cam realized she had subvocalized and then repeated what the translator gave her, without knowing she'd done either.

All at once the unholy shouting and attacking stopped.

A man had appeared in the doorway that Aveo had indicated, striding through another of the curtains that seemed to be doors here, and given an order. The soldiers dropped back behind Cam. The man was very tall, his bare breast painted nearly entirely blue, a blue helmet on his head. Cam said, "Uldunu?"

"No!" Aveo said, scandalized. "Chief of the Royal Guard." And then, "Let me."

Not that she had any choice, until the translator could

handle this language. But already it had picked up a few phrases and Cam's implant whispered, "King . . . was sent . . . woman from the sky . . ."

Aveo said to her in Pularit, "Follow him."

"Will he take us to Uldunu? No, they'll protect the king, right? I won't get to see him?"

"Of course you will see him! Kulith!"

Cam scowled. Couldn't these people tell the difference between some stupid game and real life? Was this what the Atoners wanted her to witness—that the Kularians couldn't tell the difference? What the fuck was she here for, anyway?

I don't know. But I don't want to have to kill anyone else.

On the other side of the curtain was a huge room, maybe as large as a football field, with people massed at the other end. The ceiling soared high above, the walls and floor were covered with the tiny glittering colored stones in the weird patterns, and plants grew in big triangular beds set into the floor. The plants groaned at her with their unmusical rumbling, sounding for all the world like something in minor pain. Cam approached Uldunu on his raised throne, surrounded by bare-chested men—no women—who all wore skirts and whose chests were painted red or blue.

The king was a small, muscular man in a silky green skirt with fantastic green designs covering his chest and face and legs and arms, and with green-painted toenails in golden sandals. He looked to her like a leprechaun, or maybe something from a drag show, but she kept her face stern and was proud of herself for this. The king glared at her. Amazed whispering ran over everybody else like wind in blue-and-red corn.

Aveo said, "He is angry that you do not kneel."

"And I'm not going to, either!"

"But I must."

"Don't you dare, Aveo! They'll kill you!"

"Let's hope not." He leaned slightly forward and over her shoulder began a long speech to the king. Somewhere near the end the translator started up in Cam's implant. ". . . and so to honor Uldunu Four, the (unknown) of the Goddess of All Green on (unknown) with gifts of invisible armor."

Gifts? Invisible armor, plural? This wasn't what she and Aveo had discussed! She was supposed to be a trader, with things to sell to the king. What was Aveo playing at?

The king went on glaring at her. No one in the vast room seemed to so much as breathe, and the only noise was the low, agitated, incredibly irritating drone from the plants. Then Aveo moved away from Cam, sank to his knees, and crossed his arms over his breast. She saw his eyes.

"No!" Cam cried as the Chief of the Guard strode forward. Before his long knife was even out of its sheath, Cam fired.

Everything slowed. The soldier fell with excruciating leisure. Cam saw her arm inch out to grab Aveo, who resisted with surprising strength and remained kneeling, his head lowered. Men in red skirts shifted with the speed of continental drift and spoke so slowly that the words were elongated and below hearing, like the moaning of the infernal plants. Blue-painted soldiers stretched languorously toward their weapons. The dead man lay on the floor, smelling of burnt flesh, as if motionlessly asleep.

Then Uldunu said something that Cam heard clearly, and the horror turned to horrible farce. Soldiers replaced their weapons, red-skirted men scurried to obey, Aveo raised his head and stood. A small table, its contents, and two large cushions woven with gold were set before Cam. The king descended his throne. Aveo, inexplicably left alive, tugged on Cam's hand to pull her to one of the cushions; he sat on the floor beside her. The king sat on the other cushion.

Cam stared at the kulith board and game pieces before her.

She lost, of course. Despite Aveo's tutelage, she could barely remember how the pieces moved, let alone the insanely complicated rules for trading, stealing, or destroying pieces, hers and his, that represented land and cities and crops and people. Or maybe they didn't, since which pieces represented what seemed to change throughout the game. Aveo sat silent and still, not helping her. When she had no pieces left and her stomach rumbled from hunger, the king waved his hand. Naked slaves, who had not been in the huge room earlier, sprang forward, knelt, and then led Cam and Aveo out.

"You did well," he said to her in Pularit.

"I lost!"

"I should hope so!"

So the game had been some sort of ritual, and she was supposed to lose. All those hours wasted in something predetermined . . . She remembered the conversation between the king and Aveo. Aveo said she was bringing gifts of invisible armor, which she most certainly was not. They had discussed invisible armor, but as trade, not gifts. But if she accused Aveo, he would know she now understood the language of this city, whatever it was. It might be an advantage to her if Aveo didn't know this—wasn't he already lying to and about her? She was no longer sure she could trust him.

They were led to a luxurious room with two wide couches—beds, she supposed—massive polished stone tables, and more swaths of the groaning plants. One whole wall opened into yet another noisy garden. Never had Cam seen such a public or unsecured bedroom. Food and drink sat on one table, and Aveo looked at it longingly. He whispered, "Eat or drink nothing."

"Poison?" This place grew worse and worse.

"It is not inconceivable."

"I'm starving! And why are you whispering?"

He came closer and took her in his arms, like a lover. Cam recoiled, but he held on tighter. "There will be spyholes, and by now they will have found someone who speaks Pularit." He kissed her.

A ruse. But she found herself clinging to him like a child to a father. His kiss was dry, cool, without passion, which was good because anything else would have snapped her nerves like guitar strings.

He called, in his own language, "Slave!" and a naked girl appeared, shaking. Cam remembered Obu, shut up in the supply cabinet of the shuttle on the roof. Another complication. Aveo said, "Take us to the kitchens." She did, and amid startled and terrified slaves and a bedlam of cooking, Cam and Aveo loaded themselves with waterskins and porridge intended for slaves. Back in their room, Cam ate eagerly.

Darkness fell, the swift plunging sunset of the equator. Kular B rose huge in the sky, one half blue and white and the other in shadow. Aveo took Cam's hand and led her to one of the wide beds. He pulled it away from the hectically colored wall to the middle of the room and lay on it behind her, curled around her body and within the shield that she turned off and then on to take him in. "Take him in"—even the wording was sexual. She didn't want Aveo, although she felt his cock rise against her ass. Well, probably the poor coot couldn't help that, he was old but not ancient and Cam knew quite well the effect her body always had on men. But his embrace was respectful and he didn't push. Instead he whispered in her ear, so soft that even if they had been near a wall no spyhole could have caught it, "Have you found it?"

"Found what?"

"Whatever your masters sent you here to 'witness.'"

"Shut up," Cam said in English, and was not even surprised when Aveo laughed, a low sound without mirth, eerily like the groaning of the alien plants.

15: LETTER FROM A WITNESS

Translated from Hindi by Anjor Khatri

My dear parents,

I write you to try to explain, better than I could on the telephone, why I have accepted this assignment as "Witness" for the Atoners. I know and respect your disapproval, and you are of course correct that it is a dangerous unknown. Also, I respect your concern that I am leaving my good position at the university so soon after I have been hired there. For all your sacrifices to send me to university both in India and in the United States, I will be grateful for the rest of my days on Earth. I can never repay you for all you have done for me.

But your sacrifices and support have made me a historian, and as a historian, I cannot refuse this unprecedented opportunity. Think of it, my dear parents! Ten thousand years ago humans were taken from some primitive civilization or civilizations on Earth, transported to other planets, and left to flourish as they might. At the same time, the transporters of those humans, the first aliens to ever contact Earth, committed some crime against humanity, which was not the transportation itself. How could anyone interested in the history of the human race not wish to investigate all this? How could anyone of intellectual curiosity not wish to become part of the new bridges among Earth, these lost human colonies on alien worlds, and the aliens themselves?

I so deeply regret that you are angry with me, and that you fear I may never return. You may be correct. But you raised me to use my mind as well as to honor our traditions. Never will I have a greater or more significant chance to do the former, and I will never abandon the latter. Please try to understand why I do this, and that I am still, no matter where in the universe I go, your loving daughter.

Amira Gupta

16: LUCCA

"Tell me again," Soledad said.

Lucca tried to restrain his impatience. He sat alone in Hytrowembireliaz's cold hut, half-buried under a pile of stinking blankets, which had obviously been someone else's blankets before Lucca and still smelled of him or her. Possibly the blankets smelled of several other people. The hut certainly did, including baby feces from Hytrowembireliaz's youngest. Lucca hadn't lit a lamp and so sat in darkness relieved only by the snow falling steadily outside the one small window. He clutched the commlink so hard that his fingers ached.

He said, "You reviewed the translator uploads. I think the Kularians are telepathic. Chewithoztarel—the child informant I told you about—knew things I had said when I was far out on the plain, with absolutely no one within hearing. She knew I called you *amica*! You know I'd never done that before. Soledad, this must be what we were sent here to witness. Does Cam report anything like this?"

"No, at least not yet. She linked last night and she— Lucca, are you sure? One instance doesn't seem to me enough evidence. Has this child heard—sensed, received, I don't know what word to use—anything besides *amica*?"

"Yes. She saw me piss in a corner when I was alone and . . ." He couldn't think of any other instance. Chewithoztarel had also repeated "Soledad," but he might have called that out in his sleep.

"One or two instances, both doubtful," Soledad said,

and he could hear the skepticism in her voice. "There might be some other explanation."

"Like what?"

"I don't know. What do the Kularians say is the explanation?"

"Religious. They say they can see souls or ghosts or something, people who have recently died, until the dead set out 'on the third road.' It's just another form of the afterlife myth. But the telepathy is—could be—real." He could see her, sitting at the commlink console in the Atoner ship, her intelligent gray eyes weighing the evidence, finding it insufficient.

"You need to run more experiments, Lucca."

"Yes, of course. But Cam—she hasn't reported anything like this?" Although Lucca wasn't sure Cam would even notice any covert telepathic communication. She didn't have a very subtle mind.

"Cam just survived a firefight with an entire army of soldiers, she's practically a prisoner in a palace, and her informant may or may not be lying to her. She's got her hands full."

Lucca felt a brief stab of envy. All that action, and of course it was the unseeing American who got it. Lucca knew himself to handle activity far better than inactivity. Then he was ashamed of his envy. After all, it was he who had witnessed the telepathy . . . unless he hadn't. "You're right, Soledad, I need to do more experiments. I can—" He stopped cold.

"Lucca?"

Something had changed, something significant. He peered around the dim hut and then it came to him.

"Lucca!"

"I can't smell anything."

"What?" Soledad said.

"It smells really bad here, hygiene isn't big with this village, and now all at once I can't smell any of the reek."

"Maybe you're getting a cold."

"All at once like that? I feel fine, whatever the Atoners put into our bodies has warded off all germs, but now all at once I can *smell* nothing at all."

"Maybe the Atoners did that for you, too. After a certain number of days, just cut off smell so you'd be more comfortable."

Lucca considered this. "No, I don't think so. Smell has too much survival value, especially in primitive cultures. Bad food, for instance. I don't know what this could be."

"So watch it and link to me when there's something else I should know. About the telepathy or the smells."

"And you should ask Cam to be alert for telepathy."

"Yes," Soledad said, but he heard the disbelief in her voice, and resented it.

When the link was broken, Lucca drew a deep breath. No odors. Steeling himself, he went back outside and walked toward the pen where the shaggy, malodorous, elephant-like *shen* huddled placidly. *Certo,* if he could smell anything, it would be these beasts.

Nothing.

In the lodge, he hobbled from one group to another, smiling, sniffing, brushing the stomping dancers in their warm clothing that would not be washed until spring. No scents.

His entire olfactory sense had just vanished, between one second and the next.

"Chewithoztarel, do you want to play a game?"

"Yes," she said eagerly. "What game?"

The two of them sat in the snow house that, under Lucca's direction, they had spent all morning constructing. A few other children had helped but then had gone back inside the lodge, saying they wanted to warm up. Chewithoztarel never had to warm up; she seemed to have the metabolism of Mt. Etna. Lucca had to brace himself against the snow walls to stop from shivering. He wondered briefly about parents who would let a grown man linger alone and unseen with a young girl on the cusp of adolescence, but then decided that the damn cold made child molestation unlikely—or at least unenjoyable.

"It's a game where I think of something very hard and you tell me what I'm thinking about."

She looked puzzled. "How can I do that?"

"Let's try." He brought up an image of her father, picturing the long mustache and red tooth and sun-seamed face in every detail, thinking clearly the word "Hytrowembireliaz."

Chewithoztarel said doubtfully, "Snow?"

"No. Try again."

She failed to guess—or pretended to fail—three of Lucca's thoughts and then said, "This is a stupid game. I'm going inside."

"No, wait a minute! Tell me . . . Tell me who left for the second road in the summer and fall."

"Oh . . . Ragjuptrilpent. Don't scold me!"

"I promise I won't. Who else?"

"Chytfouriswelpim. I thought you were there."

The man whose throat had been slit right after Lucca's rescue. "Yes, I was. Who else?"

"Nobody. Oh—Ninborthecam. But she was very, very old."

"Did she stay long on the second road?"

"No. Not even a minute! It was so funny!"

"Where does the third road go?" Lucca held his breath.

"How should I know? Are you teasing me?"

"No, I'm not. I just wondered where you think it goes." He gave her his warmest smile, or the warmest smile he could, considering that his teeth had started to chatter.

"Someplace nice. Maybe with summer all the time. I don't know." The child looked baffled but not uncomfortable. "You don't get to find out until you finish the first and second roads, but you should be very good because maybe on the third road you'll have to answer for what you've done here." This was said in a singsong tone, clearly parroted from adults. Then she reverted to her own voice. "Lucca, who do you know that left for the second road? Where you live?"

The question smacked him hard, although there was no reason it should. He should even have foreseen it. Everything in him revolted from telling this dirty snow-urchin about Gianna. So he choked out, "Well, my grandmother."

She looked at him keenly and said, "You're not telling me true."

How had she known that? Telepathy or just good observation? Suddenly he was sick of this. She wasn't going to tell him anything useful. A discovery important enough for aliens to have sent him halfway across the galaxy, and he was forced to rely for information on an irritating and ignorant child.

He snapped, "I am *not* lying. My grandmother died."

"Was she old?"

"Yes."

"How long did she stay on the second road?"

Lucca covered his cold face with his cold mittens, pulled away from their odorless scratchiness, and said, "Let's go inside."

"All right. This game was stupid."

"Yes," Lucca agreed. "It was."

He was going to have to use an adult as an informant. He was going to have to devise a more sophisticated telepathic experiment. He was going to have to wait for someone else to die.

Before any of these things could happen, Lucca's sense of smell returned. He was seated on a cushion in a dim corner of the lodge, eating a porridge made of soaked and boiled wild grain and dried meat, when all at once odors rushed in on him: the steaming food, the unwashed people, the sour fermented ale in his mug, the smoky peat fire. It was a rich, redolent, repulsive mixture, so strong after the total absence of smell that he almost cried out. He looked around, trying to identify something—anything—that might have caused his nose to work again. Nothing looked different.

The next moment, he went blind.

17: WWW.URGENTALIENCRISIS.ORG

• HOME | NEWS | PROTEST PHOTOS | HOW TO ORGANIZE | RESOURCES •

• STATEMENTS OF SUPPORT | CALENDAR | BLOGS | CONTACT US •

ORGANIZE TO PROTEST HUMAN ABDUCTIONS!!

If you are outraged that "aliens" would waltz in and demand human sacrifices for some "experiment" in "witnessing" . . .

If you are rightly suspicious of their vague motives . . .

If you think our spineless government has just bent over and let this first step toward Atoner domination happen . . .

If you believe they have—as they themselves admit!—abducted humans before and are doing so now . . .

THEN DO SOMETHING ABOUT IT!!

No, we can't reach their so-called "base" on the moon (if it really even exists), but we can organize massive protests on Earth—OUR planet!!!

HELP STOP HUMAN EXPLOITATION NOW

18: AVEO

To weave a blanket, you carefully intertwined warp and woof, pulling on each with just the right amount of tension. To polish a gemstone, you turned it evenly to each facet, neither neglecting nor favoring any one. To create a strategy, in either kulith or life, you both wove and turned, and if you failed with one thread or one facet, you died.

Aveo looked at Cam, eating her breakfast of incredibly rare and costly delicacies as if they were so much ber bread, and knew he could never explain any of this to her. She was not capable of understanding it. Her heart, he had come to believe, was good, but her mind was that of a child, simple and straightforward and easily distracted. She could have studied kulith for years and the roughest fisherman on the Niol Sea would have beaten her. Never would she understand that life mixed reality and illusion, and that in most people's minds these two *were* warp and woof. Including hers.

She drank off her wine, wiped her mouth, and said, "Aveo, the first thing we have to do is go back up to the roof to the shuttle. Obu's been in the supply cabinet all night! And I have to talk to my friend on the . . . the comm-link."

That last word was meaningless, but no more so than the rest of her speech. He said with the patience one would use when talking to a child, "You can't do that, *ostiu*. You can't leave these apartments until the king says you may."

"The hell I can't." She stood. "I'm not a prisoner, and neither are you. Nobody even tried to bother you last night, all night. I can't leave that poor girl in the cabinet any longer. . . . How could you even think of such a thing? She'll starve to death or die of thirst or something! And anyway, surely we should establish right now with Uldunu that I'm an emissary, an equal, not his subject?"

Aveo groaned. She had just said aloud that she was the equal of the king. She had called him Uldunu, not Uldunu Four. She had set up her will against his. She had also forgotten what Aveo had said last night about the spyholes, and even as he searched for the right words—critical words, all of which would be reported to the king almost before he finished uttering them—she jumped up and clutched at something inside her tunic.

"Sorry, Aveo, I have to—" She pulled out a small black box. He tensed, thinking it might be the mysterious weapon that had killed Cul Escio and the Chief of the Royal Guard, but it was not. Cam put it to her lips and said, "Soledad?"

The rest of her words made no sense, being in her own language. Her eyes grew wide. Her voice rose in pitch.

Had he underestimated her? If this was a performance for their unseen watchers, it was a good choice. Talking to demons through a magic box . . . Had she somehow discerned how superstitious Uldunu Four was? Nothing else could have been so calculated to impress him, or to make him cautious in the face of her gross insults. Perhaps she even understood that Aveo did not believe in demons or magic and thus her performance was a signal to him, too—a signal that she could weave the threads of deception if necessary, could play kulith like a master. Perhaps even her dismal kulith performance so far had been part of the deception.

Aveo caught the word "Lucca" several times. Cam paced the room, expressions chasing each other across her face, urgency in her voice. She presented this urgency from every possible angle, catching all spyholes. No one rushed in to arrest her, to kill her. Aveo was impressed.

Eventually she put the box back in her tunic and said, "Sorry. A friend is . . . is ill. In his nose."

"Yes." He nodded, looking as if he knew this imaginary friend with the ill nose, as if he had had as much converse with "demons" as she did, and so was as dangerous. But the false conversation had accomplished one thing; she had accumulated enough kulith points to ascend unmolested to her egg on the roof.

Aveo made the *belon* to her, the gesture of acknowledgment of a masterly game move. She pretended to ignore his gesture—which was also masterly.

His hopes for survival rose.

The hopes were dashed again inside her ship.

Cam closed the door of the tiny space and flung open the cabinet door. Aveo had already caught the stench of Obu's night soil, but the girl was in a better way than he'd dared to expect. She was not dead, not unconscious, not mad. Released from her prison, she again huddled in a terrified ball in a corner, but Cam cleaned her with water from the egg and fed her as tenderly as if she were her own babe and not a slave. It was a stupid kulith move, but there was nobody but Aveo to see. What kind of city had she come from, where slaves were treated as *rem* and kulith was not played and the king would send such a confusing emissary across the wide sea?

Cam said, "Okay, this is what we're going to do."

"Isn't that for me to say?" Aveo said, as mildly as he could. He outranked her in kulith so much it was laughable.

"You? Well, if you have anything to add— Of course, I didn't mean to be rude. I'll tell you what I'm thinking, and then you tell me. I think I should offer Uldunu some other trade goods—from Pular, if you want to say that—in exchange for letting me sort of hang around with him for a few days. As an observer. That way, I stand a better chance of seeing whatever the . . . the people who sent me here want me to witness. Look, here's what I can offer him."

She opened another metal cabinet and took out three or four boxes. Aveo, despite himself, gasped.

Jewels in colors never found anywhere on this side of the world. Cloth so soft and bright that it must have been woven by spiders he could not imagine. Small bottles of thin colored glass, or something like glass. She unstoppered one and waved it in the air. The scent of strange and unknown flowers drifted on the air, rousing even Obu. But then she opened the fourth box, and Aveo forgot all else.

Daggers. Short and mid-length, curved and straight, some with decorated hilts and some plain, and all with a wicked, sharp, thin blade. Cam said, "Not bronze. Steel, so they won't break so easily."

"Steel." Another strange word. He picked up one of the shortest and plainest of the knives. It was forbidden for a scholar, painted in red and wearing the red skirt, to touch a weapon. But by Uldunu Four's decree, Aveo was a scholar no longer. That reality was gone.

"Yes, good idea," Cam said. "Arm yourself—I really should have thought of that last night. But do you think that if we gave him these, the king might let me follow him around the court until I see whatever I'm supposed to witness?"

"Ostiu Cam, you cannot just offer him these . . . these treasures. You must not!"

"Why?"

If her innocence was feigned, it was a wonderful act. But Aveo was losing faith that it was feigned. Another illusion gone. "It would be the grossest insult. You must lose these things to him in kulith, carefully, and with the *feft* move and no other."

"With the what? Aveo, if I have to arrange this through kulith, it'll never happen! Can't you play for me?"

He pretended to consider. "Perhaps."

"Oh, good. Which stuff should we bring downstairs? Will he play now, or at least soon?"

She gazed at him from those dark eyes that were Pulari

and not Pulari, and Aveo suddenly saw that he would never understand her. Not if he studied her for a thousand years. He would never follow her thinking or penetrate her illusions, because even though she was not a goddess but a woman, she was so foreign, so strange, that she lay completely outside any reality he could ever grasp. She was her own reality, and she and all of the known world were not playing the same game. The best Aveo could do, he thought despairingly, was try to steer her away from disaster, and perhaps survive until she went back to wherever she had come from.

She said, "What's wrong? You suddenly look like your entire family plus your dog just died."

Outraged, he raised his hand. But she didn't know about Ojea. She didn't know anything. He let the hand fall and pointed to the box of gemstones. "Bring that first. Save the cloth and perfumes and knives. We can— Oh, in the name of the Goddess, let the slave carry the box!"

"I didn't know you believed in any goddesses," Cam said.

Aveo didn't respond. He moved behind Cam, and, followed by the trembling Obu, they left the egg fallen from the sky to descend back into the palace below.

19: LUCCA

Lucca was completely blind.

Even the Kularians, who usually took everything in stride, seemed concerned. After he stumbled outside Hytrowembireliaz's hut into the driving snow, shouting as loud as he could and hanging on to the open door to keep from getting lost, the villagers came running. Someone grabbed his arm and led him back inside. He could hear, smell, feel the presence of more people than the tiny hut should be able to hold, but he could see nothing, not even a glimmer of light. Someone put hands on his face, pushed up each eyelid in turn, and leaned close. Lucca felt fetid breath on his face. He groped in the dark until he found a human arm and hung on, obscurely ashamed of his need for contact.

Why blindness?

The Kularians could not provide answers. They had no real medicine, no real technology to examine his eyes. All they could offer was Hytrowembireliaz, his voice finally distinguishable to Lucca among the concerned and helpless babble, saying, "Do you wish then to set out on the second road?"

"No!" Would they listen to him, or would they slit his throat anyway? Lucca fumbled inside his tunic for his personal shield, unused for so long.

"Are you sure, my fellow-traveler-on-the-first-road? It might be easier to leave now."

"No!"

"As you say." Hytrowembireliaz's smell faded.

Over the next several minutes, the hut emptied. Cold air whooshed in each time the door opened and closed. Finally, when Lucca thought everyone had gone and left him alone, he heard Chewithoztarel's voice.

"Lucca, do you want a stone cake?"

"No. Will you—"

"Do you want me to take you to the lodge?"

"No! Will you go away and leave me alone? Please!"

He heard her get up and go out without speaking again, and he knew he had hurt her feelings. But panic didn't let him care. He fumbled with the commlink.

"Soledad— I've gone blind!"

"What?"

"Blind! I can't see anything. All at once and— What do you think it is!"

She was silent so long that he thought he'd lost the link. Then she said, "When did this happen?"

"Just now!"

"And you still can't smell, either?"

"What? Yes, I can smell. . . . So what? Don't you understand? I'm blind."

"Calm down, Lucca. Yes, I understand. First you couldn't smell, then the next day at about the same time in the morning you can smell again but not see. . . . I don't think this is natural. Or not even caused by anything in your environment."

"What do you mean?" Her tone, so even and rational, was lessening his first fear.

"A rapid rotation of sensory deprivation, and smell returns just as sight goes away, and both occur at the same time on successive days . . . what toxin or body failure does that by itself? Doesn't it sound to you like something planned? Engineered?"

Her meaning seeped into him slowly. "You think the Atoners did this to me? How? Why?"

"I don't know why. But 'how' might be through turning off and on various genes. Remember, they put drugs or nanomachines or something in our bodies to fight disease and lessen pain and speed healing— How can we know what else they put in? Remember, they did it after we were brought up to the moon for the second time, and no human doctors ever saw the stuff we agreed to. That one Witness who objected, that Japanese man—he was sent home and replaced by Tomiko. We don't know *what* we have in us now. We were willing to do anything to have this opportunity."

That sounded as if Soledad had changed her mind about the Witnesses' malleability, but Lucca wasn't interested in exploring this now. He seized on the hope in her theory. "So if they took away my smell and then restored it, they might restore my vision, too, perhaps tomorrow? But why?"

"I don't know."

"Is it even possible to cause blindness by switching off genes?"

"Yes," said Soledad. "I know that because my cousin has it. The most common form of congenital blindness is caused by mutations in just two genes. Lucca, you must wait until tomorrow and see what happens."

"They want me to 'start on the second road.' Which means, be killed."

"Keep your personal shield activated."

"I will. I don't suppose Cam has reported anything like this?"

"No."

Lucca didn't ask what Cam was doing. He didn't care. He waited for Soledad to ask, yet again, if he wanted her to bring the shuttle down and fetch him, but she said nothing. Clearly she expected him to see this through.

And he expected it of himself. He was ashamed of his momentary panic. The blindness might be gone by tomorrow. If not, he would find some way to deal with it for as long as it lasted. He had a task to do here.

But why had the Atoners done this? If they were trying

to send him a message, what could it possibly be, and why hadn't they just told him outright? The three days that the Witnesses-to-be had spent under the Atoner Dome had been packed with information. None of the volunteers had ever actually seen an Atoner; everything was spoken from behind impenetrable screens. The humans had been instructed in how to use the personal shields, the comm-links, the shuttle and ship controls, the laser guns. They had been thoroughly acquainted with the other two Witnesses that the aliens had chosen for each particular mission. They had been told about the health-enhancing injections of nanobots given while they were under anesthesia. But no Atoner had ever mentioned manipulation of the human genome. Nor even that the aliens were capable of doing so.

Lucca knew that patience had never been one of his virtues. Nonetheless, he reached for patience as he sat cross-legged on the pile of dirty rugs in the crude hut he could not see, on an alien world somewhere in a galaxy suddenly much colder than even he, so easily given to despair, had imagined.

20: ADVERTISEMENT

For the Adventurer in You

You're more curious than average, bolder than average, smarter than average. You know that this universe of ours holds marvels, and you want to see as many of them as possible. And now ... you can see more than you ever imagined. See, touch, experience.

You can go to the moon.

The ultimate adventure, dreamed about for millennia ... and now a reality.

Contact our representatives today to book your once-in-a-lifetime trip. By appointment only.

- Trip includes four nights at Earth Base Alpha and two nights at Luna Station.
- Medical prescreening provided.
- Three-day Space Orientation and Training given at Earth Base Alpha.
- Rover trip to view Selene City and–NEW!–the Atoner Dome.
- Powerful telescope at Luna Station shows amazing sky and moon detail.

FARRINGTON MOON TOURS: New York: 212-555-3765; London: 020-5577-6652; Tokyo: 03-5152-8748; farringtonmoontours.com

Licensed by Federal Aviation Administration, Office of Commercial Space Transportation, in accordance with Commercial Space Launch Amendments Act, Code of Federal Regulations, Title 14, Chapter III.

21: CAM

Cam, Aveo, and the terrified Obu were met in the long gallery by a contingent of soldiers. Aveo was pressed close behind Cam, within her shield, but Obu had no protection, and Cam had already seen one child spitted and murdered. She stopped, hoping the slave girl would not run, or drop the box of jewels that were supposed to be a gift for the king, or be attacked in any way that forced Cam to draw her laser gun. To her left the alien plants moaned and growled—how the fuck could anyone want to hear *that* from flowers all day?

"Be quiet," Aveo said in her ear. He began to talk, still not realizing that her implant was giving her the translation in her other ear. Stereo.

Aveo said to the soldiers, "Conduct us to Uldunu Four. Rem Ocama has costly gifts to present from her king."

Her king? Well, maybe you could think of the Atoners that way— No, you couldn't. And when had Cam become a *rem*? Yesterday she'd been an *ostiu*. Still, *rem* was what Aveo was, so maybe that was okay.

"A gift?" said the captain of the guard, or whatever he was.

"A kulith gift," Aveo said. Oh, Christ, more kulith. But Aveo had said that perhaps this time he could play for her, losing the jewels in exactly the way he'd insisted on: *carefully, and with the* feft *move and no other*. Like she could ever manage that.

"Come," the captain said, and even in another language, on another world, his anger and hatred and fear were clear to Cam. She lifted her chin and started forward. But evidently the anger and hatred were equally clear to Obu, already shaking. She took one step forward behind Cam, stumbled, and dropped the box she'd been entrusted to carry. The latch sprang open and jewels spilled out like brilliant rain.

Rubies, sapphires, diamonds, garnets, emeralds, topaz . . . The trouble was that as soon as the gems hit the ground, they seemed to disappear. They were the same brilliant, glowing colors as the tiny tiles set in intricate patterns on the gallery floor and walls. Cam heard the jewels strike the ground, some clattering softly . . . and then even her twenty-twenty eyesight couldn't distinguish where they'd rolled.

"Fuck!" she cried, and bent to gather them just as Aveo hissed into her ear, "No! Stoop and you lose all kulith!"

"Damn kulith— Oh!"

It happened fast, but Cam was faster. The captain leaped past her, graceful as a panther, drawing his dagger. Obu shrieked and fell to the ground. But he hadn't touched her yet, and Cam thrust herself between them, touching the shield button that rooted the shield to the ground. He hit her as if she were a solid stone wall, which was pretty much what she was, and ricocheted off, in turn falling onto the tiled floor.

Then he reversed the direction of his own dagger and thrust it into his breast.

Cam gasped. Aveo said, "Quiet, *ostiu*." Then, in his own language and very harshly, "Obu! Retrieve the gift!"

The girl crouched, motionless, and for a long moment Cam thought she wasn't going to obey. But evidently Aveo scared her more than the soldiers (why?). She scrambled on all fours, snatching at jewels Cam couldn't see, shoving them back into the metal box. Another soldier slid smoothly to the head of the military detail, knelt, crossed his arms across his breast, and said, "Please come this way, *rems*."

"Follow him," Aveo said softly.

"Obu—"

"No one will touch her now. You made good kulith, *ostiu*."

She hadn't made anything at all. Cam stepped over the body of the captain, from which blood spread in a sickening pool over the bright designs of the floor. Were any jewels caught under his corpse, in the warm, red pool? She didn't care. Nothing here made sense, least of all the captain's suicide, which everybody else seemed to think was normal and which of course was some sort of stupid, incomprehensible kulith move.

All at once Cam flashed on herself at twelve or thirteen, seated cross-legged on the rug in front of her PC, playing *Half-Life* or *Counter-Strike* or *Grand Theft Auto* with Billy and Hannah next door. Killing people and zombies and aliens in those all-engrossing games. But that was *different,* that was—

They entered the throne room.

It turned out that kulith wasn't a bad way to witness this place, after all. Aveo played the actual game for her, although Cam didn't know why. He said he was now her surrogate because she had made the "*firl* move," although Cam had no idea what that was or when she might have made it or what it signified. But Aveo moved the game pieces, steadily doling out jewels to Uldunu as forfeits for whatever, and Cam was free to watch the comings and goings of bare-chested, skirted men painted red or blue and of naked slaves, both male and female. She was free to "witness."

Witness *what*? She still had no idea. This was a savage, barbaric place, but even though her high school grades in history hadn't been all that great, she'd seen enough movies to know that her own planet could be just as savage and barbaric. The Atoners had assured all the Witnesses that "you'll know it when you encounter it." But she saw nothing like that.

By late afternoon, Cam was thoroughly bored. The kulith played on, hours and hours of it. Didn't the king have a war to run? You'd never know it. Her translator was fluent now, but she never heard anything worth noting, especially since no one spoke during the game. The vast room was as silent as a grave. Cam almost jumped when Aveo finally leaned away from the kulith board and whispered to her in Pularit, "You must leave the throne room, *ostiu,* and walk through the palace. You should have done it before now."

"I should have— God, why didn't you say so? I'm dying to get up and move around!"

His pale eyes grew weary. "I did say so. Many times. I made the *pleft* move . . . and *ostiu,* I know I told you what that means."

"You didn't— Forget it. I'm going."

The moment she stood, a solid block of blue-painted, blue-skirted soldiers formed to her left and red-painted, red-skirted advisors to her right. Cam looked at Aveo, who nodded slightly, and she set off, trailed by half the palace. She walked without awareness until she found herself in the gallery where she had killed the captain of the guard. The corpse was gone, the tiles scrubbed of blood.

Cam stared at the garden of moaning plants, her "escort" at a respectful distance, and pulled out her commlink. Fuck the reactions of these guys in their little skirts—if she didn't talk to anybody normal, she was going to go mad.

"Soledad? Things have calmed down here. Everybody's playing board games. Has Lucca's smelliness returned yet?"

"Yes. But now he's blind."

Cam drew a sharp breath. The plants whined more loudly. "*Blind?* When did that happen?"

"Just this morning. I have a lot to tell you. Are you somewhere you can talk?"

"Yes. No. Just a minute." Cam left the gallery and the droning garden, retraced her steps, and turned right. After only one false turn she found the only other room she'd visited since the interminable kulith game began: the "women's area." Not that Cam had seen any other women in it. Probably that bastard Uldunu didn't want Cam to pollute his harem or concubines or whatever he had. Soldiers and advisors stopped as soon as Cam walked through the door curtain. The room, windowless but large and airy, was tiled in soft yellow, with more curtains to pull around holes in the floor. Modesty for pissing. Warm water filled shallow basins along the walls. If there were spyholes, Cam didn't see them, and anyway, no spies would understand English. She just wanted to talk to Soledad away from the banks of impassive faces and watchful eyes.

She sat on a polished stone bench and said, "Tell me."

"Lucca's sense of smell returned exactly twenty-four hours after he lost it, and then a little while later he went blind. Cam, have you lost the use of any of your sensory organs?"

"No."

"Have you experienced any changes in your body at all? Think carefully before you answer."

Soledad's caution and doubt, even worse than usual, scraped across Cam's nerves. "I don't have to think about it! I'd know if my body changed, and it hasn't!"

"Okay. Have you observed anything strange about the Kularians?"

"Fuck it, Soledad, *everything* is strange here! What exactly do you mean?"

Soledad hesitated. "I don't want to bias your perceptions."

Cam couldn't take this; she really couldn't. Why did Soledad always have to sound so superior? But Cam tried to control her voice. "You won't 'bias' me. Tell me what you're talking about. Did Lucca see something weird? Does everybody on 'A' just go around losing senses every once in a while?"

"No. Just Lucca. And I don't think that's a result of being on Kular A. I think it's some sort of side effect of the medical nanobots we received in the Atoner Dome."

Cam had never understood about the nanobots. Also, she disliked thinking about tiny machines swarming in her blood. But Soledad was smart, and this felt important. "You mean the 'bots are screwing up Lucca's blood?"

"More than his blood—his genes. Lucca might be having genes switched on and off. That could cause both the disappearance and reappearance of various senses."

Cam struggled to understand. "But . . . why would the Atoners *do* that? And why to Lucca and not to me, too?"

"I don't know," Soledad said.

An insect of some kind buzzed past Cam's ear. She shot out one hand, got it, and crushed the small body. At least it was one thing she could grasp. "Soledad—there's something else, isn't there? What did Lucca witness that you thought I might have seen, too?"

Silence.

"Tell me, damn it! Or I'll call him and ask him myself!"

"Don't call him. While he's blind he can't get away from people safely, and his Kularians of course shouldn't see his commlink."

As Cam's already had. Well, too fucking bad. "Tell me, Soledad. I mean it."

"All right. Lucca's informant, a little girl, told him several things he did when he was absolutely alone. Things like take a sponge bath or commlink me."

The crushed insect had left slime on Cam's hand. She plunged it into the basin beside her bench. "But how could the kid know those things if Lucca really was 'absolutely alone'?"

"Lucca thinks they might have some kind of telepathy."

Cam stood so fast that water sloshed onto the floor. *"Telepathy?"*

"That's what Lucca thinks."

"You mean there's another way to think about it?" Envy washed through her, followed by a bitter emotion she couldn't name. Lucca got telepathy, and all Cam got was killing and kulith.

Soledad's voice was careful. "The Kularians themselves have a different explanation."

"What?"

"They think they can see and talk to the dead."

Cam laughed. "That's ridiculous!"

"Well, it sounds that way," Soledad said, and why did she sound so relieved at Cam's reaction? "But I think it's important to postpone committing to any sort of hypothesis without further data. The information we have so far is . . ."

Cam had stopped listening. *Talk to the dead.* Was that possible?

No. It wasn't.

But if it *was*—

Cam didn't believe in ghosts, in religion, in God. Yet, even so . . . She broke into Soledad's flow of intellectual blather. "What kind of 'further data'?"

"Lucca is running some experiments. Or he was, until this blindness came up. I'm wondering if the two are somehow related."

That made no sense. Cam said, "I want to hear all his conversations with that little girl. In English."

Soledad, sounding exasperated, said, "You could have done that already. Just download Lucca's uploads from my link the way I told you and let your translator learn Kularian A. Then all you have to do is—"

"Wait—I have to go! Talk to you later!"

A strange noise had sounded outside the door, somewhere between the droning of the god-awful garden and the chittering of demented insects. A moment later sixteen naked slave women, all looking terrified, burst into the room and surrounded Cam. None of them looked her directly in the face, none of them touched her, but from their distress and gestures it was clear that she was supposed to leave this room. One, a woman older than the rest, with a shaved head and gray in her pubic hair, held out a trembling palm. On it sat a single polished, highly carved kulith piece.

Cam was summoned back to Uldunu Four and his stupid game.

Kulith ran far into the evening. When Cam and Aveo were finally permitted to return to their apartment, the kulith board still looked cluttered and Aveo looked exhausted. Obu crouched at the foot of their bed, covering her face whenever Cam glanced at her. It was like having a cringing dog in the room.

Cam pulled out her commlink, downloaded the data from Soledad, and waited while her translator acquired the language of Kular A. She listened in English to Lucca's conversations with the kid with the long name, and then listened a second time. None of it made sense.

Unless you believed Lucca's Kularians.

Was it possible, even remotely, that those semi-savages were right? That you could talk to the dead for a little while after they died? How could that be?

Cam had stopped believing in religion when she was thirteen. But Lucca's natives never mentioned any sort of god. Only the lunatics here in Uldunu's city were religious. Still . . . strange and inexplicable things did happen in the world. In any world.

"Aveo," Cam said in Pularit, "what do you think happens when people die?"

The old man jerked his head around to stare at her. She read the clear warning in his eyes: *We are observed and understood.* The spyholes.

He said, "When we die, the Goddess of All Green takes to Her those who are worthy."

The party line. She tried again. "Can the people of this wonderful country"—a little grease never hurt, after all—"talk to their dead?"

"Talk . . ."

"To their dead. You know, to ghosts." But the translator gave her no word for "ghost" in either Pularit or Uldunuit.

"Talk to what?"

"Never mind. Let's sleep."

They got into bed, this time with her spooning him from behind, her personal shield enveloping them both. "Aveo," she whispered against his ear, "now tell me the truth. Can anyone here talk to the dead? Hear them? See them?"

"No," he said aloud, with such violence and longing that Cam was startled. But she also believed him.

So whatever the natives of Kular A did, it wasn't happening here. But even Lucca, who was smart and skeptical, thought that *something* was happening in his frozen little village. He said it was telepathy, and he'd been to some important university in England. Soledad thought it was connected with Lucas's blindness and that his genes were involved—how? And what had the Atoners done to Cam's genes, or Soledad's, or all the other Witnesses'?

Then Cam had another thought. If, just "if," the dead weren't really dead, then they could be standing here, right beside this bed on this forsaken planet, looking down at Cam and accusing her, their murderer, wishing her tortured and in pain and—

Fuck it, Soledad, why did you tell me all these horrible ideas?

But Cam had insisted on being told.

She curled closer to Aveo, holding on for dear life, wishing that Lucca's telepathy existed on Kular B so that she could take comfort from whatever let Aveo sleep like that, snoring gently in her arms.

The next day, kulith resumed in the throne room. Endless kulith, boring kulith, incomprehensible kulith, until Cam could no longer stand it. Without even asking Aveo, she left the room and walked to the long tiled gallery facing the whining garden. The same escort as yesterday followed her, and abruptly she couldn't stand that, either. Anything to get away from these lunatics! Abruptly she veered into the garden of moaning plants, threading her way among them. Small insects swarmed off the leaves and dived directly at her, but of course they couldn't penetrate her shield.

Amazed, outraged sounds rose behind her. Wasn't she supposed to enter the garden? What if the plants were poisonous? Her shield protected against any solid object, but gases . . . She scurried back toward the gallery, but all at once the soldiers and advisors on the tiled gallery walk erupted.

Cam stopped, astonished—nobody had been *this* angry when she'd killed the Chief of the Royal Guard! They gestured and shouted and began raining knives at her. The knives bounced off her shield. Cam rooted herself and stayed put, while all around her the plants' low moaning rose all at once to a high-pitched, ear-piercing wail.

Aveo plunged through the curtain, between milling soldiers and advisors, and stopped dead at the edge of the garden. He said in Pularit, "Cam! Leave the plants!"

So that was it—she'd walked on sacred ground or something! Well, big deal. Shrugging, Cam unrooted herself and moved forward, just as the plants attacked.

They were incredibly fast. In just a few seconds they'd swung vines and tendrils around her from several directions. None penetrated her shield, of course, and there didn't seem to be any noxious gases, or at least she wasn't getting sick from any. But to stand there like a dummy attacked by grass . . . the fuck with that! Cam pulled out her laser gun.

"No!" Aveo yelled, and it was in English.

Cam was so surprised that she froze, gun raised halfway from her hip, until she realized that Aveo must have heard her say that word involuntarily, probably more than once. And from his face, she knew he meant it: *No. Don't fire. Don't move.* She was so sick of doing nothing, understanding nothing, witnessing nothing—

An advisor, young and brawny, with red-painted breast and red skirt that fluttered with his abrupt movement, picked up Aveo and threw him into the garden.

Cam screamed. Aveo had landed on his feet and then sunk to his knees and he was only eighteen inches away from the tiled gallery, but the farthest plants had already sent tendrils to reach him. They wrapped around his skinny legs and waist and one snaked upward to his face. The stinging insects swirled around his face. No one moved to either help Aveo or pummel the man who had thrown him.

Cam unrooted herself and rushed forward. She snatched up Aveo, but he was outside her shield unless she turned it off, and the plants held him fast. Cam leaped onto the gallery and began firing at the people around her. She didn't know how many she hit, but some fell and some ran and in seconds the gallery was empty except for corpses piled like chickens at a butcher counter. She turned off the shield, burned the vines holding Aveo, and snatched him to her. She reactivated the shield just as the unhurt soldiers regrouped and attacked.

"Fuckers! Monsters! Madmen!" She didn't realize she was screaming at them in English until her voice caught and she stopped. She couldn't move forward because if she unrooted the shield, they would knock her over. Against her chest Aveo's body, still wrapped in the severed tendrils of the weeds, breathed shallowly. She had to get him to the shuttle, there were meds there, she knew the way to the roof—

One of the men she'd burned crawled at her feet. He reached out feebly and tried to grab her ankle. The next moment the hand fell. She could smell him, charred flesh. . . . Her gorge rose. In her arms Aveo groaned, a pitiful sound she could hear even over the shrieking of the furious plants. Despite his light weight, her arms were starting to ache from clutching him.

Carefully, so as not to shift him outside the shield, Cam moved Aveo enough to again reach her gun. She killed everyone who didn't flee the gallery. When it was empty, she turned off the shield, shifted Aveo to a fireman's carry, turned it back on, and started for the shuttle.

No one approached her on the steep staircase to the roof. No one prevented her from entering the shuttle.

Panting hard, she dumped Aveo on the floor and searched frantically for the med kit. The Atoners had carefully explained each med, but that was for use with humans— Fuck it, Aveo *was* a human! But what exactly was wrong with him?

"Aveo! Hang on, it'll be all right—"

He stared at her uncomprehendingly; she'd spoken English.

Cam pulled down the collar of his robe and slapped a patch on his neck. The Atoners had described this patch as "general use," for shock or infection or allergy. . . . God knew what-all was in it. After a minute she stuck on another patch, for parasites and food poisoning. For the first time, in a detached corner of her mind that she hadn't known was even functioning, she realized that none of the twenty-one human Witnesses were doctors or medical scientists. Was that deliberate?

Aveo's eyes opened and he gazed at her. She watched the pain clear from his eyes. "What . . ."

"Don't talk. I gave you some medicine. I don't know if it will cure you or not but— Fuck!"

The entire shuttle was rocking.

Cam jumped up and switched on the external display. Slaves—hundreds of them, it looked like—were massed outside the shuttle, pushing at it. Soldiers stood behind them, shouting orders. Fury surged in Cam like a tsunami. She commlinked Soledad and shouted, "Lift the shuttle. Immediately!"

Soledad asked no questions. A minute later the shuttle rose, and the Kularians dwindled into so many tiny, head-raised figures on the roof of a miniature palace.

Soledad said, "Cam? What's happening?"

"Tell you later. But I'm okay now. Just set us down in some empty field someplace, far away from these damned assholes!" She returned to Aveo.

He tried to sit up but fell back. Cam brought a blanket and made him comfortable on the cramped floor space. She held a cup of water for him. The shuttle settled in the middle of an empty plain. Aveo looked, bewildered, from the wall displays to Cam, back again.

"We left the city, Aveo. Here, I'm going to take off those vines that—"

"Don't touch them without your invisible armor! They're poison!"

"I thought so." She removed the dead tendrils and threw them in the disposal. Aveo's voice sounded much stronger. Maybe he would be all right.

As soon as she thought this, Cam began to tremble. Aveo might be okay, but she was a murderer. She had killed God knows how many more people, just mowed them down as if they were grass or wheat or some fucking thing, fired over and over on *people*—

Aveo said something. "What?"

"How did you heal me?"

"I put on patches that— It's hard to explain. *You* explain what the fuck happened back there!"

"The plants are mating. You went among them at the time the Goddess of All Green flows within them, or so think the people. Ostiu Cam, I told you—"

"I don't understand anything you told me," she said, still trembling. *Firing over and over, all those murdered people . . .* "I don't even understand anything I saw for myself. How can the— Aveo, we're going to stay right here for a while. You're going to get better and I'm going to listen to you tell me everything you know, so I can do the job I was fucking sent here to do!"

She couldn't read his expression—surprise, surprise. She had misread everything here. Aveo was her only success, and her only link to this so-called "witnessing" of Kular B. This weak, emaciated, intelligent old man who seemed more alien to her than the Atoners ever had.

"Yes," he said, and once more closed his eyes.

22: LUCCA

The morning after he'd gone blind, Lucca's sight returned.

It happened as he sat in a corner of the lodge where Hytrowembireliaz had dumped him on a pile of smelly rugs, and it happened instantly. One moment darkness, and the next a room full of people. Too many people. Lucca saw what he hadn't suspected in his unseeing misery and had never expected to see until spring: strangers.

Not that they looked any different from the villagers. But by now Lucca could name every one of the eighty-eight villagers, describe every one of their faces, recite their kinship ties, and even detail what each ate and how well each danced. With nothing else to occupy his mind and the Atoners' mandate to "witness," the villagers had become his library, his newscasts, his d-vid games, his e-mail, his television perpetually tuned to a boring channel. But here were actual strangers!

Three men, four women, and children dashing around in too much excitement to be countable. The adults clustered around Blanbilitwan, Hytrowembireliaz's wife. Kin, coming to visit? Lucca grabbed at Chewithoztarel as she raced past, catching the hem of her tunic and bringing her crashing down on top of himself.

"Aiiooo! Let me go, I'm chasing Yerwazitel! She's winning!"

"In just a minute. Who are these people?"

She stopped struggling to get free and peered at him. "You can see them?"

"Yes, my eyes are working again. Who—"

"Why?"

"Why are my eyes working? I don't know, they just are. Who—"

"That's very strange!" the child cried. "Yerwazitel, come here!"

Lucca scowled; he wanted to be informed, not be a sideshow. But Yerwazitel didn't come anyway, being engaged in wrestling with a small boy who was doing his best to tear her hair off her head. Lucca said forcefully, "Who are these people?"

"My cousins," Chewithoztarel said scornfully, as if he should already know this. "They came from up in the mountains!"

"Why?"

"So Plengajiaz can start on the second road, of course. Let me go, Lucca, Yerwazitel needs help!"

Lucca released the girl and she shot off to jump on the squealing and wrestling children. The adults shifted around the mass of scuffling little bodies, and Lucca saw that one of the women was very old. Blanbilitwan steered her to another corner, where the old woman eased her body onto a pile of rugs not unlike Lucca's, beaming at everyone. Lucca stood and walked over to her. He barely limped; however the Atoners had enhanced his healing process, it was a spectacular success. A few of the villagers glanced at him, but no one exclaimed that this blind man was suddenly navigating unerringly through clumps of adults and shifting knots of cavorting children. Was this what Lucca had been sent here to witness—an utter lack of human curiosity? Surely not.

And why hadn't some other disability replaced the blindness that had replaced the lack of smell?

"Hello, child," the old lady said. "You are the winter visitor. They told me."

"Yes. My name is Lucca." Up close, he saw that her hands were twisted with arthritis, the blue veins like ridges above the weathered skin. Pain shadowed her sunken eyes. Her front teeth, one of which should have been red, were both missing. "You've come here to start on the second road."

"Yes. I was born here. I want to start out beside my daughter, so my sons brought me down the mountain as soon as the snow stopped. Good boys."

"Is your daughter Blanbilitwan?"

"Yes, of course."

And there it was again—the assumption that everyone already knew everything, so that both explanation and curiosity were superfluous. Was that part of the telepathy? Lucca blundered on. "When will you start out?"

"Oh, tonight, I think. I don't want to delay."

"Yes," Lucca said. Finally his luck was turning. This woman would die tonight, and he would have a chance to carry out another experiment. A new possibility had occurred to him in the long dark hours of his blindness: Perhaps something about the presence of death temporarily aroused telepathic abilities in the villagers. A response to stress, maybe, hormonally based. Then, as the stress of changes in their small population abated, so did the telepathy.

Lucca could think of an analogy: the superhuman strength exhibited when a parent lifted, say, a car that had fallen on a child. Much more strength than could normally be summoned, and only for the brief time needed to free the trapped kid. Such phenomena had strong evolutionary survival value, and so might temporary telepathy: If a tribe or even just a hunting party was fleeing a predator that had just killed one of their number, a telepathic ability to coordinate might save all their lives.

He said to the old woman, who was starting to doze off, "Plengajiaz? I would ask a task, as a fellow-traveler-on-the-first-road."

"Yes?" Half-asleep, she registered no surprise at his request.

"Before you start out on the second road, will you tell me something that happened to you when you were a child? Something known only to us two?"

"Why?" Awake now, she looked puzzled, the deep lines of her old face wrinkled as withered grapes.

"It is the custom in the village I come from."

"A strange custom. But I will do it. I will do it now, since I start on the second road as soon as my sons have eaten." Suddenly she cackled, as if something was very funny. "When I was a girl, I killed a *pybalt*. By myself!"

Lucca knew how momentous this was. *Pybalts,* vaguely lionlike, were dangerous, and Kularian women did not hunt. "And no one ever knew?"

"No one! I used my brother's spear, and I left the body up the mountain. And now I hope that I may find that *pybalt* on the third path and apologize to it."

The third path: that delusion of afterlife where all wrongs would be righted, the childish comfort furnished by faith to the weak and the old. He said again, "And no one knows about this *pybalt*?"

"No one!" She laughed again, merrily, and fell asleep.

Lucca went over to the table, where food was being set out for the second of the villagers' daily two meals. He wasn't hungry, but he picked up a hunk of stone bread and nibbled on it. Ordinarily strongly flavored with something akin to wild onions, the stone bread was completely tasteless on his tongue, in his mouth. The Atoners had taken away another of his senses, which would undoubtedly return tomorrow.

Why?

After the meal, many villagers left for the long night's sleep. Others stayed in the lodge, but Lucca could discern no kinship pattern in who went and who didn't. Chewithoztarel, along with several other children, remained. The children quieted as they joined the ragged circle of adults.

Plengajiaz took her place in the center, half-carried by

her sons. Blanbilitwan sat close beside her, startling Lucca. He hadn't realized that women killed women. The old lady raised her hand, smiled toothlessly at all of them, and laid her head on the shoulder of her daughter, who slit her throat.

Unlike the man on the steppes, Plengajiaz's blood did not spurt out in strong jets. Maybe Blanbilitwan was a more skillful executioner. Maybe she was practiced from cutting up animals for stew, cutting bread. . . . Lucca realized he was a bit hysterical. Blood oozed from the old woman, soaking the blanket under her. Hytrowembireliaz stepped forward, wrapped the body in the bloody blanket, and carried it outside.

To dump it in the snow, and let it be mauled and eaten and . . . Sick rage rose in Lucca. This was their mother, grandmother, aunt. Their disregard for their dead struck him as horrible, monstrous, *wrong*. They were barbarians.

Gianna lay in a waterproof, lead-lined casket in an English graveyard, beneath a carved headstone planted with roses.

Now the villagers jumped up from the circle, laughing and talking, and in the confusion Lucca could not see who talked to whom. He beckoned to Chewithoztarel, who skipped over. "Chewithoztarel, what did your grandmother tell me just before she started out on the second road?"

"I don't know. Do you want me to ask her?"

His mouth tightened. More games from this wretched brat. But he said, "Yes. Now."

Chewithoztarel ran to the other side of the room, where a group of adults talked. She disappeared between their legs, dashing back to him a few minutes later. Her dark eyes were huge. "Everybody's talking to her! But she bent down and whispered in my ear. She said she told you that once she killed a *pybalt*! By herself! And nobody ever knew!"

"Yes," Lucca said. "Ask your mother to come here, please."

Blanbilitwan came over to him from the table. She

hadn't been in the knot of adults that Chewithoztarel had joined. Lucca said abruptly, "Blanbilitwan, I would ask you something. What did your mother and I talk about just before she started on the second road?"

Blanbilitwan actually looked startled. But she didn't question this strange request, saying only, "I'll ask her." She walked over to the gossiping adults, returning in a moment. "She says she told you that when she was a young girl, she killed a *pybalt*. Such an ungood thing!"

"Thank you," Lucca managed. He pulled on his cloak and went outside. It was dark, but two young boys lingered beside the lodge, looking furtive. Lucca caught sight of a necklace of polished stones, such as girls wore before their marriages, just as one boy whisked the necklace into his tunic. "Nabnopithoz, what did Plengajiaz tell me just before she started out on the second road?"

"I don't know," the boy said, caught somewhere among obedience, embarrassment, and adolescent defiance.

"Go ask her! Now!"

Both boys disappeared into the lodge. Only one returned, Nabnopithoz, to whom Lucca had given a direct order. Villager children never disobeyed. Nabnopithoz said, a little sulkily, "Plengajiaz wasn't there. She already left on the third road."

"Thank you." Lucca spun around and started toward Hytrowembireliaz's hut.

It made no sense. There was some kind of telepathy going on, clearly, unless the old lady had been lying to him and everyone had already known about the *pybalt* slain so long ago. But Lucca didn't think they lied. The villagers were too startled by the idea of a girl hunting, and their surprise felt genuine to him. But the telepathy had faded so fast, whereas when Chewithoztarel had claimed to be "talking" to Ragjuptrilpent, the phenomenon had gone on for many days. Was Nabnopithoz merely bad at telepathy, and so covering up his inability by claiming that the old woman had "already left on the third road"? Was

Blanbilitwan engaging in some elaborate cultural ritual by claiming to "ask" her mother before she pulled the information telepathically from Lucca's own mind? What the hell was going on here?

E che cazzo!

He stumbled through the twilight cold to Hytrowembireliaz's hut, only slightly warmer, where he could call Soledad and ask her to help him make sense of the senseless. A little ways out on the plain he glimpsed a small mound: a blanket already half-covered with snow. Plengajiaz's body, abandoned and desolate. Lucca looked away and kept walking.

Soledad said hesitantly, "What if they're telling the truth?"

"What do you mean?" The hut was almost completely dark, and in the distance Lucca heard shouting and laughing. Soon the family would return to sleep.

She said, "Everything you just told me, about the old lady and the *pybalt* and those two Kularians asking her about it . . . What if they really can talk to their dead?"

"Don't be ridiculous," Lucca snapped. "I'm talking science, not some fuzzy mysticism."

"Sometimes science starts out as mysticism. Like . . . like alchemy became chemistry. And this is an alien world! What if the rules are somehow different here?"

"Kularians are *human,* Soledad—you know that. And do you really believe that different laws of physics and matter hold in one part of the universe than another?"

He sensed her considering, striving to be fair. "No. I don't believe that."

"Then come up with a different hypothesis, *cara.* You talked before of my genes and—"

"That was about your blindness."

"Which is now tastelessness." He laughed, sourly amused at his own diction. The door to the hut opened. "I must go—good-bye!"

Chewithoztarel rushed in. "Guess what, Lucca? Something really strange happened!"

His breath caught. "It did? What?"

"I wrestled Yerwazitel, and I *won*!" She crowed happily and stamped her little booted feet. "Can you believe it?"

23: "SCHLEPPING TO THE STARS"

(To be sung to the tune of "She'll Be Coming 'Round
the Mountain When She Comes.")

They'll be schlepping to the stars when they go,
They'll be schlepping to the stars when they go,
Aliens ship them out
And what is that *about?*
They'll be schleppin' to the stars when they go.

They'll be witnessin' for 'Tonies when they go,
They'll be witnessin' for 'Tonies when they go,
Someone did a crime
Way way back in time,
So they'll be witnessing for 'Tonies when they go.

The crime's a great big question mark to us,
The crime's a great big question mark to us,
And why the 'Tonies fess to it
Is anybody's guesstimate,
'Cause the crime's a great big question mark to us.

Our guys'll come back to see us—so we hope!
Our guys'll come back to see us—so we hope!
And maybe then we'll understand
This weird and scary Wonderland,
If our *guys come back to see us, as we hope.*

The above is hereby officially condemned by the following
organizations: People's Coalition Against Alien Interference, Mothers Against Abduction, Fight Now! and the
state legislatures of North Dakota, Alabama, and Arizona.

24: AVEO

Small sharp stings on his hands, his legs, his feet around his sandals. And a roaring in his ears, almost as soon as the vines touched him. No, that wasn't the vines, it was Cam shouting, or Uldunu Four's army shouting—No, it was Ojea, a child again and calling for his father to come right away, it was urgent, so urgent—

Aveo knew he was dying. One always died, when mating *thrul* got you. Not the best kulith moves could save you, nothing could save you from the mating poison—The din inside his head went on and on, although maybe it was outside his head. . . . He flew through the air and someone was roasting meat, its smell the last thing he noticed as the nothingness of death claimed him.

But it wasn't death, after all. Somehow he was sitting on the inside of Cam's silver egg and she was holding a cup of water for him. The pain was leaving him, sliding away from his head and body and feet like a tide rushing out. And although he felt no motion, the strange windows showed the city falling away beneath them. . . . They were *flying*. He tried to sit up, but weakness took him and he fell back.

Cam said, "We left the city, Aveo. Here, I'm going to take off those vines that—"

"Don't touch them without your invisible armor! They're poison!" He was surprised at the strength of his own voice. "How did you heal me?"

"I put on patches that— It's hard to explain. *You* explain what the fuck happened back there!"

He groped for memory. "The plants are mating. You went among them at the time the Goddess of All Green has them in thrall, or so think the people. Ostiu Cam, I told you—"

"I don't understand anything you told me," she said wearily. "I don't even understand anything I saw directly. How can I— Aveo, we're going to stay right here for a while. You're going to get better and I'm going to listen to you tell me everything you know, so I can do the job I was fucking sent here to do!"

Everything you know. Did she really think that was possible? He had a lifetime of experiences—a lifetime he had almost lost—and she was under the illusion she could absorb them without having lived his life? Without even having lived in his part of the world? Reality was not that malleable, that you could bend it like iron in the forge to fit another's mind. So far, this woman had not even been able to understand the small pieces of reality he had shown her.

Yet here he was in her flying ship, owing her his life, and he had no idea what else to do except answer whatever she thought to ask.

"Yes," he said, and closed his eyes. "Ask what you will."

"Okay . . . you said about the plants that I walked around in them when they're mating and the goddess— Which goddess?"

"Belief holds only one: the Goddess of All Green. Ostiu Cam, you have moved her piece in kulith."

"Kulith! That's a game!"

Again Aveo struggled to sit up, and this time he succeeded. Although he was weak, it was amazing how well he felt: clearheaded, even cheerful. His fingers explored the healing cloths Cam had put on his neck, but he didn't remove them.

"Kulith is not a game. Don't you yet understand? Although it uses the things of life, slaves and crops and soldiers and wars, kulith is not a mirror of life. Kulith is a mirror of the mind that produces life."

"A mirror . . . I don't see."

"In kulith are all the thought processes, and all the results of those processes, that shape a person's destiny. We play kulith to discover who we are, and who others are, and to foreshadow and so cause what will happen between us."

"Like . . . like seeing the future?"

"No. Creating the future, by creating the interactions between players that will shape their future."

She scowled, a big uneducated woman trying to send her mind where it would not go. But how could it not go there? She said, "And this goddess . . . If you shape your own future by playing kulith, then gods don't have any say in what happens? So why is there a game piece for the goddess?"

Aveo said carefully, "Most people believe that the Goddess observes all, and affects all through her sacred servant, Uldunu Four."

"We have something like that, where I come from, only it's a God. He—"

"A male?" Despite everything, he was slightly shocked. "But how would such a belief come to be? Males cannot birth life!"

She shrugged. "I don't know. But *you* . . . you don't believe in that goddess, do you?"

Casually asked, as if it were a normal question: *Is it raining? Did you breakfast yet?* This question, which Aveo had never answered directly in his life except once, to his son Ojea, had gotten that son killed. Cam waited and finally he said, "No. I do not believe in the Goddess."

"Me, neither, only . . . but . . . Aveo, the only two things I've seen here that we don't have on Earth are kulith and those plants. All the rest is the same: wars and kings and power struggles and slavery and . . . Actually, maybe we do have kulith, someplace. There's a lot of weird religions around the world and I know that some old cultures played chess like— I don't *know* enough! I didn't even go to college! I don't know why the Atoners picked me!"

Aveo followed none of this. Also, something was happening in his head, a sudden darkening. One foot began to tremble slightly.

She was still talking. Her words blurred, came back too sharply to his ears, blurred again. And then all at once there were two voices, both female, and Cam was gazing at the window on the wall where a moment ago there had been an empty field and now all at once there was a woman's head, just the head, a monstrous thing large enough to fill the window, and the head was moving as it talked. "—and then Lucca—"

"—did he—"

"—an old lady, dead—"

They weren't words in Pularit, or Memenatit, or Uldunuit. Nonsense words, such as mothers crooned to infants in arms. And Cam's eyes were wide as a child's, as if the moving picture of the woman had— How could a picture move, but of course it was a window, still a woman's head that large . . . and such a head, with short curls the dull red of *guem* flowers how long since—

"Aveo!"

Cam knelt over him then, while the monstrous head craned to see through the window and looked both puzzled and concerned. A sharp sting . . . oh, please not more poisoned *thrul* vines . . . but it wasn't. A sharp, very thin sword slid into him, in Cam's hand, and again the darkness receded from his mind and her words created sense.

"That was all I've got, the last-ditch effort," she said, but where were the ditches? This flying ship held no ditches.

"Aveo, I think . . . I think you're dying."

"Yes," he said. "I know." Darkness soon. Pushed away for a short time, maybe, but soon.

"No!" she cried, and he had to smile. Perhaps the smile

came from some potion smeared on her small sword, but perhaps not. The young were laughable. They could never see that death might be welcome.

He summoned up the strength to murmur, "Go home, Ostiu Cam," but he didn't have breath for the rest of what he wanted to say: *Go home to that place where there are wars but you have not fought them, slavery but you have not seen it, poisonous plants but not mating in the gardens of a goddess. Go home and—*

"Soledad!" Cam was screaming at the wall. "Take the shuttle to Kular A!"

"To Kular A?"

"Yes! If Lucca really saw—" There was a lot more, but Aveo didn't hear it. The room went dark. He felt the ship lift, and then he felt Cam's arms picking him up off the floor and holding him, and then he felt nothing at all.

25: LUCCA

Lucca woke just as the first light of dawn, thin and sickly,
filtered through the hut's tiny window. His commlink vi-
brated urgently against his skin.

Soledad knew that he'd kept his tech hidden from the
Kularians; she would call him only if it was very urgent.
Close to him—too close, their reek filled his nostrils and
their snoring his nose—Hytrowembireliaz's family slept.
Lucca fumbled for the commlink, opened the link, and
breathed softly, "Yes?" The rest of them might sleep as if
drugged by winter itself, but Chewithoztarel woke easily.
As Lucca's eyes adjusted, he kept them on her corner of
the hut.

"Something's happening," Soledad said, loud in his
ears. "Go outside and dress as warmly as you can."

"What—"

"Go!"

Still watching Chewithoztarel, Lucca eased himself
soundlessly from his pungent pile of rugs and blankets.
Something's happening, she had said, not *Something happened.* The ship? The Atoners? Cam? Dread coupled with
excitement sent spasms racing along his spine.

The cold was a palpable thing, slicing at him like knives.
There was no need to "dress warmly"—he already wore
everything he'd been given. Lucca wrapped an extra blanket around himself and crept to the door. Chewithoztarel,
miracle of miracles, did not wake.

Outside it was even colder. Shivering, Lucca said,
"Soledad?"

"Cam's on her way in the shuttle to Kular A, and she's bringing a native."

"What?"

"She insisted." Soledad sounded angry, apprehensive, and fascinated, all at once. "You know that the Atoners said that you two are the mission decision makers on your respective planets. I'm just the coordinator."

"But this isn't her planet! It's mine!" A second later, Lucca heard how that sounded. He strove, teeth chattering, for a more adult tone. "Why is she coming? Why are *they* coming?"

"The native is dying, apparently. I told Cam about your discoveries of telepathy in death, and Cam wants . . . I don't understand what she wants, exactly. Maybe she doesn't understand, either—you know Cam. But they're landing three miles from your village in an hour and twenty-three minutes, and you should be there. I'm going to voice-guide you to the spot. It should be well out of sight of—"

"You told her *what* about my 'discoveries of telepathy in death'?" This was incredible, was unbelievable even for Cam. How the Atoners had ever picked that rabbit-brained girl . . .

"I told her just what you told me," Soledad said stiffly. "As per my instructions from the Atoners."

"And so now she's bringing some dying Kularian to—" What? Have his 'ghost' spoken to by a mendacious child?

"You'll have to ask Cam that." Soledad's voice sounded weary.

"Who is this dying person? Another of her lovers?"

"I don't know. I only know that they're coming. They'll be there in an hour and twenty-one minutes."

"This is just stupid. And I've been getting these . . . disabilities every day at mid-morning—what if today I suddenly can't walk, or hear, or tell if I've broken my arm and I'm way the hell out away from the village, alone?"

"You'll have Cam by then."

"Oh, *certo,* she's always such a big help. We'll be stuck there with a dying Kularian, who— What are we supposed to do with him when Cam arrives? Get him to my village?"

"Or bring a villager to him."

"It's stupid, Soledad. Stupid and dangerous. How many strangers in shuttles falling out of the sky do you think this village can absorb before the villagers get disturbed and maybe violent?"

"From what you've told me, any number."

She was right, of course. Nothing disturbed the village. But, then, they didn't have to deal with anyone as disturbing as Cam O'Kane. As disturbing, as idiotic, as incapable of rational thought . . . *E che cazzo.*

Soledad said, "Start walking, Lucca. Directly into the sunrise. I'll guide you from there."

It had stopped snowing overnight, and as the sun rose, the snow began to glitter, a pristine carpet of white diamonds. He tried to commlink Cam, but there was no answer from the shuttle. Cursing and shivering, Lucca trudged east.

The Atoner shuttle came down noisily but not hard. Lucca had never seen their landings from the outside. So this was what the natives of Kular B had experienced when Cam's shuttle landed. His own, of course, had hurtled down unseen, crippled and now rusting quietly somewhere in the vast snows.

He'd been waiting for perhaps half an hour, stamping his feet and waving his arms and walking in circles to keep warm. He was hungry and thirsty, but his fury had died down, or perhaps been frozen out. Immediately the door opened and Cam stood there, gesturing wildly. "Lucca! Come quick!"

He walked from the barren steppe back into the alien future. The shuttle was warm inside, so warm that immediately Lucca began to strip off his blanket and some clothing. Strapped into one of the shuttle's two seats was an old man with a bare, sunken chest and a skirt of some rough brown material. Even lying down he looked much taller than the small brown people of Lucca's village, and his coloring was different: light brown hair gone mostly gray, open and staring navy blue eyes flecked with silver.

"Is he dead?"

"Almost!" Cam cried. "I gave him the patches and the needle and everything the Atoners gave us, but he was poisoned by some alien plants and I don't think the 'Tonies knew how to . . . Lucca, I think he's going to die!"

"And so why did you bring him here? Leaving your mission?"

At his tone, her face changed. Fear and panic shifted into a cold anger, and that was a surprise. Before, Cam had never done anything coldly. Heat was her hallmark.

"I didn't leave my mission. It was over because there's nothing to witness on Kular B. You—"

"You don't know that. You didn't see the whole planet."

"I saw enough." To his further surprise, she shuddered, deeply, sudden pain in her eyes. "You have no idea what I saw. But right now we're talking about what *you* saw. I brought Aveo here because he is going to die and I want him to die in your village, with your villagers, so that he's part of whatever is happening here. Soledad told me that your people think they can see the dead! What if it's true, what if they really can, and after Aveo goes they can tell him— But even if it's not true, we'll see them do something and Aveo will be a part of it and we'll have actually witnessed something, at least!"

"You mean," Lucca said coldly, "you'll have witnessed something at least. *I* already did. This is about you, isn't it, Cam? About you needing to be part of this telepathy phenomenon that—"

"Fuck you, Lucca! This is about Aveo! About his life actually meaning something, he lost everything on Kular, *everything,* you have no fucking idea—"

"And so you bring him here so that my villagers can have their telepathy activated and you can delude yourself that he's not really dead. It's still about you."

"It's about Aveo! You don't know for sure what's going on here! There are strange things in the universe!" She turned away, but not before Lucca saw her tears.

The same old sentimental bullshit. Temple priests speaking through hidden holes in pagan statues, oracles at Delphi, miracles at Lourdes, séances in darkened rooms . . . It never changed. People wanted to believe and so they did and to hell with rationality. And so Cam lugged a dying alien across interplanetary space so that she could comfort herself by aiding in her own self-deception. Lucca walked over and touched the old man's bare chest. Still warm. The chest and upper arms, Lucca now saw, were crossed with scars, some old and some barely healed.

Behind him, Cam blurted fiercely, "I killed at least a dozen men on B. No—more. Maybe as many as two dozen."

He turned slowly toward her. "You killed natives?"

"Yes. Burned them with the laser gun *you* wouldn't carry."

"Cam—"

"So don't talk to me about illusion and reality like I know you were going to, Lucca. . . . Don't condescend to me the way you did every day on the voyage out—just *don't*. You're the one who's been living with illusion, staying on this safe and friendly planet, having all the miracles we were sent here to witness just dropped in your lap. Experiencing them yourself. And then whining through all of it."

"Going blind didn't feel like much of a miracle," Lucca said dryly. Her anger had steadied him. Suddenly he realized that this trait—that she made him feel more competent, superior to her—was why he'd had the affair with her on the ship. Not, as he'd thought, because she looked like Gianna. The realization rattled him.

She said, "We're taking Aveo to the village. He's going to have his chance to matter to something. Now get going."

She was hysterical. Lucca switched to soothing rationality. "Cam, it's cold out there. Really cold. Even if we wrap him up completely, he's very weak. He could die of exposure."

"Then Soledad will move the shuttle to the village."

"No," Lucca said, and braced himself for a fight. "I don't want the villagers seeing another shuttle. I fit in there now, Cam. I need that acceptance in order to go on witnessing here until I figure out what's really going on with the telepathy. I don't want their acceptance of me strained."

Soledad, her face on the wall screen, said, "He's right, Cam. It's one thing to take a stranger to a native village but another to—"

"Shut up, Soledad! It's my call, you don't have any authority on-planet!"

Lucca said quietly, "But Kular A is *my* planet, Cam."

She stared at him across the Kularian's still body, and suddenly Lucca saw in her eyes the person who had, indeed, killed a dozen men, burning them down where they stood. Had she changed, or had this ferocity been present always under her impulsive theatrics? Lucca took a step away from her, very aware all at once that he was not armed and she was. The moment spun out. Before it could break, the old man made a sound.

It was low, a rattle far back in his throat, almost a growl. Lucca had never heard such a sound before, but he knew immediately what it was. The old man was dead.

Cam knew it, too. She didn't scream, to Lucca's surprise. She looked down at him, said once, "Aveo," and knelt beside the shuttle chair, with its light alien webbing. Turning her face away from Lucca, she laid her cheek against the old man's chest and put her arms around him.

Lucca looked away. This moment was private. But only a part of his mind was taken up with her. It was himself he thought of, realizing that since Gianna had died, there was no one for whom he would have knelt, wept, felt as Cam was feeling now.

The two of them trudged across the plain dazzling with sunlight, bleak with emptiness. Cam wore half of Lucca's furs and blankets, but now Lucca wasn't cold. Partly it was the sun, strong as good wine. Mostly, however, it was anger that she was here at all, that she hadn't gotten back into her shuttle and flown to Kular B, where she belonged. There had been a terrible three-way argument there in the cramped shuttle, beside Aveo's cooling body. And Soledad, to Lucca's fury, had sided with Cam.

"You don't actually know that what you have in your village is telepathy, and—"

"And you have a better idea?" Lucca had shouted, and disliked himself for the shouting.

"—and if it is telepathy," Soledad had continued, the skin of her face drawn tight with tension, "this is a perfect chance to prove it. An unparalleled chance. Think, Lucca—you yourself said that maybe the other Kularians *did* know about that old lady's hunting as a girl. That maybe she told them long ago and forgot. But there's no way they can know about Aveo. So take Cam to the village and see what they pull from her mind."

"No."

There was a long silence, and then Soledad said in a strange voice, "Are you afraid of what Cam might discover about your Kularians?"

The suggestion outraged him. "She shouldn't have come here."

"But I am here," Cam said coldly. "And how can you stop me from following you to the village?"

He couldn't, of course. She could simply trail him. Even if he could outrun her, which he doubted, his footsteps would be clear in the snow. Lucca had no choice. He said, wanting to hurt her, "And what will you do with the old man's body? Leave it to rot in the shuttle? The ground is too frozen to bury it. Will you leave it on the plain? Go ahead, predators will eat it by noon. Or were you planning on dragging it to the village, so the Kularians can do the same thing? Then you can 'witness' Aveo being torn apart."

Soledad said, "Lucca!" Cam merely gazed at him and then turned away.

Ashamed, Lucca left the shuttle and stared at the plain until his eyes burned. Cam closed the door behind him, and for a moment he thought she had changed her mind after all, that she would instruct Soledad to lift the shuttle. But after a few minutes Cam came out, carrying Aveo's body. Still dressed in only her thin tunic and leggings, she put the body on the ground beside the shuttle and said to Lucca, "Move away. Now."

He followed her about a hundred yards. The shuttle lifted a few feet, and suddenly the bottom blazed. Lucca blinked at the bright light; he hadn't known it could do that. The Atoners had said that landings would disturb nothing, and the ground around his own crashed shuttle hadn't been scorched. But when the shuttle once again set down, the plain bore a snowless crater, and Aveo's body was gone.

"Let's go," Cam said tonelessly. All at once she shivered. Wordlessly Lucca stripped off half his fur garments and handed them to her. At least her boots looked sturdy. She put on the skins and followed him across the brilliant plain.

26: CAM

Snow. Cold. Light. She registered sensations in shards, each piercing her mind like a small knife. The plain faded in and out, and what she saw during the "out" was men dying, burned down by her gun. Falling in heaps on the tiled gallery. Collapsing in the tent at the army camp, smelling of seared meat, their light eyes staring at her in reproach, their blood staining the ground. And Aveo, his kindness and intelligence leaking out as if a person were no more than a cheap plastic bottle. Every death, even Aveo's, because of her.

She was a killer.

Panic rose in her, then. *She was a killer.* Wasn't there any way to make this right? All her life there had been ways to make things right, to undo terrible things—what terrible things? Her life, that she had thought so stunted back in Nebraska, she now saw had had no terrible things. And *no way to make it right* . . .

"Cam?"

There must be something she could do, and if Lucca's village could . . . She was drowning, and she knew it, grabbing at driftwood to stay afloat. Not drowning, not water—fire, the smell of burning flesh and men falling onto the tiled gallery floor . . .

"Cam!"

Lucca's voice rescued her from the abyss. He had stopped several yards behind her, without her even noticing. She loped back and saw him standing in the snow, his face in shadow as the sun rose higher behind him. As she approached he called in a strangled voice, "I can't hear."

"*What?*"

He made a frustrated gesture, raising one hand and letting it drop, something between a plea and a blow.

She thought quickly, grateful for something to replace the images in her mind. "Listen, Soledad told me that you already had blindness and—" She stopped. He couldn't hear her. Cam pointed to the sun and held up her chilly hands, flashing all ten fingers twice and then just four fingers on one hand. *Twenty-four: Your previous afflictions lasted just twenty-four hours.* Never mind that she had no idea how many hours were in a day on Kular A or if they even had hours. She tried to nod and smile, then pantomimed sleeping and waking up: *You'll be all right tomorrow.*

He nodded and flipped both palms angrily upward: *But why?*

She shrugged. Why? She had no idea. But it gave her something else to think about as they walked. Why would the Atoners do this to him—but not to her?

Soledad called again on the commlink. "Cam, when you get to the village—"

"What? I can't talk, we're almost there."

"Good. But leave the commlink open so I can hear, too. Just stick it in a fold of your clothes or something, okay?"

"Okay." Lucca watched mutely as Cam arranged the open link in her furs. Of course, she thought bitterly, he didn't object to *Soledad* sharing his natives—no, not at all. Only to her.

They trudged through the snow into the village. Kular B had palaces, cities, massive gates, brilliantly colored tiles, and fine-spun curtains . . . but of course that had been near the equator. This was a northern hamlet with rough stone huts and one large stone building sending smoke curling lazily against a blue sky. A pathetic excuse for a village, and now the most important place in the galaxy.

The door of the one big building opened and some children dashed out, bundled like piles of laundry. They saw Lucca, whooped, and dashed over. A little girl with very red cheeks and black eyes threw her arms around Lucca's legs. He stiffened.

"Hi," Cam subvocalized, and the translator gave her something guttural that she repeated awkwardly.

The girl turned to Cam. The other children, shyer, hung back. The red-cheeked child, clearly puzzled, said, "Where did Lucca get you from?"

How to answer that? Instead, Cam pointed at Lucca and said, "He's sick, in his mouth. He can't talk right now."

The kid didn't answer. She, and all the others, turned as one to gaze at something to Cam's right. For a long moment, everyone was still, like those dioramas of primitive life in the museums Cam had been taken to for school field trips. The children all had their eyes raised to the height of Cam's head. Cam felt the world splinter, an ice castle cracking to reveal treasures hidden inside. She turned to look at empty air.

"Aveo," the child said. "Did Lucca bring you, too? Are you long on the second road?"

A noise came from Cam's clothing. She barely heard it. She couldn't move, couldn't think. Then Soledad was talking and still Cam didn't answer. The children inched away, confused. Cam began to cry.

Soledad, for once breaking the rules, shouted, "Cam! I know what the Atoners did! I know!"

But Cam couldn't stop crying, the tears freezing on her face as adults began to stream out of the large stone building, as Lucca stared at her in disgust and anger and fear, as the terrible truth penetrated her bones and she understood that, in some form these filthy children could communicate with and she could not, Aveo stood beside her, dead and yet continuing, and so in some sense not dead, not dead, not dead after all.

27: SOLEDAD

It was the genes. It had always been the genes. The Atoners had manipulated them. Ten thousand years ago, and now in Lucca.

Soledad sat in front of her commlink, frustrated beyond bearing because she couldn't explain this to the only two people within hundreds of light-years who had the vocabulary to understand. Lucca had gone deaf and Cam was crying, characteristically more involved with her own emotions than with anything else. Soledad struck her fist uselessly on the console and broke the link.

The biggest discovery in all of human history, and no one to tell!

She paced the short corridor of the deserted ship, past the three sleeping bunks and the bathroom and back to the main room, the only other area except for Storage. Deliberately she made herself sit quietly in her padded chair, its flight straps dangling to the floor, and make sure the recorder was on. Which was dumb—it was always on. Still—for *this*.

"Here is what I think," Soledad said, heard the quaver in her voice, and decided to ignore it. She needed to work this out aloud, to hear the words take shape in the empty, stale air. "Ten thousand years ago the Atoners came to Earth. They gathered up humanity somehow, or part of humanity—" *If so, what had happened to the rest?* "—and they experimented on us. Like lab rats. They can . . . can turn off sensory genes. That's how they made Lucca lose his smell, then his sight, then taste, then hearing. That's also how they made all his senses come back. They programmed the meds in him to do that, but not the meds in Cam or me. Because it was only Lucca they were sending down to Kular A.

"And ten thousand years ago the Atoners permanently turned off another sense. The one that lets us see the . . . the essence of people that leaves their body after it dies. That essence that apparently lingers a little while, and before the Atoners came humans could see it. But not after. And the change was hereditary, like . . . like color blindness. We're blind to the dead among us. Only this blindness is dominant, not recessive like color blindness. Once before, ten thousand years ago, we had—"

We had evidence of an afterlife.

Soledad got up, paced some more, beat her fists on the wall. It was so much to take in. She sat down and babbled again.

"Some small subsets of humanity must have been taken to various planets. To binary planet systems, to create double-blind experiments. One group was allowed to keep the ability to see the afterlife, like Kular A. One planet was not, like Kular B. It was— Oh, you bastards, *why*?"

"Yes," a voice said, and Soledad screamed and looked wildly around. No one was there, and the wall screen didn't brighten. But the voice continued, the deep and vaguely mechanical voice of an Atoner.

"This is a recording. It has been triggered by the content of something said aboard this ship. You are correct in your assumptions.

"Ten millennia ago we robbed humanity of one of its senses. Our civilization was very different then, and we experimented on many races besides your own, but we know this is no excuse.

"Your science calls them your 'most recent common ancestor.' They were the most recent individuals who were the progenitors of every existing member of your species. They are also the only humans we left fertile after our visit to your planet. There were a hundred and three of them, left among various sterilized populations around the Earth. We left them fertile but with altered genetic makeup.

"Those with unaltered genomes we took to Kular A, to Susban A, to Londu A, to Fumnet A, to Lirtel A, to Junut A, to Prelbin A. All planets where humans now witness.

"There are two things you must know, and that you must tell all peoples on Earth as part of your witness. First, that the genes to sense your dead were not merely kept from expression, as were some Witnesses' other senses, in demonstration. The genes to see your dead were destroyed. They no longer exist in any genome on Earth.

"Second: We are profoundly sorry for what our race has done to yours.

"Bring any Witnesses that remain planetside back up to the ship for the voyage home."

The voice fell silent.

Dazed, Soledad thought all at once of her father, dead in a construction accident when she was six. Did she believe, then, that something of him continued somewhere, on the Kularians' "third road"? No, she did not. Death was the end. But . . . the Kularian child saying, *Aveo* . . .

Lucca attributed it to a form of stress-induced telepathy, pulling the name from Cam's mind. Telepathy was a sense, too—the Atoners could have meant that—

That's not what the Atoner recording had just said—

Soledad put her head in her hands. She didn't know what she believed, what had been seen or not seen on Kular A. Everything that had just happened went contrary to the rationality she'd embraced her entire life. But she could see now, sitting in this alien ship, what her "witness" was going to cause back on Earth. Her witness, and Cam's, and Lucca's, and, presumably, the other six teams' sent around the galaxy. The Witnesses were going to cause upheavals of faith, all faiths, all ways of life, among all peoples. It was a bomb the Atoners were sending back with these twenty-one young people, a bomb that would hit all continents at once, igniting controversies hot enough to scorch them all.

And Soledad, whose life had so far been ordinary, was going to be a detonator for all the rest of her days.

PART II

AMICUS CURIAE

28: SOLEDAD

Soledad padded from her bedroom into the tiny dark kitchen, turned on the light, and, all in the same fluid motion, hit the switches for the coffeepot and the wall screen.

"—five thirty A.M. on what promises to be a gorgeous winter morning," chirped the news avatar. She had light blue skin, black hair drawn in lines sharp enough to cut diamonds, and huge purple eyes. Her body against the constantly changing simulated background was as ridiculous as all the female news avatars', and her patter was inane. But that was what Soledad wanted when she couldn't sleep: Scorn banished anxiety. And if anything important happened, an actual person would break into the netcast.

"Temperature at forty-two degrees on its way up to fifty-six by mid-afternoon. Let's all say a big thank-you to global warming!"

Oh, right. Just what all those people flooded out and droughted out and hurricaned out by climate change were dying to do: say a big thank-you to global warming.

"And another reason to say thank you—once again it's Friday! So all you sparklies just waiting to strike the pleasure gong all weekend long can—"

Soledad let the stupid chatter fade into a soothing background, took her coffee to the living room window, and watched the first headlights start the long daily commute to New York. She had moved to this small Catskill Mountains town as soon after her return from Kular as she could, as soon as the endless government debriefings and semi-welcome protection had ended. A child of Manhattan's alphabet avenues, after months in the country Soledad still wasn't used to this silence, to the dark woods at dawn and dusk, to the steep fields without broken glass or used syringes. Sometimes an owl hooted in the branches of a huge maple, a soft alien sound Soledad had never heard before. Occasionally the gentle quiet of her three-room rented house spooked her, but usually she liked it. Her neighbors, none of whom knew her identity, were distantly polite. The good thing, made possible by her sale of the three rocks that the Atoners had permitted her to bring back from the moon, was all the time that she now had to think. The bad thing was all the time that she now had to think.

You, she thought at the swoosh of car lights hurtling past, *do you believe what The Six are saying? Do you care?*

It always amazed her that people could not care. How could anyone not be affected by— The phone rang. She glanced at the ID in a corner of the screen.

"Soledad?"

"Good morning, Fengmo."

"I knew you'd be awake. You're the only person I can call at this hour."

"And the only one who calls me." Of the five people who had her number, only Fengmo and Lucca were welcome to call, and Lucca seldom called. She was the one who called him.

"Turn on visual," Fengmo said.

"No. I look a mess."

He laughed. "Are you going to Cam's lecture in New York?"

Soledad took a sip of coffee, thinking how to answer. Fengmo would wait. He was superb at waiting because, he said, he already had everything he wanted. *Bullshit,* Cam always replied, but Fengmo just smiled. His statement might even be true.

Finally she said, "I can't decide."

"Not like you, Ladybliss."

Ladybliss. No one else had ever called Soledad—sensible, reserved, stocky Soledad—by pet names. Certainly not the family to which, when they had been children, Fengmo had been the antidote, the escape, the life raft she clung to when drama was surging at home. And drama was always surging. Love for Fengmo welled up in Soledad and she thought, for perhaps the ten thousandth time, *Damn you, Fengmo, for being gay.*

"If I go, Fengie, then Cam will only say the same overly definite things she always does and I'll be irritated all over again. But if I don't go—"

"If you don't go, what? She'll say something new that will resolve your existential dilemma for you?"

"Don't make fun of me."

"Sweetie, I have to make fun of you because no one else ever does. They take one look at all that judicious reserve and they never open their poor little intimidated mouths. And if they do, you give them a look that could chill glaciers."

"There aren't any glaciers left."

"Not true. I'm sure we still have two or three, melting quietly someplace. Soledad, she-love, you know you're going to go to the lecture, so meet me first for dinner and I'll go with you to the Garden. A bodyguard."

Soledad laughed. Fengmo stood five foot four and weighed forty pounds less than she did. "What will you do, hit them over the head with the *Te Ching*?"

" 'Nobody can protect / A house full of gold and jade.' Six thirty at Leonard's. Bye, sweetie."

Cheered—Fengmo could always cheer her—Soledad rinsed her coffee cup in the kitchen sink. A gay Taoist Chinese-American runt as her best friend—what were the odds? But then she, more than most, knew that odds meant nothing when you were the one who drew the short straw. Or hit the jackpot. Or couldn't tell which. The phone rang again.

Soledad stared at the ID. Juana. Oh God.

No one knew where Soledad was living except Lucca, Fengmo, and Soledad's government contact, Diane Lovett. The facial surgery that Diane's federal Agency had paid for ensured that nobody recognized Soledad at the grocery store, the town's one cinema, the train station. Soledad wanted it that way. But unless she wanted to lose her family entirely, she'd had to give a phone number to Juana, the sanest of her sisters. Which wasn't saying much.

"Hello, Juana."

"You have to fly into New York. Today!"

Juana didn't know that Soledad lived two hours from Manhattan by maglev. The number for her encrypted phone line appeared, on all records, to belong to a warehouse in St. Louis. Barely far enough away from Juana and their mother, who lived with Juana when she wasn't on the streets.

"Fly to New York? Why should I—"

"It's Mama! She's dying!"

Soledad's stomach heaved. She had hated her mother, pitied her, tried to help her, realized that Mama didn't want help, hated her again—all the stages you go through when you live with a drunk. The teenage Soledad had screamed at her mother that she wished Mama used junk instead of liquor so that Soledad could get her sent to jail. Mama had vomited on the carpet, drunk the rent money, attacked a cop, gone missing for days at a time. But throughout she'd remained strong as a mule. She was only forty-five. Cirrhosis already? Or had she finally moved on to street drugs and OD'd?

But Soledad's voice stayed calm as she said, "What happened, Juana?"

"Listen to you! You don't even care! She fell down the stairs and broke every bone in her body and now she's dying!"

"What hospital is she in?"

"She's at home! She wants to die at home and so I'm taking care of her, Ms. Too-Proud-to-See-Her-Family! But she wants to see the great star traveler before she goes, so you better come soon!"

"All right. All right. I'll be there this afternoon."

"Good." Juana banged down the phone.

Something wasn't right here, Soledad thought. Would a hospital really send home a woman who had broken "every bone in her body"? Maybe they would, if the woman insisted on dying at home and her daughters made huge scenes and the Universal Health facility was overcrowded and inadequate, as they all were.

Dying. Her mother. Setting out on the second road, the last door, the golden ladder, the eternal sea, the bridge to far, the deep cave. Each of The Six had brought back a different description of the afterlife as perceived by the natives on an Atoner planet. And each of them was—

"APC interrupts your morning avatar with breaking news," said the wall screen, much louder than before. The blue-skinned avatar, whom Soledad had forgotten, was displaced by a middle-aged man with the deep facial lining of serious news.

"Emma Jane Taymor, the daughter of Vice President John Taymor, has just been pronounced dead on arrival at George Washington University Hospital in Washington, D.C. The White House has not yet issued a statement, but reliable sources say that Emma, who turned seventeen last month, committed suicide. The teenager posted a WT referring to the motto of the Why Wait? Society, which asserts that—"

Soledad gripped the edge of the sink and held on. *Seventeen.* And a Web Testament, with the motto of that perverted society that had grown so exponentially in the last six months: "If a better world than this awaits us after death, why wait?"

Cam was responsible for this. Was responsible for all

the Emma Jane Taymors, all the young people offing themselves across the globe. And it did seem to be mostly the
young. Maybe the old were more skeptical. Or maybe it
was just that they could already glimpse the second road
ahead of them. "Even if a better world awaits us after
death, why rush?"

And you, Soledad? Did she believe that second road
existed? The great question, and after six months she still
couldn't decide, couldn't come down securely on one side
of the question or the other. Cam's fervent certainty, or
Lucca's equally fervent denial? Eternity for all, or "merely"
stress-related telepathy activated by hormones released in
the presence of death, the genes for which the Atoners had
cut out of the human genome ten thousand years ago? Or
something else entirely?

Soledad had always believed that, despite her appalling
family, she was lucky. She'd had Fengmo, a few caring
teachers, and a scholarship to college, where she'd had the
opportunity to discover she liked classic jazz, W. H. Auden,
and fourth-century history. Also, she had cheated death for
two and a half decades. At six she'd contracted a drug-
resistant form of staph that should have killed, the septice-
mia raging through her blood like barbarians through
Rome. But her body cured itself. At fifteen she was hit by a
car, and at twenty-two she missed her confirmed flight on a
United Airlines jet blown up over the Atlantic ten minutes
out of LaGuardia. Cheating death.

But now it turned out that wasn't what she had been doing at all, because there was no death. Of the body, yes,
but not of the essence of a person. That most unbearable
of truths, that everyone must lose everything, including
life itself, was no longer true. As in poker with a perpetual
supply of chips, everybody—those who died at 6 and
those at 106—got to stay in the game.

Maybe. Or maybe not. Hamlet had the right question
but the wrong grammatical tense. *Will I be or will I not be?*

She walked barefoot into her bedroom to get dressed for the day.

Soledad's mother sat at Juana's kitchen table, drinking coffee and picking at an olive loaf. Maria Arellano's thick hair hung in two uncharacteristically neat gray braids over an orange T-shirt. Her broad face looked yellowish and sodden, like used toilet paper, and her eyes were dull as concrete. But it was clear that all her bones were intact.

Soledad said quietly, "You told me she was dying."

Juana had moved to stand between Soledad and the apartment door. Like her sister, Juana was short and stocky, but whereas Soledad looked contained and solid, Juana always seemed ready to erupt into magma flows of whirling full skirts, ashy gobs of soft powdered flesh, flying dangerous sparks of temper. *No wonder,* Soledad thought, *that I hate the stereotype of the "fiery Latina."*

Juana attacked. "Okay, so she's not dying! We knew this was the only way you'd ever come to see her, your own mother, you should be ashamed of yourself that you move all that way to St. Louis, keeping all that money for yourself while we live like this—"

Soledad tuned out her sister. The kitchen, in a crumbling apartment building whose stairwells smelled of urine, was neat this afternoon but bare, holding nothing that couldn't be hocked or sold. The wooden table was deeply carved with unintelligible symbols, probably by Juana's kids. A garbage bag in one corner held recyclable cans. Overhead, exposed heating pipes clanged restlessly, like chains rattling in the stale air. Maria raised her head. Mother and daughter stared at each other with mutual dislike, with old resentments, with a thousand bad memories that rose in Soledad like bile. She caught the sour smell of old alcohol, so deep in Maria's pores that no shower could remove it. *Are you going to go on after death, Mama?*

Would you even want to? Soledad dammed her distaste and reached for rationality.

"Juana, there is no money. I told you that. I didn't sell my story for a book or a movie or a netcast. The moon rocks sold for only enough money to resume life here, and pretty soon I'm going to have to find a job. The government did help with resettling the Witnesses, but that was only for a few—"

"You're lying!" Juana said shrilly. "Your friend Cam O'Kane—" She flounced her skirts on each of the three syllables of the name, in grotesque mockery. "—has millions! She was on the d-vids in a necklace that cost a thousand bucks by itself! I seen an ad for it, so I know!"

Soledad said flatly, "I'm not Cam O'Kane."

"You could be! That bitch tells her story over and over, the same thing all the time, and you just sit there in St. Louis and don't say anything to nobody and can't even help your own family and—"

"I didn't go down to a planet like Cam did," Soledad said wearily. "I've told you that over and over. People aren't as interested in those of us who stayed in orbit."

"Your story still must be worth something!"

It probably was. Until Diane Lovett had taken Soledad's life in hand, journalists and researchers and assorted whackos had besieged her. She wanted none of it. She just wanted answers, certainty, to *know*. But there were no answers. The Atoners sat up there on the moon, unreachable, no longer answering radio messages but not leaving, either. Lucca sulked in his Canadian fortress. And Cam turned the holy grail into a cheap sideshow. Soledad was not going to do that.

She said slowly, "Juana, why did you drag me to New York? Just to ask for money?"

Something flitted across her sister's face, some look that Soledad couldn't interpret. But all Juana said was, "The rent is due and I don't have it."

Soledad wrote out a check, as she had done so often

before. She laid it on the table, beside the half-eaten olive loaf. Juana moved away from the door, not meeting her eyes. Something wasn't right, but no one here was going to tell Soledad what it was. She left, aware that her mother had not spoken one word to her, that possibly speech was beyond her in her present state, that Maria was merely hanging on until she and Juana were once again alone and she could have another drink.

No one had even asked Soledad to sit down, or take off her coat, or have a cup of coffee. Not that it had ever been any different . . . but God, when did you outgrow this wish for your family's acceptance, for your family's approval, for an entirely different family? Would they still be able to upset her when she was forty, fifty, seventy?

Soledad made her way down three flights of badly lit stairs. A hundred years' worth of dirt seamed the broken molding. Two sullen children with d-vid games glared at her on the second-floor landing. One of the security cameras had been shot out and not yet fixed. At the bottom of the last flight, in the miniscule grimy "lobby," he waited for her.

"Ms. Arellano."

She stared at him, and all at once she understood. A nice-looking man, Anglo, in coat and tie, not much older than she. Juana had set her up.

"I'm sorry, you've made a mistake. Excuse me, please."

"No mistake. You're Soledad Arellano. And you're going to talk to me, whether you want to or not."

29: FROM *THE OPRAH WINFREY SHOW*

November 19, 2020

OPRAH: Thank you, thank you. Today we have a very serious show, on a very serious topic: the claims made by the Atoners about human ancestry. Your ancestry, mine, no matter where we came from or who we are. Now I know that all of you out there have your own views about what the Atoners and the Witnesses, the so-called "Six" who returned to Earth, have said. What I'd like to do today is open a discussion about what scientists and theologians have to say about these important matters. With me to do that is my first guest, Dr. Jeffrey Roman-Cruz of the National Institutes of Health in Washington, D.C. Please join with me in welcoming Dr. Roman-Cruz. [applause]

DR. ROMAN-CRUZ: Thank you.

OPRAH: So let me start by asking what scientists actually know about the Atoners. No one has ever seen one, is that right?

DR. ROMAN-CRUZ: That's correct. No Atoner has come down to Earth, and the fifty people they took up to their base on the moon have—

OPRAH: That's fifty total, right? The twenty-one Witnesses and also twenty-six observers from different governments and the UN?

DR. ROMAN-CRUZ: That's right. Every one of the fifty has described the exact same setup, a closed room and an Atoner or Atoners stating that they are behind a screen, which no one has penetrated.

OPRAH: Has anyone tried?

DR. ROMAN-CRUZ: I wouldn't know. The NIH is not affiliated with, say, the CIA. [nervous laughter from the audience]

OPRAH: So how can we know anything about the Atoners?

DR. ROMAN-CRUZ: Well, that's actually the point. We can only speculate. There are four schools of thought. One— Shall I just describe all four briefly?

OPRAH: Please.

DR. ROMAN-CRUZ: One, that the Atoners have come from a planet much different from Earth, with a much different atmosphere, and they stayed concealed both to remain sealed in chambers with their own atmospheric mix and because we might find their appearance distasteful or frightening in some way. Two, that they are machines, and remain concealed because human beings might not put much faith in machine intelligence or—

OPRAH: Machines? You mean, like my computer?

DR. ROMAN-CRUZ: But of course much more advanced. Artificial intelligences, but intelligences just the same. Three, that the Atoners may be so alien to us, beings composed of gases or of electromagnetic vibrations, that we can't begin to comprehend them or their needs. Finally, that the Atoners were not behind those screens at all, but remained aboard their ship in lunar orbit, or even out beyond the solar system, sending in the equivalent of robots to interact with us.

OPRAH: And which do *you* believe?

DR. ROMAN-CRUZ: I have no idea, because there is no evidence from which to form a testable hypothesis.

OPRAH: Okay. So what about the Atoners' message: that they kidnapped human beings from Earth— [she breaks off and turns to audience] I can't believe I'm actually saying these sentences, can you? Did you ever think this would happen in our lifetime? [scattered applause, accompanied by murmurs and a few indistinguishable shouts] Okay, Dr. Roman-Cruz, what about that kidnapping of our "most recent common ancestor"? Who exactly is that?

DR. ROMAN-CRUZ: Well, you get into some confusion of terminology here, because two separate things are being talked about. We can trace DNA both in mitochondria, which are transmitted only from a mother to her children, and in Y chromosomes, which are inherited only from a father. When we do that, we find that every human on Earth is descended from "Mitochondrial Eve," a woman who lived approximately 150,000 years ago. We're all also descended from "Y-chromosomal Adam," who lived between 60,000 and 90,000 years ago.

OPRAH: Obviously they had a long-distance relationship. [laughter]

DR. ROMAN-CRUZ: What it means is that Y-chromosomal Adam impregnated more than one woman. Of course, none of this implies that these were the only two people on Earth when they each lived. The other genetic lines just died out.

OPRAH: But that was thousands of years before the Atoners' alleged kidnapping.

DR. ROMAN-CRUZ: Yes. The second relevant area of study here is work done using non-genetic models of migration patterns and population densities. Studies done as early as 2004 have been refined in just the last few years, using improved simulation software. They show that yes, there could have been as few as a dozen most recent common ancestors of all humanity as recently as ten thousand years ago. Which fits with the Atoners' claim—without, of course, proving it.

OPRAH: Now for those literal believers of the Bible who say that the Earth itself is only four thousand years—

DR. ROMAN-CRUZ: Excuse me, Oprah, I have no intention of discussing religious beliefs. Of any kind.

OPRAH: Fair enough. Then let me ask you one last scientific question. Lucca Maduro claimed, in his public statements before he retreated into silence, that on one of the alien planets he went blind for twenty-four hours. Then his sight returned, but he couldn't smell anything for twenty-four hours, and so on. I'm sure there's nobody here that hasn't heard the story! Is that possible—that genes can just be switched on and off like that inside his body to produce that effect?

DR. ROMAN-CRUZ: Theoretically it's very possible. In fact, two American scientists won a Nobel Prize over a decade ago for just that. Drs. Andrew Fire and Craig Mello demonstrated a technique called "RNA interference" for silencing genes.

OPRAH: So from a genetic viewpoint, Lucca Maduro may have been telling the truth.

DR. ROMAN-CRUZ: He may have, yes.

OPRAH: Thank you, Doctor. Now, not everybody is willing to trust what the media have taken to calling "The Six"— including my next guest. Back in a moment.

30: FRANK

Frank Olenik wanted his life back. How long should a man have to pay for a single mistake?

He finished his morning exercises in his bedroom: a hundred sit-ups, fifty push-ups, weight work. The bedroom, his since he was six years old, was painted light gray, with a single window looking out on the little yard enclosed by its chain-link fence. Frank's dresser held only the statue of Our Blessed Lady that his sponsor had given him at his Confirmation a decade ago. Frank liked the Virgin's expression: modest but no-nonsense as she crushed the serpent of evil under her heel. The blue of her painted gown matched the spread on his single bed, neatly made with tight hospital corners. Downstairs Ma moved around the kitchen, and the good smell of frying bacon wafted up the stairs. Frank showered, put on a button-down shirt and jeans, and combed his short brown hair.

Paul Olenik, dressed in his blues, sat at the kitchen table, finishing his coffee. Darla played with a bowl of cereal, fishing individual chocolate puffs out of the milk and lining them up wetly on the table. Frank's mother put a plate of eggs and bacon in front of him.

"Thanks, Ma. Morning, Dad. Darla."

"Morning, Son." Olenik smiled fleetingly. At fifty, he was still handsome and strong, a silver-haired version of what Frank would look like someday. "Got a job interview?"

"Not today." Frank never lied to his father.

"Then how come you're dressed up?" Darla said.

"I'm not. I'm wearing jeans."

"You have on a good shirt. Are you gonna put on a tie? Where are you going?"

"Stop asking so many questions," Ma said, "and stop playing with your food. You have exactly four minutes until the school bus gets here."

"But I just—"

"Don't talk back to your mother," Paul said mildly, and Darla immediately replied, "Yes, sir." She shoveled a spoonful of cereal into her mouth.

Frank said to his little sister, "I'm going to church."

His mother smiled at him. Paul nodded, finished his coffee, and kissed his wife on the cheek. "Gotta go."

She held on to him a moment, the same clutching that Frank had watched his entire life. But it was brief; Judy DiPario had known when she married Paul Olenik that a cop's life could be dangerous. For years she'd hoped he would make detective because she believed her husband would be safer that way. That he never had gotten that promotion, despite working for it, was just due to the stupidity of his captain, the same stupidity that had gotten Frank removed from the force before his probation period was even over. Paul had come close to quitting over the injustice done his son; his father's belief in him was what had gotten Frank through the hearings, the lawyers, the enmity of cops who should have been his backups. But some of those cops had been dirty, which was why Frank had been on the verge of turning them in when somebody planted in Frank's locker a bag of drugs stolen from the evidence room. After that, nobody believed anything Frank had to say.

Judy Olenik had talked her husband out of quitting. Paul served in a different precinct than Frank; he was so close to retirement; they needed his full pension. Frank had understood. He admired his father, always had.

But the injustice of the charges against himself had sent Frank around the bend for a while. It was the media, partly—they had tried him in the newspapers, on televison, and on the Internet. It all got blown up into a big thing, and every time Frank saw his dirty ex-partner's smirking face yapping about "police integrity" his anger had deepened. He hadn't known what to do with himself; a cop was all he'd ever wanted to be. And he'd been shocked and impulsive and out of control then. He admitted it. Otherwise he never would have filled out that application to be a Witness. After that, everything all just sort of snowballed. That could happen. And now here he was with the first problem of his life that he couldn't take to his father.

Judy said, "Darla, get your backpack and get out to that school bus. *Now.* Frank, if you wait until the ten o'clock Mass, I'll go with you."

"I'm not going to Mass."

She stopped fussing over Darla to gaze at him. "Confession?"

"Yeah."

"I'm glad," she said simply, and said no more. Ma didn't nag, he had to give her that. She'd been deeply disturbed when Frank started questioning his faith a few years ago, but she'd left it up to him to find his own way back. And he had, although probably not in the way his mother believed. When it came to Catholic doctrine, Judy was stricter than the Pope.

Darla, in her St. Catherine's uniform and a Scooby-Doo jacket, scuttled out the door. Frank finished his breakfast, kissed his mother, and stood. "They out there?"

"Just him." Judy shoved Frank's plate into the dishwasher. "Jackal."

"You know it." Frank left the kitchen, with its ruffled pink curtains and wall calendar of martyred saints, to peer through the slats of the venetian blinds in the living room. No TV vans. Just the one kid reporter who was there every day, still hoping for the interview Frank was never going to give. He'd said everything he was going to say to the media, and all the other reporters had eventually given up. But his mother had called it right: They were all jackals, trying to feed on the sorry scraps of his story.

All at once there rose in his mind the city on Susban A, the lovely cream-and-pink buildings laid out in graceful circles, the heathen temples, the women with intricately bound hair and pants that flowed when they moved. A gracious city, slow moving. Corrupt, of course, and on way too many drugs, and shut out from the redeeming grace of Jesus Christ. Frank wouldn't have wanted to stay there. In fact, he tried not to think about Susban too much, because it confused him. Not seeing the dead—he'd had proof that they could do that, but what was the big deal? So the dead lingered a bit before God sent them to Heaven or Hell. If that was God's plan, Frank Olenik wasn't going to question it. Everybody still got their just desserts, eventually.

No, what confused Frank about his memories of Susban was his dislike of those memories. They didn't belong in the life he wanted. He never should have volunteered to be a Witness for the Atoners, never should have gone into space like that, never should have shuttled down to Susban A. He actually envied Amira Gupta, the snobby Indian professor who'd gotten to stay in orbit around A and B. By the time the alien ship had arrived at Susban, Frank had recovered his senses and would have preferred to at least stay in orbit. But he hadn't, and now he had to make a serious confession to Father Pfender. Although in one sense it was the Atoners, not Frank Olenik, who had screwed up so royally. Had let everyone down, including him.

He went back through the kitchen and out the back door. The Ohio spring had already started, even though it was only February. When Frank had been small, snow would have still been piled everywhere; one year it had reached the second-story windows. Now the air smelled of rich earth and soft breezes, and crocuses grew by the garage. Shielded by the house, he reached the back fence of chain link, scaled it easily, and cut through the Murchisons' yard. Prince, the huge German shepherd chained to the Murchison house, wagged his tail and Frank patted him on the head. On Sycamore Street Frank cut through the Blaine yard—no dog, and Ned Blaine hardly stirred outside since old Mrs. Blaine died—to the parking lot of Our Lady of Divine Mercy.

The old stone church was dim and cold. No one noticed Frank as he slid into a side pew. On a Wednesday morning, the world was at school or work and most of the other confessors were elderly, ferried from St. Ursula's Nursing Home on the bus parked out back. Scattered among the old people were a few mothers carrying infants or toddlers in wool hats with pom-poms. If anyone even recognized Frank, they had the good manners not to say so. A confession should remain private. A lot of things should remain private. He had picked Wednesday-morning confession because Father Jonathan DiPario, who was also Frank's uncle Jack, wasn't on duty then.

When it was Frank's turn, he drew the curtain on the confessional, knelt at the grill—none of that face-to-face stuff for him or, even worse, communal confession with mass absolution. His mother could rant on that particular practice for hours.

"Bless me, Father, for I have sinned."

The papery old voice of Father Pfender said, "Tell me your sins, my son."

In the gloom Frank's fingers tightened into a fist. This was it. "Father, I told a serious lie, with serious consequences."

"Consequences to who?"

"To the United States government. Under oath. I didn't think about it that way at the time, but since then . . . things just snowballed. It wasn't all my fault, and if . . . if others had done what they promised, I might have been justified. It wasn't so much a sin of commission as of omission. Or maybe not, I'm no lawyer. But as it is . . . I think . . ."

"Yes?" The old voice had sharpened.

"I think I may have committed treason."

31: SOLEDAD

Soledad walked calmly past the man in the dilapidated lobby of her sister's building. Ice chips slithered in her abdomen. "I told you—I'm not Soledad Arellano. Please let me pass."

He followed her from the building and fell into step with her on the sidewalk. "My name is Carl Lewis. I'm a freelance journalist who's written for every major outlet in New York. I don't want to compromise your anonymity, Ms. Arellano, really I don't. I don't even want an interview with you. What I do want is for you to get me in to see Lucca Maduro, and I'm prepared to offer you a hundred thousand dollars if you do."

"I don't have any idea what you're talking about."

"Yes. You do."

Soledad glared at him. Three little girls on a stoop stopped fussing with their Bratz dolls to watch interestedly. "I'm not who you say I am. And if you don't stop harassing me, I'm calling the cops on my cell. Now."

"Two hundred thousand dollars."

She took her cell from her pocket. Carl Lewis smiled tightly and said, "I can out you, Soledad. I can tell people who you are. At first just your neighbors or maybe friends of your neighbors, and you'll never be able to prove it was me. The government provides you with minimal protection and the cops can't do anything until you're actually threatened. How long do you think that will take if, say, one of the anti-Atoner fringe groups decides to go after you, or some grief-stricken papa of a teenage suicide fingers you as part of the alien conspiracy that made Junior kill himself?"

Lewis was slime. Soledad kept her face impassive, but he had touched on her worst dread. Not the vengeful fringe groups, although God knew they were out there. Not even the danger from a grieving father gone amok, also real. What she dreaded was that the father would be right: that she and the other Witnesses had harmed the world rather than helped it. That she was guilty of promoting death over life.

Come view the amazing totally rigid conscience! Fengmo had teased her. *Stronger than diamond carbon filaments! Larger than galaxies! Ladybliss, you are not responsible for every consequence of every act you ever thought of committing. The world unfolds in its own way and you are a participant, not the designer.*

But Soledad rejected that Taoist thinking. In her view, not enough people accepted responsibility for anything. She hit 911 on her cell. By the time she'd reached the second 1, Carl Lewis was running away.

"He go behind that building," one of the little girls called helpfully. "There be an alley to the next street."

"Thank you," Soledad said. She hoped he got mugged. If he really did out her . . .

Two hundred thousand dollars. Freelance journalists didn't have that kind of up-front money. He must already have an editor lined up for an exclusive interview with Lucca. Soledad was almost tempted to try to set it up; nobody would learn anything new from Lucca. Ever since Lucca stepped onto the return shuttle on Kular A, and all through his subsequent brooding and self-imposed seclusion, he had only one note that he hit over and over: telepathy, telepathy, telepathy. No one on Kular had actually seen the dead. There were no dead to see, because there was no existence beyond the physical body. What had been observed on Kular A—on Susban A and Londu A and three other planets—was stress-induced latent telepathy activated by images, and maybe hormones, of death.

Soledad took the subway downtown, patiently queuing at the metal-and-explosive detector. On the diminutive screen of a news kiosk, an avatar repeated again and again a fifteen-second spiel about the suicide of Emma Jane Taymor. No one paid the slightest attention or paid for a printed flimsy. Most of the world, Soledad reminded herself, had not been affected by the Witnesses' reports. Not outwardly, anyway. The trains went on running, the farmers went on farming, the teachers teaching, the cops policing. People raised their kids, paid their taxes, shot their gang enemies, went dancing Saturday night, dropped their litter in the street, just as if nothing had changed. Outwardly, nothing had.

But, waiting on the grimy subway platform, staring down at the primitive tracks (no maglev in *this* part of New York), Soledad had another of the moments that had infused her ever since she returned from Luna Base. She was all at once aware of more people in the subway station than actually stood there. It was not a "psychic" sensation, not a "lost sense activating"—nothing so colorful. She didn't see or feel or smell or hear anything out of the ordinary. Hers was a purely intellectual realization, capable of slamming into her at any given moment with all the force of the A train: *There could be dead standing beside me.*

Yesterday 164 people had died in Manhattan; she had checked online. The day before, 193. The day before that, 152. Surely not all of them had immediately started on the third road (or gone through the last door or crossed the "bridge to far" or climbed the golden ladder). If not, then New York was thronged with loitering dead from yesterday, last week, last month. A shadowy realm just beside the living, fidgeting as they waited for the 1:19 downtown.

Put that way, it was preposterous. The stuff of campfire ghost stories, bad movies, "séances" held by charlatans at tawdry "psychic faires." No. Ridiculous.

But it had not seemed so ridiculous on the Atoner ship, watching the display screen as a child standing in a bleak winter landscape had opened her rosy mouth and said, *Aveo,* a name she could not have known for a man she had never met.

Seeing the dead Aveo, hearing him introduce himself?

Telepathy, pulled from Cam's or Lucca's mind under stress? But why should little Chewithoztarel have been under stress?

Was it life after death?

Was it telepathy?

Which? Or neither?

And why didn't any of these other passengers fidgeting beside her seem to care?

The train shrieked through the tunnel and came to a stop, and Soledad got on.

"Why *should* they care?" Fengmo asked.

"I don't even know how you can ask that question," Soledad said. She put down her fork and stared at him hard. They sat at a corner table at Leonard's, Fengmo's favorite restaurant, within sight of the South Manhattan levee that kept out the rising ocean. Leonard's décor, techno-camp, featured old motherboards and defunct keyboards glued to the wall in intricate patterns. A non-working rotary phone sat in the middle of their table, twined with fresh flowers. Soledad had dressed up for Fengmo, who always noticed, in a turquoise silk shirt and gold necklace. Her calamari tasted like sawdust. Fengmo ate with gusto, looking like an animated Oriental elf.

"Let me rephrase, Ladybliss. How are people's lives any different because of the Atoners' revelation? How is *yours*? There's always been life and death, and we've always had to wait for death to see what happens next, and we still do. That 'third road' of the Kularians is still a mystery. Life and death are only two sides of the same unity, just as light is the other hand of darkness. Putting words to them, trying to codify them, solves nothing. 'The—' "

"I know, I know," she said wearily. "You've told me often enough. 'The way you can go isn't the real way; the name you can say isn't the real name.' "

He grinned. "Lao-tzu would be proud of you."

"I doubt it. Fengmo, the Atoners' revelation made a lot of difference to Emma Jane Taymor."

He stopped smiling. "Yes. And there are a lot of borderline types out there who are interpreting this for their own advantage. Have you heard about Anna Romany? Or the CCAD?"

"No." She pushed her calamari around on her plate.

"Anna Romany is a psychic who claims her genes for seeing the dead have 'reexpressed.' Spontaneously regenerated, like the tails of lizards. Her TV show ratings have soared. She claims to be talking to Abraham Lincoln, who still hasn't started down the third road."

"Still? After 160 years?"

"Yes. And Honest Abe wants you to stop lying to yourself about the roadblocks to your personal spiritual growth and send money to Anna Romany. The CCAD is a lot more serious. They're the Christian Coalition Against the Devil, a cross-denominational fundamentalist group that's decided there is only one Atoner, not a whole bunch of them—"

"That's not unreasonable—"

"—and that he's really the Anti-Christ. They might be just a group of whackos, but the language on their website is pretty violent."

"What are you doing on their website?" Soledad pushed away her dinner.

"Monitoring it for you. They think you—mostly The Six, but also the other Witnesses who left Earth—have been recruited by the Anti-Christ and now you're all false prophets. Which is pretty funny when you consider that you can't even make up your own mind about the afterlife. As a prophet, you're pretty wimpy."

"Don't I know it," she said grimly.

"Soledad, are you sleeping any better? You've lost weight over this."

"No bad thing."

"Sweetie—I don't think I can visit with you any-more."

She jerked upright in her chair. "Not visit with me? What the hell are you talking about?"

His face was troubled. "I should have put it together before now, dear heart. Juana lured you to her place so a sleazy journalist could see what you look like now. Any reporter—or any nut—with the brains of a poodle could also find out that you and I have been friends since the early Triassic. They could trail me to get to you. Hasn't Diane Lovett told you that much?"

She had, but Soledad hadn't wanted to listen. She wasn't ungrateful to the Agency for altering her appearance and resettling her, but neither did she want the feds controlling her life. She refused electronic surveillance on her little rented house, and she refused to account to Diane for every morning and afternoon of her life. A daily check-in with Diane was as far as Soledad would go, and the agent had reluctantly agreed. Soledad could only hope that Diane had stuck to her agreement.

Soledad said, "I'm willing to take my chances in order to see you, Fengmo."

"But I'm not willing to put you in danger."

Soledad, as she always did in times of stress, turned impassive. Her body felt like iron. "Can we still talk on the phone?"

"Sure. And I'll go to Cam's lecture tonight. But we'll travel separately and sit apart from each other. Then I'll call you later tonight to dish."

She nodded. Life without Fengmo, without lunches and dinners and the shopping trips he loved and she complained about, teasing him for the contradiction between Taoism and the love of 500-thread-count sheets. Fengmo was the only person who ever teased her back. Fengmo was the only person who could make her laugh.

"Don't look so desolate, sweetie. It's not forever. After all, everything changes constantly, in the great flow of energy in—"

"Oh, shut up," Soledad said.

He said roughly, "I adore you, you idiot."

"I know you do." She took his hand on the tablecloth, feeling a minor peace come over her. The first peace in many days. The waitress stopped, coffeepot in hand, and beamed at the multi-ethnic young couple so ideally in love.

Madison Square Garden looked as closely guarded as the U.S. Mint. Cops in full battle gear guarded the entrance, holding back a crowd getting tired of the slow funneling through metal-and-explosive detectors. On one side of the building a moving LCD displayed a two-story-high image of Camilla O'Kane, waving and smiling. Soledad's coat, which had seemed warm enough during the February day, was inadequate now that the sun had gone down. She wrapped both arms around herself and stamped her feet. Somewhere behind her in line was Fengmo.

Who were all these people? An old woman, even less warmly clad than Soledad, looking grim and muttering to herself. A middle-aged man laughing with his teenage son. Two young girls in ridiculously high heels—please don't let them be more members of the Why Wait? Society. A pair of heavyset men in sheepskin jackets and baseball caps with beer logos. What did they all want from Cam?

What did Soledad want from Cam?

A pop-up ad leaped from the sidewalk, triggered by her body heat. The holo was a beautiful woman who winked, swigged from a can of Coke, and disappeared in a shimmer of silent sparkles.

"Excuse me, miss, you dropped this."

Soledad turned around. A man about her own age stood holding out a black glove. He was gorgeous, a blue-eyed and blond Viking unaccountably transported to gritty Seventh Avenue. Probably an actor; anybody in Manhattan who looked like that turned out to be an actor. She didn't recognize him, but that meant nothing; she went to the theater only when Fengmo dragged her.

"I'm sorry, it's not mine," she said, looking longingly at the glove. It looked warm. One glove would be better than none.

He leaned conspiratorially toward her. "Well, take it anyway. Everybody else around us already has gloves, and your knuckles are turning blue."

She glanced up sharply. Why did he want her to take the glove? Did he know who she was? The plastic surgeon had altered her nose and chin, and a makeup artist had tweezed her brows, dyed her hair, and taught her to change her skin tone. To Soledad, the image in the mirror was a stranger, but to somebody with a better eye than hers . . . Was the glove poisoned or somehow rigged electronically?

Fengmo had made her paranoid.

"No, thanks."

He shrugged. "Whatever. I hope you enjoy the lecture."

"You, too." "Enjoy" was hardly the right word for something you hated to attend but couldn't stay away from. She tried to think of something else to say, something to keep his shining masculine beauty beside her a little longer, but he'd already turned away.

All at once, two lines over, she saw Carl Lewis. He stared straight at her. When she glared back, he raised his hand to his mouth, made it into a megaphone, and pointed at Soledad.

She turned her back on him and approached the first checkpoint to the theater.

32: INTELLIGENCE BRIEFING

PREPARED FOR: PRESIDENT OF THE UNITED STATES
BY: DEPARTMENT OF HOMELAND SECURITY
DATE: DECEMBER 3, 2020
SUBJECT: ACTIVITIES OF "ATONER WITNESSES"
CONTENTS:

EXECUTIVE SUMMARY

Of the twenty-one people who were taken into space aboard Atoner starcraft, seven remained aboard ship when planetfall was effected, seven "witnessed" on planets on which the populace allegedly possessed the so-called "seeing-the-dead" gene (STDG), and seven "witnessed" on planets that did not. Of the twenty-one, twenty survived. Fifteen are American citizens. All fifteen have been provided with government contacts who have arranged whatever degree of anonymity or privacy was desired. In return, daily check-ins ensure a steady flow of information.

<u>Primary finding: Thus far, no American "Witness" has reported, or appears to have had, further con-</u>

tact with any Atoner or with the Atoner base remaining on the moon.

Of especial interest are "The Six," dubbed thus by the media because they are the ones who landed on planets with STDG. Activities of The Six are detailed below; activities of the other fourteen are included in the full report. The Six are comprised of five Americans and one Englishman. The original seven sent to planets with STDG also included Lucca Maduro (dual citizenship, Italy and England) and Japanese national Tomiko Takahashi, allegedly deceased. Maduro has been excluded from "The Six" by the media because of his consistent refusal to expand on his initial brief statement or to give interviews; he is nonetheless included here. Note: Camilla O'Kane was not originally assigned by Atoners to land on an STDG planet but did so anyway.

The Witnesses have reacted variously to their journey, to their exposure to the aliens, and to subsequent media attention. This gives them varying weight as potential avenues to reopening contact with the Atoners. Briefly (for details and sources see full report):

DuBois, Andrew Emile: American, 25, residing San Jose, CA, employed by FutureSystemsCorp, writes code for computer games. Gives interviews, and is a media favorite for his casual, eclectic POV that includes STDG, Zen, astral projection, and reincarnation. His views, though colorful, are seldom taken seriously by the media, by focus groups, or by colleagues. Check-in with Security contact: sporadic. Potential utility: low.

Dziwalski, Sara Louise: American, 26, residing Austin, TX, has returned to work as an LPN at Seton Medical Center. Ignores media attention at work and refuses to discuss her experiences with patients or staff. Does off-hours interviews with media, but these have dropped off, as she speaks in a straightforward manner and does not vary or add to her statements. Believes complete Atoner explanation for what she allegedly witnessed. Check-in with Security contact: daily and at length. Potential utility: high, since she deviates not at all from "information" that Atoners wish to disseminate.

Harden, Christina Jessica: American, 20, residing with parents in Boston, MA, student at Brown (junior in international relations), youngest Witness. Very bright but gives no interviews at the request of her parents (whom she defied to become a Witness in the first place) and of the university, both of whom appear to be trying to shield her. Privately says she is "still thinking over" what she "witnessed." Currently taking courses in comparative religion, paleontology, history, and neurology. Check-in with Security contact: daily but very brief. Potential utility: uncertain. If the Atoners value brains and independent thinking, she could be valuable; however, she is very young.

Jones, John Elijah: UK national, 27, residing Cambridge, England, doctoral candidate in mathematics. Initially gave interviews but now states he has said all that he wishes to say about his experiences. Believes in STDG but seems, incredibly, not very interested in it. Is intensely interested in adding to astronomical and mathematical knowledge through careful observations made during his journey, and for this reason enjoys celebrity among scientists in those areas. Check-in with Security contact: fairly consistent (see MI6 report under "Sources"). British willing to cooperate with us on information sharing and potential contact. Potential utility: medium.

Maduro, Lucca Giancarlo: Dual citizenship, Italy and England, 27, residing Toronto, Canada, recluse.

Maduro has consistently refused to expand on his initial brief statement, to give interviews, or to appear in public. He is supported by family money on a heavily fortified small estate (see report by Canadian intelligence, under "Sources"). Alone among those who allegedly witnessed STDG in operation, he has rejected the Atoner explanation in favor of a belief that subjects were not talking to or seeing the dead but rather engaging in telepathic acts activated by stress, which pulled the information from the minds of the living who were present. (For a discussion of this hypothesis, including its followers, see Appendix C.) Check-in with Security contact: NA. Potential utility: very low.

O'Kane, Camilla Mary: American, 23, no fixed address, parents reside Jay, NE, working the lecture circuit. By far the most visible of "The Six." Believes in STDG completely and exhorts audiences to believe. Gives interviews constantly, stays consistent with her story but presents it in a theatrical, dramatic manner. Check-in with Security contact: daily and at length. Potential utility: high, since she is aggressively spreading the "message" that the Atoners presumably wish to disseminate.

Olenik, Francis Michael: American, 24, residing Barton, OH. Ex–police officer, dismissed from Barton PD for alleged evidence tampering, just before he applied to Atoners. Application appears to be out of character. Refuses all interviews. In initial debriefing said he believes in STDG and sees no conflict between that and his traditional Catholicism. Check-in with Security contact: daily but very brief and "with much reserve" (description by contacting agent). Potential utility: low.

33: FRANK

Frank emerged from the confessional no better off than when he went in.

When he was a kid, it had been so easy. Confession every Saturday morning, say a penance of three Hail Marys and three Our Fathers, and emerge to stand on the church steps shining clean and completely safe. A sixteen-wheeler could hit you and you'd go straight to Heaven. It had been the best feeling in the world.

Frank helped an old lady in a flowered hat down the steps, holding her arm. "Is somebody picking you up, ma'am?" She didn't look capable of even seeing the street, much less navigating it.

"Oh, yes! My grandson. Such a good boy, but never goes to church, let alone confession to . . . well. Thank you, dear. Do you see a 2011 blue Toyota Tundra?" The last words had obviously been carefully memorized.

"Coming along right now . . . Have a good day, ma'am." He helped her into the car, keeping his head down so as not to be recognized by the driver.

"God bless you," she quavered, and the Toyota squealed tires and lurched off.

Punk.

Frank pulled the brim of his baseball cap very low, wondered where to go now, and began to walk aimlessly. The inactivity was the worst; he hated it. No job, and no chance of getting one. The only thing he'd ever wanted was a job in law enforcement, and now that was closed to him. No girlfriend, no friends he wanted to see. His old buddies, except for Mike Renfrew, were too careful to not mention the Barton PD suspension. Or the bizarre trip off Earth ("Did you really go? Like, why, man?" Pat Donovan had asked after too many beers). Or the stares Frank got at their old bars and ball fields. But it was the reporters that really alienated his friends, the jackals that followed Frank sniffing for scraps for their goddamn newscasts. . . .

Stop. He'd just gone to confession, and here he was taking the name of the Lord in vain. That wasn't the way out.

But what was? Confession hadn't helped, not one bit. Father Pfender was too old, too out of it, too used to petty confessions of shoplifting and fornicating and fighting. But what had been the alternative—confess to the parish's other priest, Frank's Uncle Jack? No way.

"Father, I told a serious lie, with serious consequences."

"Consequences to who?"

"To the United States government. Under oath. I didn't think about it that way at the time, but since then . . . things just snowballed. It wasn't all my fault, and if . . . if others had done what they promised, I might have been justified. It wasn't so much a sin of commission as of omission. Or maybe not, I'm no lawyer. But as it is . . . I think . . ."

"Yes?"

"I think I may have committed treason."

Did the old priest even know what treason was? He'd lived in that parish house for fifty years and he'd never been the deepest carrot in the garden, even if he was anointed by God.

"If you've lied, my son, you must set it right. Go back and tell the truth."

"To who?"

"To whoever you lied to, and to all those harmed by your lie. Lying comes from pride in oneself. Turn your pride over to Christ and you will see the way."

"But—"

"Any more sins you need to confess?"

"No, I—"

"Then make a good Act of Contrition."

Easy to say, *Tell the truth to all those harmed by your lie*—but who was that? The whole world, maybe. Nobody, maybe. Frank didn't know—that was the problem.

"Look—a Witness! It's Frank Olenik!"

Oh Christ. Some old biddy with nothing better to do than stand in front of Parnell's Grocery, and the next thing Frank knew there was a crowd of punks who should have been in school and Wednesday-morning gawkers and somebody was sure to call the fucking media on a cell.

He walked in the opposite direction—walking, not running, he wouldn't give them the satisfaction—turned the corner, and slipped into somebody's backyard. A dog rushed at him, but it was small and it stopped when Frank turned and stared at it, boot upraised. He climbed a fence, and then another, and came out on Anderson Street, beside the Blue Junction.

Ten o'clock in the morning and the bar was open. Men in it, too, slouching over their drinks, pathetic misplaced losers. Frank joined them, ordered a lager, and took it to the darkest back booth.

This couldn't go on.

He wanted his old life back, and he wasn't going to get it, and it was the Atoners' fault. Yeah, he'd gone along with the whole program, but he hadn't been himself at the time and shouldn't they have known that? They'd picked him out of millions of applicants; he cringed now to think how proud he'd been of that. Fucking idiot. But the aliens were supposed to be so super-smart, all that advanced star-faring technology, and they should have given some thought to the lives that the Witnesses were going to lead when they went home. There was that barracuda Cam O'Kane writing books and doing movie deals and yapping all around the country about the afterlife being real—like Catholics hadn't known that since Jesus Christ made his promise: *I tell you today you will be with me in Paradise.* And there was Lucca Maduro sulking in some kind of rich man's bunker in Canada and Sara Dziwalski trying to go on being a nurse and pretending nothing else ever happened. . . . Well, Sara was all right. She was pretty, too, in the modest and untrashy way that women should be. But they were letting her be a nurse and nobody was going to let Frank Olenik be a cop or an FBI agent or a U.S. Marshal or anything else he'd wanted to be since he was six years old. In the last six months, even the Border Patrol had turned him down. And he'd be damned if he'd go to the private security companies and end up a useless square badge.

So what was he going to do?

"If you've lied, my son, you must set it right. Go back and tell the truth."

"To who?"

"To whoever you lied to."

He didn't know any of the names of the government team that had debriefed him for two solid weeks. There'd been so many of them, and at first he was still dazed from the decon on the moon. Their ship—Frank's and Amira's and Rod Dostie's—had landed at the 'Tonie base, guided by whatever computers the aliens had, without any help from Amira. The three of them had pulled on their EVA suits over their personal shields and walked the half mile to the Dome. The EVA suits were human designed; NASA had insisted on that, and the aliens had agreed. Not that it had done NASA any good; in decon the suits had been wiped as clean as the Witnesses.

As they waddled in the bulky suits toward the Atoner Dome, they'd been permitted to gather rocks to bring home as souvenirs. Amira had asked about that, in her prissy singsong English, and the 'Tonies had said yes, the rocks could be sold on Earth if they liked. So maybe the aliens *had* looked ahead and seen how hard it would be for the Witnesses to get regular jobs. Frank was holding on to his three good-sized rocks because he figured that the price could only go up with time, but the money wasn't the point. Not even close. A man should work.

The screen over the bar came on, abruptly and loud. Frank actually jumped. He looked around to see if anybody'd noticed—God, he was twitchy—but nobody had.

Once they'd been inside the Atoner Dome, the aliens had knocked them all out for decon. The Voice—that was how Frank thought of it, a Voice but no body—explained that they would be scrubbed inside and out to make sure they carried no germs or anything back to Earth. All implants would be removed. Their souvenir rocks would be decontaminated, too. When he woke up from that, Frank had felt like he'd been beaten and scourged, inside and out, and so did everybody else. Then down to Earth and NASA did decon all over again, although this time he was awake and it wasn't so weakening, just long and boring, almost as boring as two weeks of debriefing by people he couldn't name and didn't trust.

Not that you could really trust anybody in government. There were honest cops, like his father, and maybe some honest low-level civil service workers, too. Frank could believe that. But the bureaucracies that ran the honest workers were corrupt, two-faced, like the Barton PD brass. You couldn't trust anybody in politics.

Frank drank off his beer and considered his personal government contact, Jim Thompson, assigned to him right after the debriefing. Jim seemed all right, not too full of himself or anything, and he spoke Frank's language. A regular guy. But that could just be to get Frank to trust him, and anyway, Jim was too small potatoes for what Frank had to confess.

So . . . call the president? This information was important enough! But a president had to be the ultimate two-faced politician. Also, Frank didn't believe—and he didn't care what anybody said, he wasn't a sexist, but Saint Paul had been real clear on what men and women were each supposed to do—that a woman should be president. So shoot him. There it was.

But he had to tell somebody. Not only was that part of the penance that Father Pfender had given him, but the lie was eating him up. He knew why he'd told it, and it was still a legitimate reason—what the Police Academy called a permissible deception. But in the months back home he'd had time to think, really think, about the whole situation, and to pray about it, too. Prayer had clarified things for him. So now he needed help to make the whole situation right, and who—

The television blared something about Cam O'Kane at Madison Square Garden—"tonight, live, and for three nights only!" That exploitive nutcase, why would anyone go to see her yammer on about—

But all at once Frank knew whom he needed to tell about the lie that could change everything.

34: SUPERMARKET KIOSK DISPLAY

International Enquirer

Top Scientists Say Coffee Restores Lost Genes!	**Florida Secretly Releases 40 Convicted Murderers!!**
Conspiracy by Tea Companies Keeping Info Secret!!	"Victims aren't really dead," says chief warden, "just on second road."
Tea Execs to Be Indicted!	Find Out if Released Killers Live in Your Area!
How Much to Drink, When, How to Get Most Effect	"Our children are at risk," says angry mom.
(To print story, press key A.)	(To print story, press key B.)
Cory to Return to Hannah!	**Diet Pill Dissolves Fat Through Brain Waves**
Berry so jealous she drives car into Chesapeake Bay!	Learn to focus your mind to melt fat away—without exercising!!
Fabulous Exclusive pics!!	"I've never seen anything like this," says stunnned doc.
(To print story, press key C.)	(To print story, press key D.)

35: CAM

Cam dreamed yet again that she saw Aveo. The old man stood bare chested in his rough brown skirt, but the flesh drooped in gobbets from his bones and the bones gleamed like knives, glossy and sharp. Aveo smiled at her with blackened lips over rotted teeth, a smile like Satan himself. He held something out to her, and rasped, "You must play kulith better than that, *ostiu*, or else . . ." Cam woke, gasping.

She groped by her side but the young man, what's-his-name, must have left after she fell asleep. The bedside clock said 4:30 P.M. The hotel bedclothes smelled of afternoon sex. Cam groaned and turned on the light. She had a performance at Madison Square Garden in less than four hours.

It was the worst of all the nightmares. And why the fuck should she be having it? Aveo's body was not rotting in a grave anywhere; Soledad had blasted it into clean oblivion on Kular A. Aveo's spirit had long since started on the third road, and anyway, the old man had never looked at her with evil, had never been anything but kind in his own weird alien way. So why the terrible dream? And why hadn't that guy—Cory, that was it, Cory—stayed after Cam had fallen asleep? That had been the whole point: to not wake up alone.

Cam's government contact, Angie Bernelli, hated it when Cam picked up men: "bad security risks." But Cam didn't do it very often. And what Angie didn't understand was that there were nights—and mornings and afternoons—that Cam simply could not get through alone. Tonight she would walk out on yet another stage and deliver the Atoners' message, and no one in the audience would know that she had been in this frantic state four hours earlier. No one in the audience would know that Cam had killed several dozen men on Kular B and that those men did not let her sleep. No one understood.

She had thought, once, that Lucca might understand. He had witnessed violence on Kular A. But it turned out that those murders were voluntary, that Lucca had not killed anybody, and that he didn't want to talk to Cam, anyway. Every time she phoned him, they argued. He just hadn't been able to accept the truth about the Atoners' message. Now he wouldn't take Cam's calls at all.

She heaved herself out of bed, padded into the hotel bathroom, and looked at herself in the mirror. *God.* She looked like a crazy woman, with wild hair and wilder eyes. Like one of those bag ladies that she'd never seen back in Nebraska and that scared her in New York.

How many men, exactly, had she killed on Kular? And of them all, why was it Aveo who most terrorized her dreams?

Taking a deep breath and letting it out very slowly—one one thousand, two one thousand, three one thousand, four one thousand, five one thousand, six one thousand—she gripped the edge of the sink. She had a show to do. It was the most important show in the world. She could do this.

Aveo—

She picked up a comb and began untangling her hair.

36: SOLEDAD

Cam's lecture was being held not in the main arena, which seated nineteen thousand, but in the Theater at Madison Square Garden, which seated only fifty-five hundred. Soledad shuffled through the expansive lobby, had her purse turned inside out, and wondered if the venue meant that not as many people were as interested in the afterlife as Cam's promoter had hoped. But if Cam really had a book and movie deal . . . On the other hand, the theater was packed, and Cam was booked for two additional nights.

As soon as Soledad reached her seat, at the front of the 201 section about twenty feet from the stage, she had the answer. A transparent shimmer spanned the entire front of the stage. For a wild moment she thought it was a huge version of the Atoner personal shield, but of course it was not. The Atoners had, so far, kept all their technology to themselves, which must really be frustrating Washington. What Soledad was seeing was no more than a huge expanse of bulletproof plastic. Cam had, of course, received death threats. They all had—but undoubtedly not as many as Cam. The smaller theater made security easier.

Music started, generic-sounding usher-them-in tunes that were neither soothing nor energetic. Soledad had lost sight of Carl Lewis, although he probably had not lost her. Fengmo, studiously ignoring Soledad, sat two rows directly behind her. Soledad took her seat. Fifteen minutes later, the show started.

Frantic music and then—Good God, what was Cam

thinking?—*fireworks* behind the screen. Gunshots couldn't have been more alarming. Half the crowd leaped to its feet. But the fireworks gave way to sweeping laser lights and a man bounded onto the stage. Some of the people standing began to cheer and whistle, while the other half shouted, "Sit down, you morons!" The man was Tam Blair, a Hollywood star who had just won an Academy Award for a stupid remake of *Siddhartha*. Soledad could imagine how Fengmo, who had hated the movie's cheap sentimentalizing of Buddhism, felt about Blair's presence.

"Good evening!" Blair called. He wore a purple tuxedo and ruffled silver shirt. His auburn hair gleamed under the lights. "How are you all tonight?"

A roar from the crowd. Was he going to work them like some evangelist at a tent revival? Evidently so, because all through Blair's meandering introduction of Cam, much of which concerned his own "search to believe," he punched the air and pranced around the huge stage. The laser lights swept in syncopated arcs, changing colors. The elderly man beside Soledad, dressed in a camel's-hair coat and carrying an expensive leather briefcase, looked quietly disgusted.

But then the mood changed abruptly. Blair finished with, "And now, Camilla O'Kane, witness to eternity!" and swept into the wings. The music died, the lights went to a low and steady blue, and the crowd quieted.

She made them wait a long time. Just as the murmuring began, she walked onto the stage, dressed in a simple full-length black gown that showcased her spectacular figure but didn't shout about it. Her wild black curls had been pulled into a chignon, and her only ornament was a white rose in her hair. Cam held up her hand to still the applause, and gazed outward solemnly.

"Hello. I'm here to tell you a story, and I'd really appreciate it if you'd listen quietly to what I have to say. It deserves attention because it's *not* my story—it's much bigger than that. I'm only a small part of it. I am, in fact, exactly what the aliens who visited our star system called me: a Witness. I witnessed things of enormous moment for all of us, and I'm grateful for the opportunity tonight to do what witnesses do, to the best of their ability. They speak the truth."

Someone had written this speech for Cam; it was nothing like her flamboyant personality. And yet it was brilliant because that flamboyance nonetheless shone through the quiet words, illuminated them with energy and passion. The combination was mesmerizing, and Soledad silently congratulated the unknown speechwriter.

"But before I begin to witness to that truth," Cam said, "I want to ask a moment of silence for all the young people who have tragically misinterpreted it, and especially for Emma Jane Taymor, the daughter of the vice president of the United States. The truth of the Atoners is about life, not death. Please observe our shared moment of silence in whatever way best, for you, honors that truth."

Cam bowed her head. So did several people around Soledad. Even those who did not remained quiet. Cam had them in exactly the mood she wanted. She was a natural.

She continued to speak simply and well, starting with the Atoners' arrival on the moon. The segue from what was known as fact to what the Atoners alleged as fact was so seamless that even Soledad nearly missed it. To Cam it was *all* fact: the website call for "applications," the kidnapping ten thousand years ago of humans from Earth, the radio conversations with SETI and the UN and NASA, the altering of genes in "our most recent common ancestors," the shuttles, the events on Kular A and B and the other "double-blind" planets, the Atoners' current silence.

"And why are they so silent now? Why have they answered no communications from Earth for the entire six months since the twenty Witnesses returned?" She leaned closer to the audience. "We can't know for sure, of course—"

Why not? Soledad thought meanly. Cam seemed so sure of everything else.

"—but one possibility is that the Atoners are waiting. They need more time to observe us, to decide what should be done next. After all, their very name indicates that they wish to atone to us! So far, they have admitted their crime, and sent us to observe it—to be, in fact, friends of the court, amici curiae—"

And *that* was a term that Cam O'Kane had not come up with herself.

"—but they have done nothing to set it right. And so, my friends, we come to the two big questions that all of this poses for humanity. Two questions absolutely without parallel in our history. First—"

The elderly man beside Soledad leaned forward; she could see that he was interested despite himself.

"—what will the Atoners *do* to atone for their crime against us? They can, and will, do something—but what? And second . . ."

She paused. Long, theatrically long, too long. Soledad, disliking melodrama, felt embarrassed for Cam, but the crowd ate it up.

"Second, what lies beyond that second road? Beyond the golden ladder? Beyond the spirit door? What we Witnesses saw was just the start of what happens after the essence of a person leaves the body at death. But what lies beyond *that,* beyond—"

"Hellfire for you!" someone shouted, and then it all happened at once.

The shout had come from Soledad's left. But somewhere on her right she heard gunfire—how had guns gotten past the metal detectors? Semi-automatic—*rat-a-tat-tat-tat*—and the crowd was screaming and pushing. Something whistled past Soledad's ear—a bullet, ricocheting off the clear plastic stretched across the stage. They were firing at Cam.

Soledad tried to duck and crawl under the seats, but the elderly man was already there. A woman screamed, a high anguished cry of pure pain. People scrambled and cried out even as a loudspeaker urged calm and order. Whirling wildly around, frantically looking for Fengmo, Soledad saw him climbing over the seats toward her, shouting something she couldn't distinguish in the unholy clamor.

A movement in the corner of her eye. A man standing at the end of her row of seats, a big man utterly still, watching, a rooted bulwark that forced the panicking crowd to flow around him. He stared at Fengmo, then at Soledad, and he raised a plastic gun in his left hand.

She saw the gun clearly, with the preternatural clarity of crisis. The man fired at her. A moment before he did, she was tackled and thrown across two seats, the arms of the seats cutting sharply into her back, and Fengmo screamed.

It wasn't he who had tackled her. Someone else, someone large and blond, and then she was under him with Fengmo on top of them both, and Fengmo's blood dripped onto her face and into her mouth, tasting of salt like tears.

37: A STATEMENT FROM CONGRESSMAN HARRY MELSON (R-GA)

"Thank you for coming this morning, ladies and gentlemen of the press. I'd like to read a prepared statement and then take your questions.

"The American people have always been prepared to defend our borders. Pearl Harbor, the World Trade Center, the Las Cruces Invasion—we have never hesitated to say in terms that anyone else can understand: 'This is ours.' And I think that history shows that the same is true for other sovereign nations, at all times and all places. This is a human trait: defense of our own.

"The moon is our own. It belongs to humanity as it circles *our* globe, *our* God-given home. Yet for six months, just as we begin to establish our own human outpost on the moon, it has been invaded by beings that admit to having kidnapped our human ancestors, meddled with our gene pool, carted off twenty-one of our youth too immature to understand the implications of those actions—and told us that one of those precious youngsters died under very mysterious circumstances. Now those same invaders sit up there on our moon, within fifty miles of Selene City, and *they refuse to talk to us.* It's arrogant, it's invasive, and it's just plain wrong.

"Yet the current administration does nothing.

"So I'm calling, right here and right now, for action. We need to demand that these aliens account for themselves and communicate with us like civilized beings. And if they don't, then we should do whatever is necessary—up to and including military force—to remove them from our territory. The American people—and all the rest of humanity—deserve nothing less than sovereignty over, and control of, what is indubitably ours.

"Now I'll take your questions."

38: SOLEDAD

"Let me up!" Her own voice but not her own: full of terror and outrage and frantic concern for Fengmo.

"Okay—he's dead," the man on top of her said, and for a terrible moment she thought he meant Fengmo. But Fengmo still breathed. Soledad scrambled out from under both of them and grabbed for Fengmo before that slight body could slip onto the floor. Blood poured out of Fengmo's head. She barely noted—and yet she saw, saw it all, her mind seemed to have become multiple cameras—the shooter slumped across three seats at the end of the row, and the NYPD cop who had been hired as security for the event standing over him with a gun in one hand and a cell phone in the other.

"An ambulance!" Soledad heard herself cry, as if from a great distance. "An ambulance—oh God, Fengmo, don't die don't die—"

"Push on this," the man said and a wadded-up scarf appeared, as if conjured, on Fengmo's head. Soledad shook her head to clear it. Focus, focus. . . . She pushed hard on the cloth over Fengmo's wound. So much blood on his head, his face . . .

"We have to get him outside," the man said. "Can you press on him if I carry him? . . . Good."

They forced their way up the aisle, now packed with fewer people, the man with Fengmo in his arms a plow all by himself. The huge lobby was bedlam. Crying patrons, security guards, NYPD, medics, the press, a nightmare kaleidoscope. Then Soledad was kneeling in a semi-sheltered corner beside Fengmo, whose eyes rolled back in his head like unmoored planets. A moment or an hour later, the stranger had commandeered EMTs and two of them carried Fengmo out to an ambulance, Soledad sticking to the stretcher like a leech. As she climbed in beside Fengmo, ignoring the medics' forceful statements that she must ride up front, she turned and blurted, "Thank you!" to the rescuer and looked at him for the first time.

It was the handsome blond who had offered her the glove while they stood in line. He said, "I'll see you at St. Vincent's, then," just before the medics gave up on dislodging her and slammed shut the ambulance door.

At the hospital, doctors grabbed Fengmo and rushed him into an OR. Other casualties were coming in as well; it was another chaos, this time overlaid with the peculiar antiseptic grimness of all hospitals. Soledad found the OR waiting room and sank down, trembling, on a green plastic chair.

If Fengmo died . . .

Her life, just barely manageable now, would be impossible without him. *Fengmo.* Whom she'd known since she was five, who had been her escape and solace as a child and her closest friend—only close friend—as an adult. Fengmo of the sharp mind and sweet heart and tranquil Taoist belief that had so balanced Soledad's perpetual doubt . . . Fengmo . . .

"Drink this," a voice said beside her. The blond man, holding out black coffee in a paper cup. Soledad grabbed it, drank it off, burned her mouth, and was glad of it. The pain helped her to focus.

"It'll be a while, it always is," the blond said.

"Cam . . . the others . . ."

"Cam O'Kane is fine. Not hit. Three other people were, ricochets or bad shots. There were two shooters, both dead now. One was after O'Kane, the one with the semi, and the other one, I think, was after you. Why is that, pretty lady? Who are you?"

He stared at her steadily from his bright blue eyes. Soledad searched that gaze, trying to see who he was, what he might want. She saw only kindness—but did she see accurately? But he had saved her life, had maybe saved Fengmo's life . . . and she was so tired of hiding. Of everything. To her own horror, tears formed in her eyes. She scowled them away.

"Hey, you don't have to say anything you don't want to," he said gently. "It's okay. But those shooters—the newscasts are already saying they were CCAD. So you—"

CCAD. She struggled to remember what that was, and then she had it—Fengmo at dinner at Leonard's: *There are a lot of borderline types out there who are interpreting this for their own advantage. Have you heard about Anna Romany? Or the CCAD? . . . They're the Christian Coalition Against the Devil, a cross-denominational fundamentalist group that's decided there is only one Atoner . . . and that he's really the Anti-Christ. . . . The language on their website is pretty violent.*

"—were their target. Are you one of the Witnesses?"

"I—"

"You are, aren't you? You're Soledad Arellano. Different nose and hair, but . . . yeah, you're her."

She stared at him helplessly. He caught the look, smiled, and took her hand.

"You're afraid now that I'll blow your cover. Don't worry, I won't. I'm a very trustworthy guy, you'll see. James Hinton."

"I'm not—"

"It's okay. Just say, 'Hello, James.' Come on, you can do that, a bright star-traveling girl like you."

Despite herself, she smiled. "Hello, James."

"Good. Perfect. Now I'm going to wait with you until you have news about your boyfriend."

"He's not my boyfriend. But he's my best friend."

"Better yet." James still held her hand. Soledad, a strange warmth creeping through her, didn't pull it away.

Fengmo was in surgery for two hours, then taken to Recovery. A doctor in bloody scrubs came out to talk to Soledad, who said she was Fengmo's sister. This was ethnically unlikely, but the doctor, harried and weary, didn't care. She told Soledad that Fengmo would be taken to the ICU and Soledad should wait outside that unit until she could see him.

"Where is it?" she asked.

"Third floor, C Wing." The doctor disappeared.

James said, "Soledad, listen. By now the press will have Fengmo's name and they'll have found out that he's a longtime friend of yours. If you go to the ICU, they'll be on you like cold on space. I'm surprised they haven't found you here. If you wait somewhere—maybe in the cafeteria—I'll go wait by the ICU and bring you word."

"Why are you taking all this trouble for me?" It came out much sharper than she'd intended.

He said, "I like you."

Her gaze flew to his. Men didn't use that tone to Soledad, at least not men who looked like James. She'd had lovers, sure—but not . . . not like James Hinton.

"Go to the cafeteria," he said gently.

She went, feeling the warmth slide along her chest, her arms, her neck, warring with the dread she felt for Fengmo.

He was in a coma, the doctors said. He might or might not come out of it, but there was considerable trauma to the head and there would probably be some brain damage. James told her this in a deserted corridor by Diagnostic Imaging, the cafeteria having closed hours ago. He held tightly on to her hand. She didn't cry, just looked at him numbly.

"I can drive you home, if you like. But if you don't want

me to know where you live, I can get you a cab, or . . . whatever you like."

It was four in the morning. The maglevs to upstate had stopped running hours ago. A cab would cost a huge amount. She couldn't think. Finally she said, "A hotel . . . if there's a cheap hotel around here. . . ."

"I wouldn't trust any cheap hotel in this neighborhood. Listen, if you'll trust me . . . my place isn't that far. I promise I'm not an ax murderer."

She studied him. Even through her exhaustion and dread she trusted her own instincts: He wasn't an ax murderer. Nor a rapist, nor a thief. *I like you.*

He took her to a very small fourth-floor apartment on the West Side. Sparsely furnished, clean. She took off her shoes and fell asleep as soon as her head rested on the sofa, barely feeling James cover her with a blanket.

But after just a few hours, she woke. Pale winter light filtering through lowered blinds, the sound of garbage trucks banging Dumpsters. *Fengmo.* She cried out. There had been terrible dreams: herself trying to kill Cam, stalking her with a spear tipped with fire, waiting for the moment when Cam's personal shield had been lowered and Soledad could spit her like a pig.

James was there, then, sitting on the sofa beside Soledad, putting his arms around her. She shoved him away, but the next moment she collapsed against him and finally, for the first time in years, let tears come in the presence of another human being.

39: FRANK

Frank called his government contact, Jim Thompson, on his cell. A cell wasn't secure, of course, so all he could say was, "Meet me at Addie's in an hour, okay?"

"You got it," Thompson said.

There was no Addie's. Frank and the agent had worked out a code to avoid the press jackals that just wouldn't quit on getting that interview Frank was never going to give. To avoid, too, the occasional nut with a gun. Although Frank had received far fewer death threats than some of the other Witnesses. In his opinion, this was because he minded his own business, was an ex-cop, and looked like a normal person, not a ponytailed leftie like Andy DuBois or a fake Hollywood starlet like Cam O'Kane or a snobby so-called intellectual like Jack Jones. The only other normal-looking American in The Six was Sara Dziwalski, trying to do her work as a nurse and be left the hell alone.

"Addie's" was actually Mike Renfrew Toyota, on Culver Road. Frank rode his Harley there; on a bike it was easy to lose any tail, although Frank didn't see anybody following him. But you couldn't ever be too sure. Mike Renfrew was an old friend and his people were reliable. He let Frank leave the Harley in the service bay, behind the tire rack, and Jim picked up Frank on the back lot.

"Hey," Jim said. "How you doing?"

"Fine," Frank said. "You?"

"Can't complain. Something up?"

"Yeah. Can we get coffee?" He wanted to sit face-to-face with Jim, easier to gauge reactions that way. Jim seemed like a good guy, but he was still government, and his interests were not the same as Frank's.

They drove to a diner out on the highway. Red plastic booths, napkin dispensers on the table, no pop-ups at the slots. Frank put on his sunglasses and baseball cap and pulled the brim low. The place was full of lunchtime trade, but nobody glanced twice at them. Jim ordered coffee and Frank added cherry pie. He had a sweet tooth, and although Ma was a good cook, she didn't bake much.

"Jim, I want to see Lucca Maduro in Canada."

The agent blinked. "Lucca? Why?"

"That's my business, so far. I'll tell you when the time is right."

Jim stirred non-dairy creamer into his coffee. "If I know what this is about, maybe I can help."

"You can help by getting me over the border with no publicity, and then in to see Lucca. You said the Canadians are cooperating with us."

"They are. But Maduro's not very cooperative."

"So I hear." Frank sipped his coffee. He took it black and hot. "Can you do it?"

"I don't know. I'm being straight with you, Frank. Maduro might be more receptive if we could tell him something, anything, to convince him that you have something important to say."

That was fair. Of course the Agency—whichever one Jim was really with, FBI or CIA or NSA or Homeland or whatever—also wanted the information for themselves. But Frank had read how stubborn Lucca could be, and Frank could well see that something might be needed to convince him.

He said, "Let me think about that for a few minutes, Jim."

"Sure." Jim drank more of his coffee and waited. The cherry pie came and Frank started in on it.

Frank didn't like Lucca Maduro. He'd met him during the orientation the Atoners had given all of them on the moon before the voyage out, in those bare gray rooms under the alien Dome. Frank had sized up Lucca as a spoiled rich kid. Smart, yes, he'd give the Italian that, after all Lucca had gone to some classy university in Britain and his English was as good as anybody's. But Lucca was too smooth, too polished in that accent that drove all the girls crazy. Frank felt that Lucca looked down on the ordinary people who'd been accepted as Witnesses, people like himself and Sara Dziwalski and Rod Dostie. Frank had felt the same way about Hans Kramer and Amira Gupta and Jack Jones. Snobs.

But then Frank found out that Lucca had been married and his wife had been killed by a drunk driver. That changed Frank's feelings a little. He hated drunk drivers, and when he'd been a cop he'd done his best to get the book thrown at every single one he caught. Irresponsible murderers, in his view. And if Lucca was grieving over his wife, then maybe that explained why he sometimes looked like he had a stick up his ass. Frank hadn't liked him any better, but he'd cut Lucca some slack.

It wasn't until they all got back home that Frank started to respect Lucca. First, the man wasn't trying to capitalize on his fame. Like Sara, like Frank himself, Lucca just wanted to get on with his life, and the jackals wouldn't let him. So he had taken a time-out and was waiting out his fifteen minutes of fame in Canada, since he was a British citizen as well as an Italian one and everybody knew that Italy was a country full of crazies anyway. Hiding wasn't Frank's way, but he could understand it. Lucca hadn't sold his moon rocks on eBay, hadn't gone all trashy glitter like Cam O'Kane, wasn't New Age goofy like Andy DuBois out there in California.

But, more important, Lucca was the only one of "The Six" who didn't believe that the people on Kular could actually see and talk to the dead. He was wrong—Frank knew what he'd seen on Susban—but Lucca stuck to his beliefs, and Frank had to respect that. Most people caved when they got a lot of group pressure from a lot of people who believed the opposite of their own conclusions. Not Lucca. He might be aloof and chichi and too snobby for his own good, but he had integrity. He wasn't any kind of politician. You could trust the word of a guy like that.

And Lucca had money. A lot of money. You couldn't believe everything in the news, not by a long shot, but that seemed true. Frank had seen the pictures of the vineyards Lucca's family owned in Italy, the bank in Rome, the department stores in London. What Frank had in mind was going to take money.

Jim Thompson was still waiting. The waitress refilled both their coffees. Frank said, "Tell Lucca that I have something to tell him that is brand-new information about something he cares about."

Jim said, "Brand-new information?"

"Yes." He met the agent's eyes directly. "Something I left out of my debriefing. And yes, I'll tell you eventually, Jim. But I need to talk to Lucca first."

If Jim was angry, if he was thinking *lies* or even *treason,* he didn't show it. The man was good. He was, in fact, what Frank would have liked to be if he hadn't discovered how government really worked. Police department politics, Washington politics—no different. But that was water under the bridge. The important thing was what Frank had to do now, to set things right with God.

To atone.

He hadn't thought of it like that before, and he didn't like thinking of it that way now. Aligning himself with the aliens— *He* hadn't committed any huge crime against humanity. Just the opposite. He was going to help humanity, by doing God's work.

"So can you get me in to see Lucca?"

"I'll see what I can do. Meet me back at Addie's late this afternoon? Say, four o'clock."

That fast. Despite himself, Frank was impressed. Jim was taking this seriously, so maybe the government—

both governments, the Canadian, too—would take it seriously as well. Jim might be able to bring this off.

But all Frank said was, "Good." Expressionless, both men put money on the table—Frank always insisted on paying his own tab—and left the diner, just as the waitress came up to ask if Frank wanted any more pie.

40: TRANSCRIPT, OVAL OFFICE
TAPE #16,845

Property of the White House

CHIEF OF STAFF WALTER STEINHAUER (WS): Madam President?

PRESIDENT: Come in, Walt. Have you seen this press statement from Harry Melson?

WS: Yes, ma'am.

PRESIDENT: He wants the U.S. Air Force or NASA or somebody to blow the Atoner base to Kingdom Come! What's wrong with those voters down in Georgia?

WS: Maybe it's the heat. Madam President, we've heard from one of the special agents assigned to the Witnesses.

PRESIDENT: What is it? Has there been contact with the aliens?

WS: No, nothing so juicy. But Frank Olenik wants us to arrange a meeting with Lucca Maduro, through the Canadians. Olenik told his handler that he has important information for Maduro, quote, "something I left out of my debriefing," unquote.

PRESIDENT: How serious do you think it is? Which one is Olenik, again?

WS: The ex-cop. He's kept a low profile, and his contact says he's pretty reliable.

PRESIDENT: Not all that reliable, if he lied in his debriefing. What do you think?

WS: I think we should do all we can to get him in to see Maduro. Olenik seems to trust his handler, and this is our best chance of finding out what this is all about.

PRESIDENT: Could be it's all about nothing.

WS: Could well be.

PRESIDENT: But I think you're right. If the Atoners won't talk to us— Still nothing to NASA or the UN or SETI?

WS: Nothing.

PRESIDENT: Well, if the aliens won't talk to us, we'll have to get information from anyone who will. Get the ball rolling with the Canadians. And Walt—

WS: Yes, ma'am?

PRESIDENT: Try to find out if maybe Harry Melson was dropped on his head as a baby.

WS: That would explain a lot, yes.

PRESIDENT: Lord preserve me from elected idiots and inscrutable aliens. I should have been a plumber. No, don't answer that, Walt.

WS: I'll just go talk to Ottawa now.

41: SOLEDAD

James said, "Soledad, I have to go to work now. I canceled this morning, but I have two patients I must see this afternoon. Are you going to be all right alone?"

Soledad scrambled to sit up on the sofa. Full harsh sunlight poured into the window, along with the honking of horns from the street below James's building. James stood before her dressed in khakis, sweater, and tie, his blond hair still wet and gleaming from the shower. She felt sleep-dazed and frowzy. "Patients? Are you a doctor?"

He smiled. "No. Just a substance-abuse counselor."

"Oh. What time is it?"

"Half past noon. Look, you can stay here as long as you like. I'll be back by six, and we can go get some dinner, if you like."

Suspicion flared in her sleep-deprived mind. "Why?"

"Why what?"

"Why would we . . . I have to go to the hospital." *Fengmo.*

James's face changed from amusement she didn't understand to concern. He sat beside her on the sofa. She smelled soap and James himself, a light spicy scent that dizzied her.

"Soledad, you can't go to the hospital. You'll be identified if you try to get anywhere near Fengmo. In fact, that may be the way the shooter knew who you were last night. . . . Did you see Fengmo earlier yesterday?"

"We had dinner in New York." Which meant she was the reason Fengmo had been hurt.

"Let me stop by the hospital on my way home and check on him for you."

Why? But this time she didn't say it aloud, just nodded. After a moment James stood, touched her lightly on the cheek, and said, "See you at six. Make yourself at home."

Soledad gave him time to reach the street. *I can't stay here. I don't even know this man.* But the strength of her longing to stay frightened her. Slowly, as if going to an execution, she walked into the bathroom. James had set out a boxed toothbrush near the sink, clean towels on the counter, a sweater folded neatly beside the towels with a little sign on it: SOLEDAD: WEAR THIS. She looked at herself in the mirror: eyes puffy from crying, hair wild, clothes rumpled on her stocky body. Fengmo's blood stained the turquoise silk shirt she had worn because he liked the color.

She picked up James's clean sweater. Sky blue, the exact color of his eyes, and cashmere. In Soledad's experience, men did not buy such sweaters for themselves. Some woman had given it to him.

Walking back through the apartment, Soledad was scrupulous. She opened no drawers, examined no closets, did not turn on the computer. She studied only what stood out in plain sight, which wasn't much.

In the bedroom: A bed with inexpensive green cotton bedspread, neatly made. Pine nightstand and matching dresser, topped with a silver brush and comb and a lamp from Sears. The sales tag was still attached to the cord. On the wall, two cheap framed prints of seascapes.

In the living room: The sofa, a plyboard desk with computer, television on a metal stand, one armchair, and a fake leather cube serving as a coffee table. Venetian blinds and two prints of landscapes. No curtains, no wall screen.

Nothing on the kitchen counter except a Braun coffeemaker and an unopened bottle of what looked like very good wine.

Soledad went back to the bathroom and again fingered

James's sweater. The cashmere was thick and soft, maybe even six-ply, with a discreet label she didn't recognize but which suggested a men's store with subdued lighting and British accents. She put the sweater down, buttoned her coat over her bloodstained shirt, and left the apartment.

James didn't live there. Not really, or not yet. Maybe the place had been rented furnished and James's personal things were still in transit from somewhere else. But if not, this was a weekday city dwelling only and James returned on weekends to wherever his real life existed. Soledad knew that well-paid executives sometimes did that, but not substance-abuse counselors. So perhaps someone else owned or leased this apartment, and if so, that woman didn't live there, either.

At the station, Soledad caught the maglev north. Two hours later, she let herself into her front door and called Diane Lovett.

"Soledad! Is everything all right? When you didn't call in this morning I wondered if—"

"I'm fine.

"Turn on visual, please."

Soledad did and Diane's face appeared. Taller and slimmer than Soledad, Diane was a pretty woman trying to appear plain. She wore her rich brown hair in a severe short cut, used no makeup, dressed in loose dark clothing of no particular style. But she hadn't surgically altered her regular features, creamy skin, or huge blue eyes. She would have been a startling beauty except for her lips, which were unusually thin and made thinner by her habit of folding them tightly together when she felt tense. Soledad respected but didn't really like Diane. Their lives had had no paths in common.

"The way you can go isn't the real way"—Fengmo's voice in her head.

Diane said, "Tell me what happened last night."

Soledad told her about Cam's lecture. From Diane's expression, Soledad guessed that none of this information was new to her. Diane said, "And after you left the hospital?"

"I'm here now," Soledad evaded. James was none of Diane's business. "Will you check on Fengmo and get back to me? You can find out things I can't."

"Okay," Diane said, and Soledad heard the usual restrained disappointment that she didn't confide in Diane. Soledad didn't apologize. She confided in no one except Fengmo.

After a long, hot shower, Soledad poured herself a glass of wine and sat with it by the kitchen window, watching dusk gather in the woods that climbed the mountain behind her yard. The moon was the slimmest of crescents, a curved slash of light in the navy blue sky. Although she listened, tonight the owl didn't hoot. At full dark she turned on the computer, fought with herself, and lost. Her e-mail account, set up for her by Diane, went through two remailers and was virtually untraceable. But James's was easy enough to find using his name and street address.

James,
Thank you again. You saved not only Fengmo's life but mine, too, in ways you probably can't understand.
S.

She turned off the computer, drank another glass of wine, and went to bed. As she lay under the blanket, she finally heard the owl outside her window, low and mournful, surely the loneliest sound this side of the grave. The bird, she imagined, was hunting. Soledad slipped farther under her blanket and hoped for sleep.

The next morning, very early, Lucca called. "Soledad! I saw the news—that was your friend among the injured at Cam's lecture, wasn't it? How is he?"

"In a coma." She tried to remember when she had told Lucca about Fengmo. It must have been aboard ship during the voyage out, in that period of cramped and overheated intimacy among her and Lucca and Cam, all three of them taut with excitement over the unknown ahead. Lucca, she sensed, had been choosing between her and Cam. Soledad had wanted to engage his attention, this moody and exotic fellow voyager with the sexy Italian accent. He had chosen Cam, of course, and after that . . . But that was another lifetime.

"I'm so sorry," Lucca said. "The newscasts say Fengmo's condition is uncertain?"

"Yes."

"Soledad, *cara*—why do you continue to go to hear Cam? It's no more than flimsy theatrics. Like Cam herself."

"Maybe," she said neutrally. Lucca was not the philosophical bully that Cam was, but he was just as stubbornly fixated on his own view of what had happened on Kular A. Soledad didn't want to argue with him. Not this morning.

"She's a perfect example of what psychologists call 'situationally acquired narcissism.' I think that by now that woman has confused herself with John the Baptist—if not with Christ himself. Savior and prophet."

"Maybe," Soledad repeated.

This time he caught her reserve and changed the subject. "Do you remember Frank Olenik? He witnessed on Susban A."

"The ex-cop? I didn't interact much with him at the Dome, but I remember him. Why?"

"My government contact is bringing him here to see me this afternoon."

Soledad sat up straighter. Lucca never allowed anyone to visit him, not even the other Witnesses. In fact, she was surprised that he took her calls. But, then, loneliness drove most people to at least some human contact. She'd always had Fengmo.

She said, "And you're seeing Frank why?"

"I'm told he has important information about his own

witnessing which he has told no one before, but which I will want to hear."

"Why would you want to hear it?" None of this made sense.

"Because," Lucca said, and she heard in his voice the very Lucca-like mix of skepticism, intelligence, and permanent underlying anger that he could not acknowledge even to himself, "Frank says his information will change everything."

42: CAM

The morning after the shooting, Cam slept late. She was shocked—ten o'clock! She hadn't slept till ten since before she became a Witness.

Even more shocking, she hadn't dreamed of Aveo or Kular.

Sitting up in the bedroom of her hotel suite, Cam put her head in her hands. No nightmares, but two more people dead because of her, and some Chinese guy in a coma. She'd been told that much late last night, or rather early this morning, by Angie Bernelli, after Cam had finished being interviewed by everybody in the world. The NYPD, reporters, the Agency. It had all gone on for hours.

The two people who'd died, and who'd tried to kill her—were they right this minute standing here in Cam's bedroom before setting out on the second road, screaming at her? *Not yet, I don't want to go, I have kids and a wife and a mission to kill you and all the other false prophets like you who—*

"Ms. O'Kane?"

—are killers themselves, you killed me you killed them all—

"Ms. O'Kane!"

"Oh! Sorry, Jen—what is it?" Her secretary, a scarily intelligent girl supplied by Angie Bernelli, stood diffidently in the bedroom door.

"I'm sorry to disturb you, but you have a visitor. Angie's not here and I didn't know if you'd want him to come up or not—it's J. S. Farrington."

Cam felt her eyes widen. "Really?"

"Yes."

"Buzz him up and give him some coffee or something. I'll be five minutes."

Cam threw on a robe, brushed her teeth, and slashed on lipstick. Good enough—the dreamless sleep had helped her appearance. Automatically—not from design, Farrington must be over sixty—she left the top buttons of her robe undone.

He stood when she entered, which confused her. Should she stay standing now, too? But Angie, who had arrived while Cam primped, stayed seated and so Cam sat, too, and Farrington followed.

"I'm very glad to meet you, Ms. O'Kane."

"Call me Cam." He wasn't handsome—bald and stooped, with ears that stuck out—but he seemed easy to be with, even a bit down-home. He had very small, very bright brown eyes.

" 'Cam,' then. First let me congratulate you on your successful lecture tour and hope that last night's mess isn't going to interrupt it."

"It's not," Cam said, although she hadn't really decided that until this moment.

"What you're doing is important," Farrington said. "I've always believed in life after death, and you're getting the word out in a way that young people can understand. There's something else I've always believed in, and that's space travel, as you probably already know."

"Yes." Why was Angie scowling?

"If humanity doesn't expand out into space, we have no guarantee that our race will continue past any catastrophes to Earth. Man-made catastrophes or otherwise. Now I'm going to come right to the point, Cam. Farrington Tours would like to offer you a free trip back to the moon. That's a two-million-dollar value. But we'll take you gratis if you let us photograph you at Luna Station and outside the Atoner Dome, for our ad campaigns. That'll mean publicity for both of us, and for space exploration. Everybody wins."

Everybody wins. Had Aveo ever described a kulith move in which everybody won? Cam couldn't remember, but she suspected not. *Kulith is a mirror of the mind that produces life, Ostiu Cam.*

Angie, still scowling, said, "Mr. Farrington, there are security risks in your proposal, and after last night—"

"We know that," he said. "But all our employees and guests are screened very carefully, Agent Bernelli, and both Earth Base Alpha and Luna Station have state-of-the-art security. I believe we can guarantee Cam's safety."

"There are no guarantees where security is concerned," Angie said flatly.

"I meant, of course, relatively speaking."

Farrington looked at Cam hopefully, and Angie looked at her disapprovingly. All at once Cam was sick of them both—what was this but more pressure? Or was it the Atoners she was really sick of? Here she was, doing her best to spread their message just as they wanted, and what were they doing? Where was the promised atonement? Or—

—something she barely dared admit to herself—

—was she it? Was this all that the Atoners were going to do about their monstrous crime, just let Cam O'Kane, alone of The Six, spread the word and get shot at while doing it?

"I think," she said carefully, "that I'd like more time to think about your offer, Mr. Farrington."

"All the time you like." But he seemed startled. Obviously he'd expected her to jump at his offer like a hungry dog at meat.

She was getting tired of jumping at bait.

Angie gazed speculatively at her, as if assessing Cam's thoughts. Well, let her. Cam was doing what she had to, what was right, but that didn't mean it was always easy. If Agent Bernelli thought it was, then fuck her.

Later, after Farrington had left and Cam had showered and dressed and they were all preparing to leave for whatever city she was supposed to perform in next, Jen came shyly up to Cam. "There's something I want to say, if it's okay."

"Go ahead," Cam said. Jen was in fact two years older than her but seemed to Cam like a child. Jen had never burned down men with a laser gun, never held a dying friend in her arms, never seen a child spitted like a chicken because it threw a pebble.

Jen blurted, "A year ago I lost my faith in just everything. It was horrible. I didn't want to live. But you've given my faith back to me. Because of your message about the afterlife, I know that God exists, and so I just want to say thank you. Because of you, I know now that absolutely everything that happens, happens for the best."

Cam stared at her. Finally she said, "You're welcome," setting out the words very carefully, as if they were fragile as non-bulletproof glass.

43: E-MAIL

Subject: recent fiasco
Date: February 13, 2021
From: J6
To: D4

what the fuck happened with that stupid raid on cam o'kane and soledad arellano?? i told you dave that we changed direction and are going after the bigger goal!! command is really pissed they say if you can't control your own people better than that then liquidate your cell *NOW*. it better not happen again i mean it and so do they

44: FRANK

The drive from Ohio to Niagara Falls took only five hours. Jim Thompson drove and Frank didn't break the silence between them very often. Jim was waiting for Frank to tell him why he wanted to see Lucca Maduro, and Frank wasn't going to tell. Eventually Jim snapped on the radio and they listened to a succession of country-and-western stations, each swelling, sustaining, and then fading out, like flowers. Or lives.

Frank wondered if Sara Dziwalski liked flowers. Probably, most women did, but what kind? She wasn't a roses kind of girl—roses were too dressy, too formal. Maybe daisies, or those little purple things that smelled so good. How much would it cost to wire flowers to Texas? Maybe he could—

"This is it," Jim said, his first words in two hours. Frank saw the blue gleam of a bridge rise above the jumble of buildings and trees of some sort of park. "You want to see Niagara Falls, as long as we're here?"

"Nah," Frank said. Although he'd never seen the Falls, he had more important things on his mind. Jim should, too—why did he want to tour Niagara Falls? It must be one more attempt to soften Frank up, get him to spill his information. Nuts to that.

"Okay." Jim disappeared into a low building. Ten minutes later, they drove across the border into Canada. Frank had no trouble spotting the car trailing them, but he felt no rancor about it. Guys were just doing their job.

They drove up the Queen Elizabeth Highway toward

Toronto but then veered north. Frank wasn't sure what he expected, but when Jim stopped the car it wasn't what actually lay in front of him. No concrete barriers, no foot patrols, nothing like the fortress he expected. Just a high adobe wall with an iron gate set into it and a single, bored guard.

Jim caught Frank's expression and grinned. "Oh, he's got it, all right. The security. It's just the hidden, state-of-the-art kind that doesn't annoy the neighbors."

The guard shot his and Jim's retinas, which annoyed Frank—how did Lucca, a private citizen, get Frank's bio-info? It must be some arrangement between their governments. Frank and Jim walked through three separate detector frames—metal, explosives, and what?—and left the car behind at the gate.

Walking up the drive, Frank said a quick prayer. He still didn't see much security, but he believed Jim that it was there. Patches of snow dotted the dormant lawn. The house was large but not really rich looking. A servant let them in, and Frank revised his opinion. He stood in a foyer built of materials he couldn't recognize but which looked expensive. Creamy white stone floor, walls such a deep, rich red that it couldn't be just paint, weird crumbling statues in niches, and a huge bouquet of fresh flowers on a fancy table that looked hundreds of years old.

"This way, please," the servant said, and Frank disliked him for his accent, his uniform, his chilly courtesy. He led them to a small room lined with books where Lucca Maduro, dressed in jeans and sweater, sat in a leather chair next to a real fire.

Maduro rose, shook hands, asked about their trip. It was the same as with the servant: chilly and polite. "Would you like some wine? I can offer you a very good Sangiovese from our own vineyard."

Frank said, "Can I have a beer?"

"Certainly. Jim?"

Frank blurted, "Jim isn't going to sit with us. He's agreed that I can talk to you alone."

"Fine," Lucca said, unsurprised, "but he can still have some wine, yes?"

"I'm driving," Jim said with his easy smile, "but some coffee would be great."

The servant brought drinks and led Jim away, and Lucca and Frank settled into the leather chairs. Frank, more and more uncomfortable, wanted to get the whole thing over. He didn't belong here. Cradling his thick glass stein between his hands, he plunged in.

"Lucca, I'm here to tell you something and to make you a proposition."

"Go ahead," Lucca said. His face gave away nothing.

"Do I have your word that you won't tell anybody what I'm about to tell you?"

"No. If what you're about to tell me is some sort of crime, or if it endangers anybody, I would feel bound to tell."

Holier-than-thou prick. But Frank needed Lucca's help.

"I don't know if it's a crime but—"

"You're an ex–police officer and you don't know if you committed a crime?"

Frank drank off his beer with one long chug and tried to hold on to his temper. "If I have, it's only the crime of withholding information from my government, which has nothing to do with you since it isn't *your* government. And it doesn't endanger anybody."

Was that true? He couldn't tell anymore. But surely not doing this would endanger a lot more souls. That thought, plus the beer going golden in his veins, steadied him.

"If those two conditions prove to be true, then I give you my word to tell no one."

"Okay. Then here it is." Frank leaned forward, clutching his empty stein. "When I witnessed on Susban A, I took something from a native. A lock of hair. When we walked from the shuttle to the 'Tonie base on the moon, before we reached decon, I hid the packet of hair under a boulder while I was choosing my souvenir rocks. The hair has a lot of follicle, with DNA."

Lucca looked stunned.

"You're rich. I want you to send me to the moon on that Farrington tourist shuttle. It costs two million dollars to go and they take you to see the Atoner Dome from the outside. I'm going to retrieve that hair and donate the genes to a biotech company so they can put them back into humans."

Lucca still stared as if he'd seen a ghost. *The ghosts he didn't even believe in,* Frank thought, and felt a petty satisfaction in having impressed this jet-setter. A long moment passed.

Finally Lucca gasped, "Why?"

"Why did I do it? Because those genes were ours. Humanity's. The 'Tonies had no right to take them from us, and it sure doesn't look like they're willing to put them back."

"But why do *you* want to restore them?"

Frank frowned. The guy wasn't getting it. "They're *ours.*"

"Not for ten thousand years!"

"Maybe not. But God put them there in the first place, and He wanted us to have them. He wanted us to be able to see our dead for a little while so we'd all experience directly His infinite mercy in providing life after death. It was a gift to aid faith, and it was taken from us."

Lucca got up and poured himself another glass of wine. It shook in his hands.

Frank said, "I know you don't believe in God or Heaven or anything. Your loss. But look at it this way: You think this is all just telepathy, and here's your chance to prove it. If I'm wrong and you're right, then after scientists put the genes back, kids will grow up telepathic and everybody will buy your version." Except that Lucca's version was wrong.

Lucca sat in his chair and stared at the fire, not drinking his wine. "I don't think you've thought this through, Frank. If you succeed in getting to the moon, the tourist agency would never allow you to go EVA. If you did, the government would discover your . . . your packet of hair and take it away from you. If they didn't, you would never be able to just hand it over to some biotech agency—those companies are under constant and intense scrutiny from your FDA, and they must go through fully documented clinical trials, and they're not allowed to experiment with germ-line cells anyway."

Frank didn't know what "germ-line cells" were—he wasn't talking about *diseases,* for God's sake. His anger returned. "Are you saying you won't help me?"

"I won't help you."

"But your—"

"You are the victim of what Freud called 'the universal obsessional neurosis'—religion. You propose to deepen this obsession among people who will believe anything. Even if I thought your insane plan had a chance of succeeding, I wouldn't help you. Have you considered for one moment the chaos that would result on Earth from reintroducing a telepathy gene to a planet—"

"It's not a telepathy gene!"

"—already groaning under the weight of seven billion people? We're already poised on the edge of war and drastic climate change and bankruptcy of—"

Frank jumped to his feet. With all his strength, he threw his beer stein into the fireplace, where it shattered. "But you're not 'poised on the edge of bankruptcy,' are you, Maduro? You've got all the money in the world, but you're too selfish to use it to help anybody else!"

Frank's rant stopped Lucca's. He stared at Frank, bleakly but also with a condescension that made Frank want to throw something else. "You have no idea whom I help or do not help, Olenik. But not this. Never this. Now I think you'd better leave."

"Gladly!" But just before yanking open the door, Frank turned. "You promised me you wouldn't tell anybody what I said."

"Yes. I promised."

"You going to keep that promise?"

"Yes."

Frank saw that Lucca was agreeing so easily because he thought Frank could never bring off his plan. That made Frank even madder. He would show Lucca. Frank could do this—*had* to do this, because it was God's work—and then rich-boy Maduro would be talking out of the other side of his fucking mouth.

Frank slammed the door behind him and went to find Jim Thompson.

Back home, Frank answered none of his parents' questions and locked himself in his room. On his computer he checked what the other Witnesses' moon rocks had gone for on eBay and got a nasty shock. The price ranged from $10,000 to $25,000. That was all; since the tourist shuttle, moon rocks were just not that special. Even people who didn't have them knew they *could* get some—the shuttle base on Luna had a gift shop. The most Frank could raise on his rocks was probably no more than sixty or seventy thousand bucks.

He got down on his knees beside his bed and bowed his head. The position felt a little peculiar; Frank had prayed sitting or standing since he turned ten. But this was a big request.

"Dear God, please help me do Your work. Guide me to the right way to get the money to set right what the aliens screwed up, and I screwed up after them. I'm willing to put myself completely in Your service. Please guide me through Your son Jesus Christ, most holy redeemer."

He waited, but nothing occurred to him.

God would help him when He was good and ready. Frank could wait. That was faith.

Meanwhile, he went back to the computer. He Googled a florist in Austin, Texas, and sent Sara Dziwalski a pretty, not-too-expensive bunch of daisies.

Atoner Attack™

**They have the dead on their side–
but you have F-weapons and Cal O'Cave.**

The best new d-vid game in five years—the
graphics will snake your mind.
                    —Dov Miller, World Champion, MLG

In Full-Dimension Holo

On sale everywhere March 1.

46: SOLEDAD

The morning after she'd e-mailed James, Soledad postponed turning on her computer. She drank three cups of coffee, listening for the owl by the window. She showered, dressed, read a biography of John Coltrane. At a decent hour she called Diane, who had just spoken to the hospital and reported that there was no change in Fengmo's condition. Soledad cooked a paella, an elaborate production that forced her to concentrate on chopping peppers and onions and garlic.

There was no reason James should even answer her ill-judged e-mail. Helping her and Fengmo had been merely the kindness of a stranger, upon which Soledad was determined not to depend. Experience had taught her how that usually turned out. As she chopped, Soledad cataloged James's possible responses to her leaving his apartment and then e-mailing him. Long ago she'd named these responses after other men she'd been involved with. You made an overture that made them feel crowded—and with some men, *anything* made them feel crowded—and you could count on one of four responses:

"The Wayne," which was total silence. Gone. Disappeared.

"The Eric," which was a short, distancing response (*Really busy at work; be well*), followed by silence.

"The Martin," which was defensive. (*As I told you, I've had a lot on my mind lately. I know I said I'd call, but my job is in jeopardy and my dog died and I have a hangnail.*)

And "the José," which was a counter-attack. (*Are you one of those women who assume too much after three nights? Lighten up, babe.*)

Fuck it. Get it over with.

Her hands still smelling of garlic, Soledad punched savagely at her handheld and brought up her e-mail.

S.,
Where did you go? I rushed home early, but you'd left, apparently without changing or eating anything. Are you all right? I'm very concerned. Can I see you again? Please give me your phone number, or call me at 212-555-3644, or *at least* answer this e-mail. If I did something to offend you, I want so much to make it right.
James

She couldn't. She just couldn't. No, he wasn't Wayne or Eric or Martin or José, but he wasn't for her, either. She was in hiding after death threats and one attempt to shoot her, and he was a gorgeous Viking look-alike whose apartment didn't match his story. To get involved with him, to even see him again, would be stupid. Diane, if she knew, would have a fit. Soledad could hear Diane now: *You ask for all the trappings of the Witness Protection Program, right up to plastic surgery, and then you take on a security risk like this?* And Diane would be right.

But Soledad was so lonely.

There were worse things than loneliness.

She washed her hands, wiped the garlic off the handheld, and keyed the wall screen to a newscast. No ditsy avatar this time, a real newscast. She listened to a talking head rehashing, for the thousandth time, the fact that the Atoners had not left the moon but had said nothing, nothing whatsoever, to humanity ever since the twenty Witnesses returned to Earth. Were the aliens still even there? Maybe they had left the moon by some means undetectable to every monitoring nation on the globe. Maybe they had, under their opaque and featureless Dome, dissolved into powdery molecules or into some unknown form of energy. Maybe they were indeed remote-controlled machines and had been turned off or turned themselves off. Maybe— Soledad changed news sites.

She watched the funeral of Emma Jane Taymor, the daughter of the vice president who had killed herself in order to arrive sooner at her teenage version of Heaven. As the screen ran clips of the girl—smiling at the Inauguration a month ago, scoring a soccer goal two years ago, climbing on her mother's lap ten years ago—Soledad silently addressed Emma Jane:

Was this suicide the end of you? Or are you somewhere on the second road?

And is it partly my fault?

She kept the newscasts off the rest of the day. Outside, a cold, steady rain fell. In the late afternoon, after Lucca must have had his meeting with Frank Olenik, Soledad called him. Lucca was uncharacteristically short with her.

"Frank wanted money, that was all."

"Money? For . . . for what?" Money embarrassed Soledad, as it did so many people who'd never had any. Once she'd found out how rich Lucca was, she'd castigated herself for even imagining they might have come together on the voyage to Kular.

"For some ridiculous scheme not even worth discussing. How is your friend, Fengmo?"

"The same." She felt the tears prick her eyelids and pushed them back.

"Is he getting good care? I know your Universal Health is very new and there are gaps in what is done. . . . If you need money for him, *cara,* you have only to ask."

But she never would. Did Lucca know that? And why was he so generous with her and so contemptuous of Frank's request for money? Was it precisely because Lucca knew she would never ask?

If she kept thinking like that, she would end up as cynical as he was.

"Thanks, but Fengmo is getting very good care. Diane—my government contact—checked it out for me. How are you doing?"

"The same. I watch the newscasts and despair. This stupidity about life after death—you would think that we've learned nothing since the Middle Ages. We can only hope that the media circus dies down soon. Although I don't see how that will happen, with Cam fanning those flames."

"Ummm," Soledad said neutrally. All at once she wanted to end the conversation, without knowing why.

Yet after she and Lucca had said good-bye, she was restless again. Three times she walked toward the handheld on the kitchen table, and three times she walked into the other room. God, she was pitiful. Hours later, as she sat reading, trying to interest herself in Coltrane's stint at the Five Spot Café, the phone rang again and her heart froze.

But of course James couldn't have gotten this number. The screen ID'd Diane. When the agent's face came onscreen, it was backed by an unfamiliar living room that must be Diane's own. Usually she kept her private and work lives separate, but now Soledad saw a rocking horse on the carpet and an orange cat on the back of a sofa. Soledad's stomach twisted. With no preliminaries Diane said, "Have you heard?"

"Heard what?"

"Sara Dziwalski was murdered an hour ago."

Soledad stared blindly at the rainy dark outside the kitchen window.

"Soledad?"

"I'm here."

"She was at the medical center working an evening shift. A suicide bomber—"

"CCAD?" Fengmo, Sara, attempts on Cam and on Soledad herself—

"No. The bomber was a woman whose son was a member of Why Wait? and hung himself yesterday. A copycat act after Emma Taymor. The mother blew up Sara and herself and three other people. As if *that* would bring back her son."

Soledad heard Diane's anger, the anger of a good person helpless to stop madness. Soledad felt too stunned for anger.

Diane said, "You're still safe, of course, nobody knows where you are. The Agency tried so hard to persuade Sara to . . . well. Just sit tight and stay home for now."

"I'm not going anywhere."

"Good. Did you know her well?"

"No," Soledad said, as always cutting off sympathy, pity, anything weakening. "Thanks, Diane. Bye."

She turned on a newscast and there it was, the whole bloody and monstrous scene caught on a Seton Medical Center security cam in Austin, as well as on somebody's handheld. Soledad watched until she couldn't stand it anymore, until the darkness outside her drawn curtains was as thick in her lighted living room as if she stood in the cold woods. When the owl hooted, she jumped and cried out.

She perceived that she had reached some sort of limit. Fengmo, Sara, Emma Jane, the incessant loneliness of her own chosen isolation—why had she ever thought that going to the stars would test her? Going to the stars had been for her—the insulated passenger in orbit—all too easy. *This* was hard, this constant hammering by her own kind on her own planet. Nobody should have to stand such hammering alone. Nobody could. And she no longer had Fengmo.

The phone rang, drowning out the owl. Lucca again, probably with the news about Sara. But Lucca, choosing his own isolation, couldn't help, couldn't hold her or stroke her or provide any of the only comfort she craved: warm human touch. It wasn't Lucca she wanted.

Soledad lifted the phone receiver two inches, set it down, lifted it again. She turned off the visual and called Manhattan.

"James, this is Soledad. . . . Yes, I heard. . . . No, I . . . *Please, stop.* Just listen. Please. If I tell you how to get to my house by train, will you come? Right away? Now?"

47: FRANK

The bastards had murdered her.

Not that poor demented mother, although she had detonated the actual bomb. Probably deranged with grief over her son. Emotionally worked-up people were dangerous—just ask any cop who ever responded to a domestic disturbance—and there were other deranged groups out there, like the CCAD, who were clear enemies. When you have a clear enemy in your sights, you don't send civilians out unarmed onto the battlefield. The government should have protected Sara. There should have been cops, FBI agents, Secret Service—whatever it took. But *no*. The protection went to senators and congressmen and mayors and even to criminals in jail, who got secure cells if they might get offed on government territory and cause a public stink. But no protection for an honest and helpless woman like Sara Dziwalski, who had just been trying to nurse sick people. "No direct death threats indicating this specific target," the law-enforcement agencies always said, covering their asses. But anybody with an IQ above the speed limit knew that the spirit of the law was being violated even while the letter was being followed. Frank was ashamed of the profession he'd once wanted to join.

He cut Sara's picture out of a flimsy, maneuvering the scissors with exaggerated care, and put it in a frame he'd bought at the drugstore. His mother called him to come down to lunch, but, for the first time ever, Frank ignored her. Judy Olenik didn't insist.

Frank didn't even know if his daisies had been delivered to Sara before she died.

He set the picture on his desk and opened his closet. The nine-millimeter Glock was where he'd left it, on the highest shelf behind a heavy box, where his little sister couldn't find it. Not that Darla ever went into his room. In his family, they were taught a decent respect for other people.

The government bastards had murdered Sara.

The phone rang and his mother called upstairs, "Frank, it's for you."

"Hello."

"Jim Thompson here. Listen, I want to say how sorry I am about Sara. She was a great girl. And also to—"

"Don't call me ever again." Frank hung up.

He loaded the gun and stuck it in his belt. Any whacko who tried to take out Frank Olenik was going to meet with more response than Sara had been able to mount. But that was periphery. The central thing was to do what he was required to do. Now, more than ever, it was necessary. Now, he was somehow doing it for Sara as well as for God.

He looked again at her picture. So young, so pretty. But they would meet again. She would pass through the last door, if she hadn't already, and Frank had no doubt that God intended someone like her for Heaven. Frank would do his best to get there, too. In fact, that was what he was doing right now, even if it involved some things he didn't want to do. Saint Peter, Saint Paul, even Christ, all had to do things they probably didn't want to. But they'd done them.

He picked up the phone and dialed Cam O'Kane in New York City.

This time the reporters, a mob of them again, had the backyard covered, too. Probably they wanted a reaction to Sara's death. Frank had Darla open the garage door while he sat ready on his Harley. He tore across the lawn and

into the street before any of the jackals could do more
than shout at him, and by the time they got in their cars he
was seven streets away. Of course, they could track him
with a helicopter, but he wasn't a big enough story for that.
Cam's reaction might be big enough, and maybe that was
why he hadn't been able to reach her by phone. No matter.
This would have required a meeting anyway.

At Mike Renfrew Toyota, he stashed the Harley and
Mike let him have a '17 minivan with 55,000 miles on it
and dealer's plates, no questions asked. Mike gripped his
hand when he handed Frank the keys. It paid to know who
your true friends were. In less than half an hour after leaving home, he was on the interstate toward New York.

"Tell her it's Frank Olenik and it's important." He hadn't
wanted to give his name, and for the last hour of phone
calls from the Manhattan pay phone he hadn't. But that
had gotten him nowhere. Now it was dark and he was
hungry and cold, and even with his cap pulled low there
was a chance that one of the people hurrying past might
somehow recognize him. Reporters came and went two
streets over, in front of the fancy hotel where Cam stayed.
Jackals.

"Frank Olenik, the Atoner Witness?" The polished
voice on the other end of the line held disbelief and a trace
of contempt.

"That's what I said, and if you don't tell her I called,
she'll chew you into little pieces." Frank had no idea if
this was true or not. How would he know how somebody
like Cam dealt with an entourage?

"I'll give Miss O'Kane your message," the snotty voice
said. "Please hold."

He did, blowing on his gloveless hands, tasting the sour
scum on his teeth. Eventually the voice returned, still
snotty. "Miss O'Kane would like some verification of
your identity. What can you tell her that might do that,
'Mr. Olenik'?"

He clenched the fist not holding the phone and spoke very carefully, very slowly, as if to a five-year-old. "Tell her that Lucca Maduro has a mole on his back." Frank had once overheard Cam tell that to Amira Gupta, and even then he'd wondered why a snobby guy like Maduro would get naked with someone as trashy as Cam. But some men would have sex with anything.

A few moments later Cam came on the line. "Frank! Is that really you? Where are you?"

"At Columbus Circle." There had been a street sign. "I need to talk to you about something, but I don't think I can get past your bulldogs."

"Talk? To me?" She sounded surprised; he'd never talked to her before.

"Yes. It's important. Tell them to let me through. And tell them to let me bring my gun in. I have an Ohio permit to carry."

"Okay! Sure!" Now he recognized the note of hysteria and inwardly sighed.

He left the minivan parked on the street and walked to her building. A man met him on the corner: big, unsmiling, undoubtedly packing. Private security, Frank guessed, and hoped it wasn't some rinky-dink square badge who was more show than brains and training. People peered at Frank and then started shoving questions and cameras in his face, but the big man hurried him into the lobby and shut the door behind him. Hotel types watched while Frank was patted down, while his piece and permit were inspected, while he was walked through the detectors. All reassuring. Good procedure.

"Frank!" Upstairs, Cam hugged him like it had been him and not Lucca who'd had the bad judgment to do her. Frank untangled himself and looked around.

The hotel suite reminded him of Lucca's place in Toronto. Big, rich looking, but not homey. Except that Lucca's place somehow looked like him and nothing here looked like Cam, not even the colors. Quiet grays and blues. The room was full of people watching him sideways. A huge screen shot news into the room like arrows, and several handhelds played avatars or newscasts, making a low constant undertone like surf breaking. He said, "Where can we talk privately?"

"Follow me." She flounced into a bedroom and closed the door behind them. Frank didn't like the intimacy of that, made worse by Cam's low-cut top—she had great breasts, he'd give her that—but it would have to do.

"You make sure this place isn't bugged?"

Her eyes got wider. "Who would bug me?"

He sighed, led her into the bathroom, and turned on the shower and water taps. About as primitive as you could get, but the government and the big corporations had stuff that could override any jammer Frank could obtain. He pulled Cam close to him, put his mouth to her ear, and was surprised when she pulled away, flushing.

"I'm sorry," she said. "It's just that someone else . . . We spoke like that on Kular. . . . I . . . I'm sorry." The hysterical note was back in her voice.

He put on the respectful, calming-down voice and body language he'd learned at the Academy. "I understand. I'm just going to move closer again. . . . Is that okay? I won't touch you."

She nodded, grimacing like she knew how ridiculous she looked. Again Frank put his mouth to her ear.

"I have to tell you something big. Try not to react, Cam, and *don't say anything out loud*. Nothing at all. I need your help. Sara died and Soledad's friend was shot because neither the Atoners nor the government care about what's really right. The government screwed Sara by not protecting her and they screwed me out of my career because the whole system is corrupt. The Atoners screwed you by just sitting up there on the moon and not doing anything to atone or to help your lectures. So *we* have to help ourselves to get back what God wanted us to have in the first place. Nobody else is helping us. You with me so far?"

She nodded slightly. Frank had rehearsed this speech during the long drive to New York, drinking Energodas and forcing himself to not clutch the steering wheel. Now he readied himself to either grab her closer or put a hand over her mouth if she blurted anything. A carefully gentle hand.

"On Susban A I took a packet of hair with DNA in the follicles. I hid it on the moon—no, Cam, steady now—before we all went to decon. It's still there. I need money to go up there on Farrington Tours, get it back, and give it to some biotech company that can get back into human beings the genes God wanted us to have. You can pay for that trip."

She took a step backward, looking dazed, and he put a finger to his lips. For a long moment he wasn't sure of her—her face was a perfect blank. An undercurrent of petty satisfaction rippled through him: He'd made Cam O'Kane shut up.

Then she said, "Yes! Oh, yes!" looking like Christmas morning. She grabbed him and kissed him full on the lips. Frank's cock rose of its own accord. But that didn't mean anything, it never did. He pushed her away gently, not wanting to offend her, but she didn't seem to mind. She whirled away from him like those spinning tops he'd had as a kid, and he steeled himself to stand his new, completely unreliable, rich silent partner.

Only she didn't plan on staying silent. That was the first shock.

"I'm going, too," she whispered into his ear in the dark. Cam had insisted on his staying at her hotel, and since the alternative was Mike Renfrew's van or some cheap hotel he didn't know how to find in Manhattan, Frank had agreed. She'd sent down to room service for a steak dinner, which he'd wolfed down. Cam introduced Frank to everybody cluttering up her suite and he'd kept his face empty as he memorized them. A "lecture manager," a secretary, a federal agent, a woman described as "personal staff," two lawyers, and the bodyguard. Everybody had left halfway through the evening, although Frank would bet his Glock that the bodyguard and the agent weren't far away, nor unconnected electronically.

He went to sleep in a small second bedroom off hers, removing only his jeans and shoes. Rare for him, he had dreamed about Susban A. The high rose-and-cream towers pierced the purple-blue sky, the women in filmy pants walked the wide streets, and every square held its elaborate dead house where spirits that had not yet passed through the last door gathered to talk to each other and to the friends and relatives who visited daily. In his dream, Frank could see the dead as well as the natives could, still laughing and scheming and advising on the elaborate political plots that controlled the city. Sara, decently dressed, walked toward him, smiling and holding out hands full of the huge, fragrant blossoms that grew everywhere, and—

"Frank!"

—she said in her sweet and feminine voice—

"Frank!" Cam stood by his bed, silhouetted in the light from the open doorway. "I have to talk to you!"

Damn her. "Okay. Your bathroom. Give me a minute."

She left, closing the door behind her, which let him pull on his pants in privacy. He took his gun from under his pillow, followed her to the bathroom, and turned on all the water. Cam wore a red silk bathrobe with dragons on it, gaudy but fairly modest. She put her mouth to his ear.

"I was so surprised by what you said earlier that I can't remember if I said that of course I'm going with you."

"No. You're not. You can't."

"What do you mean?" A new note in her voice, a Cam he hadn't met before. But he had prepared.

"It's two million dollars a pop. How could you afford to pay for both of us? The—"

"Do you really think I could have paid for even one of us?" she said dryly.

That stopped him for a minute. "This hotel . . . all that 'staff'—"

"Takes everything I make. I don't have two million dollars, let alone four, but I can arrange it."

"How—"

"I got it covered." She pulled away and stared at him, surrounded by running water.

Frank had a sudden, stomach-dropping feeling that he'd miscalculated somewhere. The last thing he wanted was Cam O'Kane with him on the moon. He needed to think of a way to ease her out of going, a way that wouldn't make her shut down the whole project. To stall, he said, "We'll talk about it in the morning. But either way, you *did* promise to fund me going. For humanity, and for God."

She jerked away from him then, her eyes colder than he would have imagined her capable of. She spoke at her normal volume. "I don't believe in God, Frank, and I never said I did. If you'd seen what I have, you wouldn't believe in Him, either. That's not what you and I agreed on."

As long as she did agree. He nodded, keeping his face calm, and abruptly she left the bathroom.

He had to pass through her bedroom to get back to his own. She already lay on her bed, still in the red silk robe, her face turned to the wall. But something in the stillness of the lush figure gave Frank pause. He had the unpleasant feeling that this issue of who was going to Luna Station wasn't any longer in his control.

If it ever had been in the first place.

48: FOCUS GROUP REPORT

Prepared for Carruthers Memorial Park, Beaton, CA,
by J. L. Salazar Marketing, Inc.

SUMMARY

Methodology

Five focus groups were held, each with twelve randomly chosen participants in their fifties, sixties, and seventies. Subjects were shown a six-minute video. The first three minutes consisted of public statements of The Six concerning the afterlife, paired with computer-generated images of "the second road," "the golden ladder," "the last door," etc. The second three minutes consisted of a simple narrative paired with computer-generated images of a newly dead "soul" standing in a hospice, listening to loved ones' comments, and witnessing burial. Every effort was made to keep all of these positive, i.e., "I know he's in a better place now," "She's still right here beside me even if I can't see her," "I know we'll all be together again someday." After the video, participants were shown pictures of four different memorial-park arrangements:

- Traditional grave and headstone
- Traditional mausoleum
- "Transition Patio," a 6'×8' enclosure within a picket
  fence and including the grave, two stone benches for

"your loved one's ease—and yours as you sit beside her presence while she prepares for the journey onward"

- "Transition House," a $10' \times 12'$ roofed and heated structure with two chairs and a comfortable bunk "to visit in privacy with your loved one as she prepares for the next stage of the final journey"

Findings

42% of participants said that they would "strongly consider" the Transition Patio as a memorial-park option, if it were available. 6% chose the Transition House, 5% the traditional mausoleum, and 47% the traditional plot and headstone (see attached chart for breakdown by age, sex, and economic self-rating).

Recommendations

There is a significant marketing opportunity here for Carruthers to develop Transitional Patio offerings. See attached list of specific recommendations and marketing strategies.

49: SOLEDAD

Soledad lay beside the sleeping James. Her bedroom in the little Catskills house was still dark, but she'd put in a low-wattage night-light just so she could have the pleasure of seeing him every time she woke in the night. Now he lay on his side, curled toward her, his bare chest rising slightly with every soft breath. His hair fell onto his forehead. His long eyelashes fluttered in REM sleep. One hand lay over Soledad's arm.

Surely it must be wrong to be this happy.

Sara Dziwalski was dead, Fengmo lay still unconscious in the hospital, the Atoners maintained their perverse silence on the moon. But the CCAD had committed no atrocities for the last month, not since the night of Cam's performance. The Why Wait? Society seemed quiescent. And here, last night and many other nights, lay James.

Soledad slipped her arm from under James's hand and turned to see the glowing clock. Five A.M. Carefully she eased off the bed and groped her way to the kitchen. She was incurably awake, but James could sleep another half hour. He had to catch the 6:17 maglev in order to be at work in Manhattan at 8:30. He made this commute many nights, and at the end of April would make it all nights when he moved in with Soledad.

His bare Manhattan apartment, a furnished sublet, had been bare because James had just arrived from California a month ago, to take the job as a substance-abuse counselor with the New York City Health Department. His own furniture and most of his belongings were still in storage in California. The expensive blue cashmere sweater had been a gift from his mother, who "had great taste." Soledad had almost allowed her suspicious nature to deny her this present, unexpected, almost unbelievable happiness.

She put on the coffee and turned on a newscast, very low. When she was sure that nothing too horrible had happened overnight, she changed the screen to obituaries.com and keyed in "Manhattan." Sipping her coffee, she read each one slowly, keeping one eye toward the bedroom. This new habit wasn't something she was ready to share with James.

> Alcozer, Jane Elizabeth, Staten Island, March 24, 2021. Survived by her son, Daniel (Jennifer) Alcozer; daughter Cynthia (Eric) Carmel; daughter Mary Alcozer; 7 grandchildren; 2 great-grandchildren; brother, Donald Hogel. Memorial service Saturday, March 27, 1:00, at Newbury Funeral Home, 274 West End Avenue. Friends may contribute to the Alzheimer's Association.

> Amanti, Angela, March 25, 2021, age 9. Friends are invited to a Mass of Christian Burial, 9:30 A.M., Friday, March 26, Blessed Sacrament Church, 152 W. 71st Street.

Jane Elizabeth Alcozer, an old lady with a long life and large family, and little Angela Amanti, prematurely dead of some terrible disease, accident, or act of violence. *Are you standing together on the second road? Or are you merely rotting corpses, awaiting cremation or burial?*

"What are you doing?" James said behind her, and she jumped.

"Nothing!"

"Really?" He studied the screen. "Soledad, sweetheart . . ."

"I wish I knew. One way or the other. James, it *matters*."

"Of course it does." He pulled her from the chair and took her in his arms. She breathed in his frowzy early-morning smell and felt her heart speed up. "Nothing could matter more."

"You understand."

"I do. Of course I do. But you won't find any answers in the obituaries."

"I know. But they could be here . . . right beside us . . . this very minute. Maybe."

"Well, if they are, they don't need coffee as much as I do." He let her go and Soledad felt the small, stupid, dangerous desolation she always did when he moved away from her, even if it was just across the room. *Be careful, be cautious, don't care too much,* went all the alarms in her head, all her past experience, but she couldn't help it.

"Lucca said something to me once. He said that once a person had had an experience, it was impossible for inner life to go forward as if it hadn't occurred. That everything that happens marks us."

"Not especially profound," James said. He often got an odd tone when she mentioned Lucca. Why was that? Maybe—this scarcely seemed possible, not over her— James was slightly jealous?

"When will you be home for dinner?"

"Oh, not tonight— Didn't I tell you? I'm sorry. There's a work thing I have to go to, and it'll be easier to stay at the apartment. I can box up the last of my things to ship here, too." He drank off half his coffee at one draught.

Was that the truth? Immediately Soledad hated herself. She had no reason not to trust James. He commuted two hours each way two or three nights a week; he spent every weekend here; he was moving in. He willingly spent nearly all their time together inside her small house, for her safety, without any signs of restlessness or boredom. She would not let her suspicious nature destroy this relationship, as it had destroyed her affairs with José and Wayne. She would *not*.

She said lightly, "Then I'll see you tomorrow night."

"Count on it." He embraced her again and she rested her head on his shoulder. *This, only this, if I can just keep this forever . . .* Outside the kitchen window, the eastern horizon began to pale.

"Listen," Soledad said, "did you hear that soft hooting? We have an owl living close by."

"What?"

"Listen . . . that. An owl."

James laughed. "Sweetheart, that's not an owl."

"It's not?"

"You're such a city girl. No, it's not an owl—it's a mourning dove. Light gray-brown with black spots on their wings, and when they mate, they preen each other's feathers." Ostentatiously he stroked her hair, and she laughed.

A dove. Not an owl.

But when he'd gone, still laughing, to the shower, she wondered. Hadn't James told her that he, like she, had lived his whole life in cities?

At dawn the sun broke gloriously over the mountains. Soledad decided to take a walk in the woods; maybe she could see the morning dove. Curious that it was called that when most often she heard it at dusk.

A walk in the woods—any woods—was a more foreign activity than the voyage to Kular in an alien spaceship. The voyage had involved cramped quarters, emotional complications, unknown dangers, technology she used without understanding it—all features of life in Manhattan. But a woods was genuinely strange to her.

She made her way gingerly between the first trees, glancing back often. The ground here rose steeply between tall pines. Soledad was surprised to see that the pine branches didn't start growing from the trunk until five or six feet off the ground, and that the lower ones were sparse and brown needled. This was good because it made it easy to walk among them, and because she could see for a fair distance all around her, including back down to her little rented house. She was proud of herself for figuring out that the lower branches must die when the growing upper ones blocked the sunlight.

And how good the trees smelled! The trees, the air, the rich loamy smell of dead leaves choking the tiny creek in a ravine to her right. Why hadn't she done this before? She was going to be a country girl now. Maybe she'd get a dog to take on walks in the woods; James said he liked dogs. A Labrador or a golden retriever. It must be over fifty degrees out, a gorgeous spring day, and, yes, that was a chipmunk darting across her path. Much cuter than city squirrels, it raced up a pine trunk as Soledad tipped back her head both to watch it and for the sheer pleasure of sunlight striking her face through a gap in the pines.

Something metallic glinted halfway up the chipmunk's tree.

She squinted but couldn't see anything more than a persistent glint. She might have just shrugged—didn't chipmunks carry shiny trinkets to their nests, or was that some other animal she'd read about?—except that this was one of the few pines with sturdy branches within three feet of the ground. Coincidence?

She hoisted her foot onto the bottom branch, grasped the one above it, and pulled herself up. Stocky, she was nonetheless strong, and by staying close to the trunk she managed to climb without sending herself crashing to the ground. Panting, she reached her goal. Her house lay in a clear line of sight to the south.

The bark had been stripped partway off the tree and then replaced to hide a dark metal box. But something had chewed part of the flap of bark that was supposed to act as a concealer—were there animals that ate bark? Soledad didn't know. She pulled the box, a cube no more than three inches on a side, free from the pine and scrubbed resin off the tiny raised writing on the bottom.

EVERKNOW SURVEILLANCE 66387-J-89

Carefully Soledad lowered herself back down the quivering branches, dropping the last three feet to release a cloud of fragrance from the needles below. No one was in sight. She started to run, tripped on a tree root, picked herself up. She had to reach the house, had to call Diane. If this was government surveillance, Soledad sure the hell should have been told about it. If it wasn't . . .

She ran faster.

50: CAM

The dream about Aveo came again. The old man stood bare chested in his rough brown skirt, but the flesh drooped in gobbets from his bones and the bones gleamed like knives, glossy and sharp. Aveo smiled at her with blackened lips over rotted teeth, a smile like Satan himself. He held something out to her, and rasped, "You must play kulith better than that, *ostiu,* or else . . ." She cried out and woke.

Why now? Now, when things were supposed to be getting better? She was going to the moon with Frank, it had all been arranged with J. S. Farrington. She and Frank were going to get the seeing-the-dead genes put right back into human beings. Scientists would add them to people or to embryos or something. . . . Cam wasn't exactly sure how that might work. But scientists would know, and they would do it, and it would show everyone that the afterlife was real and so they could stop killing each other over that controversy. And then Aveo would stay out of Cam's dreams.

Three A.M. She put her hands up over her face.

This was so much harder than anyone knew, even Angie Bernelli. The constant performing, the e-mail and death threats that Angie tried to keep from her but Cam insisted on seeing anyway, the lunatics out for her blood. Well, she could handle all that. It was the memories and dreams that got her. People thought she was so cheerful and energetic, but when the memories and dreams came and sex failed her—as it had lately, all the time, she'd given up on it—the only thing that helped was talking to someone who understood. Except that nobody really did, except The Six. And most of them, for reasons she didn't get, avoided Cam.

She wanted to be again the person she'd been before she went to Kular. Which wasn't possible. *You must play kulith better than that, ostiu, or else . . .*

She had to talk to somebody or she really was going to lose it. Hotel phones, Angie had told her over and over, were not secure, and of course a cell or handheld was out of the question. But she had to talk to somebody. *Had to.*

Cam slipped out of bed, pulled a coat over her pajamas and a cap low on her forehead. Angie lay asleep on the sofa and, tonight, Jen in the small bedroom. If either of them woke, that would be it. But neither did, and Cam crept down the stairwell to the phones in the lobby.

Who? Frank was mad about having to take her to the moon, and anyway, Frank was religious and an ex-cop and about as warm as ice. Lucca didn't believe in the second or third roads, and also it was awkward with him because he wished he hadn't slept with her. And Soledad was . . . Soledad. Uptight and disapproving of Cam. Still, Soledad was the most likely to understand. Cam suspected that Soledad had demons of her own, although of course Soledad would never say so to *her.*

An avatar of the phone company said that Soledad's number had been disconnected.

Fear licked at Cam. Had something happened to Soledad that Cam hadn't yet heard about? She shivered, even though the lobby was warm. Somewhere outside a siren, police or ambulance, rose in pitch and volume and then fell again, racing to somebody else's disaster.

"Lucca? Cam. I'm sorry to wake you at this hour but I— No, it's a landline but not— *Listen,* will you? Soledad's number is disconnected and I got worried, do you

know anything about it? . . . Oh, well as long as you spoke
to her and she's all right, you don't have to tell me any—
Yes. . . ."

Lucca called Soledad, apparently, but not Cam. Somehow, it was the final straw. Aveo's ghost, rotting and leer-
ing, shimmered in front of her, beside the door to the
ladies' room. She was so scared and so *lonely.* . . .

"Lucca, listen— No, fuck it all, can't you just listen?" It
came out a muted howl. And then everything else came
out after it and she was sobbing into the phone, the men
she'd killed, Escio and all the others, and the child spitted
on a sword and the nightmares and what if she *wasn't* doing the right thing, how could the Atoners not tell her
anything to just show her she was doing the right thing, at
least fucking *that.* . . . Sometimes the words didn't even
come out right because she was crying so hard. She told
Lucca everything, except about Frank's hair packet on the
moon. Something in her held enough to keep that to herself.

Lucca changed. He became sweet, the Lucca she remembered from the first time they slept together, before it
all went sour. He said soothing things and called her *cara*
and didn't even argue about Aveo. Cam talked to him until her knees went numb and the words ran out.

Finally she said, "I have to go now, but thank you,
Lucca, thank you. . . . When can I see you? Can I come up
to Canada to visit? I could maybe rearrange my performance schedule and—"

"No, don't do that," he said, and the distance was back.
Like a palace gate shutting her out. "But I'll talk to you
again soon."

"Promise?" she said, hating that she sounded like a
child.

"Promise," he said, and she heard the weariness, and
hated him as well as herself.

But at least she had talked it out. At least, now, maybe

she could sleep enough to be able to do justice to the Atoners' message tomorrow.

Two days later, Cam sat eating breakfast in San Francisco. Outside her hotel window, shining in the spring sunlight, the Golden Gate Bridge soared as if it went straight to Heaven. No wonder one of the Witness planets—Metan?—called the second road "the bridge to" far.

Bruce, her tour bodyguard, opened the hotel door after checking the retina-scan box. Angie entered, carrying a rolled-up flimsy, which she threw onto the table.

Cam said, "What's wrong?" But the flimsy had unrolled, flopping over a discarded orange peel. A tabloid, with Cam's picture taking up half the front page, sobbing into a pay phone.

CAM O'KANE GOES TO PIECES, DOUBTS ATONERS' MESSAGE

Shocking Midnight Call to Lucca Maduro! Revelations by Eyewitness Hotel Clerk!

WORST OF ALL— SAYS THE DEAD *REALLY* HAUNT DREAMS!!!

"What night was this, Cam?" Angie demanded. "How could you be so careless! It's online, on TV. . . . You actually went down to the lobby and made a call to Maduro in the presence of a clerk?"

"I didn't see any clerk!"

"Worse fool you! He photographed you and sold this story for God knows how much, and by now he's undoubtedly on a plane out of the country. Why didn't you come to me?"

Cam grew still. Her voice came out deadly calm. "Go to you? You mean because the government, unlike that clerk, has no ulterior motives for being around me? Is that what you mean, Angie?"

Angie didn't answer.

Cam turned and went into the bedroom, leaving the tabloid beside her half-eaten breakfast, under the window with the glorious view of the Golden Gate Bridge.

51: FROM *THE NEW YORKER*

Post-Atonement-Interference Angst

"Larry, you're doing that wrong. I've always said you aren't mechanically gifted enough to— Larry? Larry?"

52: SOLEDAD

Diane arrived at Soledad's place in less than an hour, on a motorcycle with a man riding behind her. Soledad waited as Diane had told her to do, away from windows and with the door locked. She suspected that these precautions were designed more to reassure her than for any actual effectiveness against anyone who wanted to come in, and she resented the patronization implied. But this was not the time to focus on that.

Soledad heard the bike roar to a stop and cautiously peered outside. Diane was pulling off her helmet and goggles. Both she and the man were dressed in jeans, boots, parkas—just two more crazy kids joy-riding on a warm March afternoon in the Catskills. The man wore a backpack. Soledad let them in.

"Are you all right?" Diane said.

Looking at Diane's pretty, windblown face, short hair mussed by the helmet, Soledad didn't know whether to trust her, castigate her, fear her. "How did you get here so fast?"

"Helicopter. Let me see it, Soledad."

She kept the dark metal box in her pocket. "I didn't hear a helicopter."

Diane searched her face. Finally she said, "I rush-requisitioned an Agency copter in New York and we landed in a field a few miles from here. The copter carries the bike as standard equipment. This is Jerry Torres, one of our surveillance experts. Soledad, whatever you found isn't ours. I told you right at the beginning that we would honor your request to not install any surveillance on you that you weren't aware of, and we haven't."

Soledad wanted to believe her. Jerry Torres, a tall man in his twenties with a body so thin that he looked like a war refugee, was unpacking the backpack on Soledad's kitchen table. He began a methodical sweep for bugs.

Diane continued, "I've been honest with you—more honest, I think, than you've been with me. You agreed to tell me if you revealed your identity and whereabouts to anyone."

"What makes you think I have?" But she felt herself flushing.

"James. . . ."

"How do you even know about James if you haven't been surveilling me?" Soledad flared.

Diane kept her calm tone. Jerry went about his tasks as if no one else were present. "Of course you were followed, Soledad, when you started changing the times you called in. Some days you didn't call until afternoon, and that was a change in well-established patterns. We check up on well-established patterns. But I told you we wouldn't put in electronics unless we told you about them, and we kept our word. Now, may I please see it?"

Soledad handed her the small box, and she immediately handed it to Jerry. "James is *my* business, Diane."

"Yes. But we had an agreement."

"He's the one who took Fengmo and me to St. Vincent's the night of the shooting." Soledad saw that Diane already had this information. And how much more?

Diane said, "Jerry?"

He shook his head and vanished into the bedroom.

Diane said, "Did you call him today when you called me?"

"Yes." She'd reached James before he left his office for his off-site meeting, which he'd immediately canceled, but it would be nearly two hours more before he could arrive here. All at once Soledad longed for him. To lean against him, breathe in his James-scent, feel his smile on her—it would make everything easier.

Jerry appeared in the kitchen doorway, shook his head, and disappeared again. Soledad wondered if he was mute.

Diane said, "We have to leave here, Soledad. Now. Jerry has the rest of his team on the way with equipment to really sweep the woods. He says there's nothing in the house, but this location has been compromised. Take this—" She handed Soledad Jerry's now-empty backpack. "—and pack what you need for a few days, plus your laptop. The rest of your stuff will be sent to you in your new location. Also, since they've undoubtedly seen your face—"

"Who? *Who's* seen my face?"

"We don't know that yet," Diane said patiently. "It may be necessary to relocate you to another part of the country."

"And James? James has a job here!"

"He hasn't had it very long."

"You had him investigated," Soledad said, and realized she should have already guessed this. A small fountain of curiosity bubbled up through her outrage.

"Of course we did. He has a clean record, a truthful résumé, never married, a mother and sister in Oakland, no known questionable associates. Have you ever called him on a cell phone or allowed him to call you on one?"

"No. I know better than that. I used my encrypted landline or e-mail."

"Nonetheless, I'm sure 'they' know who he is. Come on, Soledad, the longer we stay here the more unsafe you are. Start packing."

"I'm not going without James."

The two women stared at each other across the kitchen table. Diane said, almost tentatively, as if performing an experiment, "Jerry can tell him you've gone and the team can bring him to you later."

"No."

"Are you sure that after he's told about all this, James will still think it's a good idea for the two of you to be together?"

"Completely sure."

"It will mean leaving his job."

"You said yourself he hasn't had it very long. He can find another."

"Do you realize you'll be putting him in danger, not just yourself?"

"Don't do that," Soledad said sharply. "Don't try to play on guilt with me. James is an adult, he'll make his own choice."

"All right." Diane said it as a sigh, somehow giving the words sibilants they didn't have. "We wait here for James. But one more thing you should know, Soledad. It definitely wasn't the CCAD that murdered Sara Dziwalski, but that doesn't mean they've disappeared. They're still there, well organized and very well funded, and the fact that they've gone quiet since that night at Cam O'Kane's lecture is ominous. They could have killed her any number of times since then—she's a wild woman and we can't control her at all. They could have killed Christina Harden or Frank Olenik or Andy DuBois, all of whom insist on living as if they'd never gone into space. It wouldn't even be that hard to get to Jack Jones in England, not to mention the Witnesses who, like you, aren't among The Six. So why haven't they? Why have the CCAD gone so quiet?"

"How should I know?" And how had Diane, her ally, become this verbal adversary?

"We don't know, either. But any change in behavior is significant. The best guesstimate is that the CCAD is planning something really big and staying out of sight until then. I don't know if this surveillance was put there by them or by some weirdo who admires your bod, but until I do know, I think it's a good idea for you and James to be invisible."

"Yes," Soledad said.

Diane opened her jacket. Soledad saw the gun in its shoulder holster. "And now I have to ask you the daily question, because that's the drill. Have you contacted or been contacted by any Atoner, or agent for the Atoners, since we last spoke?"

Suddenly Soledad felt enormously weary. "No, Diane. I haven't. I think the Atoners are done with us. I really do."

Done, and without taking steps to atone for anything at all.

When James arrived, later than the rest of the Agency team, he and Diane eyed each other like Rottweilers squaring off. But their words were outwardly courteous.

"Of course I'm going with Soledad, wherever that is," James said. "Can I get another job?"

"If we give you a new identity, Social Security number, and credit references. All of it."

"And will you? What about medical records and retina scan?"

Diane said coolly, "You sound very practiced at changing identity, Mr. Hinton."

"I can read, Agent Lovett."

"Of course. I think we can arrange those things, if you're sure."

"I'm sure." He put his arm around Soledad. Jerry Torres came back into the house, tramping in mud on his boots. He carried three more of the dark metal boxes, one encrusted with pine needles. He wasn't mute, after all.

"Russian black-market running military-grade encrypted software piggybacking on E.U. satellites," he said, and his voice was as deep and musical as an opera star's.

53: FRANK

So he had to take Cam with him to the moon, having been unable to think of any way out of it. He'd rather take a rattlesnake into his mother's kitchen. Judy Olenik would dispatch any serpent intruder in thirty seconds, while Frank was going to be stuck with Cam O'Kane for eleven long, unbearable days.

"Please, God, let her at least keep her mouth shut so I can do Your work. In the name of Your blessed son Christ Jesus, amen." He kissed the rosary, rose from his knees in the barren little dorm room, and stopped at the doorway for one last hurried prayer. In less than an hour, Cam was due at the stupidly named "Earth Base Alpha" of Farrington Tours. Frank figured he needed all the heavenly support he could get.

At least her entourage and all the media jackals weren't allowed inside the gates. Farrington Tours had been very clear about that. Only their own people would take pictures and movies and holos and recordings: great publicity. But despite all the froufrou of advertising, this was still a serious spaceport, training people for serious trips beyond the Earth, and Frank expected—

"Hello, Frankie Spacefarer!"

Standing in the corridor, wearing a pair of green antennae on his bald head, was Charlie Spiro. Frank gaped at the famous comic, known for his deliberately stupid rendition of retro humor. Spiro said, "How many Atoners does it take to change a lightbulb? . . . None, because they kidnapped all the lamps."

"Are *you* going up to the moon?"

"You know it, kid. Two Atoners walk into a Las Vegas casino and say to a slot machine, 'Take me to your leader.' The bartender says, 'Hey, fellas, that thing isn't human.' The Atoners say, "Yeah, but at least it's familiar with the living dead.' "

Frank walked out of the dormitory into the blazing New Mexico sunshine. Spiro followed him. "Sure I'm going to the moon. You think funny men don't have a sense of adventure? I'll be the trip's comic relief. Hey, do you know how to restore to the human genome all the DNA that the Atoners cut out?"

Frank, a few steps ahead of Spiro, froze.

"You advertise. 'Lonely ATGC looking for TACG for insertion.' "

Frank didn't get the joke. Did Farrington Tours let in just anybody? Anybody with two million dollars, it looked like. He walked faster, outdistancing Spiro, toward the Orientation Center.

A motorcade pulled up to the front gate, which the guard opened. One car drove inside and people erupted from the other vehicles, shouting questions through the fence, aiming cameras, even launching a minirobocam, which immediately fell to the ground as soon as it passed over the fence and hit the jammer. Thank Heavens for small miracles, as Frank's mother often said.

The one car that had been admitted stopped beside Frank. Before the chauffeur could spring out, Cam climbed from the backseat. "Hello, Frank."

"Cam."

"Good to see you."

He couldn't honestly say the same, so he said nothing. But Cam looked different from a month ago—thinner, and very tired. She wore no makeup and her hair was shoved into a careless ponytail. Her low-cut pink top showed her breasts, but even so, the whole getup made her look younger and somehow vulnerable. Frank wasn't falling for that. She was a barracuda.

She was also his meal ticket. "That's the dorm," he said, pointing stiffly, "and that's the Orientation Center. You have to check in. They'll want to—"

"Cam O'Kane!" Charlie Spiro said, walking toward them sort of sidewise so he could both wave at the paparazzi beyond the fence and leer at Cam. "Delighted to meet you, Moon Lady. When is an Atoner hungry?"

"Hi," Cam said, and walked away toward the Orientation Center. Frank followed, surprised. But then Cam looked back over her shoulder, grinned, and said, "At launch time!"

She hadn't changed that much, after all.

Halfway across the compound he said, very close to her ear, "You didn't say anything to anybody at all when you had your breakdown? About our project?"

"It wasn't a breakdown!"

The hell it wasn't. She was about as solid as cotton candy. But he didn't want to anger her, so he didn't ask what she thought her little meltdown had been. "You didn't say anything?"

"No, Frank, I didn't say anything. God!"

"Then don't say anything here, not even to me. Anywhere could be bugged."

"You think I don't know that?" She flounced away from him and entered the Orientation building, turning on her automatic, meaningless smile as the Farrington people's cameras flashed and hovered.

Maybe she would fail the mandatory FAA physical.

She didn't, and neither did Charlie Spiro, although another would-be tourist was grounded for some kind of heart irregularity. He was an Asian businessman who looked not only healthy as an ox but also very accustomed to having his own way. Frank saw him go into a side room with a Farrington executive: probably going to throw his weight around and try to buy his way upstairs. Frank was pleased and—yes, admit it—a little surprised when the Asian went home anyway. No bribery. Farrington played by the rules.

There were eighteen of them left to "train," although each tour only carried six at a time to the moon. Frank and Cam were scheduled for the first group, right after training. Maybe Cam had paid extra for a rush job. Their group included three men and another woman, all business types in their fifties. It didn't include Charlie Spiro, for which Frank was grateful. "A lifelong dream," each of the business types said at one time or another. Nice enough people, but Frank mostly left them to their dream and their business talk and their wrinkles. To his surprise, so did Cam. She had bursts of sudden, frenzied conversation like machine-gun fire, but most of the day she was quiet and subdued.

Not so the nights.

"Frank? Open the door, *please*."

He swam up from sleep, pulled on his jeans, opened the door. A message from an Atoner, or interference from the government, had they somehow learned about the hair packet . . . "What's wrong?"

"Nightmare." She looked like shit, with smudges under her eyes so dark that it looked like somebody hit her. "Can I sleep with you?"

"No!"

"Not 'sleep with' . . . just *sleep with*. Please, Frank, you have no idea how bad it is. Aveo . . ."

His patience finally disintegrated. "You bought my trip upstairs so we can accomplish something important. My dick wasn't part of the deal."

"Fuck you!" She whirled and was gone.

Frank locked the door and went back to bed, but he couldn't get back to sleep.

* * *

The "tourists" tested out weightlessness in the fuselage of a wildly rolling and dropping aircraft. They caromed off handholds, did barrel rolls in the air, flew like Superman, made pyramids, hung upside down. One man, a doctor, threw up. Another tourist changed his mind and canceled his trip (no refund).

They experienced the one-sixth gravity of the moon, walking and jumping, and nobody got sick. They attended lectures on moon geography, reusable launch vehicles, lunar exploration, Selene City, Luna Station, and what was known about the Atoner base, which was basically nothing, since the entire thing was surrounded by an opaque and impenetrable force field. During this part of the orientation, everybody shot covert glances at Cam and at Frank, who ignored them. In fact, the only part of the orientation that really interested him was the brief demonstration of the EVA suits.

"You will *not* be wearing these," emphasized the lecturer, a retired Air Force captain with, apparently, nothing to do in his retirement but turn PR flack. "They are for emergencies only, and Luna Station has never had an emergency. But your safety is paramount to Farrington, and so a suit is furnished for each of our guests— Yes, Frank?"

"Are there suits in the rover, too? For the trip to the International Lunar Base?"

"Absolutely."

A woman said, "That same rover trip also includes a peek at the Atoner base, doesn't it? There's only one rover trip per tour?"

"That's right," the captain said. "You'll make the trip in subgroups of three, four including the driver, and each rover carries four EVA suits. Although I want to emphasize, ladies and gentlemen, that this is merely an emergency precaution. No one on Farrington Tours goes EVA. Your safety is too important to us, and you can see everything on the moon just as well from either Luna Station or a rover."

Not quite everything. Frank watched the others struggle with the EVA suits. He had worn one before, of course, since NASA had insisted on supplying them to all twenty-one Witnesses for the walks to and from the Atoner shuttle to the Atoner Dome. The 'Tonies had agreed without argument. Nothing about the space-suit design had changed in the last year.

Six days more.

Please, God, don't let me fuck up.

54: BOOK REVIEW

THE CHEERFUL DEAD AND THE HUMAN BRAIN,
by Joseph Villanova, M.D. (Random House, $34.95)

Reviewed by Carol Vanderhorn

Although this book, like so many others on the same topic, was rushed into both composition and print in just six months, it stands far above most of them. Villanova, a researcher at the respected Whitehead Institute for Biomedical Research, avoids the cheap and the gimmicky in his discussion of the so-called "seeing-the-dead" genes trumpeted by Cam O'Kane and her quieter fellow travelers. Villanova wisely sticks to the ways that current scientific understanding of the human brain either supports or invalidates the assertions of "The Six."

His overview of the literature, both physiochemical and evolutionary, is excellent. While never slighting technical accuracy, it is nonetheless accessible to the intelligent layperson. However, that same layperson is likely to end up frustrated by the "Conclusions" section of the book. The author is so careful to be evenhanded that the reader ends up little wiser as to whether seeing the dead is or is not genetically possible. After all the meticulous explanations of neural firing and neurochemical-release probabilities, I had the distasteful impression that Villanova did not want to reduce sales by committing himself either way.

Less caution and more passion would have made this a

better book. Death, it seems, is not a subject that is enhanced by being approached with cash-register timidity.

Carol Vanderhorn is a brain surgeon at Washington Hospital Center, Washington, D.C.

55: SOLEDAD

Before Soledad and James left New York, Soledad insisted on seeing Fengmo.

"It's been so long, surely by now there won't be reporters still staking out the hospital waiting for me," she said to a weary Diane Lovett, who looked at Soledad as if she were nuts.

"They won't be waiting. They'll be paying orderlies or nurses or anybody else who is there all the time to alert them if you show up," Diane said. Her tone said, *Grow up, Soledad.* Soledad flushed.

"Well, okay, but if they do call reporters, then it will take a while before any show up. I just want five minutes with Fengmo. I'm going to do this."

"I can't stop you." Diane's lack of expression spoke reams.

The Agency was moving Soledad and James to Raleigh, North Carolina, under new identities. Meanwhile, they'd been stashed in a hotel in Manhattan, which they hadn't left in three days. Soledad thought how unbearable those days would have been without James, and hugged him tighter. He was sacrificing his old life—his very identity— for her. He held her gently and kissed her eyelids. Diane looked away.

"I'll finish the packing while you're at the hospital," James said.

"Good." Not that there was much to pack. They had taken from the little rented house in the Catskills only clothes, personal electronics, and a few books. That was it. For three days these objects, this room, and an incurious room service had constituted the entire world for Soledad, and she was a bit shocked to realize how little she'd minded. Diane hadn't even visited until now, maybe to minimize the chances of leading anyone to them. Soledad hadn't asked.

A few times Soledad and James had dutifully tuned to the news, but Soledad had not paid full attention. Her mind, her senses, were filled with James, and even as that scared her, it also exhilarated her. She hadn't known she could feel like this, that all the ridiculous songs and poems could, in fact, express something as real and concrete as the battered suitcases she was busily not packing. The Atoners, Lucca, the CCAD, Cam, the surveillance in the woods—all of it had taken on the faded, dreamy shapes of background watercolors when the picture held a sharply etched, bold graphic in the foreground. At some level she knew this was wrong—out of perspective, unbalanced, maybe even amoral—but her body didn't care. She was a receiver tuned to one frequency: James. James. James.

Well, no, she amended: *two frequencies.* She still wanted to see Fengmo.

Soledad and Diane left the hotel by different entrances; a second agent silently joined Soledad in the elevator. All three reached St. Vincent's without incident, and Soledad drew the curtain around Fengmo's ICU bed to be alone with him.

He lay on his side, curled head to knees, tubes running into his nose and arm and under the thin white blanket that covered his lower body. His skin was doughy, his black hair thinned and dull. He'd lost weight. Soledad took his hand, her fingers carefully circling the weak ones that had once reached so eagerly for a keyboard, a Cuisinart, almost any book.

Talk to him, the nurse had suggested. *We don't know what coma patients can or cannot hear.* But had the suggestion come from compassion or from a desire to overhear and pass on anything Soledad might let slip?

"Fengmo, I'm here," she said softly. "It's me. I'm waiting for you to come back, Fengmo."

Ladybliss, she heard in her mind, but wasn't too deluded to know that it was only in her mind, not from him. She might never hear from him again, unless Cam was right about the Atoner message. So many kinds of death—violence, disease, accident, suicide, old age—but only one life. Maybe that life continued, maybe not. Either way, Fengmo had neither life nor death. He hung between them, and Soledad couldn't reach him in that suspended, unimaginable place.

She held his spindly hand in silence for over an hour, then said the only thing she could say: "I love you, Fengmo. Come back to me." She slipped around the curtain to where the others waited.

Something was wrong.

The second agent said, "Please wait here, miss."

"Where's Diane?"

"Please wait here."

Fear rose in her. Was this guy somehow a fake, was he CCAD, or . . . was even Diane not what she seemed? *Get a grip, Soledad.* . . . She forced her face to stay impassive, her body still.

Diane reappeared. Her lips were pressed so tightly together they nearly disappeared. She said to Soledad, "Follow me. Please."

Should she? But if she couldn't trust Diane— Soledad followed, and the male agent followed her. At the far end of the corridor outside the ICU, Diane said softly, "Lucca Maduro is on my handheld. He wants to talk to you."

"Lucca? Through you?"

"Yes. He couldn't reach you any other way, apparently."

Soledad's handheld was back at the hotel; it wasn't allowed in the ICU. "Why does he want to talk to me? What happened?"

"He wouldn't tell me." The lips disappeared completely, rolled inward like pale tortoise heads. "My handheld is encrypted, of course, but you still shouldn't take this call inside the hospital. None of this has been swept, and I don't know what Maduro's subject matter is."

The Atoners— Diane meant that Lucca might have been contacted by an Atoner. Would he be their first choice? Maybe; wasn't there a story about Christ appearing first to Thomas the Doubter? . . . "Where, Diane? Where can I talk to him?"

"Follow me."

Diane led her through corridors and up stairwells, using some sort of Agency super-chip to unlock doors, until she pushed open a metal fire door at the top of a slant-roofed stairwell. She and Soledad—the third agent had disappeared—emerged onto the hospital roof.

Spring dusk, with the lights just coming on around Manhattan. A sky dotted with wispy clouds had deepened to aquamarine, the same color as the harbor in the distance. The moon, just off full, looked misty, its craters and mare blurred. Diane keyed a code into her handheld and Lucca's face appeared.

"What's wrong?" Soledad demanded. "Are you all right?"

"I am, yes, *cara*."

There was a note in his voice that she didn't like. Gentleness? Pity? "What, then? Cam?"

"Our crazy woman is also all right. She's taking a Farrington tour back to the moon."

"I heard."

"You left your place in the Catskills."

"The Agency took me away," Soledad said. "They found surveillance equipment all over the woods and—"

"Yes, I know. Now I know. They're going to relocate you and James."

"Yes. I'd have contacted you as soon as they gave me the go-ahead, Lucca. But we've been in complete hiding and— How did you know they're going to relocate us?"

"My family has influence with the Canadian government."

Soledad stared at him. Finally she said softly, "That's a *lot* of influence."

"Less than you might think. Most things are for sale." His hand entered the visual and flipped in an odd, Italian gesture that all at once brought back vividly the weeks on the Atoner ship, the even longer weeks alone in orbit while Lucca and Cam witnessed on their planets and Soledad was linked to anything alive only through the digital sounds and sights of an alien commlink she didn't understand. That lack of understanding, more than the boredom, had kept her fighting depression, even as she tried to stay steady and sensible for the adventurers depending on her. Those endless weeks had a feel, even a taste, that rushed over her now: sterile dust, choking her nose and eyes and throat.

Lucca said, "Diane? Are you there, listening?"

"Yes," the agent said.

"Good, I want you to hear this. Soledad, it's James that I'm calling about. When you first told me about him— please don't be angry—I had him investigated. I know your government did, too, but I wanted my own answers, for your sake. Everything checked out. He was who he said he was. But no background check in the world can account for what's in a man's head, what he wants, or when he might change what he wants."

"Go on," Soledad said. A stray cloud drifted over the bottom half of the moon, ghostly seaweed snagged on pale rock.

"I'm not trusting by nature, *cara*. Maybe too much untrusting. After your government discovered the surveillance equipment, I put a man on James. A shadow. He watched—"

"There was nothing to watch! We've been in the same hotel room for three days, and James is still there! Packing!"

"No, *cara,* he's not. Not now."

Diane took another handheld from her pocket.

"Once I knew where the Agency had stashed you and James, the shadow stationed himself at the hotel. He's very good. I don't think even Diane knew he was there. Today James left the hotel soon after you did. My man went with him. But James must have been either trained himself or somehow warned, because he doubled and weaved and led Marco into an alley. Marco was armed, of course, but—"

"James! Is James all right!"

"Yes, he is, calm yourself, *cara.* But there was an . . . altercation, and something strange happened. Marco was knocked out. He reported to me that he couldn't touch James and that James hit him with a bare fist, but it felt hard as steel. It gave Marco a concussion. Also, just before that, Marco hit James with a blow that should have knocked him over, but James didn't even stagger."

"I don't understand."

"That's because you didn't go down to Kular," Lucca said.

"I still don't—"

"James was wearing an Atoner personal shield."

Diane made a small noise.

"You never wore a shield because you didn't go down to the planet. I experimented with mine, a great deal—I like to know what equipment will and will not do. I said I don't trust many people, Soledad, but I trust you. Why does James have an Atoner shield?"

"He doesn't! He can't!"

"Then you didn't know about it. Ah, *cara,* I'm sorry."

"There's nothing to be sorry about!" she cried. "What are you saying—that James is some sort of . . . of spy? CCAD or—?"

"Of course not. They don't have Atoner shields. I'm saying James is—"

"You don't even know that it was an Atoner shield!"

"Yes. I do," Lucca said quietly. "I have people who keep track of security technology, even top-secret security technology. This was nothing human made. It was an Atoner shield. I think James—who escaped Marco—is some new kind of Witness for the Atoners. A Witness here on Earth. He has a personal shield because the Atoners don't want to risk him. We earlier Witnesses don't still have our shields because, now, we are expendable."

"No, you're wrong!"

"I don't think so. And that just leaves two questions: What is James a Witness of? And why?"

In the taxi Soledad leaned forward, clutching the back of the cab's front seat as if that might make it go faster. Diane shot concerned looks at her while talking in a low voice on her Agency handheld. At the hotel, Soledad tore up the back stairs, fingers trembling as she keyed in the lock code of their room.

James was gone. His clothes remained, his handheld, his notebook, his books. She rushed into the bathroom; his toothbrush lay on the sink beside his razor, fine gold hairs caught in the blade. Soledad whirled on Diane. "Wasn't there an agent with James?"

"Of course not. He wasn't a prisoner, and it's you that we're assigned to." Diane moved closer, took Soledad's hand. She shook Diane off.

He was really gone. Without a word, a note, a meaning. She felt his absence in the very air, which all at once wasn't sufficient to inflate her lungs properly. It was all true, all Lucca's terrible statements. James had worn an Atoner shield, he had decked Lucca's man, all these days and nights with Soledad he had been other than he seemed, he was somehow connected to the Atoners . . . how?

And he was gone. How? Why?

Lucca's questions. Hers, too, only with different meanings. *How could James do this to me? Why would he do this to me?*

She was going to find out. And then—God help him.

She turned slowly and Diane Lovett, well-trained Agency operative who had seen service in the most brutal African war of the century, took a surprised step backward from the expression in Soledad's eyes.

Beyond the hotel window, more clouds veiled the glowing moon.

56: FRANK

The Farrington shuttle lifted. The bone-crushing pressure surprised Frank, despite three days of training. All of his memories of his time as an Atoner Witness were blurry, as if they happened a long time ago and to somebody else. He suspected the blurriness might be deliberate. But now the Atoner shuttle to the moon sprang to his mind sharp and clear as if under a magnifying glass: the round, nearly empty gray room with three comfortable gray chairs equipped with light webbing, the smooth upward glide like a good elevator. Amira in her orange sari and Rod in his plaid flannel shirt, all three of them staring out the window as Earth fell away beneath them. Then, after just six hours, the gentle set-down a quarter mile from the Atoner Dome.

Nothing like this, nothing.

Eight people, six of them tourists and the other two Farrington pilots, sat strapped into reclining seats in what was essentially a small van. For three days they would sit, eat, sleep, and piss in these seats. Rockets screamed below Frank, the atmosphere screamed ahead of him, and Cam O'Kane screamed beside him. What had she expected? The Langford Reusable Single Stage to Orbit Launch Vehicle was "a major breakthrough in space technology"— they'd been told so over and over. It had accelerated space travel by decades.

"Shut up," Frank gasped to Cam. She did, but she shifted her eyes sideways to glare at him.

Abruptly the pressure eased. Frank flexed his hands

and feet. A cheerful, prerecorded voice began to speak. "Welcome to Farrington Tours, ladies and gentlemen! We're so glad you're with us, and let me assure you that the worst is now over. Next up is a genuine treat. In just a few minutes, our trajectory will allow you all your *first ever* glimpse of the moon free from the distortion of Earth's atmosphere!"

Frank began to laugh.

57: FROM
WRITER'S DIGEST MAGAZINE

Bringing In the Future

Is your murder mystery getting the brush-off from editors in the new, "post-Atoner" publishing craze? Here's how to update your plot so it's sure to sell!

by Lawrence Crandell

Agatha Christie and Scott Turow don't cut it anymore. Nowadays, in mysteries that actually sell, Hercule Poirot and Rusty Sabich would just turn to the victims' ghosts and be told who killed their bodies. Mystery Writers of America reports a 60% drop in purchases of "classic" mystery plots by the big publishing houses and a whopping 40% rise in purchases of mysteries set on the "alternate Atoner Earth," in which humanity's seeing-the-dead genes were left intact.

So does this mean that your half-completed novel is deader than the corpse in Chapter One? **No!** Just follow these five tips for reworking your murder plot to reflect the new parameters, and you're already halfway to a sale!

Tip #1 . . .

PART III

THE ATONEMENT

58: SOLEDAD

Diane Lovett said, "You can't, Soledad."

"Really? Just watch me."

"I didn't think you were the type to commit suicide by crazy."

"That's not what I'm doing."

"But that's what will happen."

The two women stood in what had been Soledad and James's hotel room, one on each side of the double bed. James's things lay in neat piles beside an open, empty suitcase. On top of one pile was the blue cashmere sweater Soledad had first seen on the morning after Fengmo was shot. James had worn it since then and a small stain, catsup or grease or taco sauce, discolored the soft wool a few inches below the neck band. Soledad couldn't seem to move her eyes from the stain, but not because she was afraid to face Diane. She felt neither fear nor anything else, just this numbness that she already knew wasn't going to last.

She repeated, since it didn't seem to have taken effect the first time, "You're fired, Diane."

"You don't 'fire' a federal agent. You didn't hire me and you don't fire me."

"Fine. But you haven't charged me with any crime and unless you do, I don't have to talk to you, don't have to have you living with me, don't have to exist by your rules. That's all over now."

"If you'd rather work with a different agent—"

"That's not it." Still Soledad's eyes stuck to that stain on James's sweater. When had he gotten it? Had they been eating dinner together, laughing, casually touching, in that other time before this chasm opened in her life? There was no crossing it, this chasm. No going back.

Diane moved closer. From the corner of her eye, Soledad saw the older woman do something she'd never done before—reach toward a breast pocket and then pull her hand back. So she'd once been a smoker. Odd that Soledad didn't know that, odd that she didn't know Diane's age. She didn't know anything.

James—

So it was starting now. The numbness would wear off and the pain would begin, and it would be bad. Very bad. The only thing that might help was answers, and she was going to get them.

Diane said, "Why are you blaming the Agency? We didn't know about James—God, do you think if we'd known that he had an Atoner shield, that he was somehow *in contact with an Atoner,* we wouldn't have been all over him? I'm as upset as you—"

"No. You're not. Don't be stupid."

"Sorry." Diane moved closer still, but Soledad kept her gaze on the blue cashmere sweater. Catsup? Grease? Taco sauce? And when?

"You're going to search for James, aren't you? Well, so are we. There's no reason we can't work together to—"

"No."

"You're going to work through Lucca, aren't you? Lucca's good, Soledad, he's rich and smart and he has a lot of resources at his command, but we're better. We're the United States government, for God's sake! Don't you think we have a better chance of finding James for you?"

Soledad, unable to stop herself, picked up the sweater. But once she had it in her hands, it just hung there, limp.

Empty. Finally she looked at Diane, whose mouth was pressed so tightly closed that she looked lipless.

Soledad said, "You wouldn't be finding James for me. And you don't know where he is now, do you, or we wouldn't be having this conversation. You didn't know about his contact with an Atoner—*Lucca* had to tell you. You didn't even know about the surveillance in the woods outside my house. You didn't protect Sara Dziwalski. I know the Agency's going to follow me and record me and do everything short of crawling inside my skin and you'd do that, too, if you could, to try to get to James and so get to the Atoners. I can't help all that. But I don't have to work with you. And I won't."

She shrugged off her jacket and yanked James's sweater over her head. It was too long for her and sagged in the shoulders, but it fit across the bust. The cashmere was soft on her forearms and wrists, almost but not quite pushing her into emotion. Soledad picked up her jacket and purse and left the hotel.

She was followed, of course, although she didn't see Diane or anyone else. But she had one ally: time. This had all happened so fast, the Agency wouldn't have had much opportunity to add more surveillance to whatever they already had in place. If Soledad acted fast, she could do this.

She got a taxi and had it wait at a bank, where she drew out all the money in her account, a meager three thousand dollars. Then the same taxi on to Juana's, where the phone might be bugged, but the apartment probably wasn't, not yet.

"Soledad? Well, well, the big star traveler." Juana stood blocking the doorway. No colorful skirts this time; Juana wore jeans and a man's dirty shirt, and her pupils were big as dimes. Frilled out of her mind. What she called her mind.

So much the better.

"Juana, I want some information and I'm willing to pay you for it, plus for keeping your mouth shut."

Juana's dreamily scornful gaze sharpened; she wasn't too frilled to ignore money. "What information?"

"Who else is here? Mama?"

"Nobody."

Soledad made a quick circuit of the apartment, but Juana was telling the truth for once. Soledad faced her sister. "I'll give you three hundred dollars to tell me where to find the journalist you set me up to. 'Carl Lewis' or—no, don't even start, I *know* you did that—or whatever his real name is, plus another three hundred to not tell anybody that I asked."

"Show me the money."

Soledad had divided her money in the taxi, putting six hundred dollars in her bra. She pulled out the neckline of James's sweater, drew out the money, and held it toward Juana like a zookeeper tempting a hyena. "Tell me. And if you lie, you'll regret it, I warn you right now. I have powerful people helping me, including Lucca Maduro."

Juana's eyes flew from the money to her sister's face. Juana wasn't stupid, but Soledad had wondered if Juana ever watched the news, would even recognize Lucca's name. But apparently she did, although her next words were pure Juana: crafty and petty at the same time.

"He's cute. You fucking him?"

"No. 'Carl Lewis,' Juana—how do I find him?"

"Okay. He came to me, but I got a card here someplace. . . ." She rummaged in a drawer filled with things Soledad didn't want to see. At the back was a crumpled business card. Soledad could picture it: Lewis staring doubtfully at Juana. Weighing the risk of giving contact information to this lying user against the risk of Juana forgetting how to contact him at all when she'd lured Soledad back home. Finally handing over the card, which was Spartan in its grudging information. No graphic, holo, or occupation:

CARL LEWIS
(212) 555-6398
clclcl@xixmail.com

"Give me the money," Juana said. "All of it. I won't tell anybody what I gave you."

She'd tell everything to the next person who walked through the door, which would undoubtedly be Diane or another agent. But Soledad had planned for this. She moved closer to Juana, now smelling her sister's unwashed body plus the fruity, sick-sweet smell of frill. "Juana, did you see on the news what happened to Sara Dziwalski?"

"Who?"

Lucca was a handsome male; Sara was not. "The Witness who got blown up at that hospital in Texas last month."

"Oh, yeah, I think I did hear something about that. . . ."

"She was a nurse and they got her at work, ripping her open and killing other people who just happened to be standing near her. Blood everywhere, you must have seen the pictures. Sara got it because she told someone something she shouldn't have. And you'll be in the same boat if you tell anybody about this visit or Carl Lewis. Believe me, I know."

Juana believed her. Living where and how she did, Juana was always ready to believe in violence, in retaliation, in revenge. Fury leaped in her eyes, the welcome relief of theatrics. "You bring this on me, on Mama—"

"Shove it, Juana. I'm not interested. Just don't tell *anybody* what we said."

As she opened the door, her back to Juana, Soledad put the business card in her mouth, chewed, and swallowed. The card was filthy and the gesture melodramatic, but she didn't know who might grab her just outside Juana's door.

No one did. She walked downstairs and along the street. Litter blew in the gutter and the sidewalk was cracked, the raised and jagged edges briefly catching paper and plastic before another breeze tore them free. It was several blocks before she found a pay phone that wasn't broken. Kids hooted at her and a few loitering men made comments she ignored, but she didn't see the agents. No matter; they were there. At the phone, careful to cover the keyboard with her hand, she punched in 212-555-6398, prepared to talk fast before some unseen listening device captured her offer to him, and her offered payment.

59: GUEST EDITORIAL,
TIME MAGAZINE

Helen Keller in the 21st Century

by *Laura Kendall*

Imagine you are deaf. And blind. And mute. How can you understand sound and light and color?

You can't, except through a powerful leap of imagination. Helen Keller came to believe that others experienced what she could not—but belief is not comprehension. Helen Keller adjusted to her limitations and made of her life a magnificent success. She had others help her do this, notably her gifted teacher, Annie Sullivan. Until Sullivan transformed her existence, the isolated Helen didn't even realize that there *was* anything more to experience.

Since The Six returned to Earth, we have all become Helen Kellers. Many—perhaps most—go on living as they did before, unbelieving that the world holds a dimension of experience denied to humanity. They may be right. Certainly a "sense" for seeing the dead sounds fantastic—how would it work? What structures would the "deleted genes" have grown in our brains? Through what messenger particles would information be conveyed to those structures? Photons? Electrons? Microwaves? Something entirely off the electromagnetic spectrum as we know it?

We have no answers. We cannot imagine the experience, nor the beings we would be if we had it regularly. But a failure of imagination does not mean that the whole thing is impossible. Perhaps, as scoffers say, we are deluded and seduced by the Atoner claims.

On the other hand, we may just have been in the dark so long that we cannot imagine light.

60: LUCCA

Lucca stared out the window at the snow falling in large, lazy flakes over his walled garden. Snow clung to the tender leaves on the peony bushes, the new buds of the roses. He hated Toronto. This was an unexpected snowfall, and it reminded him too much of the village and plains on Kular, captive of endless bleak snow. The news said the snow would be gone in a few hours, but it shouldn't be here at all.

No, *he* shouldn't be here at all. He should be in London, where he had friends from Cambridge and where he could lay on Gianna's grave the roses she loved. Or he should be in Tuscany, for which he felt queasy homesickness every time he uncorked a bottle of Maduro Sangiovese. Tuscany in spring: the hills holding light in their hollows, that silvery and gossamer Tuscany light. The almond and cherry and plum trees in bloom. The hills rising one atop another, mauve in the morning and golden at noon and hazy blue at dusk . . . So what was he doing here in Canada?

Yanking closed the heavy curtains, Lucca returned to his desk, where supposedly he was working on correspondence with the Canadian distributors of Maduro wines. It was convenient to have Lucca in North America, his brother Mario had agreed—*certo,* it made personal meetings with distributors easier. Lucca took no meetings with distributors, which of course Mario knew. It was convenient to have Lucca in North America so Mario, the older brother, could make the important decisions alone in Italy. Mario and Lucca . . . . an old struggle.

So why was Lucca in Canada?

He knew the answer. The Witnesses, most of them, lived here. Jack Jones was in England, yes, Amira in India, Hans in Germany, Ruhan in China. But fifteen of the Witnesses were American, including Soledad and Cam. Fourteen now, since Sara's murder. Lucca couldn't explain why he needed to stay near to Soledad and Cam, but he did. And he simply couldn't face the difficulties of moving to, or living in, the United States, with all its peculiar politics. So he was here in Toronto, wasting his time watching snowfall in late March.

Soledad needed him.

By now she would have gone back to her hotel, found James gone, and done—what? Lucca wasn't sure. On the Atoner ship, Soledad had always been the calm one, rational and intelligent, the foil to Cam. But underneath that reserve, Lucca had sensed a great capacity for passion. She hadn't, again like Cam (or himself, a nagging voice said inside his head), channeled that passion into a definite reaction to the Atoners' lies about a so-called afterlife. But Lucca knew the question troubled her. He'd watched that search for an existential answer divert itself to James, whose storybook looks could probably ignite lust in most women. Was that why the Atoners had chosen James to approach Soledad? What were the alien bastards after now?

To think that once he'd trusted them with his life. *Che cretino.*

She would call him within the hour, he was sure. And he would do whatever he could to— *There.* The phone. He didn't recognize the number.

"Lucca, it's me."

"What kind of phone are you on?"

"A pay phone in Manhattan. It's okay."

"Probably but not necessarily. What do you need, *cara*?"

Long pause. Soledad always had trouble asking for help she couldn't pay for. Lucca said, "Do you want to get out of Manhattan?"

"The Agency is following me—"

"Of course they are. Go to the Wall Street helioport, but not for three hours. Have a cup of coffee somewhere away from that whole area until half an hour before then. Try to arrive at the helioport just when my chopper does. Don't give the Agency time to guess what you're doing."

"But I don't have my passport with me, and I don't think the government would let me leave the country now anyway—would they?"

"No. They'd trump up something, detain you at the border as a material witness or something. But you're not going to leave the country, and there's no legal grounds for not letting you get on a private chopper on a public pad." Lucca hoped this was correct; American law was so damn strange. "Don't say more now, *cara. Ciao.*"

"Ciao." There was a note in her voice that Lucca couldn't quite name, but it was not damsel-in-distress. She wasn't Cam. To his surprise, the person her tone reminded him of was Chewithoztarel.

She climbed into the chopper, shivering in a too-thin jacket and carrying nothing but her purse. "Lucca! I thought you'd send somebody, and I didn't think you . . . yourself, I mean . . ." The flurry of stammering passed as quickly as it arrived. Quietly she said, "Thank you."

"Andiamo, Aldo." The chopper lifted.

"Where are we going? And is he—" Soledad waved at the pilot.

"Aldo has been with me always. He is completely reliable. Yes, Aldo?"

"Non dire cazzate."

Lucca turned to Soledad. No tears, just that look of focused intensity, and again he thought of Chewithoztarel. "We are going to a place owned by a friend. It's not the place on the flight manifest, but we'll sort that out later. And yes, that friend is also reliable. She's an American I knew at Cambridge."

"You have a lot of friends," Soledad said, and this time he couldn't make out her tone at all.

The chopper flew west. Lucca didn't try conversation over its noise. Two hours later it set down on a tiny snow-covered field on the side of a mountain in the Allegheny range in Pennsylvania. Aldo took off. Lucca lugged his large leather suitcase through the snow and keyed in the door code of Anna Parker's parents' vacation cabin.

Anna had been Gianna's best friend at Cambridge. They'd become a foursome: Gianna and Lucca, Anna and her English boyfriend, Michael. GLAM, fellow students had nicknamed them, half-derisively and half-enviously. Anna's mother had been a semi-famous movie star who overdosed on heroin when Anna was six. Her father was a studio executive, a brash and unkind man who hadn't wanted children in the first place. Anna was waiflike, bruised looking, as if she thought her exterior should reflect her inner state. Gianna had laughed at her, mothered her, become her anchor. Michael had done the same thing. Since Gianna's death, Lucca had not been able to bear seeing Anna, but he still trusted her. It turned out that Anna, now living and working in San Francisco, had been stronger than any of them. Michael was an alcoholic, Gianna was dead, and Lucca had let despair make him the tool of aliens as deceptive as the Medici.

"It's nice," Soledad said of the cabin, and Lucca laughed. It was not nice. Crude bunk beds, propane stove, Coleman lanterns, a wooden table and four chairs, rough wooden shelves holding canned goods. Anna's father had bought the place as a hunting lodge, an exercise in old-style macho, and then never once hunted. Too busy, too important, too Hollywood. Anna had liked "the lodge" precisely because her father didn't.

"Lucca, what are we going to do here? Besides hide?"

"What do you want to do?"

She didn't answer. He lit the stove and lantern, waiting. Finally she said, "I want to find James. I already called someone, just before I called you."

He straightened from the stove. "Called someone? Who?"

"A journalist that already knows who I am. My sister outed me." Her mouth twisted unpleasantly. "He wanted an interview with you and tried to pay me to set it up. I said no. But he's just inventive enough and sleazy enough to be able to track James, and so I—"

"You shouldn't have done that, Soledad." He doubted that any "sleazy journalist" would be able to find James.

"I didn't tell Carl much," she said quickly. "Just that I'd had a lover who'd deserted me and I wanted him found, and in return I promised him a big story."

"Me?"

"No! Of course not. But James . . . If he's a new 'Witness' of some kind, the story's going to break anyway, and it might as well be Carl Lewis as anybody else. At least this way I get something out of the whole lousy deal besides more people shooting at me."

This cynicism about the Atoners was new to her. Doubt, yes—she'd had doubt before. But Lucca looked at the downturn of Soledad's mouth and the expression in her eyes, and recognized a depth of suffering she would never admit.

He said gently, "Are you really sure you want to see James again?"

"Yes." The stoniness was back. "Lucca. What do *you* think the Atoners are doing?"

"I have no clue." The stove began to warm the cabin.

"Then what are *we* doing? This cabin is so isolated. . . . You got me away from the Agency, but there's not even a phone, no way to do . . . anything."

"That's where you're wrong." He opened the suitcase. With a flourish he took out two pairs of his pajamas, six shirts, socks and underwear and toiletries, and laid them elaborately at Soledad's feet like a knight presenting tribute to a queen.

She didn't smile. Staring into the bottom of the suitcase, she said, "You have a gun."

"I do, yes."

"What are those electronics?"

"Handhelds. The beam upward is traceable, but nobody's going to be looking for it here. The calls themselves and the results of the surveillance equipment are completely untraceable, Russian black-market stuff that runs military-grade encrypted software piggybacking on E.U. satellites."

She turned slowly. "What did you say?"

"I said this is Russian black-market stuff that runs military-grade encrypted software piggybacking on E.U. satellites to—"

"You fucker."

It was said so quietly, so low, that at first Lucca thought he'd misheard. Then he understood. Americans . . . they were always so open with each other. But he had expected intelligence agents to be different.

"It was you," Soledad said in that same deadly quiet voice. "You put the Everknow surveillance stuff in the woods around my house."

"Yes. I did."

"I trusted you." And after a pause, "Just like I trusted James."

"No. Not like you trusted James, and with a big difference—" He took a step toward her but stopped when she retreated. "Listen to me. I had you under surveillance because I was concerned about your safety. I didn't tell you, no, because I did not want you telling Diane Lovett or James or anybody else. Who could know that you, of all urban creatures, would take a walk in the woods?" He almost smiled but caught himself; a smile right now would be fatal. "I am not James. I did not watch you or get close to you in order to use you. I was concerned about a friend is all, and . . . Soledad, please do not be angry with me. My reasons were of the best, only. Please believe me."

A part of his mind was astonished at how much it mattered that she did believe him.

"I don't know what I believe anymore. Not about you, not about James, not about the Atoners—" She put her hands over her face.

Lucca tried to take her in his arms, but she pushed him away. *"Cara—"*

"Don't call me that. Just . . . just let me think."

He did. He busied himself with adjusting the lantern, with putting the tiny supply of clothes on a wooden shelf, with opening a large plastic box to survey the dried food inside. Five minutes passed, maybe ten. When she finally spoke, he spun around so quickly that he almost lost his balance. Soledad had removed her jacket in the new warmth of the cabin. Underneath she wore a man's sweater, blue cashmere, with a stain near the neck band.

"All right, I believe you. I've never known you to lie to me, and you admitted it when I asked. But don't withhold any more information, okay? You have to promise me. If you won't, I'm calling Diane on one of those handhelds and going back to New York."

"I promise to not withhold any more information from you." She had revealed more than she intended. If Diane and this Carl Lewis were her only other resources, she was needy indeed.

"Fine," Soledad said tonelessly. "You're a hundred percent sure these handhelds can't be traced?"

"I am."

"Then give me one to call Carl and give him the number. And after that, I want you to teach me how to shoot that gun."

He hadn't expected that, and a sudden qualm took him. He thought he knew her, but— Sometimes jealous women— "Soledad . . . *cara* . . . you're thinking of *shooting* James?"

"Of course not." She looked directly into Lucca's eyes. "But I'll shoot anybody who tries to keep me from finding out what James and the Atoners are trying to do now."

"Ah," he said, unimpressed. Apparently even a woman like Soledad was capable of histrionics—quiet histrionics, yes—when jilted in love, but he didn't believe for a moment that she would carry through any melodramatic acts of revenge. What she needed now was to untighten, to relax a bit. Lucca pulled from off a shelf a bottle of wine, inspected it, and grimaced. It would have to do, but a California merlot—amazing. Americans, even rich Americans like Anna Parker, would apparently drink anything.

NEW!!!

"Atoner Crimson"

Vivid blossoms lasting so long into the season you'll almost believe they never die!

High-centered, classic blooms in brightest red make "Atoner Crimson" a very attractive addition to any garden. A compact bushy plant that will fit perfectly into today's smaller gardens. Z 6-10, repeat bloom, 50 petals.

Height: 3' X 2 1/2'
Fragrance: Moderately Fragrant
Year: 2021
Country: France
Item #: N487
Price: $20.95 per rosebush

62: CAM

Cam hated Luna Station.

She had hated the shuttle trip up, too, although not because of the weightlessness or anything bodily like that. No, she hadn't realized how spoiled she'd become, how used to large open rooms and—despite her entourage and Angie Bernelli—to privacy when she wanted it. On the shuttle, there was no place to *move*. Cam, an active person by nature, seemed to feel her muscles crumple and thin. Eight people were crammed into the space of a minibus for three days, listening to each other snore and talk and fart. No escape except in the tiny bathroom that smelled even worse than the rest of the shuttle as the days crawled on.

Not that the other passengers were offensive people. Nice enough, they were nonetheless middle-aged people who had nothing in common with her. They talked about things she didn't understand, "quantum evolution" and "the imperative to go stellar" and "the Higgs ocean." Atlantic, Pacific, Indian—Cam didn't remember any Higgs Ocean. These people, except Frank, were all a lot smarter and more educated than she was, and Frank, who might have helped her, went the entire three days without saying anything at all. How could a person even do that? Cam couldn't wait to land on the moon.

Which was even worse.

Farrington Tours' Luna Station consisted of six trailers on stilts plus a few towering metal silos described as "air and power plants." That was it. The trailers were connected by narrow inflated plastic tunnels, so that nobody had to go outside. The lander that came down from the shuttle, carrying four people each time, turned into a rover on the surface. It drove into a tiny inflated "garage" with an air lock at one end and a door to the largest trailer at the other. Two of the trailers housed tourists, two held Farrington people, one stored supplies, and one, bigger than the others, was a kind of living/dining room/lecture hall. All of them were crammed with things Cam couldn't name.

"I'm so grateful I've lived to see this," said Jane Kingwell, in what for her passed for an excited voice. Jane, Cam's roommate in the teeny space allotted them in Module #2, was fifty-five and motherly. Cam didn't need a mother; she needed to grab Frank's hair packet and go home. "This is much nicer than the pictures we saw of the station."

Had they seen pictures? No, Cam had not—she'd been posing for the four million publicity photographs that were the price of getting her and Frank up here. For all of them, she'd had to look smiling and thrilled. The only time she could be sure of a robocam not snapping away was when she was asleep—but then came the dreams of Kular and Aveo.

"Cam, are you all right?" Jane asked. "You look pale."

Pale, my ass. She looked like shit and smelled worse. Didn't Jane ever say what she really meant?

"I'm fine, thanks. What's supposed to happen now?"

"A lecture in the Clarke Module about Shackleton Crater."

"What's that?"

"You're in it," Jane said gently. "Remember? Both Luna Station and Selene City are here because it has sunlight seventy percent of the time and the deep shadows make ice—"

"Oh, yeah, now I remember," said Cam, who didn't. More lectures, more photos. "The Atoner base is near here, too, then."

"Yes. Fifty miles away." Jane got the look she always got when anything connected with the Atoners came up in conversation around Cam or Frank: *Tell me more, please please please, but I'm too polite to ask directly.*

"Then let's get over to Clarke," Cam said.

Aveo stood bare chested *in his brown skirt, flesh drooping in gobbets from his bones and the bones gleaming like knives. He smiled at her with blackened lips over rotted teeth, a smile like Satan himself. He held something out to her, and rasped, "You must play kulith better than that,* ostiu, *or else . . ."*

"Cam! Cam dear, wake up, you're dreaming!"

She clawed up from sleep, gasping, tears on her cheeks, and looked wildly around. Where was Aveo? Where was *she*? Luna Station . . .

"You had a nightmare," Jane said, one kindly hand on Cam's shoulder. "Do you want to talk about it?"

"No!"

The hand withdrew. "I didn't mean to pry, truly. I'm just concerned. You seem to be under so much stress. . . ."

You don't know a tenth of it, lady. "No, I'm— It's okay." Jane had read about Cam's "breakdown," of course—the entire world had read about that hotel clerk's lies. Or were they lies? Cam couldn't tell anymore. "I'm fine. I'm going back to sleep. See, this is me, fast asleep."

If only.

The next day Cam's subgroup left in the rover for their sightseeing trip to Selene City and the Atoner base. The rover held four: Cam and Frank, who had insisted on going together, Jane, and the Farrington Tours escort-plus-rover-driver, Terry Siekert. Slight and pale, Terry was finishing his 180-day shift at Luna Station and apparently none the worse for it. Cam saw Frank studying Terry intently. She knew why, and her stomach tightened.

She almost cried out with relief when she saw Selene

City. It had a big dome! People walked around inside it! True, the whole thing was no more than the size of half a football field and much of it was taken up with more of the trailer-modules, but after the shuttle and the station this seemed as spacious as Uldunu's palace on Kular.

The rover drove in and out of an air lock, and Cam bolted from the rover into the dome. Frank gave her an odd look. Cam laughed wildly. Her feet were finally again on ground— Well, no, it was some kind of hard plastic floor, but it would do. She could adapt. She had adapted on Kular, hadn't she? She could do this.

Frank said, "Calm down, Cam. Don't have another melt-down."

"Fuck you, Olenik," she said, almost amiably, and followed Terry Siekert inside a trailer for dinner with the scientists of Selene City. However, once they were seated at a long table with three men and two women, things again turned sour.

It was obvious that the moon tourists were barely tolerated here. The governments that funded Selene might welcome Farrington's hefty donations, but the scientists living and working on the moon considered the visitors to be overprivileged and intrusive nuisances. Their mood worsened when Terry posed Cam again and again with each scientist, had her make inquiries she didn't understand about each piece of equipment, videoed and photographed and holoed her from every possible angle.

"I think that's enough pictures," said Dr. Alyssa Frantz, senior something-or-other. She was about Jane's age but cold-looking and snotty. Cam had disliked her immediately, and one or two remarks she'd made since only deepened that dislike. "Surely by now you have enough pixels showcasing the glory of Camilla O'Kane back on the moon."

"Allie," a bald man said warningly.

"No, go ahead," Cam said. All at once her fidgety, half-hysterical nerves hardened and focused. She could feel it happening. This woman with a stick up her ass was every-thing Cam hated, everything that had kept her down back in Nebraska, everything that had driven her to volunteer to become a Witness in the first place. "What about the glory of Camilla O'Kane back on the moon?"

"I think I've said all I want to say on that topic," Dr. Frantz said, but her gaze flickered over Cam. *I know you, that gaze said, and you're nothing.*

And I know you. "You imagine that I'm here for glory and publicity for myself," Cam said, "while you're here for serious science work."

"I really don't want to discuss this, Ms. O'Kane. Can we please eat our dinners in peace?"

"No. We can't. Tell me, Dr. Frantz, what strikes you as more 'serious work' than spreading the truth about hu-manity having an afterlife? With all the hope and comfort that gives people?"

"Allie . . . ," repeated the bald man, but not as if he ex-pected to be listened to.

"Nothing would be more important if it were true, in-stead of a pack of wish-fulfillment lies. Tell me, Ms. O'Kane, are you familiar with the recent work by Gilbert and Schumaker at Harvard and by Murakami at RIKEN? No? I didn't think so. They've had some rather astonish-ing breakthroughs concerning the electrical field that sur-rounds the human head from brain activity, including how that field might potentially carry information via electro-magnetic fluctuations."

Cam struggled to follow this. The bald man said to her, "What Alyssa means—"

"I'm not stupid," Cam snapped, and now the entire ta-ble had fallen silent, listening. "I know 'what Alyssa means.' She's talking about Lucca's idea that what hap-pened on Kular was telepathy, not seeing the dead."

"Bingo," someone murmured, while the bald man smiled timidly and tried again. "Yes, you see, Ms. O'Kane, most of us find it a bit easier to—"

"To reject a hard truth in favor of an explanation that fits with the science you already believe. Even if you're wrong."

"Until we have any real evidence that—"

"And what I saw doesn't count as evidence?" Cam was shouting now, and Jane put a hand on her arm. Cam shook it off. "My eyewitness account doesn't mean anything? And not Frank's and not Jack's and not Andy's and not Christina's and—"

"None of you is a trained observer, are you?" Dr. Frantz said. Cam knew her type through and through—not the kind to back down from a fight, and always sure she was right. Always! Dismissing somebody like Cam even when Cam was the one who was right. . . . God, *was* she right what were the Atoners doing why hadn't they spoken to her since—

Frank, expressionless, said, "Dr. Frantz, Lucca Maduro is just one untrained observer, too."

"True," Dr. Frantz said, "and his theory is certainly unproven as yet, as well. But at least it has the merit of—"

"You mean at least it comes from somebody with college degrees and not a stupid trashy PR flack like me!" Cam shouted. "Why don't you just say that? God, don't any of you people ever say what you mean?"

"Cam, dear, you're overwrought," said Jane Kingwell, whom suddenly Cam despised as much as the rest of them.

Dr. Frantz said, "I really don't descend to name-calling, Ms. O'Kane. And, of course, you've already done it for me."

Cam launched herself across the table. It was done before her brain registered what her muscles were doing. She leaped with fist raised and caught Alyssa Frantz on the side of her arrogant, patronizing head. The scientist went down like a stone, like the stones Frank had hidden the genes under, the precious DNA this woman wasn't going to let her have, she stood with gobbets of flesh hanging from her bones. . . .

Then Frank had Cam pinned against the wall while the others scrambled and exclaimed like ants in a disturbed hive and everything—all the noises and actions and explanations—seemed to be happening a long distance away, or to somebody else. The only thing real wasn't actually real at all: *Aveo, standing in his brown skirt, shaking his cadaverous skull and saying, "You must play kulith better than that, ostiu. You simply must."*

Cam started to cry.

63: POSTED ON WHYWAIT.COM

Posted: April 27, 2021
By: questiongirl614
Subject: Web Testament

My real name is Chiara Joy Donaldson. I'm 16. I can post this infermation here now becuse by the time you read it, I will be dead. I'm writing this becuse the world needs to understand something and I feel that Ive been chosen to explain it. Thats a big honur and I want to live up to it.

What you shoud know: THIS LIFE IS ONLY THE BEGINING!!!

It's like a tree. First its just a little stick with maybe two leaves and people step on you or animals eat you or you get run over by the mow-bot. Then when the tree gets bigger, everything gets better until finally your a huge beautiful oak or maple and your all you can be. Well in this life we are just sticks and that's why its so hard with people hurt and wars and starving to deth. But in the next life it won't be like that so why wait? Like the sussiety says. You can skip the bad stuff in this life so why woodnt you??????

I'm not really dead. I'm on the second road. You can come to. See ya there!

Chiara

64: SOLEDAD

Soledad braced her feet, held the Beretta steady, and fired. The aluminum can leaped into the air. Lucca said, "Very nice, *cara*. You are a natural at what you should not be doing at all."

"*You* do it." She lowered the pistol. "How did you learn to shoot, anyway? Doesn't Italy have strict gun-control laws? You couldn't have grown up doing this."

He shrugged. "Laws never apply equally to all families."

Of course not; that was a thing she already knew. Her family had not been one of those to which laws did not apply. Soledad braced herself again, fired, and hit the second can propped on the outcropping of rock. The report echoed off the mountains and a flock of crows took noisy wing. Silence floated back through the soft April air. A breeze brushed her cheek, smelling of spring.

They stood in the small clearing behind Anna Parker's cabin, where patches of very small pink and purple wild-flowers bloomed in the sunny spots. Gray trees wore un-furled leaves of tender yellow-green like curlers on old ladies' heads. It was one of the most peaceful scenes that Soledad had ever witnessed. She didn't care.

She and Lucca had been here a week, waiting for his contacts to call him. And not once had Soledad taken off James's sweater. There was bottled water to drink but very little to wash in beyond the necessities, and Soledad could smell her own reek. She didn't care about that, either.

She shot the third can off the rock and Lucca said quietly, "You should see your face as you do that."

"Why?" she said without interest.

"You look exactly as you have been behaving."

She didn't ask further; she knew what Lucca meant. She looked cold, contained, unfeeling. Did Lucca sense the hell of emotion underneath or what it cost her to contain it? Probably, but it didn't matter. All this week he had been perfect: respectful, distant, impersonal. At night he slept in the bunk above her as if they were brother and sister, and if he heard her sleepless thrashing in the bed, if he noticed that she wore James's sweater day and night, if he was concerned that she ate almost nothing, he didn't say so. He was uniformly calm and attentive. He was playing a role, and so was she. This was the first time he'd remarked on her behavior.

"I'm fine."

"Oh, yes, of course you are. *Cara,* who are you shooting at?"

She didn't answer.

"Because I am not going to let you have the gun when we find James. I want you to know this now."

She swung around to face him, so fast the barrel of the Beretta pointed right at his chest. Lucca paled, reached out, and turned it away. He said, "And that is why."

"What is why? You know I wouldn't shoot you!"

"No, not intentionally. But in your present state of training and your present state of mind—"

"You don't know anything about my state of mind."

"Ah, Soledad, you are not that stupid."

It stopped her, if only because he seldom used her name, merely the meaningless *cara.*

He went on, "You must remember, I lost my Gianna, as you have lost James."

Fury rose in her. She pushed it down, because if one emotion broke through, they all might. Her voice stayed low as she said, "It's not the same. Don't pretend it is. Gianna didn't choose to leave you, didn't . . . Lucca, if you're not going to let me carry the gun, then why are you teaching me to use it?"

"You wanted to learn. And here we are with little to do . . . *Cara,* I ask you again, who are you shooting at? Not those helpless tins."

She said evenly, "I'm shooting at Atoners."

An unseen bird began to sing, an operatic outpouring of loud song, joyous and insistent. Lucca said, "The bird is in that bush to your right . . . no, closer to the cabin . . . yes, there. Kill it."

Soledad stared at him.

"You heard me. Fire at the bird."

"No."

"Then what makes you think you could shoot an Atoner? Assuming, of course, we ever meet up with one, which I doubt will happen." He watched her intently.

"That bird never fucked over the human race. Never promised something and failed to deliver. Never used people, never worked underhandedly to—"

"To do what, *cara*? We still don't know what the Atoners are doing with James. It may be an action for good."

"You don't believe that, Lucca. Don't try to goad me. You're the one who's distrusted them since we got back from Kular . . . and you were right. Is that what you want me to say—to admit that you were right? Okay, you were. We don't understand those alien minds, we don't know if the Atoner message is true or not, we can't trust them." She heard her own voice: dead calm on the surface, and only on the surface. "Why did they give James a personal shield? Why did they use him to spy on you and me? God knows I'd have talked to them directly. We all would have, except maybe you, and so would the governments of every country on Earth."

She opened the pistol and slid out the bullet clip. He opened his mouth to say something, but Soledad wasn't finished.

"And when I said that I was 'shooting at Atoners,' it was metaphorical. There's a difference between desire and action, you know."

"Are you sure about that?"

"Stop it, Lucca. I only wanted the gun to make sure nobody stops me from getting to James. The gun is just a threat."

"Which you will wave about like some third-rate robber in the mall branch of a bank, thinking that it will make the manager open the vault? You must know that when we find James—if we find James—your government will already be there."

The bird stopped singing. A chipmunk ran across the clearing, something in its mouth. Soledad saw Diane Lovett saying, *Lucca's good, but we're the United States government, for God's sake!* "So?"

"So they may or may not stop you from approaching James. Yes, if they wish him to stay undisturbed. No, if they don't want to blow their own cover, or if they wish to hear what you two say to each other. But they certainly will not let you shoot him. And I will not let you carry the gun. You were right—Italians do not approve of personal firearms."

"Are you going to carry it?"

"Yes."

"Hypocrite."

"Innocent."

"Lucca, don't think you can try to—" The handheld shrilled.

It lay at their feet on the new grass, a splotch of dark metal against the raw green. Soledad's head jerked to look down at the screen. She didn't recognize the number. Carl Lewis, calling from a pay phone somewhere?

No. Lucca answered and conducted a long conversation in Italian. When it finished, he said, "My people found James."

Her throat closed. She managed, "But Carl—"

"I never believed that your cut-rate journalist could find him."

"You didn't tell me that."

Lucca gazed at her. His eyes, a paler blue than James's, seemed to reflect all light back at her. "There are many things unsaid here, Soledad."

What could she answer to that? But it didn't matter; only one thing mattered. "Where is James?"

"In Brooklyn."

At first it staggered her, and then it made sense. James had disappeared after clubbing a federal agent with a fist hardened by an Atoner shield, and the Agency would have instantly watched planes, trains, and buses out of New York. And Brooklyn had changed radically in the last decade. The blacks had moved, or been moved, out of the disastrous projects. Gentrification had taken hold and then, abruptly, had failed. In the ever-changing lottery of New York boroughs, Brooklyn had reverted to what it had been a hundred years ago: the first stop for hordes of immigrants, this time most of them illegal. Brooklyn was a warren of shifting streets, alleys, lanes made of temporary structures among the crumbling permanent buildings. Some areas were nothing more than rubble; some flourished in a dozen languages; some reflected a desperate attempt to re-create the old country in the inhospitable new. There were no reliable maps of this new Brooklyn. Landlords had given up on at least half the buildings. Police did not like to go there, and so local vigilante groups flourished. Anyone could disappear into Brooklyn.

Including an Atoner?

Soledad said, "Call your chopper and let's go."

* * *

As the helicopter lifted, Aldo shouted something over his shoulder to Lucca. Lucca turned to Soledad. "Cam and Frank Olenik are on the moon."

She nodded. A sudden memory took her: Cam at the start of the voyage to Kular, looking impossibly beautiful and very young, although in fact she was only two years younger than Soledad. Cam had glowed with anticipation: *This is going to be so wonderful! We're going to the stars!* Soledad had watched Lucca raise his head to stare at her, his personal gloom reluctantly dispelled by her excited joy.

What did Cam feel now about the Atoners? Why had she returned to the moon?

The chopper approached New York. Soledad could just make out the blue of water on the horizon, blending with the blue sky. Lucca had said that of course his chopper would be tracked the second it lifted off in Toronto and that the Agency would guess where he and Soledad were headed. *They may or may not stop you from approaching James.*

Now she could see Manhattan below her: the levees holding out the ocean at the south part of the island, the skyscrapers in midtown, the half-constructed dome over Central Park. Other choppers, mostly one-person copterettes, flew low below them, an orchestrated ballet that nonetheless scared her far more than the flight in an alien ship through interstellar space, and what kind of sense did that make? But the Atoner ship to the stars seemed a long time ago.

On her lap lay James's sweater, neatly folded now, stained and smelling of too many wearings.

Aldo shouted something to Lucca, who shouted at Soledad, "We're cleared to land at the helioport in Park Slope. That's a good sign. And something else—Cam struck a woman in Selene City. Some sort of argument, and apparently Cam just went crazy."

"But I will not," Soledad said, reassuring him, reminding herself.

The chopper began its descent.

65: FROM *THE PURPLE BREADBOX*

The E-zine of Satire

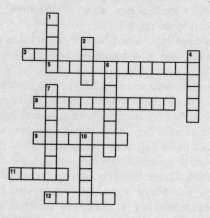

ACROSS

3. Network that don't work no more
5. Pulitzer novel that wasn't novel
8. Like Atoner information
9. Good nickname for Madam Prez
11. Greatest heist in history—or not
12. Org. named for worst senator ever

DOWN

1. Winegrower fermented very sour
2. Odd preference of certain aliens
4. City name launching 1,000 bad jokes
6. Cut-rate lunar Sarah Bernhardt
7. Reddest thing on Valentine's Day 1929
10. Worst actor on Dreamworks Holo

(answers on next page)

Answers

If you didn't know these answers, don't come out from your melting cave at Point Barrow and rejoin the world—you're too ignorant to survive out here.

ACROSS

3. NBC
5. *American Bulie*—rehashed Jay Porter, anyone?
8. Parsimonious
9. Palomino—spirited but not-too-bright blonde
11. Genes, ours
12. Green-o (self-explanatory)

DOWN

1. Lucca
2. Tyro (What—you aliens couldn't find any seasoned observers?)
4. Selene
6. Cam O'Kane: Best Supporting Actress in an Interstellar Drama
7. Massacre
10. Mallie—maybe she could play Cam O'Kane in the inevitable movie?

66: FRANK

The rover left Selene City at 9:00 A.M. EST the day after Cam attacked Dr. Frantz. Frank watched Cam, but this morning she seemed calm enough. He was surprised to find that he was the one feeling twitchy. Well, maybe not so surprised. It wasn't every day you got to set human history back on the right course.

The instant he thought this, he rejected it. He wasn't affecting history here; God was merely using him to carry out His work. Once Frank had that firmly in mind, he felt better and went back to surreptitiously checking Cam for any signs of blowing the whole scene. Although in one way, he didn't blame her for wildcatting Dr. Frantz. The woman was a clueless snob. Weren't scientists supposed to need evidence to come to conclusions? Dr. Frantz had called seeing the dead "a pack of wish-fulfillment lies," but she had no eyewitness evidence. She hadn't been on Susban. Frank had.

And there was another reason he didn't blame Cam as much as he once would have. Seeing her launch herself at that awful woman, watching her sob afterward, Frank had come to a realization: She was a child. That's how Darla might have behaved, if their parents hadn't raised her with better manners. Cam O'Kane, rich and "successful" and famous, was basically just a scared and scarred child. It didn't make him like her any better, but it did give him some perspective. *Suffer the little children to come unto me,* Christ had said, and so Frank felt bound to accept Cam in all her childish unpredictability, like it or not.

"How you feeling?" he said to her as they took their seats inside the rover.

"Great," she said shortly, "just great."

Terry Siekert, the Farrington Tours group leader who was also their driver, grimaced and started the engine.

The rover looked like a round-cornered rectangular box on tractor treads with a smaller box, the air lock, protruding out one side. Windows of clear, tough triple plastic allowed direct views out the front and side, augmented with a small display screen of images from the cameras mounted on the roof. The back half of the cramped space was all storage, life-support systems, and a chemical toilet in a closet small as a coffin. Terry sat in a seat up front, and two padded benches lined the sides, a short one beside the air-lock door and a longer one opposite. A table could be lowered between them from the ceiling. Frank sat on the short bench, opposite Cam and Jane.

"Here we go," said Jane, with cheerful pointlessness. Cam and Frank exchanged glances.

High contrasts of light and shadow meant they drove in and out of sunlight. Earth hung in the black sky and the stars shone high and cold. Frank twisted to see out the window behind him. Rocks, dust, the arid landscape of lifelessness. An appropriate setting for the Atoners; Christ's holy covenant was not here.

Terry said, "Shackleton Crater, which we're driving by right now, lies entirely within the South Pole–Aitken Basin, which is the largest known impact crater not only on the moon, but in the whole solar system. The Basin was named for the things that lie on either side of it: the lunar South Pole and the Aitken crater. The Basin is unique because—"

Terry rambled on about crustal thickness maps and geochemical signatures. He sounded much more cheerful now that they were away from Selene City. Out here, nobody except Farrington Tours could record anything Cam O'Kane might explode into. Jane, that sweet-natured soul, wouldn't set Cam off. Frank was presumably her friend. Terry would be rid of all of them by tomorrow, and what could happen before then?

Frank could have told him.

He listened to Terry's scientific information the way he listened to beach waves on his family's annual vacation to Lake Erie: as soothing background noise. Three hours to the Atoner base.

Two hours.

One hour, and they stopped for a cold lunch on the table let down from the ceiling. Cam ate heartily, which reassured Frank. Jane asked Terry what were probably intelligent questions. Finally she turned to Cam and said hesitantly, "Cam, I haven't wanted to pry and, of course, there's all that holocast material about the outside of the Atoner base and all your fascinating interviews about your experiences there, but I'm still wondering . . . can you or Frank add anything about what we're going to see this afternoon?"

Cam stopped eating, the remains of her sandwich halfway to her mouth. Frank held his breath. But after a long and painful moment—she was capable of saying anything, anything at all—Cam merely said, "No."

"Again, I didn't mean to pry."

"You're not prying. But everything that can be told about the Atoners I already said, and you just said you read it all. The rest can't be told except to people who were there . . . who saw . . ." She put her sandwich on the table and, to Frank's dismay, her eyes filled with tears.

"I'm sorry," Jane said. And then, with a tartness that Frank hadn't suspected her of, "It was a natural question, I think."

Terry jumped in with information about the elevated mineral abundance right there in the dust and rock under their rover.

* * *

When they reached the Atoner base, Frank felt his pulse quicken and his diaphragm tighten. *Steady, boy.* Soon now.

"There it is!" Terry said, with weary heartiness. "The temporary home of the only other known sentient species in the universe."

Not that there was much to see. The base looked exactly as it had when Frank last saw it six months ago, when he first saw it nearly a year ago. A gray opaque Dome, rising from the gray dusty ground littered with gray and black and dull red rocks of varying sizes. Five times before, Frank had walked between a shuttle and this strange up-turned bowl: to and from his initial interview, to and from his witness on Susban A, to his final trip back to Earth. His muscles remembered the weird spring-and-fall of walking in a space suit in the one-sixth Earth gravity. His mind remembered the childish sense of amazement: *I'm on the moon.* His soul remembered the belief that only God could create human beings and dictate their makeup: "Male and female He created them." All that, before he knew what the Atoners really were and what they had really done.

Jane peered out the window, twisting sideways on the bench beside Cam. "Terry, are you sure we can't go outside? We have the EVA equipment. . . ."

"Absolutely not," Terry said in a practiced tone. "Our license from the Office of Commercial Space Transportation of the Federal Aviation—"

Frank caught Cam's eye and nodded, and they both sprang.

Frank yanked Terry from his seat and threw him to the small clear space on the floor. The ropes, made from one of Frank's own shirts torn up just that morning, were already in his hand. He had kept in superb physical condition and he outweighed Terry by at least thirty pounds, and in three minutes Frank had the tour guide bound hands and feet. Cam had no trouble with Jane, either.

Thy will be done.

"What the fuck do you think you're doing?" Jane screamed, and Frank looked at her in surprise. Sweet old Jane.

"It's okay, nobody will hurt you," Cam said. Her face had gone so white that Frank thought she might faint, except that her dark eyes shone wildly. "I won't hurt you. I won't hurt anybody. Never again."

Terry said with an admirable willed calm—Frank could see the will— "What do you intend to do?"

"We're going outside!" Cam cried.

"You're already in violation of your signed agreement with Farrington, and going outside isn't only a danger to you and us, it will expose you to criminal prosecution."

"You'd have made a good cop," Frank said. It was his highest praise, or at least once it would have been. "But we have to do this."

Frank turned off all radio transmissions. He pulled open the storage locker and he and Cam donned EVA suits. It all came back to him, the right order for each piece of equipment, the procedures to check each other's suits, the weight of the helmet in his hands.

"If we stop transmitting to Luna Station, they'll send another rover after us," Terry said.

"I know," Frank said. After her first burst of cursing, Jane remained silent, but her expression held disgust, fear, and some other thing Frank couldn't name. He repeated, "We have to do this," and put on his helmet.

He and Cam stepped into the air lock, stood quietly for a long moment, and stepped out onto the surface of the moon.

67: SOLEDAD

The turko, an armored taxi able to stop ordinary bullets and the milder forms of roadside bombs, crept through the crowded streets of Brooklyn. Windowless, it transmitted views of the outside on a small viewscreen. The driver was a huge black man in a fez who wielded his joysticks as if they were butcher knives, in short, hard chops. He either didn't recognize Lucca or didn't care. Lucca had handed over his Beretta, which now lay on the *turko*'s sealed-off front seat until the cab reached its destination. The backseat smelled strongly of disinfectant.

Soledad stared at the viewscreen. Arab souks, jammed with hanging djellabas and bright cushions and squatting men drinking tea. On the next block, bodegas, which in turn gave way to a twisting lane of movable foamcast shelters. The *turko* could barely squeeze between them. Children darted after a soccer ball, adults swarmed like clamorous bees. Houses painted turquoise or silver, with crowds of women gossiping on the crumbling stoops. Signs in Russian, Arabic, Spanish, languages Soledad couldn't identify. Open stalls with black-market electronics and halal meat. Basement bars, Coptic crosses, gunges. Veiled women, bare-breasted women, young men in skimpy purple vests that displayed augmented muscles to the cold air. The noise was astonishing, a constant blended roar over which suddenly rose wailing from an unseen minaret. The sidewalk crackled with pop-ups.

"Soledad," Lucca said quietly, "whatever we find here, I want you to know something. I'm not helping you sort out all this in order to influence how you see the Atoners and their lies about an afterlife."

It was enough to wrench her out of her stony silence. "I didn't think that."

"Good."

"Why would it even occur to you that I'd think that? I know you're being a good friend, a . . . a big brother."

"Good," he repeated, and unzipped his jacket. The motion sent a wave of scent toward her: expensive leather and Lucca's unwashed body. Tension gave him a jawline like stone.

They turned onto a quieter street flanked by dilapidated houses that might have once been grand. In front of 1437, the old-fashioned painted number just barely discernible, the *turko* stopped. Lucca paid the driver, reclaimed his gun, and stuck it in the back waistband of his jeans under his open leather jacket.

Soledad started up the drooping steps. In her hand she clenched James's cashmere sweater. Lucca followed closely. Soledad sensed someone else fall in step behind Lucca, but Soledad didn't turn around. Let the agent follow them in, as long as he or she didn't try to stop Soledad. Let the agent witness, yes. It couldn't matter.

A dark first-floor hall with no metal detectors, no lobby, no visible security; the only surveillance camera had been shot out. A broken scooter leaned in a corner. Six reinforced metal doors, three to a side, opened off the hall. Lucca steered Soledad to 1C, at the back, and pressed the bell.

The surprising thing was that the door opened. A woman stood there, a young brown woman with short black hair crackling around her head. She smiled, unafraid, and exposed one red tooth. Lucca gave a small gasp. Soledad might have turned around then—Lucca was not the sort that gasped—but she felt rooted, as if she might never move again. The light in the hallway was dim and the light in the apartment apparently off, but Soledad could see the woman clearly. Small. Red toothed. Smiling. Pregnant.

"Pizza, yes?" the girl said, her accent very heavy. But the smile faded as she realized that there were two—three, how the fuck many Soledad no longer knew—people standing in the hallway.

"Frabilothatel!" James, completely naked, dashed into sight behind the pregnant girl, who opened her mouth to say something just as a gun fired and the end of everything began.

68: CAM

As Cam stepped out on the moon, nerves as electrified as a cow fence, she had a crazy thought: *The future depends on human hair.* Just what Sissy at the Cut 'n Curl in Jay, Nebraska, had always said: *It's all about the hair, honey. With the right hair you can go anyplace.*

Cam laughed and Frank turned in his bulky suit to look at her. Over the suit-to-suit radio he said, "Silence." She thought of reminding him that he'd turned off all transmissions to and from the rover but decided against it. He was just being cautious, his usual anal-retentive self. Well, no, not just that—the prick was also afraid she would say something out loud about hair. He'd never trusted her, she was only here because she could arrange for the trip. Well, fuck Frank. Whatever the reason, Cam was here, and together they were going to restore what the Atoners had taken away. Just spreading the Atoner message apparently wasn't enough. It should have been, but it wasn't. What it got everybody was suicides and death threats and weird cults. This way was better.

She scanned the rocks dotting the plain, hoping Frank could remember where he'd left his packet of hair. The Atoners had taken their shuttles back inside the Dome, or melted them down, or maybe sent them home—who knew? Cam didn't see any scorched area like the one Soledad had left when she used a shuttle to cremate Aveo's body. (Aveo—where was he now? *Stay focused.*) That meant there was no way, in the featureless plain, to know if they now even stood on the same side of the Atoner Dome as the shuttles from Kular had come down last summer and fall.

Frank walked slowly, scanning the ground. Clumsily he dropped to his knees and began moving stones about the size of a kitchen garbage can. Cam noted the general configuration of the closest rocks: two gray ones roughly the same size, then an even larger reddish one a yard closer to the Dome. She touched Frank on the shoulder, pointed to the rock arrangement and then farther along a circumference around the Dome, and pantomimed looking. He nodded and pointed to one of the gray rocks.

It was slow work. They had an hour's worth of air, Frank had said. No one knew what they were looking for, and Terry would have no way of knowing what they found.

"They'll search us," Cam had said.

"I'll swallow the hair if I have to. It'll take a few days to work through my digestive system, if I don't eat anything."

Eeeeuuuuwwww. But if that's what it took. . . . "Are you sure scientists can get the DNA out of your shit?"

"Yes. I researched it online."

Cam crawled around on her knees. Nothing, nothing, nothing . . . A voice on the radio. "Frank and Cam! Come back inside the rover right now!"

Terry. How had he gotten loose of his bonds to turn on the radio?

Frank's voice said inside her helmet, "We'll be back soon, Terry."

"Now!"

"How did you get loose?" Cam said, despite herself.

"Come in now! You can't get into the Atoner base—don't you think that NASA's tried?"

So that's what Terry thought she and Frank were doing: knocking on the Atoners' door. Well, good. The curve of the Dome now shielded them from the rover's sight. But what if Terry drove the rover straight at them? . . . Would he do that? Would he try to kill them?

Why not, Cam? You killed everybody on Kular who interfered with what you wanted.

"Come in *now*!" Terry sounded like Cam's mother calling her in from play when it got dark outside.

Cam risked talking to Frank. "How much air left?"

"Half an hour. Silence, Cam."

Bossy bastard. Desperately Cam searched for two gray rocks the size of a garbage can with a reddish rock a yard closer to the Dome. Nothing, nothing . . . No rover drove around the Dome. The rocks weren't hard to move in the light gravity, but her bulky EVA suit made lifting or even rolling them awkward. She couldn't remember which of the two gray rocks Frank had looked under, so in each pair she had to move both. Nothing, nothing . . . What if she missed a pair of gray rocks? *Please don't let me miss it.* . . . Some of this dust had been lying around her undisturbed for thousands of years, Terry had said. Nothing, nothing . . . *You must play kulith better than that,* ostiu . . . Nothing . . .

"Cam. Come."

A hot retort leaped to her lips—she wasn't a fucking dog!—but then her mind caught up with her indignation and registered Frank's tone. She ran toward him.

In his glove, a gleam of yellow, shocking in this gray landscape.

She stared. Yellow cloth, surprisingly filmy . . . Frank shook moondust off the delicate bundle. Couldn't he have found any sturdier cloth? This looked like it came from a negligee or something . . . *Frank, you secret stud.* Cam's head swam. She laughed out loud.

The yellow packet in one hand, Frank crossed himself with the other and lowered his head. Praying. Well, it was all right for some, but Cam felt sudden worry snap at her like a Rottweiler. If Terry and Jane were loose in the rover, they would get the jump on Frank and Cam as soon as they entered the rover in their clumsy EVA suits. They might take away the hair. Maybe Frank could swallow it in the air lock, in the brief time between repressurization and the sliding open of the inner door. Terry wouldn't kill them by fucking with the air lock, would he, or even locking the rover from the inside or—

"Cam!"

She looked up. Frank pointed over her shoulder, swinging his arm so wildly, in such an un-Frank-like way, that he lost his balance and fell. Cam almost lost hers as she spun to face the direction he pointed: at the Dome.

A section of it had opened, and an Atoner walked toward them.

69: ARTWORK IN MS. JUDY KESINGER'S SECOND-GRADE CLASS, TOPEKA, KANSAS

Gramma
If you can see this frum the sekund rode then draw
one mor flowar so I no.
thank you.
Your frend
Hannah

70: LUCCA

Lucca heard the shot, grabbed Soledad, and hit the dirty floor of the hallway. Nothing to roll behind, nowhere to hide her . . . *cazzo.* He shielded Soledad's body with his own and groped for his Beretta.

Another rapid string of shots. He was hit, his leg, it burned as if acid had been thrown on it. . . . He got the Beretta free and raised his head—who the hell to shoot at? The hallway was full of people, all of them screaming. A body fell beside him, spurting blood but still firing a semi-automatic, the bullet explosions so loud it deafened him to all other sound. Some of the flying blood hit Lucca's eyes, obscuring his vision. He swiped it away and again tried to see whom to aim at. Then he was pushed so hard that his injured leg sent fire directly into his brain, pain so intense that for a moment he barely noticed that the Beretta had been snatched from his hand. It fired inches from his head, the explosion of sound adding to the agony in his leg to create a red cloud that he could actually see, so that nothing else was visible but that crimson haze, like the finest of blood droplets shrieking and dancing in the air. . . .

Then his mind cleared, the pain became bearable, and he was looking up at Soledad, on her feet and holding Lucca's gun in the perfect two-handed stance he had taught her behind the mountain cabin.

"Drop the gun, Soledad. Now," said a voice rigid with forced calm. Lucca knew that voice, had heard it . . . His mind fumbled and he tried to turn his head, but the slight movement again sent pain racing along his nerves. But he knew the voice; he had heard it often enough on surveillance recordings. Diane Lovett, from the American Agency.

Lucca's Beretta crashed to the floor. He reached for it, but Diane said, "No, Lucca," and he let it lie. Blood poured from his thigh, but despite that, his vision abruptly expanded, as if a zoom lens had suddenly snapped on, and every detail of the hallway became preternaturally clear.

A man lying dead beside him, eyes staring sightlessly at the L-shaped crack in the ceiling, a small red-rimmed hole from Lucca's gun just above the bridge of his nose.

Soledad lurching over the body to kneel beside James, whose naked body had been so torn by bullets that it looked like the ground veal of Lucca's cook.

Diane Lovett lowering her gun, walking toward him, picking up the Beretta with two delicate fingers, glancing sharply at Lucca.

All the other people, each limned so clearly in Lucca's mind that he could have identified them even years later: the three other agents, the fat woman in the orange skirt who was still screaming, the peering boy clothed in rags and curiosity, the man with dark curly hair and full beard holding an unfired shotgun and looking uncertain whether any of the others threatened his home and, if so, whom he should shoot.

And the pregnant Kularian girl, unhurt because she wore the Atoner personal shield off which most of those bullets had ricocheted, and shouting at an empty patch of air beside the dead man's body, just at head height for a standing man, words Lucca had not heard in nearly a year and didn't expect to hear ever again: *"Kla shulathewithoz, beenitu kla!"*

Not the second road! Not now!

Diane Lovett stepped over him to go to Soledad. Another agent reached under the body beside Lucca, pulled the dead man's wallet from his pocket, and tore it open. Into his handheld he rasped, "Who the fuck is 'Carl

Lewis'? . . . Well, run it now, damn it!" In the distance si-
rens began to scream. Lucca strained to hear over the
noise—the fat woman had never stopped screaming nor
the Kularian girl shouting—but there was no sound from
Soledad.

Lucca closed his eyes and gave himself to pain.

71: CAM

The Atoner was *small*. That was Cam's first thought: *Our whole species was changed by something so small and fat!* Then she realized that maybe this wasn't an Atoner at all, just a machine or a holo or something that humans hadn't yet invented and couldn't imagine. It must not be a real Atoner because it didn't wear a space suit. It walked naked and alive on the dead surface of the moon.

Maybe a yard high, with soft, faintly green skin that looked pasty and loose. Two fat legs and four, five, six arms . . . but they weren't arms, they were vacuum hose–like things that each ended in four fingers. A head shaped like a funnel with the open top full of some writhy stuff like black worms, two eyes, a mouth but no nose . . . The fearsome Atoner, shaper of human destiny, looked like a seasick Pillsbury Doughboy on a bad hair day.

"Hello, Cam. Hello, Frank," it said, and it was the voice of Cam's first interview, of the recordings of NASA and UN radio speeches, of Soledad's tape on the shuttle in orbit over Kular the day Aveo died. "Give it to me, please."

"No," Frank said.

"Give it to me, please."

Frank ran, leaping in clumsy bounds away from and around the curve of the Dome, toward the rover. He ran, and then all at once he stopped running, so suddenly that his top half swayed back and forth, like a tree in a gale. Cam tried to lift her foot, and couldn't. She, too, was rooted to the ground. It was the same rooting her personal shield had done on Kular, only not under her control. Or Frank's.

The Atoner, or Atoner-thing, waddled to Frank. Frank's whole body stood motionless—at least Cam could move the top half of hers—but the little alien effortlessly lifted Frank's gloved hand and removed the yellow packet.

"I'm sorry," it said in that same incongruously deep, creepily polite voice, "but you cannot have this. We watch Earth, you know. You cannot have this." The Atoner waddled to the Dome. A section of the opaque gray wall slid open, revealing swirling gray fog. The alien went inside, the door closed, and Cam's body was released from the shield.

"You fuckers!" she screamed. Red mist settled over her brain—she could *feel* it, burning and stinging like a million flying fire ants. "How dare you, how could you, you—"

"Cam!" Frank called, but she barely heard him. It all rushed over her, then—all the *trying* so fucking hard, trying on Kular and trying on Earth with all those lecture performances and trying on the moon, trying and trying and trying to get it right and every fucking time sabotaged by aliens who did—who didn't— All the men she'd killed— Aveo—

"You could have helped us!" she cried at the solid Dome. "You could have been our mentors, our . . . our interpreters, our fucking guardians! Your race could have helped ours to handle the new genes again, could have shown us the right road. . . . You could have been our big brothers!"

Rushing over to the Dome, she beat on it with her gloved fists, sobbing and crying out, not even knowing what she said. "Brothers! Yeah, you were our brothers, all right— like Cain to Abel! You robbed us and then you kidnapped us and then you show up promising atonement and when there is no fucking atonement, all you do is rob us again— Those genes are ours, do you hear me, you bastards? Ours! Ours!"

"Cam!" said Frank, pulling at her, trying to put the bulky inflated arms of the EVA suit around her.

"—*ours,* and you could have been our guides, our guardians, you could have shown us how to play kulith better— What was it? Jealousy? Can we go on after death and you can't so you took that knowledge away from us, was that it—"

"We have to go, Cam. Air will run out. Cam—"

"You could have been our bridge to the next stage for our entire race!"

She let him lead her, still sobbing, back to the rover. In the air lock she collapsed against the wall. Frank stood close to her. As soon as possible—too soon, the air lock wasn't fully pressurized—he pulled off his helmet. Then hers, and he stood even closer and put his mouth against her ear. With one hand he unsealed one of the pockets on his suit, shielding the action with both their bodies, the whole thing at double speed. He forced her head to look down, whispered to her, and resealed the pocket.

Then it was over.

Dazed, she heard the inner air-lock door slide open. Terry and Jane weren't untied after all. But Terry had somehow gotten his boot off and lay on the floor, hands tied to the bench post where Frank had left him, one foot propped up on the console with his big toe on the radio key. He was talking, yelling, but Cam wasn't listening.

What Frank had shown her in his pocket was a duplicate dusty, filmy yellow cloth packet.

What he said in her ear was, "Evidence tampering isn't always a crime."

72: SOLEDAD

Numb, Soledad knelt over James. The thing below her barely looked like James. Most of his face had been shot away. His bright blond hair matted with blood, still flowing . . . how could a person have so much blood? She laid a hand on his left thigh, one of the few patches of skin not torn or bloody, a glistening expanse of smooth, pale flesh over hard muscles, warm and wet.

Wet, but not with blood. James had been in the shower. That was why he was naked. He'd been in the shower and he'd bolted out when he heard the girl answer the door because he didn't know if she really understood how dangerous that was in this place, or if she was wearing her personal shield . . . as he was not. You didn't wear a shield in the shower, how could you get clean . . . they were expecting a pizza, such an ordinary thing, but the bell rang too soon and James heard it and knew . . .

"Soledad." Very gentle. Soledad went on resting her hand on James's warm thigh.

"Soledad." Diane's hand on her elbow, guiding her, and Soledad rose. She dropped the blue cashmere sweater over James, as if to keep warmth in the body losing all warmth.

"Lucca?" The word hurt, as if it traveled up her throat with stingers unfurled.

"Shot, but I don't think it's serious. A ricochet bullet. Soledad, who is Carl Lewis?"

Soledad looked, then, at the man she'd killed. He had been spraying bullets around the hallway like a gardener hosing plants. . . . No, that wasn't right. Her mind wasn't working right. Something was wrong with her memory. Carl Lewis had been firing at . . . at the girl. Yes. The girl wearing her personal shield because the Earth *was* a dangerous place and the Atoners wanted to protect her unborn baby. And James had not been wearing his shield because he'd been in the shower—

Soledad squatted beside Lucca. His face contorted with pain, but he opened his eyes. "I'm sorry, *cara*."

"Did you know? About . . . her? Anything at all?"

His eyes went wide and she believed him. "No, I didn't know. I would not have . . . have brought you if . . ."

"Easy, buddy," said a medic who had somehow appeared, and Soledad was pushed aside. She straightened and found herself staring into the eyes of the pregnant child-woman from another planet. The girl was crying.

"Did you love him?" Soledad asked. "Or was he just the stud that the Atoners chose to get the DNA back into the human genome?" But the English words must have been too sophisticated for her; uncomprehending, she turned away.

Diane said to Soledad, "We have to get you out of here before anyone arrives. All of you."

"I'm going with Lucca. Is an ambulance—"

"Agency chopper. Come!"

Soledad heard the chopper then, although she couldn't imagine where it could possibly land. The girl—where was she from? Kular? Susban? Londu?—had begun shouting again in her own language. Soledad walked by Lucca's stretcher, reaching for his hand. He squeezed her fingers. She kept her gaze on him as Diane hustled them from the lobby, only looking back once to see if, somehow, an Atoner had appeared on the scene to witness firsthand the havoc its race had brought on hers. But, of course, there was no Atoner in the grimy Brooklyn hallway. They didn't witness in person on any human planet; it was far too dangerous down there among the savages.

73: TRANSCRIPT, OVAL OFFICE
TAPE #17281

Property of the White House

CHIEF OF STAFF WALTER STEINHAUER (WS): "Ma'am, this—

PRESIDENT: My God, Walter, what is it? You look like—

WS: This just came from Selene City. . . . They have . . . a Farrington Tours rover. . . . You better read it.

[long silence]

PRESIDENT: Did they—

WS: I don't know!

[long silence]

PRESIDENT: [barely audible] Tell Colonel Shoniker I said to go ahead with his recommendations.

WS: Judith—

PRESIDENT: Do it. Now.

74: FRANK

Frank thought rapidly about the order of what should come next. Order was critically important. If he removed the yellow packet from his EVA suit before he untied Jane and Terry, Terry might see it or spy-eyes Frank didn't know about might see. If he untied Terry first, he might have to scuffle with him. Frank couldn't drive the rover. The miniscule john had no room to remove a space suit. Terry watched him with eyes more full of anger and bitterness than Frank would have thought possible, although at least the man had shut up.

Frank began peeling off his suit. Cam's was already down around her knees. She looked too happy, damn her. The woman just didn't have a poker face. But the next moment he realized that he'd underestimated her: She was creating a distraction.

"We saw an Atoner!"

Both Terry's and Jane's gazes jerked toward her as if yanked on a rope.

"The Dome opened and it just walked out! Little, squishy-looking, a tiny bit green, it had these wiggly worms for hair, sort of, it waddled like a duck because its legs were so fat. . . ." She babbled on. Jane clearly didn't believe her. Frank couldn't read Terry's expression, but it didn't matter. Frank had the hair—the real hairs, the ones from the child on Susban, with the real genes—out of the EVA suit and clutched in his hand. The filmy yellow material with its precious burden compressed to almost nothing. That was why he'd chosen that cloth.

He said, "I'll untie you as soon as I use the can," went into the bathroom, and put the hair into the special pocket he'd sewn into the inside of his boxers. Even if he was forced to strip, the pocket wasn't noticeable unless you were looking for it, and no one would be.

When he came out, Cam had freed Jane and started on Terry. Terry stood and put his boots back on. He said nothing as he sat in the front seat and started the engine. But, of course, Cam felt compelled to talk.

"We're sorry, Terry. But please try to understand. So much happened to both of us out there, it changed us so much, and we just wanted to ask the Atoners why. But the Atoner that came out from the Dome wouldn't say anything. He—it—just stood there, looked at us, and went back in. Still, we had to do it, everything that happened out there just keeps eating away at us until we could barely even function. . . . You have to understand!"

"No. I don't," Terry said tonelessly while Frank shot Cam a look of dislike. He'd been in no danger of not functioning.

Jane said, "I think you need professional help, both of you. I know a good psychiatrist in New York who—"

"Oh, shut the fuck up, Jane," Cam said.

The trip back to Luna Station passed in total silence, three hours of it, even Cam. Frank was grateful. He stared out the window at the arid moonscape and rehearsed the next steps. Could Farrington bring some sort of lawsuit against him and Cam? Maybe. But it didn't matter. All that mattered was to get the hair to a biotech company, an ethical one with no government ties, that would agree to clone the genes and help restore them to humanity. Maybe a fertility clinic would be best, so people could choose to have them implanted in embryos—could they do that yet? Frank wasn't sure. But if they couldn't, then the hair could be saved until the technology caught up.

Maybe he should rent a safe-deposit box. Yes, that would be best. He hoped it didn't cost too much. And a lawyer—did he need a lawyer? He didn't really trust lawyers—every cop knew how lawyers could screw with legitimate charges against some scumbag and get him clean off. But the safe-deposit box, definitely—

"We're here," Terry said. The rover drove into the clear plastic "garage" and it pressurized. The four of them got out, still in silence. The door to the Clarke Module opened. Terry and Jane went first and then, before Frank and Cam could pass through, the door was slammed shut.

Cam cried, "They're going to kill us! They're going to depressurize—"

"No." Frank willed himself to calm. "No, they won't do that."

They didn't. But as his legs buckled and his head grew light, Frank knew what they had done. A knockout gas, an emergency contingency tool because tourists after all were selected only for their money and who was to say some of them might not be genuinely crazy. . . . *Hail Mary, Mother of God, pray for us now and in the hour of our death. . . .*

He went down.

When he came to, he lay strapped in the Farrington shuttle. Cam lay unconscious in the seat next to him. No other tourists occupied the space-bus shuttle, but Terry sat at the controls and three other people, a crowd in the tiny space, stood gazing down at him. No weightlessness— they were either on the moon still or else on Earth. Frank craned his neck to see a window. Earth filled the sky, a glowing blue-and-white ball. So—still on the moon.

"Can you see clearly?" a woman asked. She began resting boxes against his body and studying their small readout screens. A doctor.

"Yes."

"Trouble breathing?"

"No." Dread began its slow climb along his spinal column. It didn't matter what they did with him, but please don't let them already have the packet. . . . He wore his own clothes, a good sign. *Hail Mary, Mother of God . . .*

The doctor finished and a small man took her place. Frank hadn't seen him at Farrington Tours. He must have come out from Selene City, that was the only other possibility—how long had Frank been unconscious?

The small man studied Frank intently. He had a completely bald head like a peeled egg and very deep, almost black, brown eyes. He held up the yellow packet of hair. "Tell us about this, Frank."

Frank closed his eyes.

Terry, apparently unable to contain himself any longer, burst out, "Didn't you know that transmitters on your EVA suit operate continually to Luna Station even if you cut off rover-to-suit communication? No, you didn't, you thought you'd get away with—"

"That's enough, Terry," the bald man said, with unmistakable authority.

Enough. Too much. Game over. But Terry was right: Frank hadn't known about the continual transmission. That fact about the EVA suits hadn't shown up in his online research, probably by design. Caught in pixels, all of it: the Atoner, the hair, his switch. He'd fooled the Atoner but not his own kind. He just hadn't known.

75: FROM *THE JOURNAL OF ANTHROPOLOGY*

Publisher: Royal Anthropological Institute of Great Britain and Ireland
ISSN: 13560123
OCLC: 60577118
LCCN: 2005-236986

ROADS, LADDERS, AND MOUNTAINS: AN OVERVIEW OF AFTERLIFE MYTHS AMONG AMAZONIAN TRIBES AS COMPARED TO PRELIMINARY REPORTS FROM KULAR, SUSBAN, ET AL.

by Susan L. Jemison, Professor of Anthropology at the University of Arizona, and E. M. Kubasak, Chair, Department of Anthropology, Eastern New Mexico University

Abstract

Although described by "Witnesses" untrained in anthropology, the alleged afterlife myths reported by Andrew DuBois, Sara Dziwalski, Christina Harden, John E. Jones, Lucca Maduro, and Francis Olenik should be of interest to scholars concerned with the formation, propagation, and maintenance of cultural beliefs concerning the existence of life after death. Of particular interest are various close parallels between these "extra-solar" beliefs and myths found among three indigenous Amazonian peoples. These parallels are examined in terms of death rites, prayer, tribal religious leadership, and socialization of the young.

76: FOUR

Soledad stood by Lucca's bedside in a facility—it wasn't exactly a hospital—that she hadn't known existed. Nor did she know where it was, except that from the window she could see a rocky shore and what looked like a very cold ocean. Whatever it was, it included an OR, to which Lucca had been rushed at the same time that an entire medical team arrived by another helicopter. He now lay unconscious in this small sunny room with a bulky dressing on his leg, antibiotics dripping into his arm, and guards at his door.

"He was lucky," Diane said. "The doctor said the bullet ricocheted off the girl's shield and tore into the quadriceps of his anterior thigh, but it missed the femoral artery. He may limp, but otherwise he'll be fine."

Soledad touched Lucca's cheek. *Lucky.* Fengmo, James, Sara . . . but Lucca, at least, would recover.

"There must be more of them," she said to Diane. "More pregnant girls with the pre-Atoner human genes. The Atoners wouldn't stake their entire 'atonement' on just one pregnancy. Does the Agency know where any more of them live?"

Diane's expression gave away nothing. "The aliens don't inform us of their arrangements."

Of course not. Just as James hadn't told her about his double life, just as Lucca hadn't told her about his pine-tree surveillance, just as Juana hadn't told her about Carl Lewis. Just as the Atoners hadn't told her what would follow her romantic, quixotic, utterly insane volunteering to be a Witness.

"Then they're a lot like us," she said tonelessly to Diane, and bent to hold Lucca's hand.

Frank, freed from his harnesses, sat in the shuttle on the moon and sipped the coffee they'd given him. He knew what to expect. Questions and more questions, days of questions. He'd answer them all truthfully, because at this point, what would be gained by doing anything else? He would do his best to avoid any possible charges of obstruction of justice or interfering with an ongoing investigation or whatever else they could dream up. But he would also stick to his primary statement.

"The genes are mine, and I'll sue in federal court to recover them."

Col. Thomas Shoniker, who had indeed rovered in from Selene City, held the yellow packet in his large hand. "Frank, I feel duty-bound to tell you that if you don't cooperate, you can be detained as a material witness and a security risk, practically indefinitely."

"Only practically," he said. He wasn't giving up. You couldn't trust the government. But he hadn't trusted the Atoners, either, and eventually he'd beaten them. He'd rescued the genes that God had given to humanity from the aliens. Now, with Cam's help, he had to rescue the genes from the feds. Fighting one, fighting the government—the same thing. Stay alert, trust no one, plan for contingencies.

Just the same.

Lucca opened his eyes. He lay naked in an unfamiliar bed in an unfamiliar room under an unfamiliar yellow blanket. But there was Soledad, blessedly familiar, asleep in a chair with her head thrown back and her mouth open. His leg throbbed. He remembered everything.

"Soledad—"

Her eyes flew open. She'd been waiting for him. Something shifted in his chest.

"Are you all right? How do you feel?"

"Shot," he said. "And you, *cara*?"

"Fine. You saved my life, you know." She looked away. Sunlight from the window caught the glint of dried tears on her cheek.

He groped for firmer ground. "Who was Carl Lewis?"

"Diane says CCAD. They've shifted from trying to kill the original Witnesses to trying to kill the . . . the 'brides' the Atoners brought here."

He tried to take this in. "How many brides?"

She shrugged. "Probably a lot, all over the world."

That made sense. Young foreign brides who spoke no English were a commonplace in the great cities of the world. The Atoners knew that some of the girls might die, some miscarry, some be detected. They knew that nothing was certain and that things change.

He looked again at Soledad, dirty and bloody. Her tears were for James, but the concern furrowing her face was for Lucca.

Atoners must think a lot like humans, Lucca thought, because they were right: Things change.

Cam walked out of the main building at Edwards Air Force Base, NASA's primary shuttleport since climate change had made Florida unusable, and into a blinding blaze of light. The California day was gray and overcast, but cameras flashed and robocams zoomed and a TV floodlight caught her square. Cam smoothed her hair, smiled, and stepped to the podium waiting for her on the tarmac.

"Cam! Cam! Cam!"

She held up her hand and the reporters quieted.

"Before you ask me any questions, I want to say something. Yes, it's true that I've been answering questions for our wonderful government. Let me start by saying that

I've been treated with the utmost respect, and that I've been happy to help. And now let me say what I know you've heard rumors about."

She drew a deep breath. This was it. This was the performance of her life. Someone at Farrington Tours had leaked the story, probably selling it for a gazillion dollars, but she was its star. She and Frank, and Frank could never do this part. Only she could. Over the last few weeks she, the Agency, and an army of lawyers had worked it out: how much to tell, how much to hold back "for national security." The scripting had begun even before Cam left the moon, and it was thorough and careful and balanced.

"Yes, the story is true," she began. "I saw an Atoner on the moon. I—no, please wait, there's more!—saw the Atoner because it came out to talk to me and another member of The Six, Frank Olenik. The experience showed me something important, which I'm now going to tell you."

Colonel Shoniker watched her carefully. She could almost hear his mind: *So far, so good.*

Her mistake, she knew now, had been to believe that the aliens really would atone for their crime, really would set things right for humanity. Cam should have known better. The Atoners were just like human beings—they only went after what mattered to them. That's what Cam herself had done when she'd volunteered to become a Witness, when she'd slept with Lucca, when she'd killed Escio and the others, when she'd brought Aveo to Kular A, when she'd become a media star. Aveo had tried to tell her: *We play kulith to discover who we are, and who others are, and to foreshadow and so cause what will happen between us.*

Cam knew now who she was and what she wanted to cause. The men she'd sent onto the second road were now beyond kulith, out of the game. But Cam was not and the Atoners were not—alike in that if nothing else—and Cam was going to win. She took a deep breath and stood up straighter.

Fuck the script.

"What I learned on the moon was that the United States government possesses the seeing-the-dead genes *right now* and will not release them unless we all demand it!"

The tarmac erupted into shouting, into official fury, into just the beginning.

PART IV

THE VERDICT

77: LAWSUMMARY.COM

CASE: *Olenik v. United States,* 2022

United States Court of Appeals for the Fifth Circuit

PLAINTIFFS: Francis Michael Olenik
              Camilla Mary O'Kane
              American Civil Liberties Union

DEFENDANTS: Thomas Sean Corino, Attorney
                General
              Linda Amanda Molsky, Director,
                National Intelligence Agency
              Colonel Thomas Shoniker, USAF
              Special Agent James F. Thompson,
                NIA
              Joel Simon Farrington
              Terence Gary Siekert

Appeal from the United States District Court for Eastern Arizona

Argued January 3, 2022, Decision for Defendants

Reargued March 13, 2023, Decision for Plaintiffs

PRECIS: Olenik et al. brought an action challenging the right of the NIA and the U.S. Justice Department to confiscate, on grounds of national security, material of which the plaintiff claims personal ownership, said material consisting of hairs conveyed by alien shuttle by Olenik from Susban to Luna.

CURRENT STATUS: On Supreme Court docket for 2024

Information last updated: July 17, 2023

The chopper from LaGuardia settled onto the hospital roof. Maduro security personnel jumped out and began their preliminary sweeps. Soledad and Lucca sat quietly, knowing the wait was inevitable, Lucca pulling at the collar of his shirt in the summer heat. She smiled at him.

"You could have let me come alone, you know."

"No. I could not."

"An Italian Galahad," she scoffed.

"An American Boadicea."

She laughed. Lucca's security chief opened the door and said, *"Prego, Signora Maduro."* Soledad let him help her down and followed him through a doorway leading to the elevator.

Lucca watched until the door closed. He didn't want to be in New York—no one not insane wanted to be in New York in July—but even less had he wanted Soledad to make the flight from Italy alone. Once he had lost Gianna. He would not lose another wife, even if that meant dying with her.

Dying. Lucca scowled at the city sweltering below. How many of those poor steaming souls had been caught by Cam's nonsense? She was a huge international star now, more beautiful and flamboyant than ever, her lawsuit the cause célèbre of the century. And still a complete idiot. At least Soledad was too intelligent to talk any longer about Cam's "afterlife"; Soledad hadn't even mentioned it in over a year. Pure wish fulfillment, complete pathetic illusion. To think that once, on the voyage out, Lucca and Cam had—

Lucca pushed the thought away, as he routinely pushed away thoughts of Cam, of the Atoners, of everything that had happened three years ago. An aberration, a boil on his life. That life now was rooted where it belonged, in Tuscany with Soledad and little Angelina, now at home with her grandparents. His daughter was a perpetual astonishment, a miracle. To think that once Lucca had thought he didn't like children! *Che cretino.*

"Aldo," he said in Italian to the pilot, "there is no way to turn on AC without starting the chopper?"

"Non dire cazzate," Aldo said amiably. Lucca, sweating, turned on his handheld. He got a children's program in which cartoon animals named "Ready Freddy" and "Hurry-Up Hannah" jumped around with typical American frenzy. Ready Freddy was a scrawny chicken and Hurry-Up Hannah a rabbit in a purple hat. Lucca found a newscast.

". . . marked the anniversary of the so-called 'preggers murders,' in which three young women in three different cities were simultaneously killed while in the shower," said a blue avatar with macabre cheer. "All three women were pregnant at the time of the slayings, all three were recent brides, and all three were undocumented aliens whose entry into the United States has not been traced. Debio Stevenson, Falewithozkith Stein, and Hrill DiPetrio were in different trimesters of pregnancy, but none of their unborn infants survived the grisly shootings. One husband, American Jon Stein, also perished in the attacks. Law-enforcement agencies in New York, San Diego, and Topeka are sharing information on the three cases. Said Topeka Police Chief Darryl Mendon earlier today, 'The similar pattern suggests the same killer or killers for all three women. We *will* get this guy!' Nonetheless, no arrests have ever been made in any of the tragic murders.

"Now, turning to that wildfire still burning in Colorado . . ."

Lucca flipped his wrist. The local police never would

"get this guy." Possibly the federal government already had, just as they had gotten Carl Lewis with no one ever learning what had really happened in Brooklyn. A drug deal gone bad was the official story, an undercover agent did the shooting, an ongoing internal investigation . . . What was it Soledad said? "Blah blah blah."

Soledad had taught Angelina to say that phrase, too. On her, it was very cute.

A sudden powerful longing to be home with his daughter took Lucca. Tuscany, with the dusty vineyards and soft blue hills and red poppies . . . And yet, strangely, when he thought of peaceful Villa Maduro, he also often thought of that peaceful frozen town on Kular. Chewithoztarel would be a young woman now. Was she married? Was she pregnant?

He sat in the chopper and sweated and waited for his wife.

Accompanied by both hospital and Maduro security, Soledad moved quietly through corridors cleared for her. She nodded thanks at everyone and slipped alone into the room at the end of a hall devoted to terminal patients.

She barely recognized him. Three years in a coma had reduced his already small stature to that of a child. He lay on his side, hooked to tubes and more tubes, his mouth slightly open. His gums had receded around his teeth. His bones looked like an underfed bird.

Carefully she took his hand. "Hello, Fengmo."

Hello, Ladybliss. But she would never hear that again. This was her last trip to New York.

"Fengmo, it's Soledad. I'm here." She paused, wondering what else to say, shocked that she didn't know. After all those years of telling each other everything . . . but that was the past, a different place with a different geography. Then, all at once, she found what she wanted to say.

"I still don't know if there's life after death, Fengmo. I don't talk about it anymore with Lucca, but I still don't *know.* Maybe he's right and it is stress-induced telepathy in the presence of death. Or maybe Cam's right and it's a real perception of something we've lost. Whatever it is, it's coming back to us. The Atoners did atone, after all. But—and here's the big 'but,' dear heart—*it doesn't matter.* What matters is—"

She stopped, appalled. She'd been going to say, *What matters is life here now. That's what we should give our souls to.* But Fengmo had no real life now, and perhaps no soul left, either. She could not say those words to him. She had so much of everything now—Lucca and Angelina and their sweet life in Italy—while Fengmo had lost everything, and for her sake.

So she said instead, "What matters is that I will always love you," kissed him, and left.

Security waited for her. As she left the corridor, they admitted a woman who'd been waiting patiently to come in. She held a toddler by the hand. The two women smiled at each other, the young mother looking sympathetically at Soledad's tears.

That one, she lost a person to death, the young woman thought. *Perhaps I will be so lucky and that horrible old man will die.*

She was visiting her father-in-law, a duty visit. She had not wanted to go, nor to bring her son, but her husband had insisted. "It's Dad's only grandchild," he'd pleaded, and she had given in.

Now she held the child up for the dying man to see, and he smiled at the boy. He never smiled at *her.* Once she had heard him call her a "dirty foreigner." Her English was not good, but it was good enough for that. She set the child on the floor and sat in a chair, determined to stay the entire half hour she had promised her husband, even if the old man never looked at or spoke to her. He had no manners, that one.

They sat in mutually stubborn silence. After five

minutes, the woman dozed off. She was pregnant again and always tired.

The child gazed at his mother with big dark eyes and toddled out the door.

Fengmo stood, bewildered, by a bed with a wizened body in it. Where was he? How had he gotten there?

A child staggered into the room, a small brown boy with lively eyes. He stared up at Fengmo.

"Hi, you Weady-Fweddy, you twaveler-on-the-second-woad," he said, and smiled like sunlight on blinding snow.

TOR

Voted

#1 Science Fiction Publisher
20 Years in a Row

by the *Locus* Readers' Poll

———•———

Please join us at the website below
for more information about this
author and other science fiction,
fantasy, and horror selections, and to
sign up for our monthly newsletter!

www.tor-forge.com